UNSHAKEABLE
Copyright © 2022 by Molly MacKenzie
All Rights Reserved.

Cover Design and Interior Format

UNSHAKEABLE

MOLLY MACKENZIE

A NOTE BEFORE WE BEGIN

IN AUSTRIA, AS in many continental European countries, children of male aristocrats automatically inherit their titles at birth. In England, the Earl and Countess of Grantham's daughter would be Lady Mary; in Austria, the Count and Countess von Holstadt's daughter would be Countess Marta. Ludwig von Braumark and his father are *both* Baron von Braumark, which causes a great deal of confusion at dinner parties.

PART ONE

"Everything I do apart from music is
badly done and stupid."
-Ludwig van Beethoven

CHAPTER ONE

(In Which Our Heroine Makes Eye Contact)

May 1, 1869
Vienna, Austria
One hour before the party of the year

COUNTESS MARTA VON Holstadt belonged to the luckiest family in Vienna.

She'd been told this regularly since childhood, and generally, she agreed. After all, most people in the Austro-Hungarian Empire had to survive without a title, fortune, or impeccable lineage. Most families were deprived of eighty-room mansions and vast country estates. Vienna was the most beautiful, cultured city in Europe, and everyone who lived there was lucky—but people knew the von Holstadts were uniquely blessed.

So it was ridiculous that, on the evening of her twenty-first birthday, Marta couldn't shake off a sense of impending doom. For several reasons, the most immediate being that she had freckles on her nose.

Were those freckles, though? Or just a fleck of dirt on the mirror? Mirror dirt wouldn't set off her mother's you-have-such-beautiful-skin-why-must-you-ruin-it-you-look-like-a-peasant routine. Frowning, Marta leaned forward to inspect her nose, causing her maid Nella to pull sharply at the chocolate-colored curls she was arranging.

"Careful, milady!" Nella exclaimed, firmly pinning a lock of hair into place. "I wouldn't like to yank your hair off."

Obediently, Marta straightened her spine. "Sorry, Nella. If I have freckles Mama will be after me with the lemon juice and I really can't be bothered, not after spending half the afternoon with crushed strawberries on my face. It didn't make my skin anything except sticky." As a former royal lady-in-waiting, Countess Hannelore von Holstadt was frightfully *correct* about everything, from silverware placements to her daughter's complexion. Marta had a theory about her mother's tendency to fret. When people like Hannelore had nothing of substance to worry about, they staved off boredom by fussing about nonsense. This theory did explain the behavior of most high-society Viennese matrons.

It didn't assuage Marta's fears that soon she'd become one of them.

"I've heard that strawberry trick is one the Empress uses, so perhaps there's something to it," Nella said pensively, pulling Marta's thoughts back to the present.

"Maybe. But Empress Elisabeth will look beautiful no matter what she puts on her face, won't she?" And the empress, Marta reflected with a grimace, most likely never forgot her hat while sewing in the garden. Something Marta had done at least three times that week.

"You would look beautiful too, milady," Nella said loyally. "And the freckles aren't so obvious. We'll put on extra powder and if anyone looks too closely at your nose, wrinkle it as if you've smelled something bad."

"Are you implying that Vienna's high society is capable of smelling unpleasant?" Marta asked in mock indignation. "Though I'm sure any smell will be easily masked by the scent of that glorious birthday cake we're serving. Personally I plan to eat quite a lot of it, and if Mama complains I'll just say I'm working on my child-bearing hips." Not that she currently lacked in that department. Marta had inherited her mother's build—middling height, wide hips, large bosom—and had never received any complaints on the subject.

"That's the benefit of crinolines still being in fashion, isn't it?" she went on. "Even if I did overindulge in a bit of cake, no one could tell. I suppose if fashions from my grandmother's day come back I'll be in trouble, so I mustn't allow that to happen."

"If anyone can control the direction of fashion, you can,

milady," said Nella. "I still see ladies copying what you wore three years ago. Turn to your left, please."

Marta did so, gazing wistfully out the window as Nella fiddled with several errant ringlets. The von Holstadt house overlooked the Stadtpark, its treetops glowing gold in the sunset, and Marta wished she were down there instead of being primped for a ball she was dreading.

On paper, the reasons for the evening's festivities were perfectly sound: Marta was twenty-one now, officially of age under Austrian law and an adult in every sense. For a woman of her class, though, twenty-one translated directly to *marriageable*. Her parents had been patient and kind, but Marta knew their hopes all too well. She was expected, within the next eight hours, to find a future husband.

And if she didn't, she would probably wind up marrying Ludwig von Braumark.

Compared to that, freckles were nothing.

By the party's beginning, Marta's nerves had settled somewhat, helped along by the glass of champagne she'd snuck earlier. She looked well enough, which was comforting. Nella had worked wonders with her hair, and the dress Marta had designed for the occasion was a true masterpiece. The pale gold silk made her brown hair and eyes look much more interesting, the tulle-covered skirt had taken her and the family *modiste* ages to arrange perfectly, and the low lace-edged neckline was daring without being scandalous. Her great-grandmother's emerald-and-pearl necklace, dug out of the family vaults, set the whole affair off perfectly.

Clothes, music, dancing—those were the appeal of any grand occasion. Usually, they were enough to keep her sane.

Still, as she stood in the vast, candle-lit ballroom with her parents and brother, a small voice in the back of her mind kept whispering one word: *run*. She wasn't sure where, though. Outer Mongolia or a remote island sounded equally appealing. Both would presumably be far enough from the Vienna marriage market.

How many other von Holstadt women had stood in this exact spot over the centuries? And how many of them had been happy about it?

"Marta, dear, don't play with your hair," her mother chided. The elder countess was resplendent in a gown of burgundy velvet, her silver-streaked golden hair neatly coiled at the nape of her neck. "You'll ruin Nella's lovely handiwork, and you know how important your appearance is tonight."

Marta released the lock of hair she hadn't realized she'd been twisting. "Sorry, Mama. Deep in thought, I suppose."

"What about?" asked her brother suspiciously. Ten-year-old Heinrich von Holstadt the younger, known to all as Heini, had insisted on staying for the first hour of the party, and the long-awaited heir always got his way. "Catching a husband?"

"That's vulgar, Heini, and no. I'm thinking about…" Marta quickly cast about for a possibility, fingering the lace at her collarbone. "Lace. I need to learn to make lace. What's the word for it? 'Tatting.'"

Heini wrinkled his lightly freckled nose—for a boy, of course, freckles were perfectly acceptable. "You're always learning to make things they can make in factories. Why don't you study something useful, like shearing sheep?"

Marta laughed. "And when, exactly, would shearing sheep be useful for an accomplished young lady?"

"Marta. Heini," Their father, Count Heinrich von Holstadt, scolded, his dark, impeccably combed mustache quivering with annoyance. "Please save this discussion for when we are not entertaining half of Vienna. I will not have my children arguing like street urchins tonight."

Neither Marta nor her brother had time to formulate a witty reply, for the next moment, the ballroom doors opened to admit the ball's first guests.

"Baron Ulrich von Braumark," the butler announced. "Baroness Marianne von Braumark, Baron Ludwig von Braumark."

All disagreements with Heini evaporated from Marta's mind as the staff ushered in the three people in Vienna she least wanted to see.

Baron Ulrich von Braumark, well-known patron of the arts,

a short, portly man with a fondness for tweed suits. His pale, fragile-looking wife, Marianne. And their blond, bespectacled son, Ludwig, the classics scholar who'd been after Marta's hand in marriage since they were children. He homed in on Marta as soon as possible while his parents greeted the count and countess.

"My dear lady." Ludwig bent to kiss Marta's reluctantly outstretched hand, lingering for a moment too long. His suit, Marta thought, made him look like a blond penguin. "You look beautiful as always—and, as Socrates said, 'Beauty is the bait which with delight allures man to enlarge his kind.'"

Marta didn't claim to be an expert in Socrates, but she didn't quite think this was a compliment. Still, Ludwig undoubtedly meant well, as he always did.

"You're very kind," she said "Please, enjoy the evening." *And don't propose to me, I beg of you. Even if your parents have been lecturing you all day about the family line, do* not *propose to me on my birthday.*

Luckily, even if Ludwig had intended to propose at that moment, he didn't have the time. The butler cleared his throat once again and declared: "Mr. and Mrs. Jacob Stein. Miss Sophie Stein."

The words *Sophie Stein* nearly made Marta collapse in relief. She'd grown up with Sophie, whose father was one of Vienna's most respectable finance men, and there was no event in the world that couldn't be improved by her dearest friend's caustic remarks. Especially one where Ludwig was in attendance.

"Thank heavens you're here," Marta said, as Sophie hurried to her side. "I couldn't possibly get through this evening without you."

"Well, it seems you won't have to. And happy birthday, darling," Sophie said, pulling Marta into a tight hug. Marta had always thought Sophie, with her slim build and Mediterranean coloring, resembled a Greek goddess. Tonight, though, her royal-blue taffeta gown made her look like the heiress she was. "Listen, Mama and Papa have got you a suitably sparkly gift, but I wanted to give you something small from me." She pressed a small velvet pouch into her friend's hand, out of which Marta pulled a small, exquisitely made pincushion in the shape of a peacock.

"Sophie, it's beautiful! Where did you get it?"

"Mrs. Petrova made it. You remember, the old Russian lady who works for the *modiste*? I completely overpaid her for it, of course," said Sophie with satisfaction. "Redistribution of wealth, don't you know. It was the least I could do. She works so hard, and did you know she's got ten grandchildren in Siberia to support?" Sophie's passion for worker's rights and intense dislike of greed had always been one of her best qualities, though one couldn't tell that from her wardrobe.

"I can't say your radical politics will endear you to many in this crowd," said Marta, "but I'm sure this is the nicest present I'll receive tonight."

"I don't know about that." Sophie smirked, brushing a lock of sleek jet-black hair behind her ear. "I think the von Braumarks would buy you a diamond mine if it made you more likely to marry their precious son. How is Ludwig, by the way? Still smitten with you?"

"Don't be silly, Ludwig doesn't love me. He just thinks he does because that's what his parents have been telling him for his entire life, and he's very trusting. Would you mind dancing with him a few times tonight? I can only stand to hear so many Socrates quotes on my birthday."

Sophie rolled her eyes and groaned. "Only for you, darling, and only because it's your party. But if he tries to argue with me about metaphysics again, I am leaving."

"Nor would I blame you," said Marta. "And if at some point during this party I decide to flee to Mongolia, I promise to take you with me."

Two hours later the ball was going splendidly. The emperor and his family were unable to attend, a blow from which Marta's mother would undoubtedly recover, given a decade or two, nor was Marta's grandmother, Dorothea von Holstadt preferring to remain in the country. Nonetheless the guest list was a veritable catalog of Vienna's finest. As the evening drew on the music became livelier, the conversations became louder, and an archduchess accidentally-on-purpose spilled punch on a rival's gown. This being the kind of chaos Marta thrived on, she was having a far better time than she'd expected.

One thing, however, was still dampening her enjoyment. Ludwig had claimed a waltz on her dance card, and he couldn't be dodged. As soon as the orchestra struck up a soaring rendition of Strauss's *Blue Danube* there he was at her elbow. Inwardly, Marta cringed as he took her in his arms.

There was nothing particularly wrong with Ludwig. He was pleasant and intelligent and even handsome, in a way, and therein lay the problem. Had he been prone to drinking and gambling and flirting with actresses, her parents would never have expected their daughter to marry him, old family friend or not. As it was, Marta's primary arguments against the match—that Ludwig was the dullest person she knew, that he cared nothing for art and music and filtered all his thoughts through classical quotations— seemed awfully middle-class.

"Is the orchestra up to your standards?" Ludwig said, finally breaking the silence. "Father helped select them. He knows everyone in all the opera companies. The Odysseum Opera Company isn't quite as good as the Court Opera, of course, but it's easier to book this lot. They don't perform nearly as often. Still, music is the food of love, as Shakespeare said."

"They're very good," Marta said quickly, before the conversation could go any further in the direction of love. "I don't think I've heard of the Odysseum Opera Company, though."

"They're in the old Landfeld Theatre in Leopoldstadt. They did *Masked Ball* last month; it wasn't bad, though you know I don't go in much for that sort of thing."

To avoid Ludwig's unsettling gaze, the one that always made her feel he was studying her like a book, Marta glanced over his shoulder at the small orchestra. Its members seemed thoroughly professional and focused, even if they weren't the Court Opera. The violinist closest to her was certainly entirely absorbed by the music. Marta's gaze lingered on him, admiring his wavy dark red hair and long, slender fingers. She didn't know much about the Odysseum Opera Company, but they seemed to turn out nice-looking musicians…

Then the violinist lifted his head, just slightly, and glanced in her direction.

Good heavens. Now *that* was unfair.

If Marta ever met God, she would have to have a very stern talk with him about allowing mortal men to have eyes like that. Eyes that particular shade of blue-green, so intense they seemed to be lit from within, belonged on ancient gods from the old Celtic folktales Marta's English governess had told her—the sort who did interesting things like turning into foxes and kidnapping mortal girls to be their wives. Eyes like that had absolutely no business belonging to violin players in birthday-party orchestras.

Was he looking at her? He *had* to be looking at her, or Marta thought she might scream just to get his attention. She leaned forward, hoping to catch his eye, her heart pounding in anticipation.

"Marta? Are you all right?"

Marta came back to herself with a start, suddenly aware that Ludwig was looking at her with concern in his pale blue eyes. With a twinge of embarrassment, she realized that while she had been staring at the violinist she had nearly forgotten that she was dancing, or that there was anyone else in the room at all.

"Are you all right?" Ludwig asked again. "You're looking a bit feverish."

"No, I'm really…" Marta put a hand to her cheek and realized, with surprise, that her face was quite warm. "Do you know, Ludwig, I *am* feeling poorly. I must be tired from all the dancing. Would you excuse me for a moment? I believe I'll sit down and have a glass of punch."

"If you're sure." Ludwig's frown deepened. "Would you like me to come with you?"

"Oh, no, that's quite all right. The waltz is over anyway, and I'm sure Sophie would be delighted to dance the next one with you. Don't let me keep you." Before Ludwig could object, Marta slipped out of his grasp, hurried to one of the chairs along the walls, and settled into a seat from which she could watch the handsome violinist to her heart's content.

It was an agonizing twenty minutes before supper was announced and the orchestra was finally permitted to take a break. As guests found partners to escort them to the dining room Marta hopped up from her seat, determined to find *her* violinist before the musicians disappeared down to the kitchens or wherever the help went during breaks. She wasn't entirely sure what she would say to him since a wordless scream of admiration, while representative of her feelings, was likely to be startling, but she could learn his name, anyway. And tell him how lovely the music had been. And stare at him some more.

Luckily, it took her less than two minutes to find him. He was in the corner where the orchestra had been set up, engaged in an intense conversation with Baron von Braumark, and was nodding valiantly as the baron gestured wildly. Marta paused briefly, inspecting his clothes with a connoisseur's eye. His black suit was elegant, if threadbare, and his trousers were a bit too short for his long legs. Strangely, the air of shabbiness only made him more attractive.

"Ah, the lady of the hour," Baron von Braumark said, seeing Marta approach. "Mr. Király, I don't believe you have made the acquaintance of Countess Marta von Holstadt, the very reason we are gathered here tonight. Countess, my dear, allow me to introduce Andras Király, first chair violinist at the opera company."

Andras turned those glowing turquoise eyes towards Marta, regarding her so intently it made her breath catch in her throat. With some relief, Marta concluded that he was just as gorgeous close up as he was from afar, if not more so; he had a thin, refined-looking face, with cheekbones that had to be sharp enough to cut glass, and the longest eyelashes Marta had ever seen on a man. While his hair was too long to be fashionable, nearly down to his shoulders, it was *such* a lovely color. Even his long nose was utterly charming.

Andras Király—a Hungarian name. Was he from Hungary, then?

"Countess, it's a pleasure to meet you," Andras said politely, dipping into a graceful bow. He had a lovely voice, low and seductive, and rolled his r's just a bit.

Marta managed the slightest of curtsies—if she bent any deeper her shaking knees were certain to give out. "Likewise, Mr. Király. And you must let me congratulate you. The music tonight has been excellent."

Andras looked down at her—quite significantly down, he practically towered over her—and offered a small but sincere smile. "That's kind of you, Countess. I won't say I entirely agree, but then it's not easy to be satisfied with one's own performance, as I'm sure you'll know if you have ever played music yourself."

"You're quite right. I spent ten years taking piano lessons, and I was always terrified of being asked to play at a party because if I made a mistake I'd be furious at myself all night. I remember once at Christmas when I was eleven, I forgot what came next halfway through *Silent Night* and I wound up playing the same line five times in a row." Realizing she was starting to babble, Marta bit off the end of her sentence. "I beg your pardon. You and your colleagues have played beautifully. I don't think I've ever heard Strauss performed so well. The orchestra is lucky to have you."

"On the contrary, I think I'm the lucky one. It's an honor to be able to work here in Vienna." Andras's jaw tightened as though he was suppressing a yawn, and for the first time Marta noticed the pale violet circles under his eyes, as though it had been a few days since he'd had a good night's sleep. "Though," he added, looking away absentmindedly, "my father might disagree with me about that…"

"Would he?" Marta leaned closer, sensing a delicious hint of intrigue. "Why is that?"

Andras blinked, as if only just remembering she and Baron Ulrich were there. "Nothing important," he said quickly. "Forgive me for keeping you, Countess, Baron. I expect they'll need you to lead everyone in to supper. Allow me to wish you a very happy birthday, Countess."

He bowed again, this time kissing the back of her hand—merely brushing his lips against her gloved fingers, but even that was enough to make Marta feel her skin had burst into flame. With this he departed, leaving her to admire the lean, graceful lines of his body as he walked away.

"A pleasant young man, that," the baron remarked. "Too many

of these artistic types, especially the Hungarians, have no idea how to speak to their betters."

"Mmm," said Marta vaguely. "He works for the Odysseum Opera Company, Ludwig said?"

"Indeed. Not a bad little troupe, even if their theatre is a bit run-down. I believe their next production will be *Don Giovanni*. Your family will have to accompany us to one of the performances."

"Oh, yes," Marta agreed ardently. "I can't think of anything I would like more."

The rest of the party was both pleasant and easy to summarize.

Supper: Delicious.

Cake: Exquisite.

Her father's speech at the end of supper: very sweet and slightly too long.

Her dance partners for the rest of the evening: lovely fellows one and all, if forgettable.

Ludwig: …present and accounted for.

What Marta would really have liked to do was drag Sophie off to a corner and have a proper gossip about the handsome and mysterious Mr. Király. But when it was one's own party one had duties, and it was nearly four in the morning before the revelry finally wound down and the orchestra began to put away their instruments.

They really had done a lovely job. It wouldn't have been much of a party without them. Surely it wouldn't be inappropriate for her to thank the musicians and wish him—them—good night. Gathering up her skirts, Marta began to make her way to the back of the ballroom.

"Marta?"

Drat, she knew that voice. Turning, Marta arranged her face into the most pleasant expression she could manage. "Hello, Ludwig."

"I was hoping to find you. Are you feeling better?"

"Hm? Oh, yes," she replied. "Did you enjoy your evening?"

"Yes, yes. It's been an excellent party." Ludwig visibly swallowed, his Adam's apple bobbing in his thin neck. "Marta, I do hope you

don't mind, but I've been meaning to speak with you about…
something important. Could we perhaps talk in private?"

Marta glanced about the quickly emptying ballroom as the
guests offered their best wishes to her parents and then departed.
"Won't your family be wanting to leave?"

Indeed, the poor baroness looked about to collapse from
exhaustion, while the baron's face was red as a tomato.

"This won't take long. Marta, we've known each other a
long time, haven't we? And you know I think you're brilliant,
and Socrates said that…" Ludwig shook his head rapidly, as if
attempting to clear his thoughts. "Marta," he said eventually,
voice firmer, and reached out. "I wonder if…"

Oh no.

No, no, no, this could *not* be happening. Was he really going
to propose now, at four o'clock in the morning, when she'd just
had the most interesting encounter of her recent life? She wasn't
ready to marry Ludwig, or anyone like him. She wasn't ready
to be a dull married lady before she'd even had a chance to live.
And if Ludwig's bony hand dared touch the place where Andras
Király had kissed her, she was likely to scream.

Hastily she pulled her hand away, tucking her arm behind
her back. "Honestly, Ludwig, I am completely exhausted. It's
dreadfully late. Why don't you go along with your parents, and
we can discuss this some other time?"

"But…"

"Good night, Ludwig," Marta said firmly. "It was lovely for
you and your family to come, as usual. I will see you at the
opera soon." With a brisk, polite curtsy, she swept off, leaving the
unfortunate Ludwig sputtering in confusion behind her.

Not the most ladylike or polite of maneuvers, and she'd have
to apologize to Ludwig the next time she saw him. But it was
late, and suddenly her bed seemed like the most wonderful place
in Vienna.

For one more night, at least, she was free to dream.

CHAPTER TWO

(In Which There Are Financial Concerns, and Also Art)

May 2
The morning after

IN THE LEOPOLDSTADT neighborhood, in a cramped garret apartment in a ramshackle old house, Andras Király lay in bed and stared at the ceiling. It wasn't a particularly interesting ceiling, other than the water stain he'd always thought resembled a turtle, but he didn't have enough energy to do much else.

Despite the fact that he rarely woke up in time for church, Andras thanked God every week that he was not required to work on Sundays. Every other day involved hours of practicing and performing until his fingers felt worn to the bone, but on Sunday, Andras was able to rest.

Or, more accurately, he would have been able to rest were it not for Franz Bauer's snoring.

Rolling his eyes, Andras hopped out of bed, pulled on a pair of trousers, and made his way to the garret's other room, where he tossed a pillow at his noisy flatmate. "Up, Franz," he called. "It's ten o'clock and if I can't sleep any longer, neither can you."

In reply, Franz rolled out of bed and landed with a thump on the floor. He and his cello had also been at the von Holstadt party, though he'd partaken of more wine afterward than Andras had. "Really, Király, is it something about being Hungarian that makes you wake up at such uncivilized hours? I planned to sleep until noon at least."

"I wouldn't blame being Hungarian as much as your wheezing," Andras retorted. "You've probably woken half the building. We'll have Mrs. Lutz from downstairs bursting in here in a moment, brandishing a frying pan."

"Ah, the luscious Mrs. Lutz," said Franz, his annoyance at being awoken apparently forgotten. He hoisted himself up and adjusted his nightshirt. "She's quite attractive, under those aprons. You should have an affair with her, Andras. Some loving might do you good."

Andras rolled his eyes. Franz had been his flat mate and dearest friend since his graduation from the Academy four years earlier, and was far more talented a musician than his demeanor suggested. But his mind seemed capable of focusing on only three subjects: music, wine, and women. "You really think I would risk life and limb to have an affair with a married woman? Even if she were the slightest bit interested in me?"

"She's interested, all right. I've seen how she looks at you. It's the romantic air about you—the long hair and the expression of permanent melancholy."

Andras resisted the urge to point out that his "expression of permanent melancholy" was not so much romantic as a sign that he almost never slept well. "That's as may be," he said instead. "But I've no interest in cuckolding Mr. Lutz. The man's a builder. He could kill me with one punch." He sighed, running a hand through his hair. "Speaking of affairs, where is Brigita? Don't you usually meet her for breakfast on Sundays?"

"Usually, yes, but this is the first Sunday of the month, the day upon which she promised her grandmother she would always go to church." Franz shook his head sorrowfully. "I did try to go with her once, but I fell asleep halfway through."

"You're cursed with a worldly soul," said Andras. "But look on the bright side, Franz. If one Sunday a month in church is the only price Brigita pays for her career as a ballerina, then the opera company is very lucky."

Franz snorted, clearly contemptuous of the idea that church could be any more important than his own company. "It's not as though she's a prima ballerina… yet. But on the subject of women, didn't I see you talking to the lady of the hour last night?"

Andras blinked, trying to keep up with the abrupt change in conversation. "Pardon?"

"The countess, Andras," said Franz, rolling his eyes. "The daughter of our illustrious host? Countess Marta von Holstadt? You two seemed cozy."

In truth, Andras had been so tired that the previous evening had been something of a blur. "Cozy is an exaggeration. Baron von Braumark introduced us briefly, and we had half a conversation about music. She was pleasant, from what I can recall."

"Pretty, don't you think?" said Franz. "I can't say I go for that big-eyed ingénue type much myself, though I know you did at one point."

Andras closed his eyes, summoning up an indistinct image of wide brown eyes, dark curls, and a yellow dress. Pretty, he couldn't say, but she had seemed friendly enough.

"As I said, pleasant," he said. "Though I can't see how it matters. The important thing is we now have five gulden in our pockets that we didn't have before."

"Though of course you won't be using yours for anything enjoyable. Every penny will go right back to Hungary." Franz sat up sharply, digging his hands into his bright gold curls. "I say, I completely forgot. Give me a second." He reached under his bed and pulled out a crinkled envelope, wiping a light coating of dust off its surface. "This arrived for you two days ago."

"Give me that." Andras snatched the letter out of Franz's hand, his heart leaping with nerves as he recognized his sister Ilka's spidery handwriting. The eldest of the Király girls, Ilka worked as a maid for a bourgeois Austrian family in Budapest, and rarely wrote unless something was wrong. "You had this under your bed for two days and didn't tell me about it?"

"Sorry," Franz replied brightly. "You know how scatterbrained I am. What does it say?"

"I don't know yet, do I? Will you let me read it first?"

Franz acquiesced and sat back on the bed, while Andras dropped into one of the wobbly chairs and began reading.

Dear Andras,

I hope you're well and that everything is all right in Vienna. Thank you for the photograph you sent last month—we've hung it up in the kitchen and we all think you look very dignified, though Pa thinks you ought to cut your hair. I told him Ma would never have allowed it!

Jozefa and Kitti are working hard in school, but have started to take in work making artificial flowers in the evenings (Pa's been helping. I think he enjoys having something to do with his hands). When I am home I try not to let Kitti help after it gets dark, as she must save her eyesight, but she insists on doing as much as she can. I'm not sure Jozefa will be willing to remain in school much longer as she is very keen to set out and try to get a job of some sort. (Do you think you could convince her otherwise? I really wouldn't like her to give up her education.)

I myself am quite all right. The Grubers are good employers and I have stopped leaving smudges when I polish the silver. Mrs. Gellert says if I continue to improve I may work my way up to become a lady's maid someday. Wouldn't that be grand? I'd certainly appreciate the higher salary.

There's only one piece of bad news: Pa has been feeling quite poorly again. You know how his lungs get, especially when there's been lots of smog. The really unfortunate part, which I hesitate to even mention, is that the price of his medicine has risen somewhat. The artificial flowers help with the cost, and I truly don't want to make demands when I know how hard you've been working, but if there was any way you could help, you must know how much we would appreciate it.

Love,
Ilka

Andras dropped the letter onto the table as all the familiar, humiliating signs of one of his panicky spells began to set in— the tension behind his eyes, the twisting stomach, the increasing speed of his heartbeat. He put a hand over his eyes and breathed deeply, willing himself not to fall to pieces.

Once again, his family desperately needed him. And, as usual, he would probably let them down.

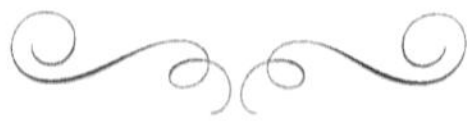

The Király family hadn't always been in such dire straits. They'd never been wealthy, but they'd been comfortable enough nonetheless. György Király, coming to Budapest from the countryside by Lake Balaton, had found good work in one of the newly opened factories, and his wife, Anna, had been the busiest seamstress on Szerdahelyi Street. Andras had been too young to remember these early years, but he still knew they'd been good.

But then had come 1848 and with it, the revolution—bloodless at first, but escalating into an all-out war a year later.

At the age of four, Andras had had a very limited understanding of why people were shouting in the streets and why his father had headed off to fight. His mother carefully explained that their friends and neighbors wanted Hungary to be a free country, not part of the Austrian empire, and that since the emperor did not listen when they asked nicely, the Hungarians would have to find some other way to be free.

They'd had such high hopes at the beginning. For a long while it seemed as though the revolution would be a success. Until the Habsburgs, fed up with the rebels, had gotten assistance from the Russian army. Budapest was shelled, the revolution was stifled, and György came home with a missing leg and ruined lungs.

His injuries made it difficult for him to return to factory work, or indeed any work other than doing some minor repairs for the neighbors—no one on Szerdahelyi Street was willing to let a patriot starve—so the burden of providing for the family had fallen primarily to Andras's mother. Anna had acted as breadwinner uncomplainingly, working longer hours, sewing until her fingers bled, while his father took it upon himself to cook and clean and look after Andras and his three younger sisters. They didn't go hungry, though one didn't have to be brilliant with numbers to see that money grew tighter every year. Finally, when Andras turned sixteen and was ready to get a job of his own, a professor from the Vienna Academy of Music had arrived in Budapest on holiday and run into Andras' mother at the bakery. She had bullied poor Professor Strobel into hearing Andras play, and the rest was history.

Scholarships from prestigious music schools weren't dropped in one's lap every day. Of course he had to go, his parents insisted.

After a few years of education he would be a real musician, a successful one, and there wouldn't be any need to worry about money. And Andras, desperate as he was to study music, to escape, had listened to them.

These days, by Király standards, Andras was a success. An education, a steady job, extra work when he needed it. A breadwinner, like his mother had been.

But it wasn't enough, was it? It was never enough.

"Are you all right?" Franz's concerned voice broke through Andras's troubled thoughts. "Not bad news, is it?"

Andras shook his head. "Not too terrible. Money problems, same as always. I just wish I could do more to help, that's all. I don't seem to be much use as things currently stand. Would you ever forgive me if I decided to give up music and become a shopkeeper?"

"I would not," Franz said. "Nor would anyone else who has ever heard you play the violin. Come on, chin up. I'll make a pot of coffee and we can think up a few financial schemes."

"*I* will make coffee. Yours is always terrible," said Andras. But he managed a smile nonetheless. If nothing else, he still had Franz.

Who was it that had said no man with friends could be truly poor? Whoever it was, they'd been onto something.

May 3
Künstlerhaus Gallery

Despite the differences in their backgrounds, there were quite a few things upon which Hannelore von Holstadt and Mrs. Stein agreed. One of these was the necessity of ensuring that their daughters absorbed a sufficient amount of culture. Not too much, not enough that they would prove intimidating to future husbands, but enough to make them good conversationalists. Thus Mondays were set aside for museums, and exhibitions, and musical recitals, or any of the myriad cultural delights the city offered. On the Monday after Marta's party, their destination was to be the Künstlerhaus Gallery, just one of a number of new artistic institutions that had resulted from the Emperor's efforts to modernize the city.

It was astonishing how much things had changed, Marta mused during the journey, gazing out the window of the family carriage as it bumped along on the streets. Only four years earlier the medieval wall surrounding the city center had been torn down and replaced by the modern boulevard known as the Ringstrasse, lined with museums, palaces, and the controversial new Opera House. Hannelore hadn't entirely approved of these changes, but Heinrich had supported them. "After all, if that Baron Haussmann can modernize Paris, I see no reason why we can't do the same thing here in Vienna," he'd declared, undoubtedly pleased that his own home would remain unaffected.

Marta herself had no objections to the emperor's modernizations. Walls and streets would come and go, but the spire of St. Stephen's Cathedral still towered over the city center, the green and gold domes of the Hofburg palace still glittered in the afternoon light, and music still drifted out of every building. It was still Vienna, still home, and she loved it. Since her birthday, in fact, the city had seemed more beautiful than ever.

Marta knew her parents hadn't considered Saturday's party successful. Nearly eight hours of dancing with Vienna's most eligible men, and not an engagement in sight. For the exact same reason, though, Marta thought the evening had been a triumph. Most of her potential suitors were only capable of discussing military maneuvers, the hunting in Tyrol, and who had the finest dueling scar. In ten sentences—not that Marta had counted— Mr. Király had proven himself more interesting than all of them put together.

She couldn't wait to tell Sophie about him.

Nor could she wait to see him again.

If only she could figure out *how*.

As their mothers proceeded down the gallery's echoing halls, Marta and Sophie hung back, the better to carry on discussions the older women might not approve of. After Sophie had gotten her hands on *The Communist Manifesto* the previous year, the girls had given their mothers a full half-hour head start in order to discuss the pros and cons of Mr. Marx's controversial book without any parental scoldings. Hungarian violinists were probably a less risky topic, but Marta wasn't taking any chances.

Sophie paused in front of a particularly lurid painting depicting Leda being ravished by Zeus in the guise of a swan, and wrinkled her nose disapprovingly. "I can't think why artists keep painting this disgusting story. Is it meant to be romantic? What woman in her right mind would want to be seduced by a swan?"

"Bird fanciers, I expect," Marta replied. "And perhaps swans are easier to deal with than some men. Speaking of men, Sophie, I have something very important to ask you about my birthday party. Did you *see* him?"

"That depends on who you mean by 'him,'" Sophie replied. "If you mean Baron von Katz, then yes, I saw a great deal of him. He insisted on dancing with me three times, and I spent ages staring at that awful polka-dot tie of his. It was only after I gave him a lecture on the treatment of workers in his family's factories that I was finally able to get him to go away."

"I did not mean Baron von Katz, though I applaud your response to him. I meant," Marta said solemnly, "Andras Király. The violinist."

"One of the chaps from the orchestra, you mean?" Sophie shook her head. "He escaped my notice. What about him?"

"What *about* him?" Marta exclaimed, drawing surprised looks from Hannelore and Mrs. Stein as they strolled ahead of the girls. Lowering her voice carefully, Marta went on. "He's *beautiful*, Sophie. The most handsome man I've ever seen. And he plays the violin so well, and he has the loveliest voice."

"My goodness, what a paragon." Sophie gave a wry smile. "I'm starting to regret that I didn't meet him. Király's a Hungarian name, isn't it?"

"Yes, and he had the sweetest accent. I wonder how he came to be working in Vienna. I expect he was a brilliant prodigy of some sort, top of his class at the Academy of Music."

"Marta, I hate to say this, but I think you are doing that one particular thing you always do."

"What thing? I don't do a *thing*."

"You most certainly do. You do a thing where you discover a

new person or idea, become utterly infatuated with it, and resort to all sorts of wild speculation about how absolutely perfect it must be. Then you discover too late that it's not perfect at all, and feel awful for days. Don't you remember the Shetland pony six years ago?"

"That thing was horribly bad-tempered," Marta said with a shudder. "It nearly bit my finger off. But Heini's done a wonderful job training it and they're very good friends by this point, so it all worked out for the best. Besides, Andras Király is nothing like a Shetland pony."

"That's true. He is a Hungarian violinist with whom you have had one conversation, which is worse."

Marta raised her eyebrows. "Are you implying something, Sophie dear?"

"There's no implying about it. I think I am being very straightforward. Please don't tell me you're in love with him, I don't think I could cope with it."

This was so ridiculous Marta couldn't even laugh. "How could I possibly be in love with him? As you say, we've only had one conversation. Besides, he's almost certainly not on my mother's list of Potential Husbands for Marta, so there could be no question of my fancying him."

"Then why," Sophie asked, her blue-gray eyes narrowing, "are you talking about him so much?"

It was a reasonable question, one to which Marta did not readily have a good answer. "I think…" she began, trying to arrange her thoughts. "Sophie, have you ever noticed how small our circle is? Over half a million people live in this city, and the only ones we ever meet are those with grand estates and 'von' in their names. I expect I found Mr. Király so fascinating because I don't *get* to talk to people like him. Not proper artists," she added, glancing ruefully at another painting, this one depicting a group of anemic-looking nymphs.

Sophie nodded, seemingly satisfied. "It's a disgrace how isolated people like us are. We're barely supposed to talk to our own servants. Perhaps you should hire Mr. Király to follow you around so you can always have someone interesting and artistic to chat with. Besides me, of course."

Marta stopped in her tracks as the vaguest sketch of an idea struck her. Sophie was only teasing, she knew, and yet, could she…

No.

Unless…

"Marta?" Sophie glanced back, brows drawing together. "Are you all right?"

"Yes, yes, of course," Marta said quickly. "And you are interesting to talk to, I'll absolutely grant you. But I've seen your attempts at watercolors, and I think you have a way to go before you reach artistic." She swatted Sophie playfully with her fan. "We'd better find our mothers. If we stay away too long they'll start thinking we've been ravished by swans."

CHAPTER THREE

(In Which an Opportunity Presents Itself)

The von Holstadt House
Tuesday, May 4

MARTA AWOKE ON Tuesday morning with a singular purpose in mind. Not just a purpose, but a scheme. Possibly her most brilliant yet.

Of course Sophie had only been joking when she'd suggested hiring Mr. Király. And hiring him as a conversation partner would be ridiculous. But as a teacher…

Musicians taught lessons all the time, didn't they? Even Beethoven had taught piano early in his career. There was no reason to think Mr. Király would turn down work as a violin tutor.

As Marta's violin tutor.

After all, what else was she meant to be doing in this strange period of her life between childhood and marriage? Not having been born a boy, there was no question of her going to university or working outside the home. But that hardly meant she had to spend her days sitting about, waiting to be proposed to, letting her passion and curiosity atrophy. She would learn and experience as much as she could before marriage and children consumed her every waking minute.

She would, therefore, learn to play the violin, and handsome, mysterious Mr. Király would teach her.

This conclusion drawn, it was with serene confidence that Marta joined her family for luncheon and informed them that she needed to learn to play the violin.

Heinrich looked up from the *Neue Freie Presse*, his brow creased in confusion. "The violin, Marta? Where is this coming from?"

"From common sense, Papa, You know how fond I am of music, and at present I can only play the piano, which isn't exactly portable. The violin is such a beautiful instrument. And most importantly," Marta said, casting a significant glance at her mother, "it's an accomplishment. And haven't you always said, Mama, that the more accomplishments a lady has the better wife and mother she'll be?"

"That is true," Hannelore said. "The ability to play another instrument would hardly be a point against you on the marriage market."

"Marriage market?" Heini asked, clearly delighted that, as was so rarely the case when he ate with the adults, there was something interesting to discuss. "Is that like the cattle and horse markets in the country?"

"Absolutely," Marta informed him. "All the young ladies of Vienna are put up for sale, and the more clever things a girl knows how to do, the more gentlemen will want to take her home. If I learn to play the violin I'll be as valuable as that gray Arabian horse you wanted so badly last year."

Heini set down his glass of lemonade emphatically, causing liquid to slosh out onto the tablecloth. "Why are we arguing about it then? You've got to let Marta take violin lessons. Maybe I should take them myself. Do fellows need to be in the marriage market too?"

"Heini, if you expect to make any kind of progress at school this autumn you've got more pressing things to worry about than marriage and violins," Heinrich said. "Though I suppose I don't have any objections to Marta studying the instrument. A girl's got to occupy her days with some wholesome activity. There's the matter of choosing an appropriate tutor, however."

Marta, secure in the knowledge that she had triumphed, went in for the *coup de grace*.

"As it happens, I met someone at my party who would be an absolutely ideal teacher," she said lightly. "A very nice young man from the Odysseum Opera Company. I don't think we need to look any further."

Six Hours Later
The Landfeld Theatre, Leopoldstadt

Andras arrived at the Landfeld Theatre at precisely ten minutes to three on Tuesday afternoon, his violin case in one hand and his lunch—a greasy spinach pastry wrapped in newspaper—in the other. His entire body relaxed as he pushed open the stage door with his foot and found himself in the cool, musty air of backstage.

The small Odysseum Opera Company had not been his first choice for employment when he'd graduated from the Academy. With all the optimism of the twenty-year-old he'd been, Andras had planned to immediately find work with the Court Opera or the Philharmonic Orchestra, or perhaps launch a brilliant career as a soloist like Paganini or Liszt. Unfortunately, the city's finest orchestras already had plenty of excellent violinists, and there were no jobs for someone just out of school without a single patron to vouch for him. Several weeks of unemployment had left Andras exhausted, hungry, and ready to return to Budapest and confess to his family that he'd failed.

It was Franz who'd saved him. Good old Franz, who'd noticed Andras's violin case and struck up a conversation at a café. He'd explained that the first violin at the Odysseum Opera Company had recently left to join the army, and if Andras could tell one end of a fiddle from the other, there was likely to be a job for him.

Franz proved as good as his word. Andras had auditioned the next day, and the Odysseum Opera Company had promptly accepted him as one of their own. Since then, he had never had a single regret. Certainly their audience consisted of shopkeepers rather than royalty. Certainly his paycheck was nothing to brag about, and he had almost no spare time in which to write music. But the Landfeld Theatre was undeniably home.

Now, as he deftly made his way through the noisy and crowded backstage, Andras offered polite greetings to the stagehands, assisted the elderly wardrobe mistress in moving a heavy basket of artificially bloodstained doublets, and bowed respectfully to Kristina Eisen. The beautiful golden-haired Bavarian lead soprano frequently showed up several hours before expected and spent her spare time flirting with every creature that crossed her path. Andras had more than once had to duck out of her way to avoid a highly inappropriate pinch.

There would be a few small operettas performed in the theatre over the next two weeks, but the premiere of *Don Giovanni* on the eighteenth of May was all anyone in the company could discuss. It had been far too long since the Odysseum had performed a work by Mozart, and surely nothing could be more glorious than to bring to the stage an opera by that most quintessentially Austrian of all composers. Andras's fingers were already itching in anticipation as he took a seat in the orchestra pit. This was why he had come to Vienna in the first place, why he had put up with bleeding fingers and sleepless nights. He would have put up with plenty more of the same for the opportunity to perform some of the world's most beautiful music.

If there was one person at the company who had fully embraced the idea of pain equaling art, it was Karl Dietrich. The wiry, black-haired conductor, who had been with the Odysseum since the beginning, had higher standards for his orchestra than all the Academy professors put together. Legend had it he'd once sacked a flautist for mispronouncing Haydn, and God help anyone who showed up to rehearsal with an out-of-tune instrument. Why this great man was working at an outfit like the Odysseum was unclear, but Andras was grateful for his presence. He'd always felt that Dietrich, underneath all the ferocity, was a kindred spirit.

They both knew music was worth sacrifices.

"Well, you pack of fools," Dietrich declared, when the orchestra pit was sufficiently quiet for his taste. "Let's get to it. Any of you who give Mr. Mozart cause to turn over in his grave will be asked to go ahead and join him there. Begin."

And with a tap of the conductor's baton on his stand, they were off.

It was three brutal hours before Dietrich finally indicated it was time for a break. A collective sigh of relief rose from the orchestra as instruments were finally placed back in cases and aching fingers stretched.

"All right. As I am sure you're all aware, you are a disgrace to the name of opera. Get out of my sight and don't come back into this pit for an hour. Not you, Király," Dietrich called, as the rest of the musicians began packing up. "Glöckner needs to see you in his office."

Andras frowned. The director of the opera company was generally too busy worrying over ticket sales and placating singers to hold meetings with orchestra musicians, and while Glöckner had always been kind to Andras, this didn't bode well. "Did he say why?"

"Yes, of course," Dietrich drawled. "And then he bought me a cake and promised to name his firstborn son after me. Good God, boy, you think the director tells me anything? Go upstairs and ask him yourself."

Sensing an imminent loss of temper on the conductor's part, Andras obediently hurried to the back of the theatre, entering the director's office after his knock was answered by an irritated grunt.

Mr. Oskar Glöckner, a thin, balding man with watery gray eyes hidden behind round spectacles, glanced up from his extraordinarily messy desk and gestured for Andras to have a seat. He'd founded the Odysseum Opera Company over eighteen years prior and, according to rumor, hadn't slept since.

"Andras Király," he sighed. "Why have I been hearing your name with such frequency lately?"

When speaking to someone he knew well, Andras had a tendency to conjure up music for them in his mind. Franz was associated with a dance tune; Dietrich's music was something booming and Wagnerian. Glöckner's was sometimes cheerful, sometimes furious… but always frantic.

"I couldn't say, sir," he said. "Is there some kind of trouble?"

"For you, no. For me, yes. First you and that Bauer lad are snatched away to perform at private parties, and now this." Glöckner tossed the letter he had been reading onto the table. "That, my boy, is a letter from Count Heinrich von Holstadt. About you. Specifically, about a job."

Of all the things Andras had expected Glöckner to say to him, this was at the bottom of the list. "A job?"

"An interview for one, anyway. Evidently the count's children have a fancy to learn the violin, and you were the first person who came to mind."

"I was?" Certainly the countess whom he had met at the party had been complimentary enough, but surely the Count von Holstadt could afford to pay a much better music teacher than a violinist at a middle-class opera company. "Are you sure?"

"Indeed I am." Glöckner pinched the bridge of his nose in frustration. "If you were to get the job, the count has made it clear that it would be in addition to your work here, not a replacement. Still, I do worry."

"I'll turn it down, sir," Andras said quickly. "My work here is the most important thing in my life, and I wouldn't jeopardize that." He felt more than a twinge of regret at saying this; Ilka's letter still weighed heavily on his mind. And if there was one family who could afford to pay him well, it was probably the von Holstadts. But there were some things he couldn't risk losing.

Glöckner shook his head. "Don't be ridiculous, Andras. Everyone here knows your situation. Far be it from me to deny you any opportunity to help your family. Arrange an interview with the count, by all means, with my blessing. I only ask that you attempt to find some sort of balance. You understand?"

"Very much so, sir," said Andras, trying to keep the intense relief out of his voice. "Besides, it's only an interview. There's no guarantee the count will actually hire me."

"Hmm," Glöckner replied, clearly unconvinced. "I suppose God may smile on me after all. I'll send word to the count that you're interested. He suggested tomorrow for an interview. Now remember, the first time you talk to Count von Holstadt, call him Your Excellency, and don't speak until you are spoken to. And for the love of God, don't mention anything about your father, you understand?"

"No, sir," Andras murmured. "I certainly wouldn't say anything about that."

CHAPTER FOUR

(In Which Our Hero Considers the Nature of Wealth)

May 5
The Day of the Job Interview

IT HAD BEEN approximately four years since Andras had awoken before nine in the morning, yet on the day of his meeting with Count von Holstadt he was not only awake, but breakfasted and moderately coherent before the St. Stephen's clock chimed eight.

Andras tried to dress as elegantly as possible, a difficult feat since he only currently possessed one and a half suits, the trousers of which were slightly too short. He kept meaning to have them altered or buy new ones, but there never seemed to be enough time or money. Still, his nicest green waistcoat and matching cravat, both of which he'd got secondhand, were clean and presentable, and his hair cooperated enough that he could tie it back. His mother had always done that for him when he was a little boy and complained about his hair being too long. No one with the famous Lázár family red hair was allowed to *cut* it. "The source of all our powers," Anna had always called it.

With any luck, those powers would include getting hired.

The von Holstadt kitchen at least was familiar, and a comforting sight after riding in the entirely-too-nice carriage the count had sent to bring him to the interview. On the night of the party

Andras and the other musicians had received a simple but hearty supper that he'd thought about for days afterward, and as he was herded through the servants' entrance Andras could smell something utterly delicious baking. On his way out he would have to see if he could beg a piece from the cook. Hell, if he was hired here, maybe they'd give him all sorts of leftovers. He wasn't starving on his current salary, but eating bread, cheese, and soup for most meals got tiresome after a while—coupled with the fact that Franz couldn't cook at all, leaving Andras in charge of all dinners.

He was jerked out of his culinary thoughts by the sound of a throat being cleared loudly. The throat in question belonged to a hatchet-faced and extremely dignified man whom, after a beat, Andras recognized as being the butler. What was his name again? Herbert? Herschel?

"Hermann!" Andras exclaimed, causing the butler to look taken aback. "Sorry. I mean, you are Mr. Hermann, aren't you? I believe we met briefly on Saturday, though you might not remember me."

"Mr. Király. Yes, I remember you," Hermann said, his tone implying that Andras did not deserve in the least to be remembered. "Normally, you would wait in the kitchen. But I am under orders from the countess to deliver you to the Blue Parlor in order to make you more... comfortable."

"That's generous, but I think I would be more comfortable in the kitchen..." Andras stopped, as the butler's expression indicated that he had no choice in the matter. "I mean, thank you. Lead on."

As he followed the butler through the house, Andras did his best not to stare like a country bumpkin at the luxury that surrounded him. This turned out to be a nearly impossible task, though in Andras's defense, how was he expected to not be overawed at everything in the von Holstadt home? He'd heard that the emperor lived in the most beautiful palace in Europe, but it was hard to picture even the emperor's home being finer than this. The walls were covered not in wallpaper, as Andras had originally thought, but in a cream-and-gold brocade fabric that was probably worth more than the entire Landfeld Theatre. And the fragile-looking vase in the entryway strongly resembled one Andras had seen in a book about the emperors of China.

For all he knew, the vase *had* belonged to a Chinese emperor. Some ancient von Holstadt had likely arrived at Kublai Khan's court and said, "Well, chap, how much for the vase? Goodness, what a bargain. Throw in a few gold candlesticks and some silk for the walls while we're at it."

All around Andras, suspicious faces glared down from meticulously painted portraits, the faces of illustrious and departed von Holstadts, presumably, as though questioning what right he had to enter their domain. He could hardly fault them for this, as he had similar questions himself.

Don't look at me. He frowned at a painting of a pointy-bearded chap in a heavily embroidered doublet—General Johannes von Holstadt, according to the frame. *Look at your descendant, he's the one who got me into this.*

Unsurprisingly, the portrait did not respond.

"Wait here," the butler said coldly, ushering Andras into another exquisitely decorated room. "I will inform the count you have arrived."

"Thank you." Andras glanced longingly at one of the armchairs. "Am I, ehm… allowed to sit down?

Hermann glanced around the room, clearly assessing whether Andras would get dirt and poverty on every piece of expensive von Holstadt furniture. "If you must," he said at last. "Don't touch anything."

Before Andras could ask how he was meant to either sit or stand if he didn't touch anything, the butler departed.

Andras exhaled deeply and sank into one of the blue chairs. Perhaps he was just tired, but the cushions felt like he was sitting on a cloud. Lord, was this how rich people felt all the time? Just… comfortable? The only armchair in the Király household belonged strictly to György, and that was twenty years old and sagging in every part.

Another reason to hope he got the job. Comfortable chairs were no small luxury.

The thought of the reason he was here made his heart thud in worry, and he quickly cast his eyes around the room, hoping to distract himself. A coat of arms above the fireplace caught his attention—a blue shield, decorated with a gold chevron, a crown, and a rose. Squinting, he took in the motto at the bottom.

Spes nos defendit.

The Italian he'd learned at music school enabled him to translate that to *hope protects us.*

That was true enough, Andras supposed. Though it was probably easier to be hopeful when you lived in a palace. Perhaps, for the sake of accuracy, it should have been *money protects us.*

What would the Király family motto be if they had one? Something like *stubbornness preserves us,* Andras reflected. Or *starvation is imminent.* Or, if his father was in charge of selecting it, maybe *Austrians can go straight to…*

"Mr. Király?"

Andras leapt to his feet, guiltily wondering if Hermann, who had just entered the room, could read minds. "Sir?"

Either the butler could read minds, or he simply disliked Andras. Either way, despite Andras being the taller of the two, Hermann somehow managed to look down his nose at him. "The count will see you now, Mr. Király. This way, if you please."

Count Heinrich von Holstadt's office was a dark, wood-paneled space dominated by shelves of books and an enormous oak desk that looked like the prow of a ship. The man seated behind the desk, with his heavy mustache and sleek dark hair, had the air of one who expected his every command to be followed with a minimum of fuss. If he wrote a song for the count, Andras decided, it would be a military march, heavy on the tubas. There was a painting on the wall just behind the desk—likely a family portrait—featuring the count dressed in a pale blue military uniform, an attractive blonde woman holding a lace-clad baby, and a dark-haired, beaming young girl.

"So," the count said finally, putting down the letter he was inspecting. "Mr. Király."

There was an awkward pause before Andras realized he was probably allowed to speak now. "Your Excellency," he said, with a bow. "I, ah … appreciate your seeing me."

"And I appreciate your coming. There, we've got the formalities out of the way. From here on out, you may address me as 'sir.'"

The count gave him a surprisingly kind smile. "After the strict protocols of court, I prefer to keep a more relaxed tone in my own home."

Relaxed, Andras understood, did not mean *egalitarian*. He therefore waited until the count gestured to the chair in front of him before allowing himself to sit.

"Now." The count leaned forward, tapping the tips of his fingers together. "I suppose you know why you are here."

Andras decided to err on the side of the obvious. "Your children needed a violin teacher, sir?"

"One of my children. My son, Heinrich, will be heading to the Theresian Academy this autumn, and must focus on more academic subjects. It is my daughter, Marta, who is keen to learn the instrument. One of the accomplishments she claims to need in order to attract a husband." The count shrugged helplessly. "I shouldn't think that would be difficult whether or not she learns the violin, but young women and their fancies… well. No harm in it."

"No, sir."

"What remains is to establish your credentials. How long have you been with the Odysseum Opera Company?"

"Nearly four years, sir. Ever since I left the Academy."

The count looked appraisingly at Andras, taking in his shabby appearance. "You attended the Academy?"

"I was a charity case," Andras explained. "One of the professors from the school came to Budapest, and Ma—that is, my mother— insisted I audition for him. He was kind enough to help me get a scholarship."

"Kind indeed. And after your years of academy training, do you feel competent enough to instruct my daughter? She is not a child, you know. She is a young woman with very high standards. There will not be any slacking off if I were to hire you."

Slacking off! As if anyone who'd spoken to him for more than five minutes could think that Andras Király, who'd gotten himself through the Academy on sheer determination and showed up to every single rehearsal ten minutes early, was capable of *slacking off.*

"I've never slacked off in my life," he blurted, adding as an afterthought, "I mean, sir."

There was a long, strained silence, in which Count von Holstadt looked at Andras carefully. Andras resisted the urge to shrink away from that steely gaze, keeping his back straight and his eyes forward. He might have needed the money, but he was Hungarian, damn it, and a Király. There wouldn't be any begging today.

"I believe you," the count said at last. "And I will say that both my daughter and your director seem to have nothing but positive remarks about you. Without making any guarantees, I'm inclined to give you the job."

"Thank you, sir. Do you …" Andras gestured at the violin case next to him. "Do you need to hear me play anything?"

"To be perfectly frank, I am a man of business, not the arts. One violinist sounds much like another to me. If you can show up on time and make my daughter happy, I don't feel I can ask much more." He stood and nodded politely at Andras. "Thank you for your time, Mr. Király. You will be hearing from me."

Years of musical training had given Andras one very important skill—he knew a cue when he heard one. And this, clearly, was his cue to leave.

"Thank you, sir," he said, bowing. "It's been an honor."

"Yes," said the count. "I suppose it has."

❧

Two Days Later
Café Voltaire, Leopoldstadt

While Café Voltaire was neither clean nor fashionable, it was both cheap and conveniently located, and for these reasons it was the preferred meeting place of most of the opera company's lower-paid members. It was here, then, that Andras hurried after rehearsal on Friday evening.

His friends were crammed around a small table in a corner of the crowded, smoky café. Franz was there, already pouring glasses of yellow wine from a dusty bottle, and next to him sat Brigita Novak, her ballet clothes swapped for a brown linen frock but her copper hair still tightly pinned up. Rounding out the group was plump, bespectacled Leo Meier, oboist, whose suburban parents were surprisingly proud of his Odysseum career.

"You're late," Brigita declared as Andras flopped into the last chair.

"Had to run home. I wanted to see if we had any post." He jerked his head in Franz's direction. "You two still on speaking terms?"

"And why shouldn't we be?" Franz asked indignantly, putting an arm around Brigita's shoulders. Andras did not dignify this with a response. Franz and Brigita's relationship was notoriously difficult to keep track of. Every so often they would quarrel horribly and insist they never wanted to see one another again, then a week later would act as though the whole incident never happened. Privately, Andras thought that if Franz wanted to keep Brigita around much longer, he'd better marry her before she took up with one of the stage-door hangers-on, but this did not seem imminent.

"Anyway, I've had a letter from the von Holstadts," Andras said, considerably more casually than he felt. "I expect it'll be about that job."

"And you're secretly a puddle of nerves so you've come to us for moral support?" said Leo with a wide grin. "Say no more."

"Not in the slightest," Andras lied. "I don't much care about it, really."

"Which must be why you've gone pale as a sheet," said Leo. "Cheer up, Király. If you get the job you'll have some extra money and if you don't you won't have to spend your days teaching the violin to bratty snobs. Either way, you can count yourself victorious."

"He's right. What are you waiting for?" Franz demanded. "Go on, open it."

Andras looked down at the envelope in his hand, which seemed to suddenly have tripled in weight. "Alternately, would it be possible for me to take a week or two to build up the courage?"

"Oh, for heaven's sake, I'll read it," Brigita said, rolling her eyes and plucking the envelope from Andras's hand. She ripped the envelope open with her fingernail and declaimed: "Dear Mr. Király. You are hereby offered the position of music tutor in the von Holstadt household. You will be expected at the family's residence twice a week for two hours, and will receive a weekly salary of five gulden."

Andras stared at her, giddiness rising like a balloon in his chest. "Five gulden! Are you certain?" For four hours of work a week, it was an unheard-of fortune. György's medicine would be paid for, Jozefa wouldn't have to leave school, Andras could finally buy new trousers...

"Five gulden indeed," Brigita exclaimed. "Heavens, they are rich. Makes you wonder what they did to deserve it. Think they need a ballet tutor as well? My gran back in Litvilov could use a new roof on her cottage."

"Unfortunately, I don't think they're hiring ballerinas. But I'll buy you a drink to make up for it. As a matter of fact," said Andras, "the entire next round is on me."

CHAPTER FIVE

(In Which There Are Many Questions and Few Answers)

May 6
Lesson the First

ONE HAD TO be cautious about accepting generosity from one's betters. As a scholarship student at the Academy, Andras had been exceedingly careful about not taking advantage of his wealthier classmates. The more often he bought his own drinks when he joined his classmates at the pub, the less guilty he felt about accepting Laszlo Klasky's family helping him pay for train fare to Budapest during the Christmas holidays.

All of this was to say that when the letter containing Andras's terms of employment generously offered him transportation to the von Holstadt home whenever necessary, he replied with gratitude and explained that unless it was pouring rain, he would prefer to walk.

Besides, it seemed a crime not to indulge in a half-hour walk on his first official day of work. The sun blazed, the domes of the old city glittered in the light, and despite the painful struggle of waking up long before his usual time Andras felt distinctly encouraged. Teaching a countess was intimidating, but it was still the violin, the instrument his entire life had centered around since he was six years old. He could probably teach the violin to a frog, given enough time and money.

His good mood was further bolstered when he was greeted at the door not by the intimidating Hermann, but by a cheerful footman who welcomed him to the staff and told him Countess Marta awaited him in the music room.

The idea of having a room just for music had always been a fond fantasy of Andras's, and he was pleased to see that the von Holstadt music room lived up to all expectations. Light from the large window at the back streamed over the pale yellow walls and illuminated not only the figures within but what had to be the most beautiful Bosendorfer piano Andras had ever seen. Even though the piano was primarily Ilka's area of interest, the sight of the von Holstadts' instrument sent a sensation close to lust rushing through his body.

"Mr. Király, Countess," the footman behind him announced, bowing deeply and reminding Andras that not only was he not alone in the room, but he had not been hired to stare at pianos. He'd been hired to tutor the young woman in front of him rising from her chair with a wide smile.

And truth be told, his new student rather looked like a china shepherdess.

Really, seeing her in the daytime and with his brain properly functioning, the resemblance to one of the figurines on Granny Erzsébet's mantelpiece was astonishing. The porcelain skin, glossy chocolate-colored curls, and generous curves would have suited a china shepherdess very well, though the young countess's pale green dress looked much too expensive for a country girl to own. And the look of intense interest in her wide dark eyes was not very doll-like.

Anyway, Andras would be able to report to Franz that Countess Marta was indeed pretty, and then forget all about the subject.

An awkward hush fell over the room, and he realized he had been so busy staring that he had completely forgotten to bow. He did so now, stiffly, without flourish. "Countess. A pleasure, once again."

"The pleasure is entirely mine, Mr. Király," Countess Marta replied. She had a bright, surprisingly loud voice. In another life, she might have done very well as a schoolteacher. "It's terribly good of you to accept this position on such short notice. I can't promise that I'm very talented, but you are, so it ought to balance out, don't you think?"

Andras nodded obediently, wondering as he did so what exactly he'd done to give the countess such a high opinion of his talent. As far as he was aware, he hadn't performed any better than usual during her birthday party. There was no accounting for the whims of the rich, he supposed.

"This is my maid, Nella Schmidt," Marta went on, gesturing at the other occupant of the room—a slim dark-haired young woman in a black dress, who looked thoroughly amused by the whole situation. "If you need anything at all, please let her, or myself, know. After all, you are our guest."

Guest was putting it strongly, he thought, though it was polite of her to avoid the word *servant*. With a murmur of thanks, he set his violin case next to the piano bench and, when Marta sat, followed suit.

She had a sprinkling of golden freckles on her upturned nose, he noticed absently. Funny, one didn't usually expect aristocrats to have freckles. China shepherdesses, on the other hand…

Seeing the expectant look on Marta's face, Andras cleared his throat and opened his violin case. "Well. Shall we begin?"

Three years earlier, Marta had been presented at court to the emperor and empress themselves, wearing a crinoline so wide she'd barely been able to fit through the door and her hair pinned up so tightly it made her eyes go a bit funny. Despite having grown up surrounded by royalty and nobility of all sorts, she'd spent the entire presentation trembling with nerves over whether she was going to trip, or sneeze, or start laughing.

Her first lesson with Mr. Királn was not nearly as significant as a court debut, not by anyone's standards. So it was difficult to explain why she currently felt just as nervous as she had then.

Actually, it wasn't that difficult to explain. Emperor Franz Joseph had been a very striking and intimidating presence, but he hadn't been so handsome that Marta felt slightly feverish from being in close proximity to him. It was good to know, at least, that her initial attraction to Mr. Királn hadn't been the result of champagne and excitement.

He'd tied his hair back today with a length of faded green ribbon, clearly in the interest of looking neat and polished. Yet, Marta noticed with amusement, a few stray dark-red tendrils had come loose from their moorings and tumbled down to his wide shoulders. She had the oddest urge to reach out and brush his escaped hair back behind his ears, but managed to restrain herself.

His long hair made him look like something out of the eighteenth century, like Mozart. Marta could just picture him in one of those long brocade coats, probably green to set off his hair and eyes.

Belatedly, she realized Andras was looking at her expectantly, presumably having just asked her a question. "I'm sorry, Mr. Király, I was distracted for a moment. You were saying?"

"Quite all right. I was asking," Andras said, "if you had your own violin, or if you would need to borrow mine." He did not, it had to be said, look very pleased at the prospect of letting someone else lay hands on his violin. Probably an attitude most musicians shared.

"No need to worry, Mr. Király, I do indeed have my own. Nella, if you wouldn't mind?"

Dutifully, Nella brought over the shiny mahogany-colored case containing Marta's new violin, purchased from one of the most renowned dealers of musical instruments in the city. It was very nice, and Marta was delighted to own it, but it was so glossy and perfect that she was almost terrified to touch it.

"That's a fine violin, Countess," said Andras, sounding relieved as Marta opened the case. "May I?"

As he picked up the instrument and turned it over in his hands, Marta quickly glanced down at Andras's own violin case, which he'd carefully placed next to his seat. It looked far more like a true artist's possession than hers did—black leather, slightly battered, with the word *Clara* embossed on it in faded gold letters.

Clara. Who was Clara? Some strapping Hungarian peasant girl who'd been Andras's sweetheart since childhood?

"You might already know that the strings are A, G, D, and E, and their pitch can be changed by—" Andras broke off and let out a muffled yawn. "I'm sorry, Countess. The pitch can be changed by—"

"My goodness, Mr. Király, you look exhausted," Marta interrupted. Truth be told, he didn't look any less tired than he had at her party, though he must have slept since then. "Are you sure you're feeling well?"

Andras shook his head. "I assure you I'm fine, Countess. Simply tired. I woke up earlier than usual."

That made sense, considering how late at night opera rehearsals must go. Marta felt a flash of guilt at having chosen ten o'clock as the best time for music lessons. It was a good two hours after she usually woke up, but apparently she hadn't considered Andras's schedule. "I am so sorry, you must be awfully worn out. Nella, could you ring for a pot of coffee?"

"That's really not…" Andras began, but Marta shook her head firmly. It was bad enough that she'd made him get up so early; she certainly wasn't going to have him fainting from exhaustion.

The coffee was duly brought up, and Andras filled his cup to nearly overflowing, gulping it down with the gratitude of a man dying of thirst. "Thank you, Countess," he said at last. "I admit I needed that."

"Your German is very good," Marta blurted. "I noticed at my party, too. I mean… It isn't your first language, I assume."

Andras looked disconcerted by the volume of this remark, but nodded politely. "Thank you, Countess. It's not really so impressive, though. We all learn German in school back in Hungary, we don't have much of a choice. And I've had plenty of time to practice, living in Vienna."

"Ah, that explains it. I've always longed to explore Hungary properly. It's a terribly interesting nation. So much history." Marta had been reading about Hungary for several days, and at this point could have carried on a detailed discussion about the nomadic conquerors and King Stephen, but Andras looked a bit too tired for this. "Where in Hungary are you from, exactly?"

"Ehm, Budapest," Andras replied, appearing mildly uncomfortable. Perhaps, Marta thought, he was one of those people who needed encouragement to talk about themselves. What luck that she was an expert at giving that sort of encouragement.

"That's brilliant. I've never been there myself, but I've heard it's a beautiful city. How long have you been in Vienna?"

"Eight years, ever since I was sixteen; that's when I started at the Academy." Andras

took a final sip of his coffee and set the cup down briskly. "Right, shall we…"

"Oh, I'm in no hurry." If he was this uncomfortable with taking a short break, Marta hated to think what his job at the opera company must be like. Never a minute's rest, most likely. "Is your family all still in Budapest? They must be very proud of you." Except his father, maybe, considering what he'd said at her party, but there was no need to bring that up now. "Being able to study at the Academy, and all that. It's such a prestigious school."

"I suppose they're pleased enough. Not my mother, she's no longer with us, but my father and sisters. But they're a long way away, you know. Which isn't always easy."

"I can only imagine," said Marta. "Is your family musical too, and have they ever come to visit you in Vienna? What does your father do?"

It seemed like a perfectly innocent question, but the minute it left her lips the air in the room seemed to turn to ice. Andras's face, already on the pale side, went even paler, and his vivid eyes widened in what could only be described as horror.

"Is that… strictly relevant?" he asked in a strained voice.

Marta blinked in surprise, the heat of embarrassment flooding her face. Clearly she'd said something wrong, but what? She'd never heard that Hungarians considered it rude to ask questions about one's family, but then again, she'd never done much research into the subject. "I suppose it isn't, but I was simply interested to hear about your history. Have I offended you, Mr. Király?"

"Not a bit," he replied, in a tone that very much said *yes, you have*. "But I do not enjoy discussing my family with strangers, and I would consider it unprofessional of me to talk about my own life during our lessons. Besides, we have a great deal more to cover today."

Something about the way he said *strangers* made Marta wince. Of course it was technically true. They'd only met once before, and he was the help. But somehow she'd expected him to feel the same way she had when she'd first met him. That spark of… friendship? Attraction?

Whatever it had been, it was evidently one-sided. Plainly, he didn't care much about them getting to know each other. He didn't even seem to like her that much.

In which case, what were they doing here?

"You're quite right, Mr. Király," Marta said after a moment of extremely awkward silence. "Do forgive me for becoming distracted. Please, continue."

"I can't do it, Franz," Andras announced, slamming the garret's door shut behind him with a force that made the thin walls shudder. "I absolutely cannot do this job."

Franz, seated at the kitchen table, looked up from the sheet of music he was studying. "And why, pray tell, is that?"

"It's not the teaching I mind," Andras said. "It isn't even the fact that they're rich enough to buy Bavaria. But good God, I don't see how I'm supposed to teach someone who is constantly talking and asking me personal questions. *Personal questions,* Franz."

"Ah," said Franz. "So you can't possibly teach this countess because she's... nosy?"

Andras pointed a finger at him. "Precisely. Nosy. She is very nosy."

"Which is a problem because..."

"First, I have never enjoyed telling new people about my personal business. Remember how difficult it was for us to get to know one another when I first moved in here? Second, how do you think the von Holstadt family would react to learning about my father's revolutionary history? I doubt they would be pleased."

"Bold of you to assume they would care what your father did twenty-one years ago. I mean, Glöckner knows about your family history and yet he's never sacked you."

"Bold of you to assume they wouldn't. These are not ordinary Austrian people, Franz, they're the Count von Holstadt's family. Practically royalty, from what I hear. Who's to say they wouldn't view my very existence as a personal attack?"

"All right, then, don't tell them. Or quit. Who's stopping you?"

Andras shook his head. "I would leave. But…well, you know why I can't."

"Then you'll have to grin and bear it." Franz offered him a sympathetic smile. "Look, it won't be so bad. I reckon the best strategy is to agree with everything she says, and if she starts to get nosy, change the subject. These rich folks want our lot to behave like agreeable peasants."

"Oh, Lord," Andras groaned. "I wasn't agreeable by a long shot. I was a bit harsh, actually. God only knows if I'll still be employed there after today. Wouldn't that be something? All that fuss over getting the job in the first place and I'll be back to where I started after one day. My family's going to be furious."

"Not if they don't know you got the job in the first place," Franz pointed out. "Have you written to them about it yet? No? Good, then you're safe. For all they know you've never had another job in your life."

There was some logic in this. Still… "I really do need the money," Andras said ruefully. "Pa's medicine…"

"Well," said Franz. "If things get really bad, you can always sell your hair."

Andras rolled his eyes and headed back to his bedroom, letting out a growl of frustration as the door closed behind him.

Of course Franz would make light of the situation. That was what he did. It was the way their friendship worked—Andras worried, while Franz joked, and it had kept them both moderately sane for years. But Andras couldn't bring himself to laugh this time, overcome as he was by fear and anger and, most of all, humiliation.

Yes, humiliation. How else was he supposed to feel after he'd completely panicked during his first day of a job he desperately needed? Not to make excuses for the countess—she had no business asking highly personal questions after two minutes' acquaintance. But after the way he'd reacted, she'd surely be suspicious of him now, and from suspicion it was only a short leap to his being back where he'd started.

With a sigh, Andras glanced over at his violin, still safely locked in its case. Sometimes, he thought, it seemed as though there was only one person—or thing—that he could rely on.

"I don't suppose you have any advice for me, do you, Clara?" he asked. "Come on, we've known one another for eighteen years. You must have some insight."

There was no reply, but after a pause Andras nodded anyway.

"You're right," he said. "What else can I do?"

Later That Day
Hannelore von Holstadt's Sewing Circle

Marta bent over her embroidery hoop with utmost concentration, blocking out the chatter of the other women in the parlor. The pattern she was working on was a Polish one, exceedingly complicated and requiring a variety of colors, and the more Marta focused on it the less likely she was to dwell on the events of her first music lesson. Which had been an incomparable disaster.

It was just as Sophie had said. *You discover a new person, become utterly infatuated with them, and then discover too late they're not perfect at all and feel awful for days.* It was Friedrich the Shetland pony all over again, except that instead of acquiring an animal who tried to bite her, Marta had hired a music teacher simply because she liked his eyes and then completely annoyed him with her nosiness.

What had she thought would happen when they were together? Had she expected him to whisk her away into a brand new world of art and adventure, or fall madly in love with her? Perhaps not, but she'd at least expected her musical education to lead somewhere good.

And she'd so been looking forward to learning the violin.

Good Lord, if she continued in this vein of thought, she was going to burst into tears. Marta shook her head and forced herself to listen to what her mother's other guests were discussing, which turned out to be the recent strikes by workers in the garment factories.

"A nasty business," Marianne von Braumark was saying, her words punctuated with a slight shudder. "Terribly bad form, taking to the streets as though they're fighting in the French Revolution."

"But they deserve to be heard, don't you think?" Sophie said. "After all, these women are dedicating their lives to honest labor and are badly treated as a reward."

"What do you know about labor, Sophie?" Marta put in irritably. "Your only experience with work comes from when we were twelve and disguised ourselves as servants at your family's Hanukkah party. Which was my idea, incidentally."

Sophie sniffed. "I learned lots from that experience, I'll have you know. Three hours of serving drinks in an itchy dress taught me more about the world than half my tutors. And anyway, it doesn't matter if I've done labor, what matters is that I know its value. What is the use of all our money if we aren't using it to improve people's lives?"

What, indeed? At the moment, Marta did not particularly feel capable of improving her own life, let alone those of the general public. "You make a fair point, Sophie. But how do you expect us to go about doing so?"

"By standing with them, of course!" Sophie exclaimed. "By making sacrifices." She glanced around at the shocked faces of Countess von Holstadt's guests and seemed to deflate like a balloon. "Or, you know. Anything we can do to help, really."

"Well, personally," the countess said, "I would like to point out that our sewing circle has made dozens of blankets and handkerchiefs for the local orphanages, which is a quite sufficient amount of charity on our parts. And as for the women from the garment factories, they are perfectly entitled to protest ill treatment, so long as they do not make nuisances of themselves or bring out the guillotine." This pronouncement done, she picked up a plate of biscuits from the table. "Who would like another vanilla kipferl?"

Once the guests had departed, Hannelore turned to Marta with a frown. "All right, my dear, are you going to explain why you're looking so downcast today?"

Marta debated with herself whether to tell her mother the

truth. It was embarrassing, certainly, and yet it was better that Hannelore knew about this than Ludwig's dodged proposal. "Frankly, Mama, I'm rather upset with myself. Tell me honestly, do you think I am the most ignorant, immature woman in Vienna?"

Her mother raised a surprised eyebrow. "My goodness, not at all. Why ever would you think that?"

"Because I'm always making the most ridiculous mistakes," said Marta, closer to tears than she would like to admit, "and blurting out whatever nonsense comes into my head, and humiliating myself. I know I'm legally of age now, but half the time I still feel like a dratted child."

"Ah, Marta, my girl." Hannelore gathered Marta into her arms, patting her hair. "I'm sorry to say that being of age doesn't make any of us less likely to do foolish things. But you are not an idiot, and not a child, just a bright and impulsive young woman."

"Thank you." Marta sighed. She leaned against her mother's shoulder, allowing some of the tension to drain from her body. "The trouble is I think I've upset poor Mr. Király. My attempts at a friendly chat backfired and I was horribly impertinent instead. He'll never want to speak to me again after that."

"Well!" Hannelore sniffed. "I don't see why it matters what he thinks of your questions. He's hired help, darling. He'll get over it, or he'll find another job. If you feel you were rude then apologize, of course, but there's no need to make a fuss about it."

Marta considered this. Andras didn't seem like mere hired help, somehow, but otherwise she supposed her mother was right. A polite apology was all she could do, and if he wasn't inclined to forgive her… Well. There was hardly a shortage of violin teachers in Vienna, even if none of them were capable of making her shiver with anticipation.

She could guarantee one thing, though. If Andras kept his job as her tutor, she would not become infatuated with him. Any feelings of desire would be firmly squashed.

After all, he wasn't the only one capable of being professional.

CHAPTER SIX

(In Which Everyone is Deeply Sorry)

May 11
Lesson the Second

ANDRAS HAD NOT lost his job.

Not yet, anyway. But if he hoped to keep it, he would have to do quite a lot of apologizing. He'd spent Sunday rehearsing an appropriately penitent speech, and repeated it to himself under his breath during the entire walk to the von Holstadt home.

Upon his arrival, as before, Andras was shown to the music room and left in the company of the countess and her maid. Marta looked much as she had before. Elegantly dressed, in lavender this time, perfectly poised—but something was different. The confidence he'd noticed in her last week had faded, replaced by something he couldn't quite name.

"Mr. Király?" she said hesitantly. "It was good of you to come back. Would you have a seat?"

Andras obeyed, taking a deep breath as he sat. "If you'll allow me, Countess, I feel I owe you an apology."

Marta looked surprised, but composed herself quickly. "Is that so?"

"It is. You have been nothing but amiable to me during our brief acquaintance, and I haven't returned your kindness one bit. In fact, I have behaved…" Damn it all, he couldn't remember the rest of the speech. He let out an awkward laugh. "I've behaved like an ass, pardon my language."

"Language pardoned. As for the apology, I appreciate it, though it's not necessary." Marta leaned forward in her seat, perfect posture temporarily abandoned. "Mr. Király, I know I tend to talk, well, a lot, and ask many questions. I am nosy, I'll fully admit to it, but I'm afraid my family and friends have grown so used to me that they no longer notice. You had every right to be annoyed, and I am extremely sorry." Two bright spots of color had appeared on her cheeks, and her hands twisted anxiously in her lap. "If you would prefer not to tutor me anymore, I understand."

Of all the things Andras had been expecting Marta to say, this was not one of them. She was utterly sincere, he realized—and not only sincere, but nice. And it would be difficult to stay angry with someone who was both sincere and nice.

"I wonder, Countess," he said, "if the wisest thing to do in this situation would be to start over completely. As we seem to have gotten off on the wrong foot."

She seemed to find this a good idea, as she smiled brilliantly and stood, dropping into a brisk curtsy. "Countess Marta von Holstadt, music amateur and asker of rude questions. It's a pleasure to meet you."

Andras laughed and bowed deeply. "Andras Király, nervous idiot. At your service."

"And Nella does not need to reintroduce herself, because her behavior has been impeccable," said Marta briskly, sitting back down. "I am sorry that you were nervous, though. I was too excited to notice. Was it because you've never taught lessons before?

Her guess was only about one-third accurate, but it was as good an explanation as any. Better than the full truth, in fact. "That was certainly part of it," he said. "And to be perfectly honest, Countess, I'm not sure why you hired me as your violin tutor. Surely you could have your pick of the finest musicians in the city instead of an orchestra violinist from a second-rate opera company."

"You're quite right. I could have my pick of the finest musicians in the city," Marta agreed. "Which is why I chose you. I heard you play in the orchestra at my birthday party. I know how talented you are—which is very, incidentally. But just as importantly, I decided to have Papa hire you because, as my English governess used to say, I liked the cut of your jib."

Andras had learned some English while studying at the Academy, but this hadn't extended to words like *jib*. "I understand most of those words separately, but not together, Countess."

"Sorry. What I'm trying to say, Mr. Király, is that you seemed like an interesting person with whom I would enjoy spending time. Something I am still inclined to think."

"Ah." It was difficult not to feel flattered, even if he wasn't certain he believed her. "I hope it won't disappoint you to learn that I am in fact a very boring person who spends every waking hour in a drafty opera house."

"Clearly, you and I have very different definitions of boring, Mr. Király," Marta said. "I can also conclude that you have never spent three straight hours practicing walking down a staircase with a book on your head at the age of nine. Compared to that, spending every waking hour in a drafty opera house sounds like a grand adventure."

Andras' lips twitched in a faint smile. "It can be sometimes. Though I wouldn't be surprised if the opera ballerinas had to walk about with books on their heads occasionally. I thank God every day that I chose to be a violinist instead of a dancer."

"May I venture to ask you another personal question, Mr. Király?" When he nodded hesitantly, she went on, "How did you become a violinist?"

Ah, now they were on safe territory. This was a question he could answer easily.

Andras had, in fact, first picked up a violin at the age of six.

The instrument in question had been a battered old fiddle belonging to Mr. Zoltán Batori, the Király family's next-door neighbor who had once played for the Vienna ballet. While during his heyday he had been well-respected and bordering on renowned, Mr. Batori's fortunes had fallen, and by 1851 he had been reduced to living in a one-room flat two floors down from the Király family and playing at the local beer hall some evenings.

Anna Király, who considered herself a dutiful neighbor, visited Mr. Batori once a week, bringing a basket of rolls and nodding along politely with all of the old man's rambling stories. Accompanying her on these visits, with the understanding that good behavior would earn him a piece of marzipan, was young Andras. And he was well-behaved, though privately he found Mr. Batori, with his bushy beard, shock of white hair, and almost colorless blue eyes, a bit frightening.

It wasn't until the fourth or fifth of these visits, while Anna busied herself in the kitchen making coffee, that Mr. Batori pulled out his violin and, completely ignoring Andras's presence, played a few haunting notes of the most beautiful song the little boy had ever heard. Andras, who had been sitting in awkward silence, leaned forward so far he nearly fell off the splintery wooden chair he was perched upon. By the time Mr. Batori set down his bow, Andras was thoroughly enchanted.

"What was that?"

Mr. Batori smiled with the rapture of a true connoisseur. "That, my boy, was the overture of *La Sylphide*, one of the greatest ballets ever written. I think I could go deaf and blind and still be able to play that tune in my sleep."

"Oh." Andras stared longingly at the instrument in Mr. Batori's lap. It might look like just a funny block of wood, but anything that could make a sound like that had to be pure magic. "Could I play it?"

"That song? No, I don't think so," Mr. Batori said bluntly. He smiled at Andras's stricken face and patted him roughly on the head. "Not yet, anyway. After all, you're just a wee chap, barely out of nappies."

"I'm *six*!"

"All right, then, you're six. Too young to be any use to music. Still, in a few years' time…" He looked Andras up and down appraisingly. "If you truly have the spark, who knows?"

Andras couldn't have explained why, but it suddenly seemed more important to him than anything else that he should someday be able to play that song, and play it perfectly. Thus, a deal was struck. In exchange for some food and free mending from Anna, Mr. Batori would give Andras violin lessons twice a week until the boy was either deemed hopeless or had learned all Mr. Batori could teach.

And, as it turned out, Andras hadn't been hopeless. Not a bit.

Listening to this story with great interest, Marta had a very pleasant realization— Mr. Király was not a Shetland pony.

She hadn't misjudged him at all. He was lovely, and interesting, and clever—and, most importantly, he didn't hate her.

Which meant that her brilliant-scheme-turned-humiliating-disaster was perhaps not a disaster at all.

"How kind of him," she said, when the tale ended. "Was Mr. Batori a good teacher, then?"

"Good? He was excellent. He used to crumple up bits of newspaper and throw them at me when I made a mistake." Andras smiled wistfully. "Don't worry, that will not happen in our lessons. But unusual methods aside, he was an excellent teacher with incredibly high standards. I wouldn't be anywhere without him."

"I imagine he must be very proud of you," said Marta. "Living in Vienna, and playing at a proper opera company, and all that."

"I like to think he is, though I'm afraid I cannot ask him any time soon. He died, unfortunately, just before I left for music school."

"Oh, goodness, I'm sorry."

"Don't be. It's not all bad news." Andras looked fondly down at the violin in his lap, running a finger across the smooth wood. "He didn't have much to leave behind, old Batori, but he did leave me Clara here. I've had her ever since."

Marta bit back a giggle, both from amusement and relief. "Clara is the violin? Oh, that explains a lot."

He blushed, quite fetchingly. "Ehm…yes. That was what Mr. Batori called her, and I…picked it up. Silly, I know, but…"

"It's not silly at all," said Marta. "It's lovely. I completely understand why Mr. Batori would give his violin a name. It must feel like a member of the family. Sorry, *she* must feel like a member of the family."

He looked gratified enough by this that Marta felt comfortable enough to ask one more thing. "That song, the tune from *La Sylphide*. Did you learn how to play it?"

"Oh, yes," said Andras. "I'm afraid I've become like Mr. Batori in that respect. I'll remember how to play that tune until I die."

"Could you play it for me now?"

To her great relief, he gave her a genuine smile. "It would be my pleasure, Countess."

With that, he lifted his violin to his chin and began to play.

The late Mr. Batori had been right, Marta reflected. It was a beautiful tune, warm and romantic and sensual, and it was hardly surprising that young Andras had been so enchanted by it. Even Nella, who had spent most of the conversation dozing in her chair, was now listening intently. Marta smiled, picturing a small, skinny red-haired boy, utterly transfixed by music, probably with the same dreamy, focused expression on his face that he had now.

She'd promised herself that she wasn't going to become infatuated with him. And she absolutely intended to keep that promise. But really, did he have to make it so hard?

Dear Ilka,

I'm very sorry it has taken me so long to reply to your letter. As usual, things in Vienna have been hectic, leaving me with little time to write. Thank you for writing to me, incidentally; I'm pleased to hear that you and the rest of the girls are doing well. Please tell Jozefa that if she neglects her schoolwork I will personally come home and throw her in the river. Surely she realizes that out of the bunch of us, she is by far the most intelligent?

Now, on to Pa. I may have some good news regarding his medicine. In the time since you wrote to me I have managed to find some extra work as a music tutor for the von Holstadt family. You likely won't have heard of them, but the patriarch of the clan is Count Heinrich von Holstadt, and his family is extremely aristocratic and sophisticated, something that I would not mention to Pa if I were you. You know how he gets about 'those Viennese toffs.'

Setting that aside for now, my primary duty is to teach the violin to the count's daughter, who is only a few years older than you. Countess Marta is a very agreeable young lady, although she does tend to talk a great deal. Frequently in English, for no discernible reason. Still, as far as aristocratic employers go, I could do much worse. I've enclosed some money with this letter, which will hopefully help with Pa's medicine.

And how are you? I'm glad to hear your employers aren't treating you too badly. Do you still play their piano when they aren't at home? It's important to keep in practice, though I suppose they might be annoyed if they caught you. When I'm rich and famous, I'll buy you the finest piano in Europe.

Your loving brother,

Andras

PS: Is Kitti still refusing to kill spiders? I know she respects them for eating insects, but she really must understand that if they are not going to pay rent they have no business building homes inside our flat.

Dear Andras,

Don't apologize—I wrote to you with a problem and it only took ten days to find a solution! Meanwhile, your Mr. Mozart wrote the overture for one of his operas on the morning before it opened so you've got him beat. The next time you're upset you can tell yourself "I am more efficient than Mozart."

I thought the name von Holstadt sounded familiar, so I peeked in one of Mrs. Gruber's society papers and sure enough, there they were. My goodness, they sound illustrious. Did you know that they own a coal mine? And that their estate in the country has the largest hedge maze in Carinthia? Compared to them the Grubers seem like—well, us. The Countess sounds quite sweet. Does she dress very beautifully?

I won't tell Pa any of the details about your new job. Can't guarantee that the other girls won't, but I'll give them a talking-to about upsetting Pa when he's ill.

Oh, an idea just occurred to me. Perhaps you could get the von Holstadts to be your artistic patrons. All the great musicians have patrons, don't they? Like Beethoven and that prince whose name I've forgotten. Or if they don't want to be your patrons, they could be mine. Everyone likes the piano.

Love,

Ilka

PS: I will have you know the Grubers like it when I play their piano.

They almost never play it themselves so they appreciate that I keep it in tune.

PPS: I've talked to Kitti about the spiders but she's given them names by now. It's hopeless.

(Note attached to box of slightly squashed chocolates)
Dear Ilka,
Don't get your hopes up re: patronage.
—Andras
PS: As far as my uneducated eyes can tell, she dresses very beautifully.

CHAPTER SEVEN

(In Which the Opera Company Sells Four More Tickets than Usual)

THE RUMORS THAT Oskar Glöckner had not slept since he'd founded the Odysseum Opera Company in 1850 were, Andras suspected, exaggerated. Whether he slept well was another matter entirely. Running an opera company in a city already so saturated with musical talent, combined with a lead soprano who was nearly always upset about something, a lead baritone who was constantly missing his cue, and the ever-fluctuating ticket sales, surely resulted in fitful nights for the unfortunate director.

Andras had no desire to make Glöckner's life more complicated than it already was, though he knew his new job didn't make matters easier. So when he was summoned to the director's office for the second time in as many weeks, he ascended the theatre's back stairs with a heavy heart.

"Sir?" he said cautiously upon arrival, lowering into the office's other chair when Glöckner gestured for him to have a seat.

"You're not in trouble, Andras," Glöckner said. "I only wanted to briefly discuss your other employment. How is everything with the von Holstadts?"

"It's…" Andras paused. His new situation was oddly difficult to describe. "Fine, actually. Not entirely what I was expecting, but I have no complaints."

"I am very glad to hear it. You have," said Glöckner, "quite an opportunity here, you know."

"Sir?"

"What I mean is the von Holstadts are a very influential family.

It wouldn't hurt to have their name associated with ours. If, by any chance, you could convince them to take an interest in our little production…" Glöckner raised his eyebrows significantly.

"Ah. You'd like me to talk them into seeing *Don Giovanni?*"

"If possible. Of course I don't expect you to overstep any boundaries. Propriety is of the essence. But if you could work it into conversation. Listen, Andras, you know *The Barber of Baghdad* didn't do as well as we'd hoped, and some good publicity would do wonders for this place. There is the lease to consider," Glöckner said mournfully, "and Miss Eisen keeps threatening to go to the Court Opera. Not that I think she would, but I wouldn't like to risk it."

"Say no more," Andras said quickly. "I'll bring it up to Countess Marta tomorrow. She's enthusiastic about the theatre." *And everything else.* "I'm sure she would be happy to oblige us."

Glöckner breathed a sigh of relief. "Thank you, Andras. If there's anything at all I can do for you. "

"Pay to send my sisters to finishing school," Andras suggested. Glöckner's eyes bulged, and Andras laughed and shook his head quickly. "Only joking. You've done enough for me as it is. If I may, I believe Dietrich might need me back in the pit."

"Yes, yes, of course. Thank you for your time."

The minute the office door closed behind him, Andras let out a low growl of annoyance—with himself rather than Glöckner. Hadn't he learned by now not to make promises he couldn't keep? Advising aristocrats on what theatre tickets to buy was certainly not what he'd been hired to do, and it had a chance to backfire horribly.

He'd do it anyway, of course, to preserve the opera company he loved. But perhaps he should have asked Glöckner for more money after all.

May 13
Lesson the Third

Andras arrived precisely on time and looking, Marta was pleased to note, less exhausted than usual. His hair was mussed, but it suited him. Best of all, upon entering the music room he gave her a genuine, wide smile.

"Good morning, Countess. And Miss Schmidt," he added in the direction of Nella, who briefly glanced up from the ladies' magazine she was absorbed in and nodded. "You look well, Countess. That's a nice frock, the… the color suits you."

Marta flushed with pleasure at the compliment. She quite liked the dress she had on herself, a pale green one with pleats on the bodice, but she hadn't expected Andras to notice. He didn't seem the sort to think much about clothes.

"How kind of you to say so, Mr. Király." She scanned his clothes, looking for something new to remark on. Same trousers, same jacket… ah. "I do like that bow tie, I must say. What an interesting pattern. Are those horseshoes?"

"Are they?" Andras asked, trying and failing to look down at his own neck. "I keep buying secondhand ties and I've got an odd collection at this point. One's got to have some small luxury, and I use the term very loosely. But on another subject, I have a favor to ask of you, if I might."

He looked so nervous Marta was momentarily terrified. Was that why he'd complimented her dress, to flatter her so she would help him? Perhaps he owed money to criminals, or he was deathly ill, or something awful like that.

"I'm under strict orders from Glöckner—the Odysseum's director, you know," Andras went on, "to ask if your family would like to come and see *Don Giovanni* later this month. It's opening on the eighteenth and Glöckner's convinced your support will mean a world of difference, since you're so well-respected. I'll completely understand if you have no time, but Glöckner would be disappointed if I didn't ask."

Marta laughed in relief. "Is that all? Mr. Király, of course we'll come to *Don Giovanni*. We've been planning to for ages. The von Braumarks have practically insisted on it." It wouldn't be as enjoyable to go to the opera with Ludwig hanging about and not enjoying it properly, but still, an opera was an opera and Mozart was Mozart. And it would be delightful to see the differences between the opera company's costumes and the ones she'd been idly sketching. "Only… oh, drat. You say it opens on the eighteenth? No, that's out, I'm afraid, the Steins are having a ball and they're always so keen for us to come.

"But don't worry, we are absolutely going to attend one of the performances," she added, noting Andras's disappointment. "How long does it run? We'll come later. And I'll talk about it to everyone. It might wind up in one of the society papers and your next production will be sold out for weeks."

"I didn't know they put things like that in the society papers," Andras said, with a slight smile. "It might make for an interesting headline. Something like *Aristocrats Patronize Second-Rate Opera Company Out of Pity for Daughter's Violin Teacher.*"

Marta couldn't hold back a snort of laughter. "If I saw a newspaper with that headline I would buy it immediately. But you'd be surprised at the kinds of things that make it into the society papers. When I wore peacock feathers in my hair at a ball three years ago, it was written about for weeks."

"It must have been a slow month for news," Andras said. "But I appreciate your help. It's not as though the opera company is on its last legs, but Glöckner does tend to worry; one never knows how each production is going to turn out. Audiences can be fickle, after all."

Marta smirked. "I suppose now you'll say they're just like a woman." She'd heard her father and Ludwig say similar things far too often and always struggled to find a sufficiently contemptuous retort.

To his credit, Andras appeared genuinely confused. "Why would I say that? I have three younger sisters and they're all so stubborn, I don't think they have ever been fickle about anything. I remember once," he said, smiling fondly, "my sister Jozefa was so convinced her teacher had the wrong answer to an arithmetic question that she threw her slate at him. She got a few slaps across the knuckles with a ruler for that one, but she was right after all, so we were all quite proud of her."

"I don't know your sisters," Marta said thoughtfully, "but I already feel as though we would get along very well. And you have three of them, you say? Are they all younger than you?"

Andras's eyes lit up, and he fumbled around in his pocket before pulling a worn photograph from his wallet. "There they are," he said proudly, handing it to her. "Ilka, Jozefa, and Kitti. They got that photograph taken as a present for my last birthday. A handsome bunch, aren't they? At last count they're seventeen, fourteen, and ten, which is shocking, if you ask me. They really need to stop growing."

They *were* a handsome bunch, and not less so for their marked resemblance to their brother. The tallest girl, on the far left, had dark wavy hair but Andras's tall frame and high cheekbones, while the pigtailed girl in the middle was shorter and stouter but had the same direct, intense gaze. The sweet-faced little girl on the right was all long limbs and big eyes, just how Andras must have looked when he was young. Marta felt a prick of envy. She'd always wanted a sister. And Andras was lucky enough to have three.

"They're lovely," she said. "Ilka looks so much like you! Kitti too, though Jozefa not quite as much."

"Jozefa takes after our father's side of the family. Ilka and Kitti and I got the Lázár blood from our mother, which unfortunately translates to gangly."

"I don't think there's anything unfortunate about it. Your sisters are all very pretty girls. Are they musical too?"

"Ilka is. She's brilliant at the piano. I think if she had been a boy she would have followed me to the Academy. As it is, she's working as a maid, though fortunately her employers have a piano for her to practice on. Jozefa wants to be a writer. She's desperate to go to university and study literature, and Kitti is too young still to know what she's good at, but she's very clever."

"Quite an age difference between you and your sisters. Because you're… twenty-five?" As far as she knew he hadn't actually mentioned his age, but it seemed a good guess.

"Twenty-four, as it happens. And yes, there's a bit of a gap, but only because, you know." Andras gestured vaguely, with a hint of embarrassment. "Pa was ill for a long time, and he and Ma didn't think it convenient to have more children for a while."

"Say no more," Marta replied quickly. "It was the same with my family. Apparently having me was hard on poor Mama, and no one was sure if she'd be able to have more children. It was such a relief when my brother Heini was born. Having no male heir would have been a disaster. The entire estate would have gone over to my uncle Siegfried and he's sort of an adventurer. He spends most of his time in the Orient these days. Now he can keep eating dumplings in Shanghai while Heini gets trained to take on the mantle of responsibility when he'd really rather spend all day with the cows." She shrugged. "Anyway. You mentioned that your mother passed away? I'm awfully sorry."

"Yes, four years ago," Andras murmured. "It was difficult for our family. Not least since she was essentially the breadwinner after Pa… well, after he took ill."

"She sounds like a very hardworking woman. What was she like, if you don't mind my asking?"

"She was loud," Andras replied with a chuckle. "Opinionated. Bit of a squawky voice, big laugh, very bossy. Didn't take any nonsense from anyone. Kitti and I got the red hair from her, and the height. She was taller than Pa, which all the neighbors had a good laugh at. The one thing I didn't get from her was the musical talent. Excellent woman, my ma, but no ear for music."

Marta would have been perfectly happy continuing in this vein, but unfortunately Andras chose this moment to look at the clock and raise an eyebrow. "My goodness, is that the time? I had better start teaching you the violin, or your father will accuse me of slacking off."

"Oh, yes, he's very invested in the outcome of my musical education," Marta said with mock solemnity. "If I'm not ready to perform at the new Opera House by this time next year, he'll have the pair of us tossed in prison. Go on, explain to me what *scordatura* is, I've been wondering for weeks."

It wasn't until the violins were back in their cases and the sheet music was put away that Marta was finally able to resume their earlier conversation.

"Mr. Király? I forgot to bring it up earlier, but thank you for telling me all of that, about your family. You didn't have to."

Andras opened his mouth and then shut it again quickly, apparently having decided against whatever he was about to say.

"You're very welcome, Countess. I know how much you value learning about other people's lives."

"You mean how nosy I am, I expect. Quite all right, I've learned to accept it."

"No," Andras said quietly. "I admit I thought so at first, but not anymore. If you are nosy, well, I imagine it's because you care about people."

It was rare that Marta was struck dumb, but this was just about enough to do it.

He understood. After she'd annoyed him so much, he still *understood*.

"That's kind of you to say, Mr. Király," she said. "And I do hope you know that the questioning goes both ways. You can feel free to ask me anything you like."

Andras raised an amused eyebrow and folded his arms. "Anything, eh? Nothing too scandalous. We wouldn't want to shock Miss Schmidt."

"I don't think Nella will mind." Marta glanced in the direction of her maid, still absorbed in her magazine. "Will you mind, Nella?"

"No, milady," Nella replied, not looking up. "It's not my place to mind."

"Thank you, Nella. You see, Mr. Király? It's quite all right. Ask me anything."

"Hmm." Andras leaned back in his seat, tapping his long fingers together thoughtfully. "All right, then, I'm game. What do you do when you're not playing the violin and going to balls with archdukes?"

"I find other people to pester with endless irritating questions." Marta said. "Really, though, I enjoy making things. Sewing, especially, and thinking of ideas for clothes."

"Is that so?" Andras asked with interest. "That's wonderful. My mother was a seamstress, you know. Best in the neighborhood. I always thought it looked like awfully hard work."

"I'm hardly a professional," Marta said, with a modest shrug. "But I am fond of embroidery. I made that cover on the piano, as it happens."

Andras glanced over his shoulder at the delicately crocheted and embroidered decoration laid across the instrument. "You made this?"

"I did. It was one of those days when it was snowing too hard for me to leave the house and as a result, I was highly focused."

"I have to say, I think my mother would be impressed. It's beautiful. You're very talented, Countess."

"You're very kind. I don't suppose your opera company needs a new costume designer?"

She hadn't been entirely joking, and so was relieved when Andras didn't laugh. "I'm afraid not, though I'm sure you're highly qualified," he said, with a kind smile. "Our wardrobe mistress is getting on in years, so if she retires soon I'll certainly recommend you to Glöckner."

Even if he was being serious, Marta thought with a pang of regret, she'd never be allowed to make costumes for opera singers. Sewing was a perfectly acceptable pastime for a well-brought-up woman provided she didn't make any money from it. The fantasy was awfully nice, though.

Either Andras could read minds or Marta's ability to hide her emotions had not improved with age. Whichever it was, Andras looked at her with sympathy. "We couldn't offer you the salary you deserve anyway, judging from this beautiful piano cover." He lifted up a corner of the decoration in question and squinted at the initials Marta had embroidered on the pale linen. "M.D.E.R.v.H. Are all of those *your* initials?"

"Tragically, yes. I have an extraordinary number of middle names, from lots of illustrious female ancestors who will presumably come back to haunt us if they're not honored. My full name," Marta said, rolling her eyes, "is Marta Dorothea Elisabeth Reinhild von Holstadt."

"And here I thought there were no downsides to being an aristocrat."

Marta could think of several downsides to being an aristocrat— the inability to get a freckle, let alone undertaking a career in the arts, without one's mother throwing a fit being one—but she elected not to say this aloud. Whatever her struggles, they weren't as bad as supporting a sick father and three young girls.

"It's not so bad, being a countess," she said lightly. "Though one doesn't get much personal freedom. Too many expectations to live up to. When I was younger and my family would go abroad, I'd always want to wander off and explore, but they would never let me."

"I can understand that. Your family wouldn't want to see you hurt, and I can only imagine the ransom they would have to pay if you were abducted."

"Good point," Marta admitted. "But it's still a shame. If I was a man I could go on a proper Grand Tour and spend my inheritance on absinthe and loose women, and no one would say a thing about it. Not that I have any desire for absinthe or loose women," she added hastily. "But it would be nice to have the option."

"I've always liked the idea of traveling myself," Andras said, his voice wistful. "I've only ever been to about three places in my life: Budapest, Vienna, and my gran's house by Lake Balaton. Always thought Paris sounded rather nice."

"Oh, Paris is lovely. Mama has half her clothes made there. If you ever go there you've simply got to visit the Louvre museum. It's full of beautiful art that Napoleon stole from all over Europe. And…" Marta trailed off, embarrassed. It was awfully unfair for her to talk about what Andras should do in Paris when he might never be able to go.

"You needn't feel guilty, you know, Countess." Andras's quiet voice broke into her thoughts and Marta looked up, surprised. "About being able to go to Paris and things, I mean. I enjoy hearing about it, even if I can't travel much myself."

"I do feel a bit guilty," Marta admitted. "It's not right that my mother has her clothes made in Paris while you only have one pair of trousers." She clamped her mouth shut, guilt flooding her at such an uncouth observation.

"Now wait a minute." Andras's eyes narrowed, though he looked mildly amused. "Why would you think I only have one pair of trousers?"

"My one area of expertise is clothing, and I know for a fact that the trousers you have on are the ones you've worn every single time I've seen you. Black wool and slightly too short."

Andras let out a low whistle. "You're wasted in the aristocracy,

Countess. They ought to put you on the police force. You'd be able to catch every thief in the city just because you recognized his jacket."

"Yet another job that my education inadequately prepared me for, I'm afraid," Marta replied. "But I am sorry for being rude about your trousers. If it helps, short breeches were very fashionable a few generations ago. In fact, I think you'd look quite dashing in one of those eighteenth-century suits. Dark green, I think, to suit your coloring."

"Green," Andras said thoughtfully, "is my favorite color."

It was incredibly trivial information, barely more intimate than talking about the weather. There was no reason at all for the warmth in his voice, the faint smile on his lips, to make Marta feel as though she'd stumbled upon buried treasure.

"My favorite color is yellow," she offered up quietly. "Gold, to be specific."

"Like you wore at your birthday party, if I recall correctly," said Andras. "Though if I recall incorrectly, you'll have to forgive me. I was exhausted that evening." He frowned slightly as the clock began to chime, signifying half past noon. "I'd better be on my way if I want to cook lunch before rehearsal. For the record, I'm very pleased with your progress, Countess. Your assignment for next time is to practice today's scales at least twice, if possible."

Marta nodded, privately giving herself another assignment—writing *I will not become infatuated with Mr. Király* at least fifty times.

With any luck, it would be effective.

Later That Evening
The von Braumark mansion

"I'm disappointed in you, Ludwig."

Ludwig von Braumark winced, not glancing up from Marcus Aurelius's *Meditations*. "I know, Father. You've been very clear about that."

"And who can blame me?" Baron von Braumark demanded. His round face was red as a cherry, either from emotion or the imported Scottish whiskey he'd been imbibing all afternoon. "You had a job, my boy. The simplest job in the world. And yet you couldn't get up the courage."

"It wasn't about courage," said Ludwig. He hated how much his voice was shaking, but all the wise words he'd studied seemed to disappear when his father got like this. "I tried to propose to her, truly, but I didn't have the chance. She simply… slipped away at the end of the party."

"Slipped away?" his father snorted. "She's a girl, not an eel. I'd never have stood for that sort of thing when I was courting your mother. Why, I remember— "

As Ludwig did not enjoy picturing his parents' courtship, he interrupted quickly. "I should be more firm with her. I know. And next time I will be, I swear."

The baron rolled his eyes, which was to be expected. *Firm* did not come easily to Ludwig. He couldn't be firm with his father's hunting dogs, or the servants at Schloss Braumark in the country. He couldn't be firm with his own parents, and certainly couldn't be firm with the beautiful, chaotic, and terrifying young lady he'd been told since childhood would be his future wife.

That was the appeal of philosophy, in the end. Great philosophers didn't need to be firm. They were thoughtful, reflective, and open. They didn't need to fuss about marriages and family lines.

The trouble was, barons did.

"Enough waiting, Ludwig," said his father, his voice steely. "I know you're fond of Marta, so propose to her, before someone else does. You know your duty. Do it."

"I will," Ludwig said quietly. "I promise."

CHAPTER EIGHT

(In Which Marta Pronounces a Word Correctly)

May 18
Lesson the Fourth

ANDRAS, FIVE MINUTES late, rushed to the music room and flung the door open, prepared to make his apologies. Instead of Marta, however, he was greeted by the sight of a very small, sausage-shaped dog with long silky hair and large, soulful eyes. Noticing Andras, the dog let out a small bark and trotted over, looking up at him expectantly.

"*Szia*, love," Andras greeted it delightedly, reverting to Hungarian as he always did around animals. Kneeling, he reached out a tentative hand and stroked the small creature's soft fur. "You're very sweet, aren't you." The dog snuffled happily and licked his fingers, making him laugh. "Yes, you're a lovely little beast, you are. Who do you belong to?"

"Liebchen!"

Andras looked up sharply and flushed at the sight of Marta, looking very fetching in a cream-colored frock patterned with flowers, frowning down at him. He quickly stood and brushed a few stray dog hairs from his trousers. "Pardon me, Countess. Er... *liebchen?*" Had she just called him *darling*? And if so, why did he feel so pleased about it?

But she was looking at the dog, not him. "Liebchen," she scolded. "Have you been bothering poor Mr. Király?"

"Ah," said Andras, rather stupidly. "Liebchen is the dog. No, she hasn't been bothering me, she's very nice. Yours, is she?"

Marta smiled, bending down to pat Liebchen on the head. "My mother's, really. But we're all very fond of her. Heini would love to have a really big dog like one of those St. Bernards from Switzerland, but Mama's convinced that it would eat poor Liebchen alive, so here we are. Have you got any pets back in Hungary?"

Andras shook his head. "Unfortunately not. We never had enough room in our flat. The closest we got was the neighborhood pigeons. I remember there was one particularly fat one I used to feed when I was small, who I thought of as a pet—I called her Erzsi. To this day I'm not entirely certain if she appreciated all those breadcrumbs."

"Oh, I'm certain she did," said Marta. "She would have to be a fool not to. I'm sure by pigeon standards you are considered a great philanthropist. There will be pigeon libraries and museums named after you."

"I'd pay good money to see a pigeon museum."

"Who wouldn't? But on another topic, I have been thinking, Mr. Király," Marta said solemnly, passing the dog to Nella and taking a seat. "I have a favor I'd like to ask of you."

Several different possibilities flashed into Andras's mind, ranging from the mundane (teaching her how to play a specific song) to the outright scandalous (kissing her). He wasn't sure where the last possibility came from, but the thought of it made his cheeks heat up embarrassingly.

"What favor is that, Countess?" he asked, in as even a tone as he could manage.

"You look quite nervous, Mr. Király. Don't worry, it's nothing untoward," Marta said, smiling. "I just hoped you might teach me a few words of your own language."

Andras looked at her in surprised amusement. "You want to learn Hungarian?"

"Why not?" said Marta. "The empress speaks Hungarian, after all. Surely if I'm going to be an educated citizen of our dual empire, I must learn a bit of Hungarian."

"Good point, though I should warn you, it's considered a very difficult language."

Marta waved a hand dismissively. "Nonsense. I learned English, which makes no sense whatsoever. I see no reason I cannot learn Hungarian just as well."

"If you insist, then, I suppose I can teach you the basics. We can start with 'hello.'" Andras leaned back in his chair with a wry smile, the ghost of an idea making its way into his mind. It was risky, but possibly worth a laugh… "Say *tántoríthatatlanság*."

Marta's mouth dropped open in horror. "That's hello?"

"As I said, a difficult language. Go on, give it a try."

"Tantorith…" Marta swallowed hard and tried again. "Tantorithata…No, don't give me that look, I can do this!" It took several more tongue-twisting attempts, but she finally spat it out. "*Tántoríthatatlanság!*"

For reasons Andras did not care to examine, hearing Marta speak Hungarian was not only entertaining, but more than a little arousing. Surreptitiously he adjusted his trousers, hoping Marta wouldn't notice the effect she was having on him. "Well done, you're a natural! Of course, *tántoríthatatlanság* really means *unshakeability*, but still."

"Wait." Marta frowned. "It doesn't mean 'hello'?"

"Oh, no. Hello is *szia*. But you've really proven that you've got a Hungarian tongue, and that's exactly what I was hoping to discover—" He was cut off suddenly, as he dodged the crumpled piece of paper Marta had thrown at him.

"You are terrible," she cried, hands on hips. "Just think, if I'd gone to Budapest tomorrow and tried to have a friendly conversation I would have been using that awful word all over the place and everyone would think I'd gone mad. I'll never forgive you as long as I live.

"Oh, not really," she added quickly. "But now that you've had your little joke I insist you give me a proper Hungarian lesson one of these days. What did you say 'hello' really was? *Szia*? I can say that easily enough."

Andras grinned in relief. "But of course you can, Countess. As I said, you have a Hungarian tongue."

"Well, Mama always said I had to be good at something," Marta remarked. "But I say, *Don Giovanni* opens tonight, doesn't it? Are you feeling prepared?"

"Ehm," Andras replied eloquently. "I suppose I do, but I can't testify to the readiness of the rest of the company. I don't know if you were aware of this, Countess, but every single opera company is at least fifty percent lunatics."

"I always suspected as much," said Marta. "But the rest of the orchestra must have half a brain between them, or else I doubt you'd ever get through a performance."

"Debatable. Franz is all right—he plays the cello. You might have seen him at your party. Got me the job in the first place, as it happens. Mind you, living with the fellow is an entirely different affair. I'm always a bit grateful that we don't make enough to buy many new clothes or his half of the garret would be even messier than it is. I'm surprised Brigita tolerates him as much as she does."

"Who's Brigita?"

"Another friend of ours, one of the opera ballerinas. You'd like her, she's very no-nonsense. And then there's good old Leo on oboe, he's probably the most well-behaved one of all of us. He comes from one of those good suburban Jewish families, very well-brought-up, though that doesn't stop him from drinking with us at Café Voltaire in the middle of the night."

"And what is Café Voltaire? It sounds like a den of iniquity."

"More of a den of underpaid nocturnal bohemians. But it's cheap and close to the theatre and has both coffee and alcohol, so we're all quite fond of it."

Marta let out a sigh of what sounded like longing, though Andras was sure he'd misinterpreted it. Longing wasn't an emotion anyone usually associated with Café Voltaire, unless it was a longing for cheaper wine. Then again, to someone who'd grown up drinking champagne in ballrooms, maybe cheap wine and a den of nocturnal bohemians sounded tantalizingly exotic.

"What an interesting life you lead, Mr. Király," she said at last. "I should dearly love to be a fly on the wall at this Café Voltaire. But we'll have to discuss it another time, I suppose, or I'll never learn another tune on the violin. Shall we get back to work?"

He agreed and launched into an explanation of proper hand placement, contemplating as he did so that whenever he visited the von Holstadt house, it took him longer and longer to remember that he was there to work.

Later That Evening
The Stein Mansion

In general there was nothing Marta enjoyed more than a good party. And if the Stein family knew how to do one thing, it was host a good party. That particular Thursday was no exception, as Jacob and Rachel Stein had invited the crème de la crème of Vienna's financial world, hired a perfectly decent orchestra, and had their cooks whip up a selection of dishes that wouldn't have been out of place at court.

But unlike the majority of the occasions when she was at the Stein house, during this particular party Marta's mind was a thousand miles away. Or rather, about a mile away in the Landfeld Theatre, contemplating the opening night of *Don Giovanni*. Had they sold enough tickets? Would poor Mr. Glöckner, who sounded like such a nice man, finally be able to rest? Andras would be able to tell her about the performance during their next lesson, but it was hardly a replacement for being there.

"Marta?" Sophie waved a hand in front of her friend's face. "Are you awake?"

Marta blinked, quickly taking stock of where she was. Sophie's house, ballroom, party. "Yes, just deep in thought. What were you saying?"

"I was saying," Sophie said, "that not only has my cousin Miriam become engaged, but her parents used a matchmaker as though they live in some tiny village fifty years ago. I worry my parents are going to get ideas."

"If your parents want to pay someone to find you a husband, they should simply ask me," Marta replied. "For one thing I'm acquainted with half of Vienna, and for another I know what you like."

"Oh, you do? What do I like?"

"Factory workers, of course. Preferably ones who are on strike."

"I stand corrected. You do know what I like. You're hired." Sophie took a long swig of her drink and looked out at the swirling crowd before turning back to Marta. "What were you contemplating so deeply?"

"Nothing much, just that…well, it's the opening night for *Don Giovanni* at the Odysseum Opera Company, and I hope it goes well. Their last show didn't make much money and their lead soprano is always throwing fits."

"Marta von Holstadt, I am shocked. I believe you'd rather be in some dusty theatre watching people sing Italian at each other than here at my parents' extremely lovely party."

"That's not true," Marta protested. "I adore your parents' parties, you know that. Only Mr. Király works for the Odysseum and I've got invested in their goings-on."

"Ah, yes, good old Mr. Király. How are the famous violin lessons progressing?"

"Brilliantly. He's much less shy around me now. He's told me all about his sisters back in Hungary. His family sounds terribly sweet. I hope I'll be able to meet them someday. And today he told me I have a Hungarian tongue. Wasn't that kind of him?"

"I don't know what a Hungarian tongue is, but I don't like the sound of it," Sophie said. "Does it mean you have a high tolerance for pepper?"

"No, darling, it means I'm good at pronouncing Hungarian words. It's actually a funny story. I asked him how to say hello in Hungarian and he taught me some horrible long word as a joke."

"Amusing. Do you actually play the violin in these lessons, or do the two of you just toss witticisms back and forth like a pair of French novelists?"

An involuntary shiver passed through Marta's limbs at the memory of Andras adjusting her hand placement during their lesson, his warm fingers gently moving hers into place. "I'll have you know," she said primly, "that I can play the entire *Minuet in G* now with no mistakes. I may still be an amateur, but an amateur is someone who's having a good time."

"Is that the exact French translation?"

"Precisely."

Sophie let out a tired sigh. "You know, I hate to say it, but I'm a bit envious of you."

"It's because of my childbearing hips, isn't it? A mixed blessing, I assure you."

"Don't be ridiculous. And this is empty." Sophie gave an

irritated glance at her wine glass. "Marta, you and I get along so well because we're both always causing trouble, yes? Yet you're also brilliant at sewing and music and languages, everything our mothers approve of, and I … Well, I'm not artistic like you. All I do is cause trouble."

"You mustn't be so hard on yourself, Sophie," Marta said. "Ladylike accomplishments are all well and good, but they're not the only measure of brains. You're brilliant, and you care about people. That's nothing insignificant."

"What good is caring about people if I can't actually do anything? Last week we had a professor at one of our dinner parties and I asked him very nicely if he thought universities would start allowing women professors soon, and Papa changed the subject immediately. He told me later he didn't want me to start another one of my arguments." Sophie looked to be on the verge of tears. "What's the point of trying to do good in the world if it's unacceptable for me to simply ask questions at a dinner party? Sometimes I really do think I should just run off to America. Maybe I'd be a touch more normal there."

Sophie's face was oddly reminiscent of Andras's during his first two lessons with Marta—that strained, pale look of anxiety. Perhaps, Marta thought wryly, it was simply her destiny in life to serve as a counselor to insecure friends. "It's certainly not your fault that we have such strict rules for behavior. But you help me a great deal simply by being the finest of friends. Very few people would be as willing as you are to listen to my endless babbling." Marta smiled and elbowed Sophie gently. "Does that help?"

Sophie pursed her lips, obviously suppressing a smile. "I suppose. Though you're so rich and spoiled that being your friend may actually be a disservice to the general public. Who's next on your dance card?"

"Leopold Meissner. And if you'd like to perform some good deed tonight, you can give me some cotton wool to put up my nose. That fellow bathes in cologne."

As Sophie laughed and turned back towards the refreshments, Marta allowed herself to send one more hopeful thought in Andras's direction. With any luck, the Odysseum Opera Company would triumph.

Physically nearby but socially a thousand miles away, *Don Giovanni* had reached its intermission, giving the exhausted musicians, singers, and stagehands a chance to stretch, use the lavatory, and consume vast quantities of coffee.

Though Andras didn't want to jinx the show by saying so, the first half had gone surprisingly well. Stefan Stefanowski and Kristina Eisen had both shown up early, sober, and reasonably calm, and the number of tickets sold was perfectly respectable. Inexplicably, Andras found himself glancing out towards the audience as he headed backstage at intermission, hoping to see... who?

Well, Marta, truthfully, and he couldn't help being disappointed that she wasn't there. It would have been nice to see her, ask her what she thought of the show. Undoubtedly she'd have countless opinions about the music and costumes. He could just imagine what she'd say. Something like *I don't think people in Don Giovanni's day really wore stockings like that, do you? Though Mr. Stefanowski sang well enough that it barely bothered me.*

"What are you thinking about so deeply, Király?" Franz asked, clapping him on the back. "I've always wondered why you think so much. Is it because you're so tall that all your thoughts take ages to get anywhere?"

"Franz, I want you to do me a very important favor. Never become a doctor," said Andras. "And I was thinking about nothing in particular, really. Relieved we're halfway done with tonight, I suppose."

"I couldn't agree with you more." Franz groaned. "I've just spent ten minutes being lectured by Brigita. She's been dropping hints lately about getting hitched, and I have to say, Andras, I don't think I can handle that. I mean, you know me. I can barely look after a pot of coffee."

"This seems like a conversation you should be having with Brigita."

"I know, but it's comforting to talk to you about these things. It's like confiding in an older brother."

"Good God, Franz, I'm three years younger than you," Andras

said irritably. "Do I have to be your older brother as well? Haven't I got enough siblings constantly in need of my help? Being taller than you doesn't make me wiser."

"All right, all right." Franz held up his hands. "I'm sorry, I shouldn't have put it like that. I trust you is what I meant to say." He regarded Andras critically, brow furrowed. "What has gotten into you lately? You're distracted all the time and prickly as a hedgehog. Is teaching that countess really so awful? I know you said she was all right, but if the work's making you miserable—"

"This has nothing to do with Countess Marta," Andras interrupted, surprised by the harshness of his own voice. "As a matter of fact my lessons with her are the only time I get a bit of damn peace in my life. The second I step into this theatre I've got Glöckner begging me to use social influence I don't have, Dietrich working my fingers to the bone, singers making rehearsals drag on with their tantrums, and my friends asking for advice that I can't give. Not to mention my sisters' educations and my father's illness and the fact that I only own one damn pair of trousers. Spending four hours a week in the von Holstadt music room having conversations about pigeon museums feels like paradise."

"Pigeon muse…? Never mind." Franz shook his head, looking hurt. "I'm sure I'm sorry we've been asking so much of you. I know you haven't got an easy time of it. That said, I hope you know you're not the only one here who struggles, though you are the only one also working for one of the richest families in Vienna."

Hot, painful shame rose up in Andras's throat, nearly choking him. "Franz, I'm sorry, I…"

"Time to get back in the pit," Franz cut in quietly. "Don't worry, Király, you'll land on your feet. You always do."

CHAPTER NINE

(In Which Café Voltaire Serves a Higher Class of Customer)

May 20
Lesson the Fifth

ON THE MORNING after opening night, Andras strongly considered canceling his music lesson with Marta on grounds of illness. It wasn't entirely a lie. He'd spent most of the opening-night party alternately avoiding Franz and drowning his sorrows, and had been rewarded with a throbbing headache. A hangover, though, was not nearly a good enough reason to lose five gulden. Besides, Marta's bright smile when she saw him was nearly enough to cure all his ills.

"Good morning, Mr. Király!" she said. "You are exactly who I need to see. I was up half the night reading this brilliant book on Hungarian folk costume that I found in the library, and I've been desperate to talk to you about it."

Funny, Andras thought, how "Good morning, Mr. Király" had become one of the phrases he most looked forward to hearing. "I expect you know more about Hungarian folk costume than I do, at this point," he said. "I wish my father or grandmother were here—they'd have plenty of opinions to share with you."

Marta's eyes narrowed as she sat. "Are you telling me you've never worn one of those charming suits with the wide sleeves and colorful waistcoats? That is deeply disappointing."

"Oh no, I've certainly worn one of those. To every wedding and party in the neighborhood, in fact. Ma did all the embroidery herself," said Andras. "Though not with the wide sleeves. I insisted she leave those out. A fellow can't play the violin with sleeves like that."

"I suppose you couldn't. Is this wonderful suit back in Hungary, or could I convince you to wear it at some point?"

"Back in Hungary, I'm afraid. I wonder if it still fits me," Andras mused. "Ma made it six years ago, and I don't believe I've grown much since. Though my growth spurts have always occurred at highly inconvenient times." This elicited a slight chuckle from Nella, though when Andras glanced in her direction she'd already gone back to reading.

"Really, you're lucky," said Marta. "I haven't grown an inch since I was about fourteen. Except sideways, of course." She gestured vaguely at the bodice of her lavender dress, which molded neatly to her full breasts and narrow waist.

Do not think about that, Andras. "Did you enjoy your evening with the Steins?" he asked quickly. "A pleasant party, all in all?"

"It was quite nice, if not very exciting. And how was your opening night? No sore throats or bat infestations?"

"You laugh, but we have had bat infestations," Andras replied with a grimace. "I remember one particularly horrible performance of *The Marriage of Figaro*—but we don't need to go into that now. Opening night went well, thank Saint Cecilia, and it doesn't appear that we'll be out on the street any time soon. *Madamina, il catalogo è questo* went particularly well, if I say so myself."

"Words can't express how disappointed I am that I wasn't there," said Marta, without a hint of irony. "Nor can they express how excited I am to finally see your company perform. Now then, Mr. Király, what are we working on today?"

"I thought we'd work on the *Minuet in G* some more, considering you've nearly mastered it," he said as Marta began to flip through the sheet music on the piano. "If we make it through enough of that, perhaps we could move onto something more challenging, like…"

He was interrupted by an exclamation of "Ouch!" from the piano bench, and looked up to see Marta staring at her index finger in horror, her face pale with pain. At the sight of the long, painful-looking cut across her skin, a few drops of blood leaking out, Andras felt his stomach clench in worry. He pulled a handkerchief from his pocket and, without thinking, grasped Marta's hand, wrapping the cloth tightly around her injured finger.

Lord, her hands were warm. And she had the softest skin he had ever felt. And the way her big eyes were fixed on him, in a combination of surprise and gratitude, made him feel a bit dizzy.

Vaguely he heard Nella say something about fetching some gauze and then the sound of the door gently closing behind her. When she was gone, Marta let out an embarrassed giggle.

"How clumsy of me, getting paper cuts in the middle of a lesson," she said. "I do appreciate your valiant handkerchief, Mr. Király."

"My pleasure." He was still holding her hand and didn't particularly want to let go, to keep her cut from opening again, he told himself. And indeed, Marta didn't seem to object at all.

After a moment of heavy silence, she blurted, "While we're alone, I've been meaning to ask. Would you let me meet your friends?"

Andras dropped her hand in surprise. "You mean my friends from the opera company?"

"Yes. Could I come to Café Voltaire with you some evening and meet them? They all sound so interesting, and it's rare that I meet people who aren't part of my parents' circle."

"Countess," said Andras carefully, "I appreciate your interest, but surely you understand that it wouldn't be appropriate for someone like you to be out with a bunch of musicians and performers. For one thing, your parents would never allow it. And if you did try to sneak out and were caught, then what?"

A wave of guilt washed over him as Marta's shoulders slumped, and she looked dejectedly down at her injured finger. "I didn't intend to ask my parents for permission," she said quietly. "It wouldn't be too difficult to leave discreetly. But of course you mustn't bring me along if you think it would be too risky."

Damn those big eyes of hers and what they were doing to his common sense. "I assure you, it's not because I don't want you to come. But how would it work?"

"As a matter of fact, I've got a scheme." She leaned toward him and lowered her voice. "I can leave by the servants' entrance once everyone has gone to bed and sneak back in before they wake up. I've got a key, you see, something to do with teaching me responsible household management. It'll be all right as long as I'm quiet."

This did sound reasonable, though Andras was not entirely convinced. "And what about your, well, your appearance? With all due respect, in your current attire you would stand out."

"Ah." Marta tilted her head thoughtfully. "I see what you mean, my clothes are somewhat flashy. But I have a few plainer dresses, or I could borrow something from Nella."

"And if we're caught? I'd rather not upset your parents."

"If I get caught I will make it abundantly clear to my parents that this entire escapade was my idea," Marta insisted. "They'll believe it, too. When I was younger I got into all sorts of scrapes with my friend Sophie, and my parents always knew whose fault it was. I wouldn't let you lose your job, you must know that."

Clearly she noticed the skepticism on Andras's face, because she smiled kindly and moved her hand a bit closer to his. "Really, I swear. If we're caught, I'll tell them I ordered you to help me escape, and you were so dutiful you agreed to it. Which is barely a lie."

Andras could have given any number of cockamamie justifications for what he said next. He couldn't deny a request from someone of Marta's status; he still felt sorry for being rude to her previously; it could somehow help the opera company. But the truth was none of those excuses came anywhere near to the real reason. He wanted her to come. He wanted to spend time with her outside the confines of the von Holstadt mansion. It didn't make sense, and was an enormous risk, but he couldn't help it.

"All right," he said at last. "If you're able to get away, I'll meet you in the Stadtpark tonight at eleven o'clock. Do you know where the statue of King Francis is? I can meet you there."

Marta let out a squeak of delight. "Brilliant. I'm so excited. I promise I won't cause any trouble. Oh, one more thing." She leaned towards him conspiratorially. "If I'm going to pretend to be just a common person, if you'll pardon the phrase, you really ought to call me by my Christian name."

Andras blinked. "Can I do that?"

"You should, really. If you go about calling me Countess in front of all your friends they're hardly going to…find anyone better than Carlotta diAngelo to play Dorabella in *Così Fan Tutte*," Marta said loudly, as Nella re-entered the room. "Nella, you're so kind to fetch that gauze, but I think my finger is all right now."

The maid rolled her eyes fondly and returned to her seat, casting Andras a suspicious glance. He arranged his face into the most innocent look he could muster and adjusted his sheet music authoritatively.

Good God, what had he just agreed to?

True to his word, Andras was waiting by the statue of King Francis when Marta had successfully slipped out the servants' entrance and made her way to the park. She did have to stop a moment to admire him. She wasn't going to become infatuated with him, but he did cut a rather dashing figure in the dark with the lamplight reflecting on his red hair.

There was something almost romantic about the scene. If someone who didn't know them happened along, they might think they were observing a lovers' tryst. Which it was not, Marta reminded herself emphatically. It was an adventure, a potentially scandalous one that made her stomach flutter with nerves, but it was not a tryst.

She cleared her throat softly, making Andras jump slightly in surprise. "Ah," he said, upon sighting her. "Hello, Countess. You came, then."

"Do you remember what we talked about? I'm just Marta tonight," she reminded him. "First names only, Andras."

Was it her imagination, or did he go a bit red when she said his name? But he simply nodded, and held out his arm for her to take.

"You know, in Hungary, we put the family name first and the

personal name last," Andras told her as they walked, keeping to the most well-lit streets that were still bustling with late-night revelers. "So if we're being technical, Andras is my last name, not my first name."

"You do *what* in Hungary?" Marta shook her head. "Every time I learn something new about your country, it sounds like a stranger and stranger place. You're telling me that if I were to visit Budapest everyone would be saying my name backwards?"

"It's not backwards," Andras replied in mock offense. "You Austrians say your names backwards. How am I supposed to immediately know who all your relatives are if you put your family name last?"

"That's not so much a problem for me. Everyone knows who my relatives are. I'm a von Holstadt."

"Not tonight, apparently."

"That's true. Actually, you should probably practice saying my name so it sounds natural by the time we get to Leopoldstadt. Go on, say Marta."

Andras hesitated, then cleared his throat. "Marta."

Oh, she liked the way he said her name, rolling the *r* just a bit. "Very good," she said. "But you should probably say it a few more times, just to get used to it, *Andrrras*."

"Ah, making fun of my pronunciation, very ladylike, *Marrrta*."

"You made fun of the perfectly correct order my name is in. I'm just evening things out. Where would all my middle names go in Hungarian? Would they be after Marta or scattered around like birdseed somewhere?"

"If you were a normal, sensible Hungarian girl you would only have one middle name instead of three. You aristocrats really must stop hoarding all the middle names when some people have to get by on none at all."

"You sound like my friend Sophie with all her talk of redistribution of wealth. Well, the general populace is welcome to a few of my middle names, I have more than enough."

"You see, this is why your parents would disapprove of your meeting my friends. We've been outside your house for ten minutes and already you're becoming a socialist."

"My governess always warned me about night air," Marta said with mock solemnity. "But I suppose it's too late to do anything about it now."

Not ten minutes later they reached the café, an unassuming place from the outside, with a faded sign depicting a young woman holding up a glass of something green. Inside, it was crammed full of people in cheap, colorful clothing—mostly men, though Marta spied a few garishly dressed women among them—laughing and shouting and smoking. Somewhere in the background someone was scraping on a fiddle that did not sound nearly as nice as Clara.

Marta tried to take it all in, unable to quite believe she was truly there. She'd spent all day imagining what Café Voltaire would be like, but she hadn't been prepared for how different it would be, or how real.

If her parents knew where she was, they might die from pure shock.

There was a joke to be made about this, somehow, but when Marta opened her mouth all that came out was a smoke-induced cough. Andras looked down at her with a sympathetic smile.

"Sorry about that," he said. "The smoke's irritating, but where we usually sit it isn't quite so bad. Shall we?"

She clung to his arm more tightly than was probably necessary as they passed through clusters of theatrical-looking people. She didn't think anyone would do her any harm, but she couldn't shake the feeling that she was completely out of place.

And people were looking at her. Mainly out of curiosity rather than malice, but Marta couldn't help but worry that any minute someone would shout out "What's that useless aristocrat doing here? Toss her out onto the street." The plain dark blue dress she'd worn was hardly showy, but it was much less shabby than what everyone else had on.

She did enjoy holding Andras's arm, though. He had lovely arms, all lean, firm muscle. All those years lugging musical instruments and carrying baby sisters and moving opera scenery must have made him much stronger than he appeared at first glance. These contemplations came to a halt just as Andras did in front of a table in the corner.

There were three other people already seated at the table—two young men, one round-faced, dark-haired and bespectacled and one slim and fair-haired, and a wiry girl with copper hair pulled into a tight knot on top of her head. The fair-haired fellow's eyebrows went up when he saw Marta before his face split into a wide grin.

"Well, well, Király," he drawled. "And who is your charming guest? I didn't realize you ever spoke to anyone outside our little circle."

"Quiet, Franz. Everyone, allow me to introduce Miss Mar… Maria Weiss," Andras said. "Miss Weiss, this is my flatmate Franz Bauer, who plays the cello, Miss Brigita Novak of the opera ballet, and Leo Meier, oboist."

All three of Andras's friends nodded politely, murmuring pleasantries, while Brigita inspected Marta carefully as they took their seats.

"Well, in that dress, you're no chorus girl," she said. "Let me guess. Lady's maid?"

"Yes," Marta said immediately. Silly of her to not have thought of an explanation beforehand, but really, Brigita's assessment was perfect. A lady's maid could have fine clothes and good posture without calling undue attention to herself. "Excellent guess. I am a lady's maid. In a… in a very good family."

"Thought so," said Brigita with satisfaction. "Goodness, Király, you're associating with a higher class of people these days. Where did he pick you up, Maria dear?"

"Ah." Marta glanced frantically at Andras, who appeared just as stuck as she was. Why hadn't they sorted out their story already? It was entirely too difficult to think of lies at the last minute like this.

Finally, Andras cleared his throat. "We met at the secondhand bookshop," he said. "I was buying *The Sorrows of Young Werther* and we got to chatting about it."

Recognizing her cue, Marta nodded. "I advised him not to buy it. Awfully gloomy book. I mean, really, the poor boy spends the entire tale moping over someone who doesn't love him when he could have easily found a nice young peasant girl to marry him."

"And I didn't listen to this very good advice and bought the book anyway, only to discover that the c…Maria had been right the entire time," Andras finished. "And so we have been the warmest of friends ever since."

His friends appeared to accept this explanation without complaint, though the young man with the spectacles—Leo, she thought—looked at her with interest. "So, Miss Weiss. Which of Vienna's illustrious families do you work for? Perhaps you could talk them into becoming patrons of our little company."

Marta cast about wildly for an answer. "Er… the Steins. You know, the financiers." She regretted this as soon as she said it. Leo Meier was Jewish, she remembered Andras saying, as were the Steins, and what if they attended the same synagogue or some such? She'd be found out instantly. "Do you know them?"

"But of course, my dear," said Leo with a twinkle in his eye. "All Jewish people in Vienna are the very best of friends, you know."

There was a second of silence before Andras and all of his friends burst into peals of laughter.

"Don't mind Leo," Andras chuckled. "He likes to think of himself as one of Vienna's great wits, and doesn't mean a single word he says. Isn't that right, Leo?"

Leo tried to bow in reply, but as he was sitting down, all he managed to do was knock over his glass of wine, much to the horror of the rest of the table. There was a brief scramble as things were set to rights.

"Mind you don't get any of that on your shoes, Miss Weiss," said Leo, wiping the table with his napkin. "That's authentic Vienna wine. It'll burn holes in leather. Nothing like the weak French stuff you get in some restaurants."

"Just be grateful it's not Cuban rum, eh?" said Franz, with a wink at Andras. "We wouldn't want a repeat of last time."

"Last time?" Marta asked eagerly.

"Oh, of course Andras hasn't told you about the time he was arrested." Brigita cackled. "What was it for again? Right, disorderly conduct."

"It was a misunderstanding," Andras protested. "That constable completely overreacted."

"I'm thoroughly intrigued," said Marta. "Go on."

Andras grimaced and shook his head, though Franz seemed willing to pick up any narrative slack. "Allow me to set the scene for you, Miss Weiss. It was four years ago, when Andras had just joined the opera company, and we only knew him as the quiet Hungarian chap who'd saved our orchestra when Rudy decided fighting the Prussians was preferable to playing the violin. A few weeks after he was hired, we'd just finished up a very successful run of *Così Fan Tutte*, and to celebrate we headed out to the pub and somehow got our hands on a bottle of Cuban rum. Beautiful stuff," he said wistfully.

"We spent most of the evening interrogating Andras, of course," Leo put in. "I will say you were an awfully good sport about it."

"It's hard not to be a good sport after ingesting half a bottle of Cuban rum," Andras muttered. "I barely remember a thing about it."

"Well," Franz said with a shrug, "you couldn't hold your liquor nearly as well back then. Not eating enough, probably. Anyway, once we'd heard all about Andras's sisters and his father's injury and all two hundred and seven ways paprika can be used in recipes, we decided to head home. Except Andras wasn't entirely done with revelry yet."

Andras buried his face in his hands. "Please stop telling this story."

"No. We were walking past that horrible old fountain with the statue of Maria Theresa, and Andras decided to hop up on the edge and treat us to a rendition of some Hungarian folk song. I don't know what it's called, but it was something along the lines of springtime and planting, and somehow it's a metaphor for something very bawdy. I don't know if you're aware, Miss Weiss, but Andras is both a very good and very loud singer when he's been drinking."

"I will keep that in mind," Marta said, with a wink in Andras' direction.

"You will never hear me sing, I can assure you."

"Spoilsport."

"So anyway," said Leo. "We were making such a ruckus that a constable came along and tried to hush us—well, Andras—up, and instead of shutting his mouth and going home like a good boy, he shoved the constable into the fountain."

"The constable was nice about it, thank God," said Franz. "Only made Andras spend the night in the jail instead of hauling him off to court, and he let him out in time to get to rehearsal the next day. Still, the lesson of the story is, Andras pretends to be a sensible and dignified chap but he is actually not in the slightest."

"I hope you're happy with yourselves," Andras scolded. "Miss Weiss will think I'm the worst sort of person and never speak to me again."

"Oh, no, not a bit," Marta assured him. "As a matter of fact, I like you much better now." It wasn't a lie; she genuinely did like seeing this side of Andras, away from the relative formality of the von Holstadt home. He was in his element here, among his friends from the opera house, and it was endearing to see.

Besides, he was so very adorable when he blushed.

CHAPTER TEN

(In Which a Number of Secrets Come to Light)

Still at Café Voltaire

"YOU'RE LOOKING RUN down, old boy," Brigita remarked after another round of drinks, eyeing Andras critically. "Do your gears need winding up?"

"Gears?" Marta asked.

"Ah, I forget, you're not up on all the opera house gossip. There's a theory going around that our dear Andras is actually a clockwork automaton that Dietrich, the conductor, built to make the rest of us look bad."

"All lies, of course," said Andras. "I assure you that I am not an automaton."

Brigita raised an eyebrow. "Aren't you, though?"

"It would explain a lot," Marta put in. "I do hear creaking sounds whenever you move."

"That has nothing to do with being an automaton," Andras said primly. "That is because I have the joints of a seventy-year-old man."

"And the mind of an infant," said Franz.

Marta let out an involuntary snort of laughter which, thanks to several glasses of wine coupled with the excitement of the evening, turned into an uncontrollable fit of giggles. It took only moments for Brigita, Franz, and Leo to join in, until the entire table was in an uproar. It was a wonder that Andras managed to maintain his mildly disapproving expression until the hilarity had died down—though Marta did notice his eyes crinkling with suppressed mirth.

"Now, now, we mustn't tease poor Andras," Brigita admonished them, wiping her eyes with great dignity. "He's the most responsible person at this table. Working every hour God sends, poor dear, and with three sisters and an invalid father back home…"

"Truly a martyr," Franz drawled. "Saint Andras of Budapest. I'll have to write a letter to the Vatican."

Ordinarily Marta would have laughed, but something Brigita had said sparked a vague memory. Invalid father.

"Wait a minute. I knew I meant to ask you about that, Andras," Marta said. "Your father's injuries, Franz said earlier. Was he in an accident? Is he all right now? I do hope…" She stopped at the sight of Andras, who had suddenly gone very pale.

"Goodness, Miss Weiss, has he not told you that story yet?" asked Leo, oblivious to any tension. "I'm surprised. It's quite fascinating. Mr. Király the elder was a proper rebel, not like us lukewarm bohemians. Lost his leg fighting for Hungarian independence when Andras was just a—"

"Leo," Andras said through gritted teeth. The glass gripped in his hand shook slightly against the table. "Enough."

"You mean your father…" Marta frowned. "You mean your father fought in the revolution? That horrible violent one back in '49?"

Andras rolled his eyes heavenward, as if asking for guidance. When none immediately appeared, he grudgingly muttered, "Yes, if you must know."

Marta sat stock-still, thoughts swirling around her mind. She'd been born in the same year as the revolutions that had raged across the Empire began, and knew the essentials, but her education on the subject had been mostly limited to three points:

1. Emperor Franz Joseph ruled by divine right and was not to be questioned.

2. Hungary, Bohemia, Moravia, and all other sundry nations were lucky to be ruled fairly and sensibly by the Austrian crown.

3. Revolutionaries were violent, immoral thugs.

As Marta had grown older her views had become more nuanced, but it was still difficult to hear the word revolution and not imagine the kind of guillotine-toting monster she'd had nightmares about as a child. And Andras—polite, cultured Andras—was the son of one of those people?

Did that make him dangerous?

"You didn't tell me," Marta blurted, her voice harsher than she'd intended. "Why wouldn't you tell me something like that? Why would you lie to me?"

Andras set down his wineglass with enough force that every other object on the table rattled. "I don't need to explain my father's sacrifices, especially not to you," he growled, pushing back his chair. "Excuse me, won't you?"

With that, he stalked away from the table, disappearing among the café's other customers.

I should go now. Marta stared at her glass, hands shaking slightly. *Hire a cab or beg someone to take me home.* She couldn't walk home with Andras now, couldn't even speak to him after he'd been so dishonest. Had he ever planned to tell her? Or had he thought that if he was charming and cultured and polite enough, no one would ever discover what kind of family he came from? Now all she could think of was her father declaring that revolutionaries, and anyone who associated with them, were barbarians and no better than common criminals.

She couldn't take music lessons from a common criminal. She'd be sitting there frozen with nerves, wondering when he was about to do something terrible. Steal the family silver, cause a riot, destroy the piano.

Except…

Except no one who'd met him could call Andras a barbarian. No one could listen to the way he described his family, so loving and honest, and picture a bunch of thugs. His clever sisters, his kind and funny mother, even what little she'd heard of his father—they didn't sound like villains.

They sounded like people worth protecting.

Even, much as she hated to admit it, if protecting them meant lying.

Whatever his father had done, whatever the morality of the revolution, Andras seemed to have turned out extraordinarily well. And Marta, as usual, had been an idiot.

"Oh, Lord," she said aloud. "I handled that terribly."

"Don't feel too bad about it, Miss Weiss," Brigita said kindly. "Andras is sensitive about his family, particularly his father. I suppose living in Vienna is tricky for him. Not that Glöckner is bothered much about old Mr. Király, but there are plenty of folks in the city who might take offense. That fancy family he's been giving music lessons to, for one thing."

Marta froze, her hand clenching the edge of the table, her mouth dry. "That count and his family, you mean?" she said, as casually as she could manage. "The von somethings?"

"The very same. Imagine how a family like that would react to the whole business. Apparently even Glöckner advised him to keep it quiet, so the poor boy wouldn't be at risk of getting sacked. Well, you can't blame him for not wanting to discuss it, can you?"

"No," Marta murmured. "I can't." With a heavy sigh, she pushed back her chair. "I need to talk to him. Do you know where he might have gone?"

"If he hasn't gone back to our flat, then I expect he'll be by the fountain in the square, one block from here," said Franz. "But Miss Weiss, I'm not sure if you should…"

He was probably going to say something about being a woman alone at night, but his advice was lost on Marta, who had already leapt from her seat.

It was fortunate that the fountain was only just around the corner from the cafe, or Marta would have been considerably more frightened to be walking around in the dark on her own. As it was, her knees went weak in relief when she finally stumbled upon the small, round fountain topped with a highly unflattering depiction of Maria Theresa and spotted Andras sitting on the edge, staring at his feet.

If he heard her approach, he didn't show it. Marta hesitated briefly, not wanting to send him fleeing like a frightened deer.

"Is this where the infamous policeman-shoving occurred?" she inquired finally.

Andras glanced up at her in surprise, looking utterly exhausted. "Yes, and I have to admit I was hoping that would be the worst thing you found out about me today. I shouldn't have brought you here, I see that now. Silly mistake on my part."

"I wouldn't say that, especially since it was my idea in the first place," she said. She cautiously took a seat beside him. "In general, I've had a lovely evening. I'm just worried about you. Are you all right?"

"Better now. I'm sorry for fleeing like that," he said. "You'll think I'm very rude, I expect, only if I had stayed…" His voice faded.

"If you had stayed?" Marta prompted.

"You see, I occasionally get these, well, I've always called them panicky spells, though that doesn't do them justice. Something will set me off, even something minor, and suddenly it's, it's as though I become a cornered animal. Everything around me sort of shrinks, and I can't really cope." He shot her an embarrassed half-smile. "I am technically sane, I swear. But I'm sorry if I frightened you."

"So this time," she said slowly, "what set you off was talking about your father, I imagine? About how he fought in the revolution."

"Yes, he did." There was an odd edge to his voice. Relief, perhaps? Or defensiveness? "And I prefer not to bring it up in front of people like you, for obvious reasons."

"People like me?"

Andras exhaled wearily. "Yes, Marta, people like you. People who are born-and-bred Austrian and part of the establishment and who might very well view me as a danger to society based on what my father did twenty years ago. But we may as well lay everything on the table now. Yes, my father fought in the revolution. Yes, it cost him a leg and destroyed his lungs, and no, I'm not ashamed of him. I don't much care for violence but Pa was right to follow his conscience and he was incredibly brave, and I'm proud of him, damn it. If you think that—"

"Stop," she interrupted. "I'm sorry, I don't mean to be rude, but…" She shook her head. "I'm sorry. You can't have a very good opinion of me after how I reacted. My education wasn't exactly politically balanced."

"I assumed as much," he replied dryly. "Which is why I never told you. I was scared out of my wits that you'd find out and have me sacked."

"I wouldn't do that," Marta said. "Not after all our time together. I expect I was just angry you hadn't explained the situation to me. We're, well, friends by now, aren't we? I'd like it if we could be honest with each other."

"Honest. I see." Andras gazed at his feet for a few seconds, before lifting his head and looking into her eyes. "Marta, do you know why I became a musician?"

"Because you're good at it?" she suggested.

"That's a factor. And thank you, incidentally. But that's not the only reason." He sighed and pushed back his hair. "There are a great many things in this world that don't make sense to me. It doesn't make sense that my mother, the bravest woman in the world, died of typhus at the age of forty-three. It doesn't make sense that my father lost his leg in what turned out to be a pointless war. And it doesn't make sense at all that my sisters should have to spend their childhoods working to keep food on the table. But music… I understand music. It takes everything I feel—or everything people like Bach and Mozart felt, I suppose—and it puts it on paper in lines and notes and it makes sense. I can control it." He laughed self-consciously. "Only thing I can control, really."

"I'm sorry," Marta whispered. "I wish you and your family had never had to suffer like that."

"You have nothing to apologize for," said Andras. "And for the record, I'm sorry for not telling you about all of this earlier. I assumed that if you or your family knew about Pa and the revolution, you'd be disapproving at best."

"Mama and Papa would be, that's true," she said. "But I promise I'm not going to like you any less because of this. Is this why, when we first met, you said your father didn't entirely approve of your living in Vienna?"

"Did I say that? Lord, I must have been tired. But yes, that's about the size of it. Pa's never had any issue with my being a musician, but he's disappointed that I'm not doing it in Hungary. I've tried to explain it all to him—how much more opportunity there is here, especially in music—but he's a Királv and we're a stubborn lot. So he grumbles, and I tolerate it."

"Well, for what it's worth, I am glad you came to Vienna," Marta said. "But I'm afraid I'm going to ask you a nosy question now. After living in Austria for a few years, what do you think of… well, us?"

Andras smiled wryly. "Have I inherited my father's grudge against Austria, you mean? Here's what I think, Marta. I understand the reasons for the revolution and I'm proud of my father for fighting in it. I think the Compromise was a step in the right direction, and I think the prime minister is a good man. Most importantly, I love Vienna. I have lived here for eight years and it feels like home. Is that a satisfactory answer?"

"Hm." She tilted her head to the side and regarded him thoughtfully. "All things considered, I think you may remain in my family's employ. But if you decide to start any new revolutions, do please give me twenty-four hours' notice so I can hide my jewelry."

"I don't have the slightest interest in your jewelry." Andras snorted. "Your piano, on the other hand."

"As certain as I am that you would appreciate the piano as much as I do," said Marta, "I have a nasty feeling Clara would be jealous if you brought another instrument home."

"She might well be. Coun… Marta." Andras reached over and awkwardly patted her arm. "Thank you. For being so understanding, and for not sacking me when I was so rude to you during our first lesson."

"After I was so pushy about your family? Really, I'm surprised you weren't ruder. If I'd known then what I know now, I'd have let you get away with throwing newspaper at me."

He laughed, before standing and holding out a hand. "Listen, panicking in public is an exhausting business, and I'm on the verge of collapse. Shall we go in and say good night to everyone, and I'll escort you home?"

"If you insist." Marta rose to her feet reluctantly. "I hate to cut the night short. I had loads of ballet-related questions for Brigita. But there's always next time. If…" She looked up at him tentatively. "If there is a next time?"

"I suppose there could be. Though I have a question for you first, if we are going to be friends." Andras looked at her intently, his eyes almost glowing in the dark. As usual, that gaze made Marta mildly weak at the knees, and she had to force herself to listen to his words. "Why did you want to come here tonight, really? If I'm going to be risking my livelihood helping you sneak around the city, I'd feel better knowing it's not solely out of your desire to see how the other half lives."

She ducked her head in hopes that he wouldn't detect her face flushing from shame. "I'm sorry if I've seemed selfish," she said. "And I'm afraid you'll be disappointed in me. I did want to see how you and your friends live, but it wasn't to laugh at you, I swear. Only…"

"Only?"

"I know I live well," she said quickly. "And I'm grateful for it, I truly am. But I'm sure you understand that for someone like me, life is quite restricted. There are only about three things I'm allowed to do: go to sewing circles, repeat the same polite five phrases in every conversation, and marry Ludwig von Braumark. I suppose I wanted to see, just for an evening, what it was like to be you. To be independent and artistic and laugh at stories about Cuban rum. This has been, without a doubt, the most interesting night I've had in a long time."

To her relief, Andras didn't roll his eyes or laugh, just slowly nodded. "Yes," he murmured. "I believe I understand. Who is Ludwig von Braumark?"

"Baron von Braumark's son, an old family friend. They all expect me to marry him, but." Marta shrugged. "Anyway, it doesn't matter. My point is, doing things like this—seeing a new part of the city, meeting your friends, being treated like an ordinary person—it makes me feel more alive, somehow." She looked at Andras and smiled. "You're not the only one who sometimes feels you haven't got any control. But I don't have your musical talent. I find other ways to master my fate."

He regarded her for a long moment, his face unreadable. "I have to say, Marta," he said at last, "if there's any woman alive who can master her fate, I have no doubt that it's you."

Walking back from the Stadtpark after delivering Marta home, Andras had the odd feeling that he'd lost a great deal of weight.

Had he really spent the last few weeks torturing himself over what Marta would do if she knew about his father? He'd been certain she'd send him away, or tell her parents. But she hadn't.

She'd said they were *friends.*

"Friends with a countess," Andras muttered with a laugh as he opened the door to the garret. "I've certainly come up in the world."

"What's that?" said Franz from the kitchen table, nearly making Andras jump out of his skin.

"Nothing. What are you doing back here? It's barely midnight."

"We all decided to head home early. Be responsible for once," said Franz. "So, did the countess enjoy slumming it with us?"

Andras froze in horror. "Did the what?"

"Király, I may be drunk more frequently than I ought to, but I am neither blind nor incapable of remembering a face. Did you honestly not think I would recognize her? We were both in the orchestra at her birthday party, you know. In fact, I distinctly recall having a conversation the next day over whether you found her attractive."

"Ehm…"

"If you're trying to formulate a clever lie, don't bother. You're the worst liar I know. Don't worry, I'm not going to tell anyone," Franz said . "I'm just flattered that an illustrious von Holstadt would grace one of our little parties. Whose idea was it to bring her along? Fallen in love with her, have you?"

"Don't be ridiculous. We've just become friendly over the last few weeks, and she practically begged to come and meet all of you. I imagine it's boring, being an aristocrat all day. I didn't think it would do any harm, so I brought her along."

"She doesn't seem to have reacted too badly to your revolutionary revelation. Didn't I tell you not to worry about it?"

"Yes, you were right about a great many things." Andras swallowed and went on. "And you were right about what you said opening night, too. It was rotten of me to spend so much

time complaining when things have been going decently for me
lately."

"You know what your problem is, Király?" Franz said cheerfully.
"You're a martyr, just as I said earlier. Suffering alone as though
that makes you a better person. Trouble is, you're not alone
because you have a family and friends and rich acquaintances
who are dashed fond of you, and if you sat down and thought for
a minute you'd realize you're not too badly off."

"Fair enough. Am I forgiven?"

"Since when do I have anything to forgive you for? Go get
some sleep, you fool. I'm sure you'll conjure up another crisis
before dawn."

As Andras dropped into bed, though, his final thought before
drifting off to sleep had nothing to do with crises, and everything
to do with what Marta had said to him on the way home, about
mastering her fate. Even as they'd grown closer, he'd still thought
of Marta as another flighty aristocrat, someone who could never
truly fear the future.

Well, a fellow couldn't be right about everything.

CHAPTER ELEVEN

(In Which Heini Enhances his Vocabulary)

May 25
Lesson the Sixth

UPON ARRIVING FOR the next lesson, Andras dropped onto the piano bench with a deep and profoundly discontented sigh.

Something was troubling him, that was certain, and Marta knew he wanted her to ask about it. "How are you today, Mr. Király?"

"Oh, you know," he said, with a tired shrug. "Same goulash, just reheated."

She laughed before composing her face into something resembling sympathy. "I'm sorry for laughing, though that was funny. But go on. What's, er, reheating your goulash?"

"Nothing too terrible, but if I may complain a moment?"

"Please do."

"Things at the opera company have gone a bit mad lately. Well, madder than usual."

"Ah." Marta nodded. "Bat infestations again?"

"If only. Bats would be easier to deal with than Kristina Eisen in a snit. Not only has she been jilted by her latest protector, but she overheard Stefan Stefanowski calling another woman the most talented member of the cast. As a result, she's been throwing tantrums for three days straight." Andras sighed once again, this time less dramatically. "I enjoy my job, truly, but I can't say it's what I always dreamed of. Watching singers cause trouble isn't as gratifying as being a famous composer."

"That does sound exceedingly frustrating," said Marta. "Do you compose as well as play, then? I shouldn't be surprised. You seem to be an expert at everything musical."

He smiled ruefully. "I used to, anyway. When I was at the Academy I seemed to get a flash of inspiration every week. I could stay up for three days straight writing a new piece. Unfortunately, the muse has been fickle for the last few years. You're artistic, I'm sure you know what that's like."

She flushed and shook her head. "That's very kind, though not true. I'm not like you, anyway. You perform glorious music that inspires everyone who hears it; I embroider handkerchiefs and sketch ball gowns."

"Exactly," said Andras quietly. "You work hard to create beautiful things which bring people joy. If that doesn't make you an artist, I don't know what does."

For no discernible reason, Marta suddenly felt close to tears. "Are you certain? Everything I do seems so frivolous. In the grand scheme of things, who cares that I based the design of this dress on an old Dutch painting? The only one it'll bring any joy to is me."

"My mother used to say," he remarked, "that if something you've made pleases you, then you ought to be proud of it. But if it helps… " His gaze flicked over her in a way that made her ache with longing. "I may know nothing about clothes, but that frock certainly pleases me."

Marta limited her reply to a grateful murmur. If she opened her mouth any more, she'd either start crying or try to kiss him, neither of which would be appropriate.

Every single conversation she had with this man made her feel like a genuine human being, someone intelligent and talented and important. Not simply a wind-up doll whose only job was to smile and curtsy.

Hiring him was, without a doubt, the best idea she'd ever had. Though she regretted only insisting on two lessons a week.

"Have you noticed," Andras said, "that we tend to spend at least as much time during these lessons talking as we do actually playing the violin?"

"That's my fault," said Marta quickly. "Unfortunately, I am a brilliant conversationalist. A skill I occasionally use for evil. For example, talking to you about opera house gossip rather than admit that I haven't practiced for the past two days."

He shook his head in exaggerated disapproval. "Really, Countess, I expected better of you. When your father hired me, he made it clear there would be no slacking off tolerated on my part if he were to hire me. Apparently the same standards don't apply to you."

"I really am sorry. Would you like to take a leaf from Mr. Batori's book and throw some paper at me? I wouldn't blame you if you did."

"Tempting, but I'll resist. For now, just get out your violin and play the first line of that piece we worked on last week. Depending on your number of mistakes, I may throw some paper after all."

"How is my progress so far, Mr. Király?" Marta asked at the end of the lesson, as Andras efficiently tidied up. "Am I the next Paganini, do you think?"

"Not at all. You're much better looking than him," Andras said without thinking. His mouth dropped open with embarrassment as he realized what he'd said. But really, could anyone blame him? He didn't know a thing about clothes in Dutch paintings, but Marta's crisp dark blue dress did contrast stunningly with her pale skin and brown hair. She looked like something from a painting herself.

She laughed, not noticeably offended. "You're right. He wasn't the most appealing of chaps, was he? I was teasing, anyway, I know I'm only a beginner. I won't be at his—or your—level for years yet. But am I making decent progress, do you think?"

"In my honest opinion? I would say that while obviously there's still work ahead, you're doing well. You've got a good ear for music and despite your forgetting to practice for the last few days, you've clearly been working hard. Full marks, Countess."

Marta's cheeks went pink. "Goodness, thank you. I owe it all to your excellent teaching. I wonder if…" She paused and glanced over her shoulder as the door creaked open, revealing a young boy clad in a militaristic blue suit. Though his hair was a few shades lighter than Marta's and his features more angular, the family resemblance was obvious. This could only be the younger brother Marta had mentioned. The long-awaited heir.

"I have two questions for you, Heini," Marta said sternly, hands on her hips. "One, where is Nanny? And two, don't you know it's rude to interrupt when people are practicing music?"

"Nanny's lying down with a headache. And you're not practicing now," the boy pointed out. "You're just talking. Why can't I come say hello?"

Marta sighed and rolled her eyes. "Fine. Mr. Király, this is my younger brother Heinrich, whom we all call Heini to avoid confusion with my father. Heini, this is my violin tutor, Mr. Andras Király. Please be polite, he's a guest here."

"A guest?" Heini frowned suspiciously. "Isn't he a servant?"

"For heaven's sake, what part of *be polite* did you not understand?" Marta growled. "I'm sorry, Mr. Király. As I'm sure you know from your own sisters, ten-year-olds have absolutely no manners."

Andras heroically refrained from laughing at Marta and Heini's identical expressions of annoyance. "I assure you, Countess, I'm not offended." He bowed in Heini's direction. "It's an honor to meet you at last, Master Heinrich. Your sister tells me you're an expert on animals. I must say, I'm jealous."

"Really?" said Heini, looking gratified. "But you're Hungarian. I thought everyone in Hungary knew loads about horses."

"That's true in the country," Andras said. "But I grew up in the city, unfortunately. All we had were pigeons and rats. Have you got many cows, out in the country? I've always liked cows."

"Oh yes, all sorts," Heini said eagerly. "We've got the Holsteins—those are best for milk and butter—and the Hinterwalds, which have really good meat, and this spring we had a bunch of new calves, and Marta and I got to name some of them. What did you call yours, Marta?"

"Dorabella and Fiordiligi. From *Così Fan Tutte*," Marta said, with a wink in Andras's direction. "One of my favorite operas."

"Boring," said Heini. "Mine were named Genghis and Attila. After the Mongolian kings."

"I know all about Attila the Hun," Andras replied solemnly. "He's a distant relation, you know."

"Is he now?" said Marta, quirking an eyebrow. "And how in the world do you know that?"

Andras shrugged. "Pa's always maintained we're descended from Attila, and frankly, I can't think of a better explanation for why our family is the way it is."

The look of combined admiration and envy on Heini's face was deeply gratifying, as well as reminding Andras of his younger sisters. "You're lucky," the boy said with a deep sigh. "We're not related to anyone interesting."

"That is simply not true, Heini," said Marta. "What about great-great-great-great grandfather Albrecht? He had six fingers on his left hand. I was never jealous of him," she told Andras, "until I started learning the violin. Now I would be very grateful for a few extra fingers."

"I wouldn't mind a few extra fingers myself," Andras mused. "Though I think some more hands would be even better. I've always thought octopuses had the right idea."

Heini nodded approvingly. "You're all right, Mr. Király. Even if you haven't got a horse. Can you teach me a swear word in Hungarian?"

"Heini!"

"It would be my delight," said Andras, ignoring what was plainly a token protest on Marta's part. "But as I'm sure you know, these sorts of words are not fit for a lady's ears. If you'll come over here, I'll whisper one to you."

Heini leaned in close, and Andras, in the quietest voice he could manage, muttered "*Lófütty.*"

"Brilliant!" Heini whispered back. "What does it mean?"

"It's something you say when you think someone is lying. Use it wisely."

"I will," Heini said solemnly, as though committing to a blood oath. "Thanks, Mr. Király. I'd better be off before Nanny wakes up. Good luck with the music, Marta."

"What did you just say to him?" Marta demanded as Heini departed. "I hope it wasn't anything too bad because I know for a fact he'll be telling it to everyone, including our parents and all of his tutors."

"Repeat a curse in front of a lady? I would never," Andras said. "Don't worry, it was quite mild. Nothing my mother wouldn't have said."

Considering his mother's vocabulary, this was not particularly limiting, but Marta seemed placated nonetheless. "You have a knack with children, if you don't mind me saying so."

"As do you," he returned with a smile. "Despite the bickering, which is an older sister's prerogative anyway. But yes, I'm fond of children. Can't afford to not be, in my family."

"Do you think you'll have children of your own one day?" Marta flushed and shook her head. "I'm sorry, that was another nosy question. I've got to stop asking those."

"No, no, it's all right. I think…" What did he think? Marriage and children had always been abstract concepts, to be contemplated at three in the morning when he couldn't sleep. Still. "One day, I expect. Though I had probably better wait until I don't have to share a flat with Franz. I can't see him being a good influence."

"No, I shouldn't think so," she said. "I intend to have at least three children, and I'll have to keep them as far away from Franz as possible."

"I'm sure any children you had would be very lucky," Andras said absentmindedly. The words were barely out of his mouth before humiliation hit him, hot and sharp. He and Marta may have been friends, but he had no business remarking on her mothering abilities.

Marta looked stunned for a moment, then laughed. "You're too kind, Mr. Király. I've always worried that I'm too flighty to be a mother, but I suppose there's time to improve." She glanced at the clock and frowned. "Half past noon already, what a shame. I was hoping we could have some lunch sent up. But duty calls, I expect?"

"Duty calls," Andras said ruefully. "A pleasure as always, Countess."

"As usual, the pleasure is all mine," she replied. "And Mr. Király, I…" She stopped, and shook her head rapidly. "Never mind."

"Is something wrong?"

"No, no. Quite the opposite." Her smile was like a ray of light, like the beginning of a symphony. "Only, I truly do mean it, Mr. Király. The pleasure really is mine."

Later That Night
After Don Giovanni

"Brigita, how much would I have to pay you to kill me?"

"Andras, you know I would pay you for the opportunity to kill you," Brigita replied brightly, adjusting the laces on one of her slippers. "Why the long face? I thought that went well, actually."

"The show was fine. I'm exhausted, that's all." He yawned and ran a hand through his hair. "This having-two-jobs business is a mess. Going to bed at two o'clock, waking up at nine, working every single hour in between—it's a wonder I'm still standing."

"You only go to bed at two because you spend every night with us at Café Voltaire," Brigita said reasonably. "No one is making you do that."

"*Au contraire*, my dear. You and Franz and Leo would be miserable without me."

"True enough. But speaking of Café Voltaire, when are you bringing her again?"

"Bringing who?"

"That friend of yours, Miss Weiss. The maid."

"Ah." Andras had not recently considered the possibility of another meeting between Marta and his friends. "Not sure. Why do you ask?"

Brigita shrugged. "It was fun having her along last time. She's a nice girl. Stylish, too. Perhaps I ought to become a lady's maid, if one gets clothes that nice."

"Brigita, I mean this in the nicest possible way, but I shudder at the thought of you as a lady's maid. You'd do much better being the lady herself."

"Yes, well." Brigita's shoulders slumped. "If things keep going the way they're going with Franz, I may be tempted to find a husband who can make me a lady."

"Brigita," Andras said gently. "I don't mean to pry. But is everything all right with you and Franz?"

To his surprise, a tear slipped out of Brigita's eye. She sniffed hard and wiped her cheek. "I don't know," she whispered. "Look, Andras, you know I love ballet. It's the whole reason I came to Vienna. But one can't do ballet forever. Eventually you get old and your legs are gammy and then what are you supposed to do with your life? I'd hoped that once I'd had a bit of success I'd be happy to retire, get married and have a family, maybe start a school or something. But I don't think Franz wants to marry me. He just wants…well, a bit of fun, I think."

Andras wished he could have said something comforting, but honestly, he wouldn't be surprised if Brigita was right. Franz was a good chap, but he wasn't the sort to settle down for a long, long time. And Brigita was, at this point, practically one of his sisters. He didn't want to see her hurt.

"Look," he said, putting a comforting hand on her shoulder. "I can't say what's going to happen with you and Franz. But no matter what, you and I are always going to be friends. All right?"

She nodded, wiping briskly at her eyes. "All right. Thank you for talking to me about this. You're certainly the most trustworthy man I know."

And with that, Andras supposed, he would have to be content.

CHAPTER TWELVE

(In Which Don Giovanni *Tragically Perishes)*

May 29
The Closing Night of Don Giovanni

THE ONLY VON Holstadt who was not pleased about attending the opera was Heini who, while eager to stay up past his bedtime, preferred to resist all attempts to make him cultured. Had he been younger, Marta might have referred to the look on his face as he watched Nella dress her hair as pouting.

"Lousy old opera," he grumbled. "All that wailing and shouting. It's going to sound like a bunch of sheep with the flu."

"Oh, come now, Heini, it won't be as bad as all that," Marta said encouragingly. "It's a very interesting story, for one thing. There's a sword fight and a ghost and all sorts of delightfully awful things going on. Besides, Mr. Király will be in the orchestra, and you're fond of Mr. Király, aren't you? Remember, he taught you that swear word in Hungarian?"

Heini's eyes brightened and he opened his mouth, eager to repeat the excellent curse Andras had taught him. A stern look from his sister, however, stopped him short. "Yes, Mr. Király's all right," he said grudgingly. "But I don't see why he only gives you music lessons and not me. I might be a natural at music, for all we know."

"You're the heir, darling, and you won't be able to run the estate when you grow up if you spend all your time playing the violin. And next year you'll be in school and studying mathematics, and Latin, and history."

"But I don't want to learn those things." Heini's lower lip

trembled. "I don't need to know Latin to run the estate and look after the animals and the crops. Besides, I'm not very clever. I'll get horrible marks and the other boys will laugh at me and Papa will be upset."

Fortunately, Nella had finished arranging Marta's braids at this point, allowing her to hurry to her brother and envelop him in a hug. "Don't you dare say such awful things about yourself, " Marta scolded. "Everyone knows you're absolutely brilliant and will be a fantastic count. And if the other boys at school laugh at you, why, I'll get Mr. Király to come to the Academy and shout at them in Hungarian. All right?" When Heini didn't reply, she kissed his cheek and ruffled his hair. "I said, all *right*?"

"Ugh, all right," Heini said, wiping off his cheek. "I get your point. School might not be so bad, and neither will the opera."

"Of course it won't be. Not when we know all the secret backstage gossip. We'll probably be able to meet all the performers as well, and I happen to know they lead very interesting lives."

"Fair enough," said Heini. "But you'll need to tell me what's going on, you know. I don't speak Italian."

"It's fortunate for both of us that I had to learn Italian to prepare for the Marriage Market," said Marta solemnly. "Don't worry, I'm delighted to translate. Go let Nanny help you get ready. We've got a performance to get to."

One performance of Don Giovanni *later*

There was nothing, Andras thought proudly as the final curtain went down, quite like the feeling of participating in a performance that had gone really and truly well.

It hadn't been the easiest of runs, that was for sure. Even after Stefan Stefanowski had apologized and repeatedly told Kristina Eisen she was the most talented woman in all of Vienna, the soprano had still been constantly on edge and had more than once started crying during intermission. Not to mention that the wardrobe mistress had fallen ill the previous week and had been forced to turn all her duties over to her eighteen-year-old niece, who was woefully unprepared.

But in spite of everything, *Don Giovanni* had undoubtedly been a success. Tickets had sold well, there had been a multitude of standing ovations, and as far as Andras was aware, he hadn't played a single sour note. To top it all off, much to Glöckner's ecstatic delight, the von Holstadts had come to the final performance.

Andras rarely ventured into the front of the house after a show. That was generally the territory of the ballet dancers and female singers looking for a wealthy protector. But the von Holstadts had been kind enough to attend, just as they'd been begged to do, and as they were Andras's rich patrons in a way, he decided it was only polite to go and greet them.

He spotted them almost immediately. How could he not? The assorted von Holstadts and von Braumarks stood out from the usual Odysseum crowd as easily as swans among geese, clustered on the other side of the room amid an admiring crowd and sipping the champagne Glöckner had wisely provided. From this distance Andras could identify Marta's parents, both dressed very handsomely, chatting with a rotund man Andras vaguely recognized as the Baron von Braumark. No sign of Marta, though. Until a man standing near the baron shifted to the side and Andras spotted her, wearing a pink gown that somehow made everything else in the room look drab.

He grinned in relief and headed in her direction, eager to say hello, to ask her what she'd thought of the opera. And then, perhaps ten feet away, he stopped dead in his tracks, feeling as though he'd been slapped across the face.

Intellectually, he'd always been aware that Marta was beautiful, in the same way he knew that Buda Castle and *Für Elise* were beautiful. But in all the time he'd spent around her, he'd never entirely allowed himself to notice her looks, apart from a few brief, embarrassing moments. He still turned red whenever he remembered Marta speaking Hungarian. Tonight, though, it was impossible to stop noticing. Because in the dim golden light of the Landfeld Theatre Marta was, for lack of a better word, ravishing. Her hair was twisted up into some complicated, glittering style that resembled a halo, and that dress, good God. Perfectly decent, but one couldn't ignore the amount of smooth, creamy skin that low neckline revealed. She really did have a mouthwatering figure, lush and curvaceous, not a hint of sharp edges anywhere. Andras could only imagine how satisfying it would be to hold her in his arms, to run his hands over every lovely inch of her.

Of course she chose this moment, when his thoughts were veering into what could only be described as lustful territory, to notice him. Not only notice him, but shoot him a smile as bright as the sun and exclaim, "Mr. Király. I was just wondering when you were going to appear. How lovely to see you."

As Marta's voice was naturally far-carrying, Andras experienced the uncomfortable sensation of having every single eye in the immediate area turned in his direction. At least this was nerve-wracking enough to diminish any state of arousal. Gathering his wits, he bowed and murmured, "A pleasure as always, Your Excellencies, Baron. It was kind of you to come."

Count von Holstadt smiled kindly. "Naturally, Mr. Király. We wouldn't have missed it, now that we know you so well. And a fine show it was, too. Who was that nice young woman singing Donna Anna? Brilliant performance from her."

"Ah, you must mean Kristina Eisen. Yes, she is very talented, and I'm sure she would be overjoyed to meet you, sir. As would our director, Mr. Glöckner." An understatement. Glöckner would not only fall over himself to impress the count, but might very well propose marriage to him.

The sound of a throat being cleared drew Andras's attention back to Marta, whose arm was now in the grip of a pale, thin young man with straw-blond hair and thick spectacles. Though Andras couldn't recall having met him before, something about his eyes, coupled with the almost disdainful way he looked around the room, made his identity quite clear. This could be none other than Ulrich von Braumark's son, Ludwig. The one Marta had said her family expected her to marry. A dull and supercilious looking fellow, really, and the possessive way he held onto Marta's arm was utterly infuriating.

"Marta," Ludwig said, nodding at Andras with a vaguely suspicious air. "Who is this?"

"Oh, yes, you two haven't met yet," said Marta, settling into society-hostess mode. "Baron Ludwig von Braumark, allow me to present Mr. Andras Király, first violin at the opera company. Andr—Mr. Király, this is Baron Ludwig von Braumark, an old friend of my family."

"Ah, yes," said Ludwig. He had a high, reedy sort of voice, not one a woman would like to hear every day for the rest of her life. "Not a bad show, not at all. Though I can't say I've ever been an opera connoisseur."

"Ludwig, you needn't be a connoisseur to appreciate *Don Giovanni*," Marta said with a roll of her eyes, carefully detangling her arm from Ludwig's. "It's Mozart. But you played beautifully, Mr. Király. You must be so proud."

"Thank you, Countess, though it's hard to believe you could pick out my own playing among all my talented colleagues."

"Don't be ridiculous. I'd recognize Clara anywhere. Do give her my love."

He smiled, an odd warmth flooding his every nerve. "I will pass along your compliments."

Ludwig cleared his throat once again, plainly tired of being ignored. "Would you care for another glass of champagne, Marta?" he asked loudly, reaching for her arm again as if to guide her away. Andras experienced a sudden, overwhelming urge to haul off and knock him to the ground, though fortunately before he could do this Marta deftly stepped away.

"Yes indeed, Ludwig, would you mind getting me one? I had a few questions I wanted to ask Mr. Király, and I know how little the minutiae of music interests you," she said. Ludwig glanced from her to Andras, began to say something, and then shut his mouth again.

"Very well," he said. "I will be back shortly." With a brisk bow and a click of the heels he was off, leaving the atmosphere behind him considerably lighter.

"I'm sorry about that," Marta said, lowering her voice. "Ludwig's not a bad sort, but he does tend to cling. Now, I do think Heini wanted to ask you something, where is he… Heini!"

The small figure of Marta's younger brother appeared from in between two stout matrons, dashing over to his sister's side and giving Andras a brisk nod. "There you are. Mama and Papa are talking to Baron von Braumark and it's the most boring conversation imaginable. What in the world is a Victor Emmanuel?"

"Heaven knows," Andras replied, holding back a grin. "Glad to see you, Master Heinrich. You had a question about the opera?"

"That's right." Heini crossed his arms sternly. "The bit at the end, where the statue comes to the dinner party. Why was he a statue and not just an ordinary ghost? Statues are awfully heavy, aren't they?"

"I've wondered that myself," Marta put in. "Whereas ghosts generally weigh nothing, don't they? If I were a spirit from beyond the grave I know which one I'd rather manifest as."

Andras stroked his chin thoughtfully. "An excellent question. I couldn't tell you for certain, but I believe the Commendatore's ghost manifested as a statue so that if he trod on Don Giovanni's toe it would be very, very painful."

Marta made a noise that very much sounded as if she was trying not to shriek with laughter. "A very sensible answer, Mr. Király. Thank you. Any more questions, Heini?"

Heini shrugged. "Not now. If I think of any more I'll come to your music lesson next week."

"Run along to Mama and Papa, then. Mr. Király and I are going to have a conversation that will probably involve words like 'overture' and be thoroughly boring."

Heini appeared to consider this. "All right. I'm going to find that chap who played the ghost and ask him what he thinks about the statue." He waved politely at Andras before darting off into the crowd.

"So," Andras said after a moment. "You enjoyed the opera, then?"

"I adored it, the costumes were excellent. With the exception of Don Giovanni's orange jacket in the first act. There's a painting of my ancestor Count Wilhelm wearing something very similar just before being arrested in the 1740s."

Andras tried and failed to suppress a laugh. "Was he arrested because of the jacket?"

"I believe the official reason was embezzling, but really, I think that shade of orange ought to be a crime." Marta looked up at him, eyebrows raised. "What's so amusing?"

"Nothing much. I just had a strong suspicion that when you finally saw the production, you'd have plenty of opinions about the costumes. If you weren't a countess, I think I'd insist that Glöckner hire you."

Marta smiled wistfully. "If only that were possible. But listen, Andras, I had something I'd like to talk to you about."

Would his heart ever stop leaping like that when she said his first name? It was probably some sort of medical condition. "Anything you like, Countess."

"You can call me Marta, you know. No one's listening to us. Anyway, I wondered…" She lowered her voice carefully. "I did have such a lovely time with your friends at Café Voltaire last week, and I was wondering if I might visit again sometime. If it wouldn't be too much of a bother."

"Actually, Brigita told me she quite enjoyed having you around last time," Andras admitted. "I think everyone liked seeing a new face. If you were able to get away, you could come along tonight."

"Brilliant. Shall I meet you in the park again? At eleven? Mama and Papa always go to bed right away after a night at the theatre, so I shouldn't have to worry about them."

"That should be all right. Do you, er…" What perfume was it that Marta was wearing? Something spicy and highly distracting. She smelled like a Christmas pastry. "I mean…"

"Goodness, I'm sorry, I must go to my parents," Marta interrupted. "They're talking to Kristina Eisen. I should go say hello, it's only polite. I promise I won't mention her recent tantrums. I'll see you tonight, all right?"

She gave him a polite pat on the arm before heading into the crowd, turning back just once to shoot him a wink.

Andras nearly let out a groan of frustration. What right did she have to go around winking at fellows like that? Especially when coupled with that charming little smirk of hers. Now all he could think about as he headed backstage was pulling her into some quiet part of the theatre and kissing that smile off her full rosy lips, unbuttoning her dress and sliding it off her shoulders, letting his fingers trail over her lovely breasts…

"Oh, for the love of Saint Cecilia," Andras growled as he adjusted the front of his trousers, which had become uncomfortably tight. "What in the hell is wrong with me?"

"The same that's wrong with everyone: human nature," said Brigita brightly, poking her head out of the ballerinas' dressing room. "Or did you mean something specific?"

"No," Andras replied quickly. "I believe my friend Miss Weiss is coming along to Café Voltaire again tonight. I assume you don't have any objections?"

"None whatsoever. I ought to ask her," Brigita said, "if she ever inherits any old dresses from her employer that she could pass along to me. She won't need all those old clothes, will she?"

The subject of Marta and clothes was not one Andras felt like discussing, considering how much he had just been fantasizing about taking them off her. "Do whatever you like, Brigita. I need coffee."

"I admit I'm pleasantly surprised," Marta's father remarked on the carriage ride home. "For a company I hadn't heard of until about two months ago, those Odysseum folks have plenty of talent."

"Quite," said Hannelore. "Did you enjoy yourself, Marta?"

Marta, who was gazing out the window with one arm around a dozing Heini, looked up. "Oh yes, very much," she replied. "And it was nice to see Mr. Király again outside of the usual circumstances."

"Hmm." Hannelore's eyebrows drew together quickly before her face fell back into its usual smooth mask. "I don't like to bring it up, dear, but I did notice you were rather familiar with Mr. Király."

Marta winced at her mother's tone. If Heinrich was military-strict about schedules and accounts, Hannelore was even more so when it came to manners. And Marta's sin, in this case, was obvious—she'd been friendly to a servant. In public.

And Andras was, technically, a servant. It was dangerous to forget that, at least when her parents were in earshot.

"I don't believe I was too familiar," she said carefully. "Surely it's only natural that we've gotten acquainted. After all, we spend four hours a week together, and we do end up making conversation."

"It's only right for you to be cordial to him. But…" Hannelore paused. "Remember, Marta, the position our family is in. We live separate lives from people like Mr. Király for a reason. Treating him as you would treat Ludwig would be completely inappropriate, and I'm certain Mr. Király doesn't expect it."

Nor should he, Marta thought. Andras was a dear friend, whereas Ludwig was, well, something of a friend when he wasn't after her to marry him, and a minor nuisance when he was. There wasn't much chance of her treating them the same.

"You have nothing to worry about, Mama," she said. "There's nothing improper between myself and Mr. Király; I simply enjoy talking to him."

Marta couldn't see her mother's face clearly in the darkness, but she knew what expression would be on it. That pursed-lips, eyes-narrowed look that indicated pure disapproval. However, when Hannelore finally spoke, all she said was: "That's nice, dear."

Café Voltaire was more crowded than usual. It appeared the entire Odysseum Opera Company had taken over the place. Marta could see Stefan Stefanowski, the baritone who'd sung Don Giovanni, sipping a glass of something bright green and chatting with one of the chorus girls. He looked very different without his luxuriant false mustache. And there was that conductor fellow who resembled a scarecrow, still with his baton in hand and gesticulating dangerously with it.

Marta hadn't spotted Franz, Brigita, and Leo yet, but she hoped they were present, as she was desperate for an actual conversation. Andras had been oddly quiet on the entire walk from the Stadtpark, and more than once she'd caught him looking her over with an expression that was hard to place. Of course, it was possible he was simply exhausted after working so hard during *Don Giovanni*'s run. At one of her parents' dinner parties, Marta had once heard a very distinguished professor of music explain that the art carried with it a high toll, both physically and emotionally. That considered, a few odd looks in the park were hardly surprising.

"There's Brigita," Andras said with relief. Marta got the feeling he did not particularly like crowds. "We'd better go join her and the others, before…"

"Wait just a moment, you two," called a loud, musical female voice. Glancing over her shoulder, Marta stopped in her tracks at the sight of plump, golden-haired Kristina Eisen weaving determinedly through the crowd in their direction.

"Oh, damn," Andras muttered, and Marta felt him let go of her arm and take a step backwards. Considering the look in Kristina Eisen's eyes, Marta couldn't really blame him.

It was far too late for Marta herself to escape, though, as Kristina was now directly in front of her with a smile that bordered on flirtatious. "My dear girl, welcome," the soprano trilled. "I had no idea our own Mr. Király would be bringing a guest tonight, and such a pretty one at that."

Holding out hope that Kristina wouldn't recognize her, Marta dropped into a deep curtsy. "Good evening, Miss Eisen. It's an honor to meet such a wonderfully talented singer."

"You look extraordinarily familiar," Kristina said, pursing her lips thoughtfully. "Yes indeed, I could swear that I've seen you somewhere before. Quite recently, in fact. You weren't at the theatre tonight, were you, dear?"

"I was, er," Marta began, unsure whether or not to lie. She had spoken to Miss Eisen at the theatre, but a drab dress and sensible hairstyle did tend to change people's perceptions. "I did see the opera, yes."

Kristina frowned, her fan fluttering in indecision, before her face lit up. "You most certainly did," she exclaimed. "And my goodness, what an honor it is to see you at our little party, of all places. Tell me, Countess, do your parents know you're here?"

To Marta's chagrin, the volume at which Kristina said this, coupled with her timing, precisely as the musicians in the corner fell silent, resulted in every single head in the café swiveling in her direction. Including those of Andras and his friends, all of whom looked horrified.

Drat.

There was only one thing to do. Marta's years of training in etiquette had primarily prepared her for handling disagreements at dinner parties, but she could still handle this situation like a countess.

"How clever of you to recognize me, Miss Eisen," she said brightly. "I must say, I thought my disguise would be more effective. Nevertheless, you are quite correct. My parents are indeed unaware of my presence here tonight. I would so appreciate if we could keep this between us. This is a thoroughly innocent adventure, but my family does worry, and I'd hate to cause them any distress. Wouldn't you?"

Kristina looked at her for a second, eyes narrowed, and it occurred to Marta that the lead soprano was quite a bit shrewder than she led people to believe. At last, the other woman let out a tinkling laugh. "Gracious, how courageous you are, my dear. I am most pleasantly surprised. Don't worry, your secret is safe with me. With us," she corrected herself, glancing sternly around at her colleagues. "No need to worry, Countess."

"Marta," said Marta, grinning with relief. "When I'm here, I'm just Marta."

Kristina might have thought the whole thing was a grand joke, but based on their faces, Andras's friends decidedly did not. Brigita in particular looked as though someone had run her pointe shoes through a meat grinder.

"Andras, you lying sneak," Brigita snapped. "When did you plan to tell us that Miss Maria Weiss was in fact the countess you're tutoring?"

"Never," said Andras promptly. "I was never going to tell you, not in a thousand years. The whole thing was entirely up to Marta. I will say I am a bit surprised that none of you except Franz figured it out sooner."

"Franz knew?" Leo shot a dirty look at Franz, who was attempting to go unnoticed. "You sly dog. Why didn't you say anything?"

"Because Andras would never have cooked me dinner again. Making sure you lot are up on all the gossip isn't worth starvation.

But I am glad it's all in the open now. I've never liked keeping secrets."

"For what it's worth, I'm sorry," said Marta. "I also don't like keeping secrets, but I didn't have much of a choice. You never would have told me that story about Andras getting arrested if you'd known I was a von Holstadt. But now that you know the terrible truth, I hope we can remain friends. I've become quite fond of you all, you know."

"Well, personally, I feel terribly betrayed," said Brigita, shaking her head. "To think we've had a rich acquaintance this entire time, and we have not been properly taking advantage of her."

"No indeed, we've been most cruelly used," said Leo. "I can't say we'll be likely to forgive you, unless…"

"Unless?" Marta asked.

"Unless you buy us a bottle of wine," Brigita said firmly. "Not the cheap stuff, either. A very, very expensive bottle of wine. Once we're a bit less sober we'll be in a much more forgiving mood."

Marta felt the tension drain from her shoulders at the sight of Franz and Leo's grins. "I'll buy you the most expensive bottle of wine this place has, which I assume isn't saying much. And in case I haven't said it enough, thank you. You are some of the most interesting friends I've ever had."

Franz, Brigita, and Leo all had the good manners to look flattered by this remark. "Likewise, I'm sure," said Franz. "And now we'd better get back to our table, lest someone pinch it while you're getting our drinks. Come along, you two."

"I have to say I'm relieved," Marta remarked as she watched their retreating backs. "Your friends are much calmer about this whole revelation than I expected they would be."

"Hmm," Andras said vaguely. Not for the first time that night, his gaze swept over her from head to toe, his face unreadable.

"Why do you keep looking at me like that?" Marta demanded. "Have I got mud on my dress or something?"

"What? No," said Andras quickly. "I've got a lot on my mind, that's all. Nothing to make a fuss about."

Marta frowned, not entirely convinced. "There is something wrong with you tonight, Mr. Király."

"There's been something wrong with me since the day I was born," Andras countered. "Yet you've put up with me this long. Shall we?"

He really was one of the oddest men she knew, Marta thought. Quite thoroughly eccentric. Strange, really, that she liked him so much, liked him more than anyone else she knew, with the possible exceptions of her family and Sophie. As a matter of fact, she—

Marta shook her head briskly to clear her thoughts. There was no point in analyzing her feelings now, not when she had a party to attend. With a smile, she followed Andras back into the crowd.

PART TWO

"Love, love, love, that is the soul of genius."
-*Wolfgang Amadeus Mozart*

CHAPTER THIRTEEN

(In Which Marta Throws Money at a Problem)

June 3
Rehearsal

"I CANNOT," KRISTINA DECLARED. "I absolutely *cannot* work like this."

This was not the first time she had said this, nor would it be the last, but it was unfortunate that she had interrupted a duet during a rehearsal of *La Traviata* to say it. At the sound of the lead soprano's furious voice, much less beautiful in complaint than it was in song, the orchestra fell silent, though a few muffled laughs could be heard.

"Kristina, my dear girl," said Dietrich, in the syrupy tone of voice he used only when talking to temperamental singers. "What's the matter?"

"What's the matter, Dietrich?" Kristina snapped. "What's the matter indeed. Will you kindly tell this oaf"— she gestured sharply at the skinny young tenor singing Alfredo— "that the next time he steps on my toe while I sing I will have my cat scratch his eyes out?"

Andras watched this with amusement, not particularly disturbed by the interruption. He did like *La Traviata*, the tragic tale of a courtesan who sacrificed everything for love, but the Odysseum had done it two years prior and it was old hat at this point. Kristina Eisen's outbursts, while inconvenient, were still highly entertaining.

Out of the corner of his eye, Andras noted Franz gesturing wildly, and ducked out of his seat to go to him.

"We're off to the dance hall after rehearsal tonight," Franz whispered loudly. "In case Miss…Weiss would like to come. Might not be her sort of place, but—"

"As a matter of fact, I think she'd enjoy it," Andras interrupted, unwilling to admit how often he had imagined dancing with Marta. With her education, she had to be a wonderful dancer, probably enough to make up for Andras's occasional clumsiness. He'd made plans to meet her in the park tonight anyway, and it would be a nice change from the café. "I'll bring her."

"All right. Oh, and you've got a letter from your sister." Franz pulled a crumpled envelope out of his pocket and stuffed it apologetically into Andras' hand. "Forgot to give it to you when you came home for lunch."

There was no time for opening letters at the present, as the conflict between Kristina and her colleague had been solved, and Dietrich, eager to make up lost time, struck up *Un Di, Felice, Eterea* at an inappropriately rapid pace. As he lifted Clara to his chin, Andras allowed himself to fall into a pleasant fantasy of dancing with Marta to music it wasn't his job to provide.

Not until rehearsal ended several hours later did Andras finally have a chance to look over his letter from home. Purloining an apple from a backstage tray, he settled into a corner and began to read.

One minute later, the apple dropped out of his hand and rolled into the dust under a prop armchair, utterly forgotten. Andras sat frozen, his eyes fixed on the paper in front of him.

"Oh no," he whispered. "Oh *no*."

Something was wrong.

Marta could tell the minute she arrived at their usual meeting spot in the park. Andras was sitting on a bench, barely illuminated by a lamppost, his face in his hands, and as Marta approached she could see his shoulders were shaking.

"Andras?" she said cautiously.

He started at the sound of her voice and looked up with tired, red-rimmed eyes. Good heavens, he had been crying. Marta's stomach clenched in worry. Anything that could make someone as carefully composed as Andras cry in public couldn't be anything less than terrible.

"Andras," Marta said again, more softly this time, taking a careful seat next to him. "What's wrong?"

"Good evening, Marta," he replied, voice shaking slightly. "Forgive me if I'm not quite myself, it's been a difficult night. I'll be all right shortly, and we can be on our way."

"I do not want you to apologize, nor do I want to be on our way when you're in this state," she said. "Surely we've become good enough friends that you can tell me why you're crying on a park bench."

Under better circumstances, Marta might have spent more time appreciating the blush that spread rapidly across Andras's high cheekbones. "I appreciate that," he said. "And you're kind to ask. But unfortunately there isn't much you can do this time. It's my father, you see, he…" Andras took a shuddering breath and wiped furiously at his eyes. "I got a letter from Ilka today. Pa's lungs are much worse, he can barely eat or sleep, he can't stop coughing. It's looking bad, Marta. Ilka is asking if I can come home as soon as possible, just in case he—if he's not going to get better."

"Oh, Andras." Marta blinked back the tears that had sprung up. She had no desire to make him feel worse. After all he'd done to provide for his family, this would be an unimaginable blow. "Isn't there anything that can be done? A doctor he could see, or a sanatorium?"

"We haven't got the money for doctors or sanatoriums," Andras said. "Besides, I'm not even sure if I'll be able to go home and see him. It's not easy for me to get time off from the opera company, and I can't, I *can't* decide between my family and work. I don't trust myself to make the right choice." His voice dropped to a whisper. "I didn't last time."

This sounded ominous. "Last time?"

He blinked in surprise, as if just remembering she was there. "Last time," he said heavily. "That's a long story."

She shrugged. "Do I look as though I have anywhere else to be?"

After awkwardly running a hand through his hair—a gesture, she had come to realize, that meant he was deeply nervous—he nodded.

"My time at the Academy," he said, "was probably the happiest period of my life. I was a charity case, and a few of the other boys would poke fun at me for being poor, and I had to study every hour God sent. But for the first time in my life I was free of all other responsibilities, and I could spend every waking hour learning about music. Not to mention that I was getting three good meals a day and a comfortable dormitory to sleep in. Sometimes I think I would have been happy staying there forever.

"But the scholarship money was limited, and when I turned twenty it was made clear to me that I was expected to take my exams and move on, or be tossed out like yesterday's rubbish. So I worked my fingers to the bone preparing, staying up at all hours, practicing and writing until I couldn't see straight. I wrote an entire sonata and didn't sleep for three days during the process. And then..." He trailed off, staring into space.

"And then?" Marta prompted gently.

"And then," said Andras, "my mother died. I knew she hadn't been well, but she was always so strong and healthy when we were children, and her letters were so cheerful, that I didn't think it was serious at the time. I assumed she'd be back to her usual strength in a matter of weeks, so I didn't bother going home to visit. Then." He made a noise that sounded as though he was choking back a sob. "Then she died. Completely without warning, just before my exams."

Marta drew her shawl more tightly around her shoulders—the air around them seemed to have grown much colder. "I am so sorry, Andras. Truly I am. What did you do?"

"Something I'm not proud of. My family wanted me to come home, practically begged me to. But my professors, my classmates, everyone in Vienna told me that if I left, I would be losing my last chance to graduate from the Academy. They told me that my exams had to be the most important thing in my life or I would never be a real musician. Deep down, I…I agreed with them." Andras looked at her with such pain in his eyes it felt like a physical blow. "I didn't go to her funeral, Marta. I missed my own mother's funeral, because I am utterly selfish. And to make matters worse, I scraped by in the exams, but my marks were nothing special. What a damned waste."

"Oh, Andras. I am so sorry," she said again. "And there was nothing at all you could do? They wouldn't let you reschedule?"

"Of course they didn't," he said, so bitterly she winced. "You don't understand, Marta. I was let into that school entirely by their good graces, and it was made very clear to me that the minute my dedication wavered that would be it for me. But I still had a choice, didn't I? And I chose to stay here. I chose to be a terrible son."

"All right, perhaps I don't understand, not entirely," said Marta. "I don't understand how the Academy could treat you that way. I don't understand what it's like to be a scholarship student, or to lose a parent. But I do understand you by this point, a little, and I know that you are not selfish. You never should have had to make that choice, but I think your mother would have been proud of you for being so dedicated to music. It doesn't mean you don't love your family."

"So what do I do this time?" Andras asked, looking at her pleadingly. "If I have to make the same choice now?"

She bit her lip, thinking. A semblance of an idea was forming, and it could work, but she would have to phrase it just right. "What if you didn't have to decide this time?"

"I'm sorry, how?"

"It's quite simple, really," she said. "You need money to help your father, and time to go visit him. My family has plenty of money, and enough influence that we can surely convince the opera company to give you a few weeks of leave." She smiled indulgently as he blinked in confusion. "I mean we're going to help you, Andras. In any way we can. It's going to be all right."

Andras shook his head. "You're very kind, but I couldn't accept charity."

"Call it a loan, then. Believe me, you will not be robbing us of any hot meals."

"I can't let you do this for me," he said, though it was clear his resolve was weakening. "You don't even know my father."

"No, I don't," she agreed. "But I do know you. And I know that you're my friend, and a good and loving son. You've worked far too hard to help the people you love to be kept away from them now. Anything I can do to help you, I will."

Andras stared at her in silence, the light slowly returning to his eyes. "I…I don't know what to say."

"'Thank you' is customary, I think," said Marta. "Or if you want to get more poetic, you could say something like 'my heart is an ocean of gratitude.' That might be nice."

"A lovely metaphor. Though I think I have a better one." His voice was so earnest it made her heart flutter, and it certainly didn't help when he leaned forward and softly squeezed her hand. "Marta von Holstadt, you are an angel."

He was so close to her now, close enough that she could feel the faint heat of his breath on her skin, smell a hint of his soap, his lips only inches away from hers. And she very, very much wanted him to kiss her.

As if he'd heard her thoughts, Andras leaned in closer and then looked at her searchingly, eyebrows raised in question. Although almost frozen by excitement and nerves, she managed the tiniest of nods. Obediently, he took her face in his hands and brushed his lips against hers.

The last time Marta had been kissed—the only time, in fact, she had ever been kissed—had been at a court ball when she was eighteen. It had not been a particularly romantic experience. The young French vicomte who'd managed to get her alone on the balcony had haltingly informed her that her eyes were like moonlight before grabbing her shoulders and forcing his tongue between her lips. After a moment of being frozen in shock, she had managed to push him off and flee back into the ballroom, where she proceeded to hide in a corner for the rest of the evening.

"This is what happens when you don't have me to look after you," Sophie had remarked, upon hearing of the incident. "You get kissed by strange Frenchmen. It just goes to show what I have always said: Never trust anyone from France."

But that hadn't really been a kiss at all, Marta was realizing. That had been an aberration. Real kissing was what Andras was currently doing to her, and it was glorious. The gentle but firm pressure of his velvet-soft lips, the faint trembling of his fingertips against her temples, the slight groan he let out when she tentatively began to kiss him back were setting off fireworks in her every nerve and making every inch of her skin burn with want.

What she really wanted was to wrap her arms around him and beg him not to let go of her, ever. She settled instead for burying her fingers in his hair, stroking the silky waves gently. He needed gentleness right now, she could tell, and she could give him that. She could and would give him absolutely anything he needed.

Because she loved him.

The thought hit her like a ton of bricks, and she knew immediately that it was true. Of course she loved him, had loved him for ages. Perhaps it had started when he'd taught her that horrible Hungarian word, or when he'd told her about his father, or even when she'd learned how he first picked up a violin. But what did the exact moment matter? After promising herself that she wouldn't become infatuated with him, she'd skipped infatuation altogether and gone straight to this new emotion that was nothing like the shallow desire she'd felt when she first met him. This was like art, like music—something that came from the depths of her soul.

It was love, pure and simple.

To her disappointment, Andras drew back all too soon, his beautiful eyes dazed and his hair mussed from her fingers. "Marta," he said hoarsely. "I'm sorry, I shouldn't have."

He looked so nervous, so utterly adorable, that it took all Marta's self-control not to grab him and kiss him again. She so desperately wanted to tell him, to pour out everything she was feeling, but this wasn't the time.

"You have nothing to apologize for," she said. "First thing tomorrow I'll go to my parents and sort out the money, and then we'll contact Glöckner and arrange for your time off. Your job is to pack your bags and stay hopeful. As long as your father is alive and getting help, you are not allowed to despair."

Andras's lips quirked into a smile. "Hope protects us. Though to be honest, I always thought *money protects us* might be more accurate."

"Very true. And this time, the person who the money is protecting will be the elder Mr. Király." She gave his hand a gentle squeeze and stood. "He's going to be all right, I can feel it. Write to me now and then when you're home, won't you?"

"Of course. I'll tell you the minute I know anything about my father. And Marta…" he hesitated, then shook his head. "Thank you. I don't think I'll ever be able to express it properly, but please know that I am truly grateful."

"You're welcome," Marta said softly. "You are very, very welcome."

There was nothing more to say. Except the obvious. She loved him and wanted him, and would do anything to help him, anything at all.

Marta didn't say this, but she thought it, all the way back to the house.

CHAPTER FOURTEEN

(In Which the Prodigal Son Returns)

MARTA HAD BEEN in love once before, at the age of fourteen.

The object of her affections had been a Burg Holstadt stableboy named Karl, whose wavy golden hair and blue eyes made him look like a fairy-tale prince and more than compensated for the smell of horses. Marta had spent most of her trips to the country ruining her shoes with dung and mud just so she could watch Karl look after the horses, bringing him glasses of lemonade without being asked to and bewildering the poor boy deeply. This went on for some time until Marta's mother finally sat her down for a serious talk.

"You are a young lady now," she had told Marta. "And that means you must be careful about your reputation. It's not seemly for you to be chasing after young men, especially those who are not of your class."

"But I love him, Mama," Marta had wailed. "He's beautiful. And he's so good with the horses, and the dogs love him…"

Hannelore conceded that this was true, but Marta's behavior was still far from appropriate. "He is our servant, and while it is right and proper to be courteous to him, he is not the sort of person a young lady marries." She'd patted Marta's hand in sympathy. "You are still very young, my dear. When you truly fall in love, it will be with someone worthy of you, someone of your own rank."

Marta had listened carefully to this advice, and possibly even believed it. From that point on, she left poor Karl alone, limiting their interactions to polite pleasantries, and her parents had been able to rest secure in the knowledge that she had learned her lesson.

And here she was, seven years later, proving she'd learned nothing at all.

She probably should have felt more guilty about it than she did.

Her parents couldn't know, of course. By von Holstadt standards a Hungarian violinist was as much of a marriage prospect as one of the beggars whose feet the emperor washed at Easter. It was possible the beggars were slightly superior, having touched the emperor. If Marta showed the slightest bit of improper interest in Andras, he would be out of a job and she would be in a great deal of trouble. But it was dreadful, feeling this way and not being able to discuss it with anyone. Sophie was a possibility, but even that was a risk. She didn't quite think that Sophie's support for the working class, while sincere, extended as far as Marta marrying one of them.

Her parents had, fortunately, been thoroughly understanding of Andras's unfortunate situation. After Marta had given them a detailed and emotionally wrought explanation of György's illness, the von Holstadts had agreed to lend Andras a small sum to pay for a sanatorium. What was more, Heinrich had written to the Odysseum Opera Company and made it abundantly clear that Andras's taking time off from work was a necessity, and he, the count, would personally take responsibility for any difficulties Mr. Glöckner might have as a result. The director, overwhelmed by the honor of being personally addressed by the Count von Holstadt, had enthusiastically granted Andras four weeks of leave with the understanding that more time could be given if necessary.

With the issue settled to everyone's satisfaction, Heinrich and Hannelore declared the family in need of fresh country air, and summarily arranged a trip to the family seat at Burg Holstadt.

June 8

Andras was determined that he would not spend a minute longer contemplating what had happened in the park. He had been overwhelmed by gratitude, and Marta had felt sorry for him, and that was all there was to it.

Therefore, he spent the entire train ride to Budapest thinking of nothing else.

Why, though? It was just a kiss, an innocent one at that, and it wasn't as though Andras had never kissed girls before. There had been Franci from school when he'd been seven, who had kissed him on the cheek and told him he was going to marry her. And Agnes, the daughter of one of the Academy professors, who had insisted on helping him turn pages. And Carolina, the ballet dancer who'd been his sweetheart three years prior. Lovely girls, one and all, and yet he couldn't remember feeling this shaken after kissing any of them.

None of them were Marta von Holstadt, though, which might have explained it.

She was an unfairly good kisser for someone who'd grown up in a highly sheltered environment—a kissing virtuoso, as it were. Far from being horrified and shoving him away, she'd been startlingly enthusiastic. Really, it was a good thing she'd left when she had. Any more kissing of that caliber, and it would have been extremely difficult to stop. He hadn't wanted to stop. What he'd wanted to do, if he was being honest, was pull off her dress, lay her down on the grass, and make love to her until she could neither walk nor think. Even now, as Andras was being jolted around on an uncomfortable second-class train seat, the thought of her gasping out his name made him so aroused he could hardly bear it.

They ought to put a commemorative plaque up in that damn park. *On this spot in 1869, Andras Király lost his head over a perfectly innocent kiss because he is an idiot.*

Though, Andras thought with a smile, if the von Holstadts stumbled across that particular plaque he would have a lot of explaining to do.

The train pulled into the station at dusk, the setting sun's glow gilding even the plainest buildings in the New Town. Waving off the shouts of the cabbies on whose services he had no intention of wasting a penny, Andras hoisted up his faded carpetbag and set off down the familiar streets leading home.

In the two years since he had been there, the neighborhood where he had grown up had altered very little. The same smell of spices and smoke and horse hung about like a fog, the same shouts from hawkers, neighbors, and children filled the air, and the buildings were as soot-stained as always. If one thing had changed, it was that the place seemed even more crowded than usual.

At least he still recognized plenty of the residents. As Andras stepped into Number 27 and made his way up the stairs, a few familiar faces peered out of doors and called out greetings and invitations. And questions too, plenty of questions. He waved them all off with a smile as he passed. There would be time for visiting the neighbors later, but he had priorities.

Reaching his family's flat, he barely had to knock once before the door flew open, revealing a thin young woman in a black dirndl and frilly white apron, tendrils of her crinkly light brown hair escaping its knot. At the sight of Andras, her eyes widened in delight and shock.

"Andras," she cried. "You came!"

"Of course I came, Ilka," he said, giving his eldest sister a tight hug. It was extraordinary, how much Ilka had changed in the years since he'd seen her, and not entirely for the better. She was still undoubtedly a nice-looking girl, with their mother's height and father's coloring, but she also looked tired.

Not surprising, considering the situation.

"They couldn't keep me away, not with Pa doing poorly," Andras went on. "I got a few weeks off from the opera company, came as soon as I could."

What joy there was on Ilka's face disappeared at the mention of their father. "Yes, you'd better come in. Pa's not very well today, but I'm sure he'll be dying to see you." She clapped a hand over her mouth in horror, her eyes filling with tears. "Oh, Lord, Andras, I'm so sorry."

"Don't be." He gave her shoulder an encouraging squeeze. "We mustn't give up hope yet. I've got good news."

"We could use some of that around here. Come in, Jozefa and Kitti are getting supper ready." She stepped aside to allow Andras to enter.

What hit him first was the smell, a warm, spicy, slightly burnt scent that could only be the goulash his sisters were making. He breathed in deeply, momentarily transported back to his childhood, when he had helped his mother and father make dinner every night after school. But that had been a long time ago, and the two girls standing in the kitchen—one short, sturdy, and brown-haired, the other a small gangly redhead—were not his mother. Still, Andras could think of very few people he would rather have seen.

He cleared his throat, causing the two girls to abruptly stop cooking and look up at him in surprise. After a second of stunned silence, the smaller girl let out a squeal of delight and threw her arms around Andras's waist.

"You're here, " she cried. "See, Jozefa, I told you he would come. Jozefa thought you would be too busy, Andras, but I knew you wouldn't."

"I've always said you're the most intelligent person in this family, Kitti," he replied, picking the little girl up with effort. "Good Lord, young lady, you've doubled in size since I saw you last. This may be the last time I'm able to lift you."

"Don't care," Kitti declared, clinging to his shoulders. "You have to keep trying, you're my brother. And anyway I don't think I am going to keep growing. I haven't grown a bit for six months."

Not for the first time, Andras was torn between appreciation and guilt that his youngest sister had become so attached to him. By all rights, she shouldn't have been. He'd left for Vienna when she was practically a baby and had seen her only occasionally for visits ever since. Yet somehow, Kitti had decided she adored him and made sure he knew it. He wondered if, when she was older, she would be disappointed in him.

"Nonsense, Kitti," he said, setting her down. "You've got the

Lázár blood, just like Ilka and me. Just you wait, by this time next year you'll be a foot taller than all the boys in school." He glanced at Jozefa, who was eying him with suspicion. "Hello, Jozefa. All right?"

Jozefa shrugged. "As well as can be expected. Didn't think you'd show up this time."

Andras winced. Kitti might not have been disappointed in him, but after their mother's funeral, Jozefa certainly was. Grudges formed by highly intelligent girls were not easily dropped.

"I'm sorry about what happened with Ma, Jozefa," he said, lowering his voice. "But I'm here now. Shall we try to make peace?"

"I'm sure I don't know what you're talking about," she said. "But fine. The longer you stay this time, the more I'll believe you actually give a damn about this family."

"Don't swear," he replied automatically. "Can I go see Pa? Is he awake?"

"He's in the other room," said Ilka. "He was resting when I last saw him, but I heard him moving about a minute ago. He'll be delighted to see you, I'm sure."

As soon as she had said this, the door to the other room creaked open, and the hunched figure of a middle-aged man emerged, wrapped in a worn quilt and leaning on a cane.

"Well," said György Király gruffly. "Look who's back. And not a day too soon."

"Pa, you should be resting," Ilka scolded gently. "Moving around sets off your coughing, you know that."

"Don't see that it makes much difference now," György wheezed, but nonetheless he sat in the armchair Ilka pulled out for him. While he wasn't one for obvious affection, his eyes when he looked at Andras were kind. "Glad you could make it home, son. Wouldn't like to go without seeing you first."

Andras swallowed hard, willing the lump in his throat to go away. Ilka's report that György was not doing well hadn't been exaggerated. His usually ruddy cheeks were hollow and pale, and his sturdy frame was diminished, as though he'd shrunk in the laundry. The only thing about him that looked healthy was his wooden leg, which appeared to have just been polished. He had always been proud of his leg, saw it as proof of his patriotism and sacrifice. "Bury me with it," he'd often said, "so the good Lord will see what I gave up for my country."

But Andras was not going to give in to despair, not when he'd promised Marta. *Hope protects us.*

"Nonsense, Pa, you're not going anywhere," he said brightly. "Except to a sanatorium, to get some rest and medicine. You'll be all right in a few weeks, I don't wonder."

György let out a harsh laugh, which turned into a coughing fit. "A sanatorium, eh?" he said, once he was finally able to speak again. "And where are we getting the money for this miracle cure, eh, boy? Going to conjure it out of thin air?"

Andras grinned and reached into his jacket, producing with a flourish a thick envelope fastened with a scarlet seal. "Nearly," he said, handing it to his father. "Count it, Pa. That's enough for a good long stay at St. Luke's, with some left over."

Though his face was skeptical at first, his father's eyes widened in wonder as he opened the envelope and inspected the contents. "My God, Andras. Where did you get this?"

"Nothing for you to worry about, Pa," Andras said soothingly. "I picked up some extra work, that's all. Why don't you get some rest, and the girls and I will finish making dinner and start packing your bag."

"Huh." György looked as though he might like to say something else, but was cut off by a deep yawn. "All right, then. Thank you, lad. Can't say how much good a sanatorium will do me at this point, but I appreciate the effort."

While he may have had more to say, he was deprived of the opportunity as he almost immediately drifted off to sleep.

If their father proved too ill and exhausted to ask many questions about his son's newfound wealth, the girls were not. As soon as the door to the bedroom closed, they surrounded Andras, arms folded and eyes narrowed in suspicion.

"All right, out with it," Jozefa demanded. "How did you get all that money all in one place on five days' notice?"

"Have you become a highwayman?" Kitti asked eagerly. "Do you stop rich people's carriages on the road and threaten to play the violin at them until they give you their money?"

He laughed and ruffled his youngest sister's hair. "No, but that's not a bad idea. I wish I'd thought of it."

"Andras, please. Tell us the truth," said Ilka, her wide gray eyes filled with concern. "You haven't been doing anything unsavory, have you?"

Other than kissing my employer's daughter? part of his brain suggested nastily. Shaking the thought away, he put a comforting hand on her shoulder. "No, Ilka, nothing unsavory. I didn't tell Pa because I thought he might get upset, that's all. The von Holstadts lent me the money."

Jozefa wrinkled her nose. "You mean that horrid rich family you give music lessons to?"

"Now, Jozefa, when have I given you any reason to think they're horrid? They're all right, no matter what Pa says about Austrians. Countess Marta was perfectly happy to get her parents to help us."

"Hmm," said Ilka. "And are they expecting you to pay this back in two months with fifty percent interest?"

Andras tried to ignore the heat rising in his cheeks as he shook his head. "Not that I am aware of. In fact, M... the countess insisted on giving us the money, and I can't be certain that isn't how she phrased it to her parents. I've called it a loan for pride's sake."

"I see." Ilka looked at him thoughtfully. "This Countess Marta seems to have become very fond of you. You must be doing an excellent job teaching her."

"I do my best," he said, turning away quickly. "Who's hungry?"

CHAPTER FIFTEEN

(In Which We Enjoy a Rural Interlude)

A GUIDEBOOK TO THE province of Carinthia, published in 1860, had described Burg Holstadt as "a building in impeccable taste, a palace of yellow stone surrounded by exquisite gardens and placed in a setting of soaring green hills and crystalline lakes that seems copied from Paradise itself." The entry had caused mixed reactions in the von Holstadt family. The count had rolled his eyes and declared it much too flowery, the countess had been flattered but worried that being in a guidebook was common, and the Dowager Countess Dorothea, Grandmama, had been aghast at the thought of holidaymakers tramping around her exquisite gardens.

Marta had felt then as she felt now, in total agreement with the guidebook. Much as she loved the city, it was still difficult to believe that anywhere could be more beautiful than the family estate. As the carriage rolled down the winding, tree-lined drive to the main house, her mind was flooded by a thousand memories of past visits to the countryside— Christmases, birthday parties, lambings, and all the time spent with her grandmother.

Upon alighting from the carriage at Burg Holstadt's grand entryway, the von Holstadts were greeted, as usual, by Dowager Countess Dorothea von Holstadt, resplendent in a plum high-necked gown and holding a fluffy white cat at the sight of whom Liebchen whimpered and hid behind Hannelore's skirts. While Dorothea had spent the last ten years living in the country and rarely entertaining, she still insisted on keeping up appearances.

"Well," she said loudly. Getting on in years she might have been, but the dowager countess's voice could still carry farther than a foghorn. "Look who's here. I haven't seen you since Easter. A fine dutiful son you are, Heinrich."

It was entertaining to see how the usually dignified Heinrich seemed to revert to being a schoolboy around his mother. "Be fair, Mama," he said pleadingly. "I've got court duties and business interests in the city. Neumann's doing a fine job of managing things out here…"

"Neumann!" Dorothea sniffed. "That man calls himself an estate manager? A low-life swindler if you ask me, which no one did, unsurprisingly. Never mind that I'm the only one who lives out here year-round, I'm just a useless old woman sitting around and gathering dust…"

"Of course you're not, Grandmama," Marta interrupted, deciding this had gone on long enough. "But could we finish this discussion indoors? It's very hot outside."

At the sight of her favorite and only granddaughter, the dowager countess's face relaxed into something that was not quite a smile, but close to it. "Marta, my girl, there you are. And twenty-one years old, my goodness. A shame I couldn't come to the party, but it went well, I hear. Come inside, I've got a present for you."

Trailing after her grandmother through the castle's main hallway, Marta felt a rush of warm familiarity at the sight of the various family heirlooms crowding the halls. There was the painting of the ancestor after whom she was named, the first Countess Marta, whose menagerie had been the grandest in the province. And there was the statue of Great-great-great-grandfather Albrecht, he of the six fingers and rakish smile. And the medieval tapestry of a self-satisfied-looking knight playing the lute for an unimpressed lady. Things never changed at Burg Holstadt, not a whit.

Marta's grandmother's own apartments, located in the west wing, were simply and comfortably furnished. The only extravagance was the nearly life-sized portrait above the fireplace of Count Gerhardt von Holstadt the Third, Marta's late grandfather. Marta had never met Grandfather Gerhardt—he'd died three years before she was born—but the portrait didn't make him look like the sort of grandfather who bounced children on his knee and told stories.

Upon entering her sitting room, the dowager countess took a seat upon her favorite overstuffed armchair, placed the cat on the floor, and snapped her fingers imperiously to summon a maid, who promptly returned bearing a black velvet box.

"There you are," Dorothea took the box and presented it to Marta. "Thought you might like to have that. It was mine when I was your age."

Marta opened the box and gasped as she pulled out a silver hairpin, decorated at the end with a small cluster of diamonds. "Grandmama, this is beautiful!"

"It is, isn't it? I'm too old for such things, but a young girl like you ought to have it. Wear it to parties and such."

Marta threw her arms around her grandmother, who stiffly but fondly patted her on the back. "Thank you, Grandmama. I couldn't ask for anything nicer. But listen, I've been meaning to ask. Why are you always so hard on poor Papa? He's doing his best, you know."

"Oh, I know perfectly well," Dorothea replied. "But when one has the wealth and power your father does, it's always important to be reminded that there are some people you can't boss around."

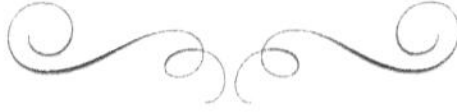

June 9

The good people at Saint Luke's Sanatorium in the suburbs were more than happy to take Andras's money and accept György as a patient, despite the older man's insistences that medicine and fresh air would be wasted, and it was no use fussing over an old fellow like him with one foot in the grave anyway. To the younger Királys' relief, these protests were duly ignored, and the doctors assured Andras that they would give him the finest care available.

The painful pit of anxiety in Andras's stomach hadn't entirely disappeared by the time he and his sisters returned to the apartment and made dinner, but it had lessened. He was with his family, where he belonged, and he was doing something this time instead of staying in Vienna and feeling guilty.

"Well," said Jozefa, gracelessly plopping into a chair and nearly spilling soup all over her dress. "Now that Pa's off getting doctored, you can tell us everything."

"Everything about what?" Andras asked.

"About your aristocratic Austrian employers, of course. The ones who Pa can't find out lent us money," said Ilka. "And we do want to know everything. How gorgeously they dress, how many houses they own, how many servants they have…anything that will make us gasp in horror at the extravagance of the rich."

"I'll do what I can," he said with a laugh. "Their house in Vienna is extremely beautiful and full to the brim of expensive art, and I know they've got a place in the country as well. It's more like a palace, so I've heard, though I doubt I'll get a chance to see it."

"I think you could get invited for Christmas," Kitti put in. "Tell them you'll play all the holiday songs for them and they can pay you in cakes. They'll never say no to that."

"Kitti, you are a font of good ideas as always, I will suggest that to them. Now, what else did you need to know? How many servants do they have? Lots, though I haven't met many of them. There's the butler, a very stiff and proper fellow, and a few maids who are not nearly as good at their jobs as Ilka, and then there's Nella, whose job appears to be taking naps during Countess Marta's music lessons."

"That's the job for me," said Jozefa approvingly. "She must be getting paid well, to sleep through your racket."

"One certainly hopes so. The family is nice enough, from what I've seen of them. Count Heinrich has an impressive mustache and is very stern with everyone, and his son Heini—that's the one who's your age, Kitti—has very strong opinions about cows."

"What's Countess Marta like?" Kitti asked. "She sounds nice, if she helped pay for the sanatorium."

"Depends on what you mean by nice. She's bossy and nosy and refuses to take no for an answer ever, but she's also cheerful and hardworking and astonishingly generous, so nice might very well be the word for her."

"So essentially, she's Ma," said Jozefa. "You could have just said that, and saved us some time."

The connection to their mother was one that Andras hadn't previously made, though now that he thought about it, there may have been some truth to the notion. "I suppose, in that they're both somewhat alarming to be around. Not much similarity in looks, though."

Jozefa nodded with satisfaction. "Is she pretty?"

"Very pretty," he said, emphatically enough to surprise himself. "She has curly dark hair and brown eyes and freckles on her nose. And she's very well-dressed. Ma would have been in raptures over her clothes."

"How adorable," Ilka said with a grin. "Have you taken a fancy to her, Andras darling? Are we going to be hearing wedding bells soon?"

"Oh, yes, there's no reason at all why I shouldn't marry a countess," Andras drawled. "No one could possibly have any objections to that. Franz Liszt married a countess, after all. Well, not legally married, but they had three children together so I suppose it counts."

"None of that talk in front of Kitti, if you please," Ilka said primly. "Now, I've got to be heading back to the Grubers' soon, so if there's any important family business to discuss, I suggest we do it now. Andras?"

"Nothing urgent springs to mind, except that there's still a fair bit of money left over after the sanatorium fees, so you girls will all be getting new boots. Now, now, don't argue, it's my money—well, the count's money—and I intend to use it for good. Kitti, wait until you hear about the von Holstadts' dog."

The fact that Kitti was now a young lady of nearly eleven did not prevent her from begging Andras to tell her a bedtime story, nor did it prevent her from falling asleep halfway through his cleaned-up retelling of *Don Giovanni*. With a fond smile, he patted his smallest sister on the head and carefully left the room, closing the door of the girls' bedroom quietly behind him.

Ilka had headed back to her employers' house in order to be

on time for work the next morning, leaving behind Jozefa, who sat at the dinner table, reading a tattered book by the sputtering light of a candle. She glanced up at the sound of his footsteps.

"She needs glasses, you know."

Andras looked at her quizzically. "Who, Kitti?"

"Yes." Jozefa set down her book and rubbed her eyes. "She's had trouble in school lately, and when I asked her why, she said the words were blurry. So I thought, maybe, well." She shrugged. "Glasses are expensive, and I really don't need new boots. I figured if there was any money left over, you could use it for Kitti instead."

"That's very kind of you, Jozefa," he said gently, sitting across from her. "Though I hope there will be money for both. If necessary, I won't buy myself seven new neckties, much as I deserve them."

Jozefa let out a snort of laughter. "Never had you pegged for such a dandy, but I suppose Vienna can change a person."

"I'm hurt, I really am. Now." He leaned forward. "What's this I hear about you planning to leave school?"

The smile faded from her face. "Where did you hear that?" she demanded. "Is Ilka telling tales on us? She's got some nerve."

"Jozefa." Andras cut her off. "Don't go blaming Ilka. She was right to tell me that you don't want to stay in school. My only question is, why?"

"Why stay? I'm old enough to work, and don't pretend we couldn't use the money. You and Ilka have been working hard to provide for us, and I should contribute too."

"Absolutely not," he said. "Ilka and I work hard specifically so that you and Kitti can get good educations. You're intelligent, Jozefa, and if you finish school you could become a teacher, or go to university, or marry an educated man." He laughed when Jozefa wrinkled her nose. "All right, you needn't get married if you don't want to. But it isn't your job to support this family. You could be a great writer if you wanted to."

Jozefa's face remained neutral, though Andras felt sure he was getting through to her. "I think you might be overestimating my brains, Andras."

"I can assure you I'm not, having known you for fourteen years. But are we agreed that your education is important, and I'll hear no more about you leaving school?"

Jozefa rolled her eyes. "If you insist, you old mother hen. Fine, I'll stay in school like a good girl. 'Til I'm sixteen, at least. That's three years longer than Ilka lasted, so you won't have anything to complain about. Deal?"

He shook her hand firmly. "Deal. Now get some sleep, and come find me if you need a bedtime story as well."

The crown-shaped hedge maze at Burg Holstadt was famously difficult, though it was child's play to Marta by now. She'd spent enough time exploring the gardens as a girl that she could probably have made it to the center of the maze blindfolded. This skill had come in handy when she'd been eight and, during a game of pirates, had buried her mother's prized ruby necklace in the herb garden. Hannelore had been understandably upset, as the necklace had been a gift from an archduchess, and Marta had spent the afternoon cowering in the center of the maze to avoid punishment.

Her motivation for entering the hedge maze on this fine day, though, was simply to be afforded privacy. She had a lot of contemplating to do, on subjects for which privacy was absolutely necessary.

Marta had assumed that being away from Vienna would distract her from thoughts of Andras, a hope that had turned out to be futile. Without the distractions of city life, Andras was practically all she could think of. At dinner, she imagined him sitting beside her and discussing Hungarian food. In the evenings, when the family gathered in the parlor, she imagined playing duets with him on her grandmother's old piano.

And at night…well. At night, alone in her velvet-curtained bed, Marta ran her hands over her body and imagined Andras touching her, his long fingers cupping her breasts and parting her legs, his mouth on her heated skin. It was a relief that her rooms at Burg Holstadt were far from the rest of the family. If anyone overheard her whimpering Andras's name as she stroked herself, they would be horrified. Truthfully, she was mildly horrified at herself, but not nearly enough to stop.

Enjoyable as these moments of indulgence were, though, they weren't entirely satisfying. Not without Andras holding her afterward, running his hands through her hair and whispering words of love in her ear. It was unbearable to think he might not return her feelings, that she'd never spend a night in his arms.

But she could, at least, still write to him. Even if she was never his lover, she was still his friend. And if she had any say in the matter, he'd never doubt for a minute how much she cared about the Király family.

So as the midday sun blazed down upon the hedge maze, Marta pulled pen and paper from her reticule and began to write.

Dear Mr. Király,

I trust it's not impertinent for me to write to you, but you and your family have been in my thoughts a great deal. How is the elder Mr. Király? Has his stay in the sanatorium been doing him good? I've been praying for him and have talked Heini into doing the same. He does tend to rush through his prayers so I cannot be certain exactly what he's requesting on your behalf, but I assure you he is filled with as much empathy as a ten-year-old can be.

This letter is coming to you from a different location than usual, as we are spending a few weeks at the family seat of Burg Holstadt, built by my ancestor Johannes von Holstadt in the 17th century. An interesting fact about General Johannes: he founded the family fortune in 1619 when he saved the Emperor from choking on a fish bone, for which he was rewarded with a title. So you can see how odd we've always been.

You know how much I love Vienna, but it's lovely to be out in the country again. The weather is extremely nice this time of year. And it's delightful to spend time with my grandmother, even if she is a bit bad-tempered. I can only hope I'm half as self-assured when I'm her age. You also have a grandmother out in the country, don't you? Yet another thing we have in common. I hope your granny is less formidable, though.

I don't have much more news to impart, except that two of the tenant farmers have had babies, which are adorable.

Please tell me absolutely everything about Budapest, and give my fondest wishes to your family. I'm sure they are delighted to have you home, as they certainly should be. Has Jozefa thrown any more slates at her teachers? Kindly inform her that as far as I know, that behavior is frowned upon at the finer universities.

And give my love to Clara, as well.

Yours sincerely,

Countess Marta von Holstadt

CHAPTER SIXTEEN

(In Which Ludwig is Both Surprised and Disappointed)

FOR SOMEONE WHO'D always taken pride in his work ethic, Andras was adjusting surprisingly well to his temporary state of unemployment.

Not that there wasn't work to do in the Király family home. With their father at St. Luke's and Ilka busy with her own job, the role of mother hen fell firmly to Andras. There were cooking, shopping, and washing to be done, and helping Jozefa and Kitti with their schoolwork.

He loved it. Loved the neighbors dropping by to ask him about Vienna, loved his sisters' complaining, loved the undeniable sensation of being home. Vienna was home too, in its own way, but everyone on Szerdahelyi Street had known him since he was a baby. In this neighborhood he wasn't a paragon of wasted potential, he was the one who'd got out, who'd become a success. To them, his life of rehearsals and late nights seemed as exotic as it had to Marta.

It was funny how frequently Andras thought of Marta, considering how caught up he was in his old life. Not all the time, but every so often he would overhear a snatch of music, or dissolve into laughter at one of his sisters' jokes, or catch a glimpse of the old castle across the river on one of his walks, and think *I wonder how Marta would like that?*

She would enjoy Budapest. Maybe not the Király family flat, which seemed even more cramped and dingy compared to the sprawling, light-filled von Holstadt mansion, but she would like the city. With her adventurous, artistic spirit, she'd fit right in.

He could just picture her velvety brown eyes lighting up with excitement at the food, the music, the language... And she'd certainly appreciate his mother's old embroidery. Ma had left behind plenty of her old sewing supplies, though none of the girls used them much, and the idea briefly flickered through Andras's mind that Marta might like to have them. Until he remembered that giving a countess hand-me-down sewing supplies would probably be a breach of etiquette.

When he wasn't cooking sausages and washing dishes and arguing with Kitti about spiderwebs, Andras wrote.

He hadn't written any music in...what had it been, months? Years? Longer than he cared to admit, anyway. But now it was as though a dam had burst and released every ounce of inspiration he'd kept pent up. He would sit down after dinner to spend a few minutes working and then glance up at the clock to find it was midnight. Jozefa and Kitti teased him endlessly at the ink stains he managed to get all over his hands, but they understood nonetheless that when the green composition notebook came out, Andras was not to be disturbed.

Perhaps all he'd needed was time away from the noisy chaos of the opera company. Whatever it was, he was grateful.

June 9
Saint Luke's Sanatorium, Budapest

"Evening, Pa," Andras said cheerfully upon arrival at his father's bedside. He'd been visiting as often as he could, and it was heartening to see what good the rest and fresh air were doing his father. "Feeling better?"

"I suppose so," György replied. "As much better as an old man like me can be feeling. Surprised they keep letting you in here, though. Aren't you worried you'll get sick?"

"Me, sick? Nonsense, I've got the constitution of an ox. Only unlike an ox, I have a violin named Clara." Andras lifted up Clara's case, which he'd brought along with him. "Thought you might like a bit of music before bed."

"Violin named Clara," György said with a good-humored huff.

"One of these days you're going to find a real woman, not some musical instrument that can't give me grandchildren. Very well, go on and play something. An old tune, mind, not one of these fancy new ones by Mozart and such."

Andras resisted the urge to point out that Mozart had been dead for over seventy years, and instead unpacked Clara and began to play an old folk song, the sort the old men at the beer hall sang when they'd had a few too many and were feeling sentimental— the very music, in fact, Andras had always associated with his father. György hummed along for a few minutes, before closing his eyes and nodding off.

"It should have been me, you know," he remarked out of nowhere, a few minutes later.

Andras, who had been halfway dozing on the chair beside the bed, looked up in surprise. "What's that, Pa?"

"It should have been me who died," his father repeated. He looked very old, suddenly, and very tired. "Not your mother. I was already short a leg and with these useless lungs, seems as though if the Lord had any sense he'd have taken me instead of Anna. She was the one who did the raising of you children."

"Pa, you can't think I'd agree with that," said Andras. "Yes, your health was poor when we were children and you weren't able to take us places as often as Ma did. But how could you believe you had nothing to do with raising us? You told all the best stories, and taught us to read, and to be proud of our country. You lost your leg fighting for Hungarian independence, for goodness' sake. Do you think that means nothing to us?"

György shrugged. "The girls are too young to understand about the revolution. I think they'd rather have your mother back. And you…well, you haven't been back from Vienna much since Anna died, have you? I suppose there isn't much point, now that she's gone."

"You think…" Andras shook his head, stung. "You think I haven't been back home because I don't love you as much as I did Ma? First of all, Pa, you need to understand that I have very little time off. Second, how can I show my face around here when I didn't come home for Ma's funeral? The shame of that has been torturing me for four years. Every time I come back to Budapest, I remember how I wasn't here when I needed to be."

His father was silent for a beat before he reached out and tentatively patted Andras's arm.

"Your ma…" he said hoarsely. "Your ma was proud of you for being so talented. She thought you could be famous if you put your mind to it."

Andras couldn't hold back a snort of bitter laughter. "Looks like she was mistaken there, wasn't she."

"Mistaken? Your mother? Lord no, that woman was right about everything. You wait, sooner or later you'll be a right success."

Andras felt his heart swell with a warmth he hadn't felt in— well, years. "I'll count myself a success if you get better, Pa," he said lightly. "That's all my ambition at the moment. After all, you've still got plenty of children at home who need you to boss them around."

His father chuckled roughly before closing his eyes, drifting off into what looked like a deep and much-needed sleep. Andras, meanwhile, leaned back in his chair and considered what a strange and complicated thing family could be.

June 11
Burg Holstadt

"Marta, get up. The von Braumarks are here."

For Marta, who had been enjoying a peaceful morning sitting on the porch overlooking the lake and embroidering music notes onto a scrap of blue linen, this announcement from her mother was roughly equivalent to a firecracker set off under her chair. "The von Braumarks?" She sat up so quickly she nearly toppled over. "What in the world are they doing here?"

"They've come for a visit, like any good neighbors would," Hannelore replied patiently. "Hurry now. Go freshen up for luncheon."

Resisting the urge to roll her eyes, Marta reluctantly pulled herself out of her chair and followed her mother inside. It wasn't surprising the von Braumarks should visit. Their estate was nearby. There was, however, a pit of dread in the bottom of her stomach.

The ominous feeling didn't lessen as the two families took their seats in the dining room. The pale, thin baroness seemed even more on edge than usual, and had the baron somehow grown louder? But it was Ludwig whose behavior was truly concerning. He barely spoke a word the entire meal, picking at his food, and every so often Marta would look up to find him gazing at her with a look in his eyes she did not enjoy.

At least he wasn't quoting Socrates.

It wasn't until the meal was over and the servants had cleared away the pudding dishes that Ludwig finally spoke up, his voice strained with nerves.

"Count, Countess," he said. "Might I request a minute of Countess Marta's time in private?"

Marta widened her eyes at her parents, silently pleading with them to refuse, but neither seemed to notice. In fact, they looked unbearably pleased.

"But of course, Ludwig," Heinrich said graciously. "I am sure Marta would be pleased to speak with you, would you not, my dear? Come, Hannelore, Baron, Baroness, we'll retire to the gardens."

One by one the other occupants of the room departed, until it was just Marta and Ludwig, both frozen into place like frightened deer.

Ludwig was doing his best not to panic, though it was difficult. This was the moment he'd spent what seemed his entire life preparing for. The entire carriage ride to Burg Holstadt, he'd contemplated how to achieve his goal, while trying to ignore his parents' incessant suggestions.

If he wanted to marry Marta von Holstadt, he would have to propose to her. Today.

And he did want to marry Marta.

Of course he did.

How to begin, though? One had to be cautious when asking someone for their hand in marriage. He knew young ladies could be bashful and timid about such subjects. Better to start slowly, then, ease her in.

"You know, I suppose, that I've finished my studies at the university recently," he said cautiously.

"I remember your father saying so. Well done. It must have been very hard work."

Ludwig shrugged modestly. "Oh, I don't know. I quite enjoyed it, really. But the point is, now that I've finished with my education, it's high time I started thinking about my future."

Was it his imagination, or did Marta edge away from him slightly?

"Really?" she said. "And a very good future it will be, I'm sure."

"I hope so, though it depends. Once my father dies I will take over Schloss Braumark, and naturally I will not be able to do it alone."

"But you won't be alone. You have a wonderful family to guide you."

"But Mother and my cousins and so on won't be precisely what I need. What I am going to need," Ludwig said, "is a family of my own. I'll need an intelligent wife from a good family, and hopefully an heir and a few spares later on. I plan to be a responsible estate owner and will need the right sort of woman to help me. Someone like you, Marta. As Epictetus said, 'The key is to keep company only with people who uplift you, whose presence calls forth your best.' That is the sort of person you are."

This time he definitely did not imagine the look of panic that crossed Marta's lovely face. Modesty, Ludwig assured himself, simply modesty. He had better make this quick before either of them lost their nerve. "Listen, Marta, you must know what I am trying to say. I don't expect it to come as any surprise. We've both known this is inevitable. But I'll put it properly anyway." He cleared his throat and straightened his spine. "Marta, will you marry me?"

There was a silence, one that seemed to last about a year. Then...

"Oh, Ludwig," Marta said. "You're very kind, and I *am* fond of you, but I can't."

Ludwig only just managed to keep his mouth from hanging open like a fish. "You can't?"

Marta shook her head. "I really can't. It wouldn't be right, you see. I don't love you in that way."

"But Marta," Ludwig said desperately. "For God's sake, be sensible…"

"I *am* being sensible. Do you really think we would be happy together? I can't bear discussing philosophy and you don't care much for music, or the theatre, or art. What would we talk to each other about?"

Ludwig resolutely ignored the part of his brain that said she had a point. "But Marta," he said again. "You're the only person I have ever wanted to marry." The only person he could marry, in fact. He barely knew any other women who didn't terrify him.

The sympathy on Marta's face made his stomach twist. "That's only because no one has ever allowed you to consider marrying anyone else. But you deserve to be with someone who truly loves you. You'll do better than me, Ludwig. I'm sure of it."

Rejection, Ludwig might have been able to take. Even if it was a rejection of everything he'd been raised to assume, everything he'd thought his future would consist of. Even if all the wisdom he'd studied for years seemed to have vanished into thin air.

But he could *not* abide pity.

Straightening the collar of his jacket, he gave Marta the most dignified look he could muster. "Very well then. Thank you for your time."

Later That Evening

"I don't understand, dear," said Hannelore, her face flushed with irritation. "I'd always thought you were so fond of Ludwig."

"I am," Marta replied, with all the patience she could muster. It had been a very, very long afternoon. "But being fond of something does not mean one wants to marry it. Frankly, I think Liebchen would be a better match for me than Ludwig."

"Now, Marta, I want you to think seriously about this," Heinrich told her. "Your mother and I would never force you to marry, and of course Ludwig's family is not quite as high-ranking as ours. But they are respectable people, with a fine estate and a good income. You'd never want for comforts."

"Their lands are so very close to ours," her mother put in. "Not to mention that their house in Vienna is practically around the corner. It would be so easy for you to visit us once you were married. And the baron is such a supporter of the arts, there's no reason you couldn't be as well. Oh, Marta, are you quite certain you won't consider Ludwig? You could be very happy with him…"

"But I don't love him." Marta swiped at her eyes, which were beginning to fill with tears. How could she make them understand the unbearable panic that filled her every time she pictured being married to Ludwig? There was no practical explanation. On paper, the alliance made sense. But even if she hadn't been in love with Andras, she couldn't forget the pure terror that rose up inside her when she contemplated living as Ludwig's wife, letting him touch her, having his children. It was wrong. "Mama, Papa, please don't keep asking me, I can't, I just…" Words failed her, and she dissolved into tears.

"Leave the poor girl alone," ordered Marta's grandmother, thumping her cane emphatically on the floor. "You know perfectly well you have no right to force her into marrying someone she doesn't like, Heinrich."

"As I said, I have no intention of forcing her, Mother. But as a girl gets older she's got to think about these things…"

"Older? Nonsense. Marta has plenty of time to turn down proposals until she finds a chap she likes. Not to mention that if you'll recall, my dear Heinrich, I was twenty-six before I married your father. And a good thing I did, or where would you be now?"

"Saints preserve me from the women in this house," Heinrich grumbled. "Very well, we'll say no more about it for now."

"How generous of you to say so." She stood and held out a hand to Marta. "Come, my dear. Let's go upstairs and have a chat."

"So," Dorothea said, dropping into one of the overstuffed armchairs in her sitting room. "You have no desire to marry Ludwig von Braumark."

"Not a bit," said Marta, wiping her eyes. "I hope you're not going to tell me why I should consider him."

"Of course not. I turned down loads of proposals before I met Gerhardt, and I'm glad I did. There was this one very insistent fellow, I remember, a horrible Polish prince with a mustache like a walrus and a laugh like a donkey, but my parents were desperate for me to marry him because he had an estate on the Baltic and fifty thousand *thaler* a year. Three times he proposed to me, and every time my parents reacted just as yours."

"What did you do?"

Dorothea shrugged. "What could I do? I said no, and I said no again, at ever-increasing volumes until they knew I meant it. Locked myself in my room for an entire week at one point, just to make myself clear. Eventually my parents gave up, and the next year I met your dear grandfather, and we had many contented years together."

"Well, I hope Mama and Papa give up after this. Because I won't marry Ludwig and spend the rest of my life in an endless cycle of quoting Socrates."

"Nor would I expect you to. A useless lot, the ancient Greeks, with a thoroughly sordid mythology. But may I ask you something?" Dorothea's flinty eyes bored into Marta. "You didn't reject Ludwig because you've fallen in love with someone else, did you?"

Marta nearly laughed. Someone else? *Oh, yes, Grandmama, there is someone I have feelings for. Only the loveliest, kindest, most talented man in Europe. And he's penniless.*

"No," she said quickly. "I only thought that if someone did come along whom I loved, wouldn't it be better to wait for him, instead of marrying Ludwig just because he's suitable?"

"You're absolutely right," her grandmother said approvingly. "I'm glad someone in this family has a brain in their head. And really, I never liked the von Braumarks. Too bourgeois for my taste."

This, it seemed, was all there was to be said on the subject. Of all the things Marta's future husband was supposed to be, bourgeois was not one of them.

Lucky she'd gotten that part right.

CHAPTER SEVENTEEN

(In Which Music Soothes No One)

June 17

IT WAS A typically lovely day at Burg Holstadt, the skies a glorious blue and the lake sparkling like diamonds in the sunlight. Marta *had* had plans to sit by the lakeside and alternately read and daydream, but Grandmama had rejected this idea on the grounds of wanting to spend time with her grandchildren. Thus the afternoon found the family in her favorite parlor, Marta embroidering and Heini absorbed in *Journey to the Center of the Earth*. Marta's parents, who had not mentioned Ludwig in several days, still seemed to regard Marta with suspicion.

Two hours passed before the silence was finally broken by one of the young footmen, who cleared his throat at the door and bowed.

"A letter for the countess, milady."

"Which one?" Dorothea asked sharply. "In case you haven't noticed, Beyer, there are three countesses in this room."

The footman flushed, but maintained his composure as he said: "Countess Marta, milady."

The dowager's lips pursed. "Why didn't you say so? I don't stand for my footmen wasting time."

"Thank you, Beyer," Marta said, and shot the lad a sympathetic smile. She took the letter from his outstretched hand, her heartbeat speeding up as she took in the Pest postmark. With trembling hands, she opened the envelope.

"Is that from Mr. Király?" Heini demanded. "Is he going to

bring us back any presents from Hungary? Can you tell him I want…"

"Hush, Heini!" Marta snapped. "I will tell you what it says when I've read it." Unfolding the letter, she rapidly absorbed its contents.

Countess,

It was very kind of you to write, and I appreciate your asking after my father. I'm sure he would be pleased to know that he features in your and Master Heinrich's prayers, incomprehensible as your brother's may be.

As it happens, I have good news. While my father is still unwell, the doctors at Saint Luke's have informed us he's on the mend, and he is expected to make a reasonably good recovery in a few weeks. We expect him home in less than a fortnight. My sisters, as you can imagine, are delighted, and are very grateful for your family's help.

Burg Holstadt sounds like a fine place. My sister Kitti, who likes to think of herself as my manager, is of the opinion that I ought to offer myself up as your official estate musician this Christmas, and so if she negotiates fiercely enough with your father perhaps I will be able to see the place myself in a few months. (I am, of course, joking, unless your family did in fact have some use for me there.)

Budapest remains much as it was in my childhood: crowded, noisy, and full of well-meaning neighbors. It's quite a different city from Vienna, but it's difficult not to love a place when your entire family is there. And, without meaning to sound arrogant, I firmly believe that Hungarian cuisine is the finest food in Europe and makes Austrian food taste like wet cardboard in comparison. Meaning no offense, obviously.

Respectfully,
Andras Király

"My goodness, Marta," her grandmother said sharply. "Bad news, is it? Are you in need of a handkerchief?"

Marta put a hand to her face and realized her cheek was damp with tears. Until this point she hadn't realized how terrified she was on Andras's behalf. And here she was, crying with joy over a man she'd never met. "It's not bad news, Grandmama. Quite the opposite. Mr. Király says his father's on the mend." She sniffled joyfully and wiped her eyes. "He's going to be all right. Isn't that brilliant?"

Aside from Heini, who whooped with delight, the rest of the von Holstadt family was less affected by this news than Marta would have liked. Dorothea let out a harumph and muttered something about other people's health being none of her business, while Heinrich merely nodded and continued to read the newspaper. Hannelore, at least, gave Marta a fond smile. "I'm glad to hear it, darling. Has Mr. Király said when he plans on returning?"

"He didn't say exactly, but it should be before the end of the month. It will be awfully nice to see him again." And what would she say when she saw him again? In all her etiquette lessons, it had never been discussed how to converse with someone you hadn't seen in a month and were in love with.

"You really must show off your musical skills at our next dinner party," her mother said. "I'm sure any number of suitors will find your violin playing charming. I was skeptical at first," she added to Dorothea. "In my day girls were only expected to play the piano. But Marta seems to enjoy it, and her future husband will most likely find it more entertaining than her embroidery."

Future husband.

It was ridiculous that those two words should make Marta's stomach clench painfully. That had, after all, been her rationale for learning the violin in the first place. She would have another accomplishment, something with which to charm a man of her class into marrying her. Her future husband would be rich and titled, perhaps even an archduke or a prince, someone with a grand country estate and a wardrobe full of military uniforms. A man who never wore trousers that were too short, whose ancestors hadn't caused any political trouble for centuries.

Marta hated him already. She didn't even know him, this mysterious future husband, and yet she wanted to find him and scream that she would never love him, that he could never inspire her or make her laugh. And every time he touched her, she would close her eyes and remember the way Andras had kissed her in the park.

"You're crying again," Heini pointed out. "Are you happy or upset this time?"

With a furious sniff, Marta shook her head. "I'm fine, Heini. Everything is *fine*."

Andras had not expected to hear back from Marta anytime soon. Surely she was busy with garden parties and other things aristocrats did in the country, so he was pleasantly surprised by the arrival of a letter bearing the von Holstadt seal shortly after he'd sent his last missive.

Dear Mr. Király,

If you think Austrian cuisine is bland, I shudder to think how you would react to British food. I was in Oxford some years ago visiting Mama's cousin (a professor, and too dull to describe further) and the only spice they used on anything was salt. Horrifying!

I am very disappointed in myself that the first thing I wrote was about British food rather than your father. I wish I could convey in words my relief at hearing he's on the mend! I'm overjoyed for you, truly I am. And I'm so pleased that you're enjoying your home city. What became of Erzsi the pigeon? I expect she's passed on by now, sadly, but wouldn't it be wonderful if she had a few grandchildren who flocked to you?

Your sister is right, you absolutely must come to Burg Holstadt for Christmas this year. Mama and Papa would be delighted to have you, and I'm sure you know many lovely Christmas songs we could play together.

Of course we'll have plenty of time to discuss this upon your return, which I hope will be soon—though not so soon that it will cause your family any trouble.

Fondest Wishes,

Marta

PS: Heini would like you to know that if you have any relics belonging to Attila the Hun lying about the house, he would like some. I told him he will probably have to wait until Christmas.

Andras shook his head with amusement as he finished the letter, tucking it into the back of his composition notebook.

How funny that she'd remembered Erzsi the pigeon after their brief conversation. But then, that was Marta all over. Nosy, but with purpose.

"What are you grinning about?" inquired Ilka from her position by the stove. It being Sunday, she was out of her maid's uniform and clad in an old plaid dress of Anna's, and the sight was oddly comforting.

"Just a letter from a friend in Vienna," he said lightly. "What are you cooking for us tonight?"

"I thought I might make *langos*," Ilka said. "I haven't had a chance to make it in ages, and it would be a shame not to have it while you're home."

"Ah, *langos*." Andras sighed rapturously. That particular dish of fried flatbread topped with sour cream had been one of his childhood favorites. "That's one thing I'll miss like mad when I head back to Vienna."

Ilka set down the pan she was holding, biting her lip. "You wouldn't have to go back, you know."

Andras glanced up from his notebook in bemusement. "Sorry?"

"You don't have to return to Vienna, I mean. Listen, Andras, I've been thinking," Ilka said hurriedly. "I know you left because you wanted to be a successful musician. But it hasn't been as easy as you thought, has it? Vienna's not the only place where you can play the violin, and it's been so good for Kitti and Jozefa to have you home. I know how much Pa's missed you, and so have I." She smiled wistfully. "Remember when we used to play duets on Father Jonas's piano?"

Andras winced at the reminder. Ilka was just as talented a musician as he was, and if only things had been different... "I know, Ilka. But it's not as simple as that. I have responsibilities and friends back in Vienna, and with my extra work, I'm making much better money now. That's nothing to be sneezed at."

"I know, and you're the only one who can decide what's best. It's just been a while since I've seen the younger girls this happy, that's all." Ilka looked up at him, her eyes pleading. "Would you think about it?"

"Yes," Andras said quietly. "I will."

Twenty-four hours later, Andras set down his notebook and gazed with astonishment and no small amount of pride at what lay before him.

It was a waltz, what he'd written. Bright, charming dance music, but underneath the sprightly cheerfulness there was something else. Something passionate, and exuberant, and a bit wild.

It was, in fact, Marta.

Perhaps he hadn't thought of it while writing, but there in front of him was Marta von Holstadt in musical form. Her joy, her wit, her way of bringing everything around her to life. It was almost certainly the best piece of music he'd ever written, and the fact that it had been so effortless…was concerning.

Andras slammed his notebook shut and strode to the window, flinging it open. The neighborhood assaulted his senses immediately: the chatter of old ladies leaning out of windows, the smells of the neighbors' cooking, the thin layer of grime that seemed to coat everything, clinging to people like a second skin. Andras had spent sixteen years barely noticing the dirt. Anna had always insisted the Király children keep as clean as possible in spite of the soot in the air. It wasn't until he'd arrived at the Academy that he'd realized what other people expected clean to look like.

That was who he was, deep down, despite all those years of education and music. A grimy, badly dressed, overly ambitious boy from the slums who could never hope to reach any level of sophistication. He was about as different from Marta as his own violin was from a brand-new Stradivarius.

Really, he should have thought of that before he'd started falling in love with her. Though falling wasn't quite the right word. It brought to mind images of a leaf gently tumbling from a tree, while Andras's feelings seemed more like an avalanche in the Alps. Triggered by a single sound and impossible to stop.

"Damn it all," Andras said aloud, and winced as Mrs. Farkas from downstairs, who had been pinning up her stockings out the window below him, looked up in disapproval.

"You watch your language, Andras," she scolded loudly. "This isn't Vienna, where anything goes."

Andras bit back a sharp retort. Couldn't the old busybody see he was in the midst of a personal crisis? "Sorry, Mrs. Farkas. I've just realized I'm an idiot. You know how it is."

Before his neighbor could reply, Andras ducked back inside, shutting the window with a thud.

He leaned against the wall, giving a deep sigh as he considered his next move. There were several things he felt like doing— writing an incoherent letter to Marta explaining his feelings, fantasizing about bending her over the piano and making her scream with pleasure, going to the pub and getting extremely drunk. Only one seemed right.

"Well, Clara," he said, reaching for his violin case. "Shall we see if this works?"

The minute he began to play, it was clear he'd been right. The waltz was beautiful. Possibly even a masterpiece.

Not surprising, considering who'd inspired it.

Much as the elder Baron von Braumark remained suspicious of the usefulness of Ludwig's university education, years at school had taught Ludwig one very important thing— how to draw a logical conclusion from scarce information. And he was determined to apply this deductive thinking to the issue of why Marta wouldn't marry him.

The trouble had started recently, he was sure. There had never been any sign of Marta disliking him during his years at university. Her occasional letters to him had been perfectly kind. In fact he could only trace her coldness back a few weeks. To her birthday, perhaps? Or a bit after? Something, anyway, had changed.

Ludwig paced back and forth in his bedroom, racking his brains. There was something strange going on, something he'd noticed just recently. The last time he'd seen Marta…

"Eureka," Ludwig cried aloud as it hit him. The Landfeld Theatre, when they'd gone to see that terribly melodramatic performance of *Don Giovanni*. Marta had ignored him and spent most of the evening talking to that music tutor of hers, that Hungarian, whatever his name was. There had been something odd there, something rather conspiratorial between them.

He wasn't sure what it was, but he could find out.

Half an hour later he'd found his way to Leopoldstadt and managed to discover the theatre, becoming lost only twice on the way. Disappointingly, the place did not seem to be open; Ludwig's knocks on the back door went unanswered.

Perhaps they couldn't hear him? He wiggled the doorknob, finding it locked. It was old, though, so maybe… Ludwig leaned against the wood, hoping he might be able to pop it open.

The stage door swung open, nearly knocking him off his feet. He looked up to see a copper-haired young woman dressed in a ballet costume looking at him with some contempt.

"Yes?" she said.

Ludwig drew himself up, arranging his face into some semblance of dignity. "Miss," he said imperiously. "I am looking for a colleague of yours. Hungarian chap, plays the violin. Anders something."

The ballerina, who had a rather striking face, now that Ludwig thought of it, and very intense green eyes, shrugged. "You mean Andras Király? He's gone, back to Budapest for a spell, to visit his sick pa. Ought to be back once the old man's either back to health or with the angels."

"I see." This was disappointing news, though perhaps it could be turned to his advantage. This dancer, after all, might turn out to be a useful source of information. "Forgive me, miss, I forgot to introduce myself. I am Baron Ludwig von Braumark."

"That so?" the ballerina asked with interest. She curtsied abruptly and smiled up at him. "I am Brigita Novak, of the opera ballet. You may have seen me in Verdi's *Masked Ball* last month."

"My family did indeed attend *A Masked Ball*, though you must forgive me if I don't recall you specifically. You were, I presume, masked."

"How very astute of you." Brigita cocked her head to the side. "If I may ask, sir, why are you asking after Andras? Has he done anything wrong? I know he's a bit of an idiot, but he's a nice chap."

Ludwig hesitated, unsure how to phrase his concerns. "I believe it's somehow his fault that Marta won't marry me" seemed more like the speculations of a madman than a sensible reason for investigation, and he knew these theatre types stuck together like glue in the face of any threat from outside. "My father was curious about him," he said at last. "Father thinks of himself as a patron of the arts, you know, and I think he was considering hiring Andras to play again."

"My goodness, how nice for him. And I expect you'd like to confirm that Andras is not some swindler who's going to steal the family silver."

This interaction was going much better than Ludwig had predicted. "Well, yes, I suppose that was what I was thinking. After all, one never knows…"

"Can't trust us show folk, eh?" Brigita winked. "All right then, I'll give you all the reassurance you need about Mr. Király if you take me to lunch."

"Take you to lunch?"

"But of course. I've got an hour free and I'm starving. Let me slip into something more comfortable and we can go get some noodles."

"I…" Ludwig began. But there was no chance for him to protest, as Brigita had already shut the stage door.

Never in his life had Ludwig met someone who could eat more food in less time than Brigita Novak. In the time it took him to finish his meal at Witzler's, Brigita devoured two dishes of noodles and a heaping serving of schnitzel, and was now on her third cup of coffee with cream.

"Ballet must be very tiring work," Ludwig ventured at last, once Brigita finally reached a point where she was able to talk.

"You don't know the half of it," said Brigita, taking an unladylike slurp of coffee. "When I first got my pointe shoes, I spent a month rubbing my feet in the bath and sobbing."

"But it's very rewarding, I imagine, working for the opera. All that," Ludwig gestured vaguely, "art."

Brigita shrugged. "It has its good points. Anyway, we've all got to make a living somehow. Even your lot, meaning no disrespect."

"Well, yes, I suppose we do," said Ludwig. "But with my kind of people it's more to do with managing than working."

"Mmm. And what do the von Braumarks manage, if I might ask?"

"Mainly the estate in Carinthia, crops and tenant farmers and so on. I believe there are also a few textile mills in Moravia."

"Moravia." Brigita's eyes brightened. "Why, that's where I'm from, you know. Where in Moravia?"

"I believe…" Ludwig's brow creased. "I believe we have one in a small town by the name of Litvilov, though I could be wrong."

"Holy Saint Theresa," Brigita said excitedly. "Your family owns Litvilov Mills? You know both my parents worked there, God rest their souls? Barely had a bad word to say about the place, too. Why, half our town would be out of work if the mill shut down."

"Well, then," said Ludwig, feeling oddly gratified. "We'll have to make sure it doesn't. If I may ask, have your parents been gone long?"

"Ever since I was six. It was the cholera that got them. But I had Granny Ester to look after me, so it wasn't so bad. Wisest woman in the village, my gran. She's got some clever sayings, all right."

Peasant wisdom. Well, there was some cultural interest in that, Ludwig thought. "Such as?"

"Hmm." Brigita thought for a moment. "'A hasty marriage is like a two-headed calf. If it lasts the night you can sell it to a circus.'"

Ludwig couldn't help it. He burst into uproarious laughter, the sort he hadn't indulged in since…Lord, how long had it been? Since he'd started university, at least. Plato and Socrates didn't lend themselves much to laughter.

"Your gran's a wise woman," he told Brigita once he'd calmed himself. "If she's ever in need of work, I think the University of Vienna might have a job for her in the philosophy department."

"I'll mention that to her," Brigita replied, in perfect solemnity. "And speaking of philosophy, here's a puzzler. Do you ever wonder how we know everything in our lives is real? How do we know it isn't all a dream?"

Ludwig's eyes widened in delight. "I think about that all the time. We wouldn't know, would we? Some people say that emotions and physical sensations are proof that we are real, but couldn't those be simulated?"

"Exactly. I might think my feet hurt after five hours of practice, but I could just be some sort of science experiment rigged up to think I have feet that hurt. Like in that British book, that scientist, what was his name? Frankenstein, that's the lad. I could be a Doctor Frankenstein experiment and not even know."

Of all the places Ludwig had expected to find himself that week, a café in Leopoldstadt discussing *Frankenstein* with a Moravian ballerina was not one of them. It was surprising how much he was enjoying it. "If you are a science experiment, Miss Novak, might I say that you are a very intelligent one?"

"How kind of you," Brigita said, giving him a broad smile. "Care for another slice of cake? I could use one. Or two."

It was an hour later before they finally made it back to the theatre, and Ludwig felt oddly disappointed when they reached the stage door. Brigita tossed her shawl back over her shoulders and winked at him. "Same time next week, then?"

Ludwig had every intention of saying no. What good would it do him to see her again? But when he opened his mouth, what came out was "Absolutely. I'll meet you here."

"Wonderful. It's been a pleasure, sir." With another brief curtsy, Brigita flounced back inside, shutting the door behind her.

It was only when Ludwig was halfway home that he realized they hadn't once brought up Andras Király.

Andras had not been looking forward to his next conversation with Ilka, which was a rarity. He and his oldest sister had always understood each other, always shared the same passion for music and concern for their family's welfare, and it was painful to know that he would be disappointing her. Again.

Unsurprisingly, the minute Ilka arrived for dinner on Sunday, she took one look at his face and asked, "Oh, Lord. Now what?"

"Well," said Andras, wondering briefly if it was too late to change his mind. "I've been thinking about what you asked me last week, and while I do understand—really, I do—there are so many other things to consider, and—"

"You're not going to stay, are you," Ilka interrupted, her voice soft.

Andras exhaled heavily. "I'm afraid I can't. I've missed you all more than I can say, and it's not easy to leave, but I have to. Vienna is where I belong, at least for now."

"I can't say I'm surprised. It's your home now, I suppose, as much as Budapest." Ilka smiled sadly. "I wish I could go with you, just for a little while. It would be wonderful to finally see Vienna."

"You will," Andras said immediately. "I promise, as soon as I have enough saved, I'll pay for all of you to come visit. We'll eat spinach strudel and wander around the Stadtpark and visit the new opera house, and Pa will complain for hours about how none of it is Hungarian enough."

"That would be a perfect holiday, but I won't hold you to it," said Ilka. "I'm sure Countess Marta is going to keep you very busy when you get back, making up for all those missed music lessons. It sounds like you've become indispensable."

Hearing Marta's name sent a jolt of pure desire through Andras's body, an emotion that was highly out of place in his current situation. In only a few days he'd be in the von Holstadt music room with her again, hearing her laugh, basking in her warmth, and he was going to make an absolute ass of himself the minute he saw her. He'd thought of her nearly every waking moment for the past week, dreamed of her nearly every night.

Apparently, he was much further gone than he'd thought.

"Andras?" He realized Ilka was looking at him with eyebrows raised. "What are you thinking about?"

"Nothing much," he lied. "Just that I'll miss you all when I leave. I suppose I haven't been much of a brother for the last few years."

"There's an easy solution to that," said Ilka. "Let us back into your life, won't you? I know you've kept us at a distance since Ma died, but you can't keep torturing yourself with guilt. We love you, Andras, and we're proud of you, and we forgive you. Is that enough?"

The look on her face transported him to eight years prior, the day he'd first left for Vienna. Ilka had been nine then, far more aware of what was happening than her sisters, and she'd clung to him like a vine on a tree all morning. She hadn't cried. Even back then, Ilka had known how to keep her feelings in check. But the look in her eyes had still broken Andras's heart.

"All right," he said. "I'll try to do better, I swear. And Ilka, I truly am sorry. Not just about Ma, but about you. I wish you could have come to the Academy with me. You deserve much more than being a servant."

Ilka laughed gently. "There are worse things than polishing silver. I'm happy enough. At least until you have another stroke of amazing luck and become the toast of Vienna. Then I'll have higher expectations."

She turned back to the stove where the evening's dinner was bubbling, and Andras's thoughts turned, as usual, back to Marta. If he couldn't hide how he felt, and he probably couldn't, he'd have to tell her the truth, which would undoubtedly be a disaster. At best, she'd laugh kindly and tell him she was terribly fond of him but they would be better off as friends. At worst, she'd slap him across the face and order him out of her life forever.

Then again, if simply hearing her name had him aching with longing, it wouldn't take long for her to discover his feelings anyway.

And if she loves you too? a small, treacherous voice in the back of his head asked. What will you do then? Andras ignored the flare of hope that lit up in his chest. There was optimism, and then there was delusion.

God, he was an idiot.

CHAPTER EIGHTEEN

(In Which an Irreversible Decision is Made)

June 27
Vienna

*M*ARTA,
  I've just arrived back in Vienna, and would appreciate a chance to talk with you in private. Could you possibly meet me tonight at ten, in the usual place? Otherwise, I will see you on Tuesday.
  A

This letter, delivered to Marta by Nella shortly after their return to Vienna, was all she had been able to think about for hours.

Andras was back. After all this time, she'd finally be able to see him again.

Waiting until Tuesday was simply not an option, of course. The minute the rest of the household was asleep Marta was out the door like a shot.

She'd thought she was prepared to see him again, but she had been entirely wrong. Nothing could have prepared her for the sheer physical effect of the sight of him, leaning against a lamppost and smiling as though there was no one else in the world he'd rather see than her. Just the sight of that smile made her feel as intoxicated as if she'd just drank an entire bottle of champagne.

"Andras. You're back."

"I am," he replied, smile broadening. "And glad of it, too."

"Your father, is he…"

"Still not the picture of health, but he's on the mend. All thanks to you," Andras added, suddenly serious. "If it weren't for your help he might not be with us now."

Marta shrugged, embarrassed. "Anyone in my position would have done the same."

"No," he said. "I don't think they would. Just you."

There was a silence, during which Marta struggled to find what to say next. "So. Now that you're back, shall we head to Café Voltaire? I'm sure your friends will be delighted to see you."

"I've said hello to all of them already. They're busy anyway, Leo's visiting his grandmother, and Franz and Brigita are at some party. We'll have to see if they can make it through the entire affair without splitting up. I was wondering, though, if you would like to come back to the garret and have a glass of wine with me? There's something I want to discuss with you."

Marta took in a sharp breath of surprise. In all the time she'd known Andras, he'd never mentioned the possibility of her visiting where he lived. Which wasn't surprising. Marta might have been reckless, but she was still a lady. If anyone she knew saw her entering a strange man's home, she would be ruined forever.

She wasn't sure what it meant that Andras had just invited her to his flat, knowing the risk it posed. But no matter what, she was going to find out.

The garret was small, only two rooms with a tiny kitchen off to one side. The main room had both a rough-hewn wooden table and a badly made bed, which Andras was quick to point out belonged to his messier flatmate, Franz. There couldn't be any doubt that musicians lived here, Marta thought wryly. If the sheet music scattered over every available surface didn't give it away, the strong smell of coffee and the ink stains everywhere certainly did.

There was a window, though. Marta couldn't resist going to it, pushing aside the ragged curtain, and gazing at the faint twinkle of the street lights below.

"What a lovely view you have," she said. "It must be beautiful at sunset."

"It is," said Andras. "The entire city seems bathed in gold, like something from a fairy tale. It's even more beautiful from the rooftop, though we wouldn't get much of a view right now." He reached out and tentatively touched her shoulder. "Would you care to sit down? I'll get us something to drink."

She obediently took a seat at the table as he bustled about the kitchen, pulling out a bottle of yellowish wine and glasses from a cupboard.

"I'm afraid it's not very good wine," he said, eyeing the bottle's dusty label. "As a matter of fact, I think it's from Serbia. If it's awful, you needn't drink any of it."

"I'm sure it will be fine. Honestly, I really can't tell one wine from another." Marta laughed nervously. "Don't tell Papa. He's quite a wine connoisseur."

"Your secret is safe with me," Andras said with a wink. He poured a measure of the pale golden wine into two chipped and mismatched but fortunately clean glasses, handing one to Marta as he sat across from her. "*Egészségedre.*"

"Eggs-esh-a…cheers." Marta raised her glass to his and took a long gulp of the wine. As he had predicted, the taste was not particularly nice, but she drank it anyway, in hopes that it would calm her pounding heart. This proved ineffective, and she was forced to hide her hands in her lap before Andras noticed them trembling.

"You wanted to talk to me," she said. "What about? Nothing bad, I hope."

"Oh, Lord, I don't even know where to begin," he said. "I… well, first of all, you must know that I missed you when I was back in Budapest. Very much so. I always found myself wanting to talk to you about things, but you weren't there, and it wasn't the same writing letters."

"I completely agree. It's much nicer to be able to talk in person. I missed you too, I hope you know, and next time we go to Burg Holstadt, it would be lovely if you could come. Is that what you brought me here to discuss?"

"No, it isn't. Well, it sort of is, because it's a symptom of the larger problem, if you will. A big problem. Not your fault, I don't blame you, but it has to do with you, so. " He sighed, his face flushed with frustration. "Damn, I can't seem to…"

"Andras, you know how much I enjoy hearing you talk, but if you don't speak in complete sentences I can't understand you," Marta said, more sharply than she'd intended. "Would you please just tell me why you're so upset?"

He pushed a lock of hair out of his eyes. "I'm sorry," he said with another sigh. "I'm not upset with you, I promise. I'm upset with myself. I can't seem to find the right combination of words in German."

"Would it help, perhaps, if you told me in Hungarian first? Not that I would understand that either, but that sort of thing always helped me when I was learning English."

"It's worth a try." Andras leaned forward, and to Marta's surprise, gently placed his right hand over hers. "Marta," he said, his voice low and intense. "*Imádlak teljes szívemből.*"

Gibberish, of course, absolutely incomprehensible. And yet the way he was looking at her, the way those extraordinary eyes were focused, unblinking, on her face.

If he was saying anything close to what she thought he was…

"Oh, goodness," she blurted. "Oh, Andras, I love you too."

She was horrified with herself the minute the words left her mouth. Why was that the conclusion she jumped to? He could have been talking about anything! He certainly seemed as surprised as she was at herself as he dropped her hand like a hot coal.

"Wait a minute," he said. "Since when do you speak Hungarian?"

"I don't," she said. "That was a wild guess on my part, but you were looking at me like…" She paused as realization hit her. "Do you mean to say I was right? That you…you…"

"I love you." An unbearably beautiful smile spread across Andras's face. "That's what I said. Specifically, I said I love you with all my heart. You did ask to learn some Hungarian a few weeks ago."

"I can't learn any new words, not while I'm trying to explain that I love you too," Marta said. She struggled to stay outwardly calm, while her heart was nearly bursting with relief and joy. "Oh, God, Andras, I've probably loved you ever since you said

I have a Hungarian tongue, and I've been aware of it ever since you kissed me in the park."

"I shouldn't have kissed you," he said with a sigh. "The trouble is, I really did want to. And I enjoyed it, too much." He looked up at her again, a slight frown creasing his brow. "You mean to say you really love me? Are you sure?"

This conversation was clearly not going anywhere at all. Marta could spend hours expressing in minute detail how passionately, intensely, and hopelessly she loved this odd and beautiful man, but there was no guarantee he would believe her. And truthfully, she couldn't blame him if he didn't.

So to clear up any confusion, she leaned forward and kissed him.

For a second Andras did nothing at all, freezing with shock as her lips touched his, but when it became obvious that Marta had no intention of pulling away, he let out a growl of pleasure and began to kiss her back without any restraint, no pretense at propriety. When he pulled her onto his lap, Marta let out a surprised laugh followed by a huff of annoyance at the way her heavy skirt blocked her from feeling anything.

She'd been trained since birth to never let a man glimpse even her ankle, and yet she wriggled to a more comfortable position on Andras's lap and pulled up her skirt, giving her the freedom to straddle him. At the sight of her legs, half clad in lacy cotton drawers, he let out an incoherent, desperate noise and captured her mouth again.

He had the loveliest hands of any man on earth, Marta thought dazedly. One was resting on her bottom, his arm wrapped around her, while the other was deftly untying her hair ribbon and loosening her braid, letting her hair fall heavily around her shoulders. He buried his fingers in it and carefully teased her lips open with his tongue. Marta moaned against him, letting him devour her, pressing down harder with her hips so she could feel that shocking hardness between his legs.

Until, to her horror, he pulled away.

"What's the matter?" Marta's heart thudded in worry. "Did I do something wrong?"

"No, no," he assured her, brushing a stray lock of hair off her cheek. "You're perfect, Marta, absolutely wonderful. The trouble is, the more time I spend kissing you, the harder it is for me to stop."

"Who says we have to stop?"

Andras shook his head. "I can't get greedy. I've already had more from you tonight than I ever hoped for. Much as I would like to…well, you know."

"I don't know," Marta replied, feeling thoroughly foolish. "What would you like to do?"

Her breath caught in her throat at his expression. Smoldering, that was the word for it. Absolutely smoldering. "To be shockingly blunt, Marta, I'd like to take you to bed and make love to you. I've been thinking of nothing else for weeks. But of course that's out of the question."

He wanted to…

Good Lord.

Andras was a gentleman, of course, and would never insist on anything. If she wanted to, Marta could leave now, go home an innocent. Well, fairly innocent, if she could ignore the heavy, damp sensation building up between her thighs. She wondered with a twinge of embarrassment if she'd managed to stain Andras's trousers.

But if she stayed.

If she stayed, she would be giving up her supposedly expensive virginity to someone who loved her, whom she loved. Not someone who would only sleep with her to produce heirs. There was no competition, no decision to be made. She'd wanted this since before she could even put a name to the feeling, probably since Andras had first looked her in the eye at her party.

"I wouldn't say it's out of the question," she said slowly. "Not at all."

Andras stared at her, wide-eyed. "Marta, are you saying you want to…"

"Yes. Andras, I love you, and I want you." And when he still seemed hesitant, she added, "*Please.*"

There was an agonizingly long pause, during which he appeared deeply conflicted. Finally, he shook his head. "God help me. I know this is wrong, but I have to have you. I think

I'll die if I don't. One last thing, though," he said, holding up a finger. "Before this goes any further, I don't want you to have any regrets. You're nearly royalty, and I'm…" Andras ran a frustrated hand through his hair. "I'm…"

"You're Andras Király," Marta said softly. "And you're poor. And you are also a brilliant musician, the most loving brother and son in the Empire, and the only man to whom I could even consider saying the following sentence." She took a deep breath and steeled her nerves. No turning back now. "For heaven's sake, will you stop worrying and feeling inferior and please, please make love to me?"

Several emotions flickered across Andras's face—shock, fear, joy—before he settled into a look that would not have been out of place on one of his marauding nomadic ancestors.

"Well!" he said. "In that case!"

Making Marta squeal in shock and delight, he lifted her at the waist, slung her over his shoulder, and carried her into the other room.

Had things been different, Marta might have had an opinion about the cramped nature of Andras's bedroom, consisting as it did of a narrow bed, cheap dresser, and single window. Certainly it wasn't the bridal suite she'd envisioned. At the moment, though, she had much more important things to consider. Specifically, the way he set about undressing her immediately after he closed the door and lit a candle.

"God, Marta," he groaned, as he deftly undid the buttons along her back. "I've been aching for you constantly, ever since *Don Giovanni*. I had no idea how I was going to come back and try to teach you twice a week when all I'd be able to think about was having you like this." He trailed off and gently pushed her dress off her shoulders, letting it fall to the floor in a puddle of heavy blue fabric, and his gaze grew even hotter at the sight of her shift-and-drawers-clad form. "No corset?"

"I got dressed in a hurry," Marta explained. "I was hardly going to bother with layers and layers of undergarments when it's the middle of the night and I had you waiting for me, was I?"

Andras laughed softly. "You truly are prepared for everything, aren't you? Now sit down, let's get those boots off." His voice was gentle, but there was a note of command in it that made Marta weak at the knees, and she all but collapsed into a seat on the bed.

With a heart-stopping smile, he knelt at her feet and set to work unbuttoning her boots, casting them aside when he'd finished. Her stockings soon followed, the silk sliding down her legs and making her shiver with pleasure, and then—*good Lord!*—his hands found the waistband of her drawers.

Marta instinctively lifted her hips and let out a faint whimper as he pulled the fabric down over her bottom and thighs. His hands were driving her mad, and if he'd asked she would have let him take her right there and then, no further preparation or undressing necessary. Even if it hurt, as she'd been told it would the first time, she wanted him so badly she no longer cared.

Clearly Andras was more patient than she was, for once her drawers were gone he didn't simply climb onto the bed and have his way with her. Instead he guided her upright once more and slid his hands up her thighs, catching the end of her shift in his hands. His hands traced over every curve of her body as he slowly lifted the thin white garment. Too slowly for Marta's taste. When his hands finally reached her bosom and lingered for a moment on her nipples, she'd had enough.

"Hurry," she whispered, "or I'll rip this damn shift in half."

He laughed and tapped her on the nose. "Adding swearing to your list of bad behavior, are you? And here I thought you were such a lady. Lift your arms, now."

Marta did so, and in the blink of an eye her shift was gone, tossed into the corner, and she was utterly exposed. A small part of her wanted to curl into a ball and pull the covers over herself. Yet another, more wanton, part wanted to show off, to make Andras want her as fiercely as she wanted him.

"Lord, you're beautiful." Andras's gaze roamed greedily over her body, lingering on her breasts and hips. "Everything I imagined and more."

Marta flushed with embarrassment and delight. His words were encouraging, but even more was the way he'd begun to roll his r's very badly, his accent far more pronounced than usual. "Are you going to join me? Only I think you're a bit overdressed."

Andras glanced down at his clothes, as though surprised they were still present. "I say, you're right. Avert your eyes if you don't want to be too disappointed."

Marta, of course, did *not* avert her eyes, preferring to watch in awe as Andras efficiently removed his threadbare clothes. Though when clothed he might have looked almost too thin, undressed he was all lean, fine muscle, without an ounce of spare flesh on him. Marta's gaze swept over his wide shoulders, his toned arms, his flat stomach, before she glanced lower to see…

Well. If what she'd learned about marital relations was correct, he *definitely* wanted her.

"Oh, goodness." Marta reached out and, when he didn't protest, carefully wrapped her hand around the rigid length of his erection. Extraordinary, that combination of hardness and softness. "Are you planning to fit that inside me?" Of course she was aware of the basics of sex, but it didn't seem possible. He looked so large, surely he'd split her in two.

"With your permission, yes," Andras replied through gritted teeth as Marta continued to delicately stroke him. "But not if you keep doing that. Oh, God, especially not if you do *that*. I won't last a minute if you keep this up." Gently, he reached down and uncurled her hand. "Let me take care of you, my love."

If Marta had had any resistance left, the sound of Andras calling her my love would have melted it entirely. She lay back and relaxed as Andras climbed onto the bed, carefully straddling her hips.

He gazed down at her, a frown creasing his face, like a chess player contemplating his next move.

"Do you need a suggestion?" Marta inquired. "You could kiss me again."

"I could," Andras replied, a wicked grin spreading across his face. "A good place to start, anyway." He pressed a kiss to her half-open mouth, then moved to trace his lips over the sensitive skin of her neck and shoulders. Finally, after what seemed like an eternity, he made his way down to her breasts and took one nipple in his mouth. He sucked gently at first, and then harder, encouraged by Marta's whimper of delight, switching to her other breast when she groaned and wriggled her hips.

She nearly screamed with disappointment when he lifted his mouth away from her, only to relax once again when he began kissing his way down her front. When he reached the inside of her hip he glanced up quickly, as though confirming she was all right. And then to Marta's astonishment, he buried his face between her legs.

"Andras," she gasped. His lips gently nuzzled her, sending a sharp jolt of arousal through every nerve. "What are you doing?"

He lifted his head and shot her a wicked grin. "Preparing you, my love. I can almost guarantee you'll enjoy it. Shall I continue?"

What an education she was getting this evening. She caught her breath. No one had ever told her there were so many variations on kissing. "Yes I want to try everything."

And then he was at her again, and that beautiful mouth was doing extraordinary things to her, licking and sucking at her sex, not letting up for a moment. Had Marta been thinking more clearly, she might have been embarrassed by the sounds she was making—low, desperate moans that she barely recognized as emanating from her own throat. But she was far past shame by now. Every rational thought was blocked by the pure sensation building up within her, intensified by every flick of Andras's tongue on her heated flesh. It was building up to something, even if she couldn't put a name to it, and the anticipation was almost torturous. If she had been capable of speech she would have begged him for more, more, anything that would bring her release.

Until pure ecstasy took over her body, and she let out a cry that was almost a scream, loud enough she worried she'd woken everyone in the building.

Andras lifted his head, his hands still holding onto her trembling legs and his lips quirked in an amused smile. He wiped his mouth. "Everything all right?"

"That's an understatement," Marta breathed, sanity slowly returning. "You're a magician. Am I still in one piece?"

"Indeed you are." He lovingly ran a hand down her thigh. "A

very lovely piece, at that. We can stop here, if you'd like. You're not entirely ruined yet."

"Aren't I? How disappointing. But I'm not going to let you stop now. We von Holstadts never give up halfway. General Johannes never gave up when…" She trailed off, mind blank. "When he did something. The point is, you are not allowed to stop."

His eyes lit up, and he lowered himself gently on top of her, spreading her legs slightly wider. For a second he paused, just nudging against her entrance, before he finally pushed forward and slid into her. A sharp gasp escaped her lips as she felt her inner muscles stretch to allow him entrance.

"Was that uncomfortable? Too fast?" he asked, eyes wide with concern.

Marta shook her head rapidly. It didn't hurt, much to her surprise. There had been a twinge at first, but after the original shock had passed, having him inside her was far from unpleasant. It seemed Marta's English governess, who had told her the facts of life three years prior, had been sorely mistaken on several points—specifically, the amount of pain a girl could expect on her wedding night.

Then again, this was not Marta's wedding night. Mrs. Montcrieff hadn't said anything about what to expect when you were in bed with your illicit lover.

"Marta," Andras whispered, his voice strained. "I rather need to continue, could I…"

"Yes," she said hastily. She'd barely thought about how he must have been feeling, but the wild look in his eyes and the throbbing hardness inside her indicated that he was very strongly affected. "Please do. I promise I'll be quite all right."

"More than all right, I should hope," he said with a wry smile. "Now lie back and think of Austria, darling."

"If I'm with you, shouldn't I be thinking of Hu…oh!" Marta let out a squeak of surprise as Andras lifted her legs and wrapped them around his waist, pushing himself even deeper into her. He began to move again, thrusting steadily, one hand moving down to rhythmically stroke the same spot he'd caressed with his mouth earlier.

The way he touched her was the same way he played the

violin, Marta thought dazedly, that mix of deliberate expertise and pure passion. If she'd been a proper woman of the world, she might have known how to touch him with as much skill. As it was, she simply lay back and let waves of pleasure wash over her, bringing her ever closer to that same astonishing peak he'd brought her to with his mouth. It was mere seconds until she cried out again and convulsed around him, her release nearly agonizing as it flowed through her like molten gold.

Andras held on valiantly, his jaw tight and his fingers trembling as he fought for control. It wasn't until she let out a sound resembling *please* that he gritted his teeth and pulled out of her with a jerk. He exclaimed something in Hungarian, his voice rough with lust, and to Marta's surprise she felt a sudden wet heat hit the soft skin of her belly before he collapsed on the bed beside her, gasping for breath.

That was it, then. She no longer had any claim to being a virtuous young lady. She was, in fact, ruined.

Good.

CHAPTER NINETEEN

(In Which Everyone is a Critic)

THROUGH MARTA'S HAZE of exhaustion and pleasure, she was vaguely aware of Andras rolling out of bed and heading to the basin, returning with a damp cloth that he used to gently wipe any traces of stickiness off her abdomen.

"I hope I didn't shock you too badly," he murmured. "Only I didn't want any risk of a baby, considering the circumstances. How are you feeling?"

Marta pulled him back down next to her and curled up against him, soaking up his warmth. "I feel… extraordinary. And exhausted, but in a good way. How are you?"

"I was just thinking," he said. "Do you remember how Chopin thought that every time he made love to George Sand, he was depriving the world of an etude?"

"Ah… I think so?"

"Frederic Chopin was an idiot," he said fervently. "An absolute buffoon. I feel as though I could write a symphony right now." He kissed the top of Marta's head, sending another shiver of pleasure through her body. "Is it wrong of me to be so utterly content? After all, I have just ruined you."

"Funny, I don't feel ruined," she remarked. "Well, I do a bit, but I have no business being ashamed for making love to you when it's all I've wanted to do ever since we met."

"Wait. I thought you fell for me when I started teaching you Hungarian."

"I said I fell in love with you then. I've wanted to bed you since the minute I first saw you." She laughed, mildly embarrassed.

"Is that an awful thing to say? I swear, I didn't only fall for you because you have eyes like a lecherous Celtic god."

"Is that what my eyes are like? I've been trying to put my finger on it for years," Andras teased. "For the record, I didn't only fall in love with you because you have loads of money and a glorious figure, though the latter was hardly a point against you."

"Honestly, I'm surprised that you fell in love with me at all. I wasn't sure that I was the type you fancied," Marta said, trying to keep her tone lighthearted. "I'm terribly flighty, and I'm not a brilliant musician at all. Not to mention these unsightly freckles."

"I happen to adore your freckles," he said. "You wouldn't be you without them. And it should be noted that even if you are flighty, you are also the kindest, bravest, most passionate person I know. I doubt it's possible for anyone with a brain and a beating heart to be around you for four hours a week and not fall in love with you."

"But…" Marta stopped, unwilling to say aloud what had arisen in her mind. *But I'm not good enough for you. But you're a genius, and I'm useless and spoiled, and you'll be tired of me in a month.*

She wouldn't speak these thoughts aloud, because there was no need to. Because Andras had said he loved her. And he was a terrible liar.

"Marta?" Andras asked. "Is something wrong?"

"No," she said firmly. "Everything is perfect. The real question is where did you learn to do all of that? Have you secretly been a famous ladies' man all along?"

"Absolutely not," he sputtered. "I've really only had one lover, and that was years ago."

"What was she like?"

"Must we talk about this?" At Marta's nod, Andras let out an exasperated sigh. "Fine. Her name was Carolina, she was a ballet dancer, and we split up after six months because she decided to move back to the country. Last I heard she was married to a farmer and was very happy. So it all worked out for the best. She got the life she wanted, and I…" Andras smiled and pushed an errant curl of Marta's forehead. "I got you."

"You certainly did, and if I catch you chasing after any ballet dancers after what we just did, I'll run you out of town." She yawned, utterly drained of energy. "If I fall asleep now, will you wake me up in time for me to sneak back home?"

He laughed and stroked her hair. "Anything you want, my love."

The St. Stephen's clock was chiming eight and the sun's first rays were just beginning to illuminate the city when Andras finally awoke. For a moment it seemed like the beginning to any other day, albeit earlier than usual, until he felt something warm and soft pressing against his arm and realized who was in bed with him. And what they had done the night before.

Marta looked utterly angelic in sleep, her cheeks flushed and a faint smile on her face. He ought to have been consumed with guilt, yet it was difficult to feel anything other than deep content as he watched the woman lying next to him. He gently brushed a lock of her tangled hair away from her face and she stirred, her brilliant eyes opening slowly.

"Oh, good, you're still here," she said, in a voice still slurred with sleep. "I was worried that I would wake up and this would all have been a dream."

"I was concerned about that myself. But believe me, I have no plans to go anywhere." Andras pulled her closer and kissed her forehead. "How are you feeling?"

"A little sore. Nothing too awful." She grinned and ran a finger down his chest. "Why, were you hoping for another round? I probably shouldn't say that I'm longing for it, but I absolutely am."

How on earth did someone raised to be as proper as Marta know precisely what to say to drive him wild? "I can't think of anything I'd like better, but I don't think it's a good idea," he said, reluctantly suppressing a wave of desire. "If you're sore it might be painful, and anyway, the sooner you get home the less likely you are to be found out. I'd hate to get you in trouble."

She let out a disappointed sigh and pulled herself upright. "Oh, heavens, I suppose you're right. If I'm going to sneak in the servants' entrance I had better get a move on. Round two," she added, rolling out of bed, "will just have to be postponed for another day."

He looked at her in surprise, not certain he had heard her correctly. "Another day? You mean, you want to do this again?"

Yanking her chemise down over her head, she eyed him incredulously. "Of course I want to. Did we not establish quite thoroughly last night that I love you? I'm hardly going to be satisfied with bedding you just once."

"Marta," he said. "What you're proposing is an affair. Is that really what you want? Because I have it on good authority—from you—that you could do much, much better than me."

"An affair," she said dreamily. "How scandalous that sounds. I love it. And I can't think why you would believe I can do better than you. Financially, perhaps, but not otherwise." Now fully dressed, much to Andras's disappointment, she bent over the bed and kissed him, only pulling back when they were both out of breath. "I would rather have an affair with you, Andras Király, than marry the King of Bavaria."

"Probably wise on your part. I hear he isn't particularly interested in ladies. Though he is known for being cultured."

"Much as I love gossiping about the crowned heads of Europe, that is not the point I am trying to make. I love you, and I want to be with you. If we have to keep it a secret for now, so be it."

And that, it appeared, was all that was to be said on the subject.

She was going to be in so much trouble. *So. Much. Trouble.*

That is, she would if she got caught, which was looking increasingly likely as she made her way home. Her family might not be awake yet, but the servants would, and there would be questions asked regardless of whether she used the servants' entrance or the front door. Questions she would not be able to answer if she didn't come up with a story, and quick.

I was taking a walk, Marta mentally rehearsed as she slipped around the back of the von Holstadt mansion. *I felt faint and needed some fresh air, so I went for an early-morning walk. And I didn't bring Nella because…because she'd twisted her ankle.*

Not the best of lies. She'd definitely get in trouble for walking around by herself sans chaperone, and it might be tricky to convince Nella to feign a limp. But that sort of trouble would be far less than what she'd be in for sleeping with her music teacher. She felt as though everyone would be able to tell right away what she'd done. If anyone stood too close, surely they'd detect Andras's scent clinging to her skin, or notice the slight stiffness in her gait.

The servants' entrance was unlocked, thank God, and she was able to avoid any prying eyes as she carefully sneaked through the back corridors and up the stairs to her room. It wasn't until she opened the door to her bedroom as quietly as she could manage and slipped inside that she noticed Nella standing by her bed, arms folded and looking distinctly disapproving.

"Good morning, Countess Marta," Nella said coolly. "May I ask where you've been just now?"

"I…um... I went for a walk?"

"A walk, milady?" Nella's eyebrows went up. "It must have been a very long walk, as you weren't in your bed when I went to wake you up half an hour ago. A bed that did not appear to have been slept in, might I add."

Marta's heart thudded in terror, as well as annoyance with herself. Why couldn't she have put a few pillows under the blankets to make it look as though she was sleeping there? Though Nella most likely wouldn't have been fooled by that.

"Listen," she said at last. "What I say needs to stay between us, all right?"

Nella bit her lip thoughtfully. "If your life is in danger, I can't say I won't tell. But otherwise, I'll keep my mouth shut."

"Thank you, Nella darling." Marta took a seat on the bed and took a deep breath. "I was away all of last night, Nella. I left right after you went to bed. I sneaked out the servants' entrance."

"If you don't mind me asking, where did you go, milady?"

"To the park, at first. You see, I'd just got word from Mr. Király that he'd arrived back from Hungary and I had to see him."

Nella raised her eyebrows again at this, but said nothing.

"You'll remember I told you his father was ill, and he had to go home and see him? Well, his father's better now. That's what he came to tell me."

"I see. But why couldn't he tell you about his father at your next lesson?"

"Wait until Tuesday? Not a chance. But that wasn't all he wanted to talk to me about." Marta could feel her face heating up as she contemplated the most significant part of this confession. "He told me he loves me, Nella. He *loves* me."

The look on Nella's face nearly made Marta laugh. "He does what?" the maid squawked, her eyes nearly bulging out of her head. "He said that to you? The cheek of it. I hope you slapped him."

"Under some circumstances, I might have. But in this case I couldn't, because the thing is, I love him too."

"You," Nella said slowly. "You love him."

"Yes."

"Your violin teacher."

"So he is."

"And you *love* him?"

"Believe me, I'm as confused by this as anyone," said Marta. "But we seem to be going in circles here."

"I'm sorry, milady. It's surprising, that's all." Nella frowned uncertainly. "So last night, when you disappeared, were you with him?"

"I was."

"*With* him, I mean? As in…well." Nella's hands fluttered in embarrassment. "You know what I mean, I think. Did you go to bed with him?"

Her cheeks warming with pleasure at the memory, Marta nodded.

Nella did not reply immediately. She sat perfectly still, hands folded, eyes downcast. Marta swallowed hard, trying not to sob from anxiety. Nella had been the best of servants, but she was a moral, well-brought-up country girl. It would be understandable if she decided her ultimate loyalty was to Marta's parents, and a scandal of this magnitude was too much to bear.

Finally, Nella shook her head. "Mary, Mother of God. Forgive me, Countess Marta, but that's not information I was expecting to hear today. I don't know."

"Please, Nella," Marta blurted. "I know it's wrong of me, I know

I've behaved terribly, but I am utterly, hopelessly in love with him. I want to marry him, have a family with him, everything. If my parents find out, if they separate us, it honestly might kill me."

"My goodness." Nella blinked, eyes wide. "You really do love him. I was worried it was just an adventure for you. He's certainly, well, different, isn't he?"

"Yes," Marta whispered. "Different from everyone I know."

"I'm glad you think so. Because listen, milady," said Nella. "My loyalty is to you, of course it is, but I like Mr. Király. He's a good, honest man. And if I had cause to believe you were just using him somehow, I'd have to put my foot down."

Marta made a mental note to tell Andras immediately how highly her maid regarded him. If he had any sense, he'd be honored. "I understand completely, Nella."

"Good. Now, I am going to ask you a question, and you must tell me the truth." She leaned forward, regarding Marta sternly. "How was he?"

"Beg pardon?"

Nella grinned, her eyes twinkling. "Really, you can't be surprised that half the girls in the servants' quarters have been speculating about him for months. He's terribly good-looking. Lovely hands, nice eyes. Petra in the scullery is convinced he must be the best lover in Vienna."

"Well," Marta said primly. "If he is, Petra won't be hearing about it from me. His skills as a lover are entirely my business."

"But between the two of us?"

"I can't say I have much to compare it to. But personally, I'm of the opinion that Petra is absolutely right."

Nella let out a squeak of scandalized delight. "I'm glad we haven't been misled. So," she said. "I've read enough melodramatic novels that I know what you're going to ask me. You want help sneaking out to see him, don't you?"

"Well, yes," Marta said. "I hate to ask this, I know it's not within your line of duty, but I can't give him up."

"Say no more, milady." Nella lifted her chin determinedly. "I'm glad to help. If you really love him, then I'll do what I can."

"Good heavens, Nella. I can't think what I did to deserve you, but I'm extraordinarily grateful. I only wish I could repay you…

ah!" She snapped her fingers. "There is one thing I can do. Is there anything you'd like from my wardrobe? Anything at all, it's yours."

"Oh no, I couldn't… "

"I insist. Please, it's the least I can do."

"Well, if you insist," said Nella, flushing slightly, "then I suppose I've always admired that purple velvet dress from a few years ago. It's such a lovely color."

"Of course, my Queen of the Night dress. I always called it that because it looks just like what the Queen of the Night from *The Magic Flute* would wear if she was alive now." At the sight of Nella's raised eyebrows, Marta laughed. "The point is you're welcome to it. It'll suit you perfectly. Though it can't possibly express my gratitude enough."

As Nella departed with a brisk curtsy, Marta let out a sharp sigh of relief. The first confession hadn't been as bad as she'd thought.

The next… well, time would tell.

June 29
The Stein Mansion

"You should have seen his face, Marta," Sophie crowed. "I've never seen Baron von Katz look guilty before. The minute I'd finished lecturing him he immediately promised ten thousand gulden to the war widows' fund. I only wish you'd been there!"

"It sounds like quite a triumph," Marta murmured. Delighted as she was by the baron's comeuppance, it was hard to summon up her usual enthusiasm. She'd been shaking with nerves from the minute she entered the Stein house.

Sophie's brow furrowed. "Are you all right? You don't seem quite yourself today."

"I'm fine, I promise," she said, hoping she wasn't blushing. "Still just a bit worried about the marriage-market fuss. My parents aren't pleased I rejected Ludwig."

"Ridiculous. Ludwig's harmless, certainly, but you two would be terribly unhappy together." Sophie eyed Marta searchingly. "Is that all? You do know that you can tell me if something's gone terribly wrong, don't you? It's not as if I have any right to judge you."

Several memories arose in Marta's mind. Herself at age eleven, confessing to Sophie that she was afraid having a baby brother would mean her parents no longer cared about her. Seventeen-year-old Sophie, incandescent with rage over discovering one of her father's partners had cheated people, begging Marta to help her to come up with a revenge scheme. Marta after her disastrous first kiss, crying on Sophie's shoulder, terrified she would never really fall in love. Nearly two decades, and barely a single secret between them.

"Sophie, listen, I…"

"Milady," a soft voice interrupted. Marta glanced up sharply to see one of the Steins' maids, standing at the parlor door with coffee on a tray.

"Oh, thank goodness," said Sophie. "I'm utterly exhausted, you have no idea. What were you about to say?"

Marta, frozen with fear, did not reply. If the maid had arrived only one minute later, she would have heard Marta's entire confession, and gossip in Vienna traveled like lightning. It would only take one careless word to set off a chain of rumors that would reach her parents in a matter of days.

Nella knew because it was unavoidable. Andras's friend Franz undoubtedly knew, though he wasn't likely to tell the world. But no one else could. Not even the person in whom Marta had confided all her life.

"Marta?" said Sophie. "Are you sure you're all right?"

"Yes," she replied quietly. "Nothing for you to worry about, I promise."

There was some small comfort to the situation, she thought. When and if Sophie found out, she would probably be forgiving.

Now all Marta had to do was forgive herself.

CHAPTER TWENTY

(Of Which Attila the Hun Would Be Proud)

July 20
Three weeks into the affair

ANDRAS HAD NEVER touched opium. His life was confusing enough without chemical interference. But if he did, he thought it would feel similar to having an affair with Marta.

She was, in a word, addictive.

Not only physically, though it was astounding that a woman as strictly brought up as Marta could be so enthusiastic and inventive in bed. The scent of her perfume and sweat lingered on his skin for hours, making him dizzy with desire every time he noticed it, and the breathy moans she made when he was inside her were more beautiful than any music Beethoven had ever written. More than that, though, it was simply being with her, spending all night talking about whatever came into their heads. And afterward, the way he slept far better with her in his arms than he ever had on his own.

He couldn't give her up, not in a thousand years. He'd never felt so alive.

But like all addictions, this one would undoubtedly ruin his life if he didn't get it under control. Even if Chopin's theory regarding lovemaking and creativity didn't hold water, there were plenty of other things to worry about. He was sleeping even less than usual, he'd had to drop a considerable amount of money at the apothecary sorting out various preventative measures, and Franz was becoming increasingly annoyed at how often Andras kicked him out of the house. And there was the small matter of how the von Holstadts would react if they found out.

Usually this would have sent Andras into a spiral of panic. However, he was having a hard time thinking about the future at the moment.

Especially at this particular moment, when he was proving Chopin quite thoroughly wrong.

Marta, lying beneath him, let out a gasp of delight and dug her fingers into his shoulders as he moved inside her. Her full, luscious breasts moved with his every thrust, and he couldn't resist reaching up to stroke her smooth skin, flicking his thumb over one hard, rosy nipple. The way her skin flushed when he touched her was glorious, unbearably so.

At last she cried out and shuddered, her eyes losing focus as she came. Through his haze of lust, he felt a surge of pride. Any of Marta's other suitors might have been able to offer her jewels and castles and prestige, but he was the only one who could do this to her. And if nothing else, perhaps he could bring her enough pleasure that he could ensnare her as unshakably as she had done to him.

It took only a few more thrusts for him to succumb as well, his climax tearing through him like a wildfire and leaving him lightheaded and breathless. When the last tremors had ceased, Andras gathered her into his arms and buried his face in her abundant dark curls. God, he loved her hair. Why did she even bother with those expensive frocks when she had hair like this?

She sighed contentedly and nuzzled against the hollow of his shoulder. "Deep in thought, darling?"

"Just reflecting on how if I were emperor I would make it illegal for you to wear anything but your hair."

"You'd find that a difficult law to enforce," Marta replied. "I'm liable to catch a chill."

"Nonsense, *drágám*." Andras pulled her closer and kissed the top of her head. "I'd keep you warm."

"*Drágám*? Is that another Hungarian word I need to learn? Let me guess, it means dragon. I don't think that's a pet name I approve of."

"It means darling, I'll have you know. And I intend to call you that quite frequently when we're alone, so you'd better get used to it."

"Mmm." She appeared to contemplate this before sitting up sharply. "Andras, speaking of being alone. You and I have been sneaking about for three weeks, and it's been lovely, but I don't think we can go on like this without trouble. We need to start thinking ahead, coming up with a plan for how to tell my parents."

Hearing the von Holstadts mentioned when Andras was naked in bed with their daughter was similar to having a barrel of freezing water dumped on his head. In short, unpleasant. Which was why, when he opened his mouth, what came out was, "Tell them? Have you gone mad?"

It was the wrong thing to say. Marta crossed her arms irritably and regarded him through narrowed eyes. "Think, Andras. What we have isn't sustainable. Do you realize how difficult it is for me to keep sneaking out every other night? Nella covers for me, but I've had plenty of near misses. I'd prefer my parents find out on our terms rather than catching me creeping in the back door at four in the morning."

"I…" He was having difficulty forming a coherent answer, as not only did the flickering candlelight turn Marta's skin to gold, but her folded arms pushed her breasts up enticingly, making her look like a gilded statue of Venus. Eventually he managed, "I don't see that it matters how they find out, they'll still be furious. You're in bed right now with a penniless violinist instead of at home obediently waiting to be married off to a baron."

"If that's your attitude then perhaps I should be at home waiting to be married off." She sniffed. "Ludwig von Braumark proposed to me while you were away, you know."

Andras froze, hit by a wave of panic. She couldn't be considering accepting, could she? Not dull-as-dishwater Ludwig von Braumark? She could never be happy with someone like that, not in a thousand years. "Did you say yes?"

"Would it matter to you if I did? Clearly you can't be bothered to make any attempts for my hand in marriage."

"I most certainly would mind," Andras shouted, making Marta sit back in shock. "Blast it all, I love you, have I not made that clear? Am I meant to let you treat me like a nobleman treats his mistress? Because I won't stand for that. If you're going to marry someone, I would strongly prefer it to be me."

"How can I marry you if you won't propose to me? If you won't even help me figure out how to tell my parents that we're lovers?" Marta wiped angrily at her eyes. "I can't do this forever, Andras. I want us to have a life. I want to hold hands in the daytime and go dancing and I want to tell everyone how much I love you. I don't want to keep lying day in and day out."

"I want those things too.. Believe me, I do. I want us to be together properly, have a life, a home. But I also don't want your parents to disown you or throw me in prison." He reached up to stroke her cheek, relieved when she didn't move away. "I'm only asking for time. A bit more time for us to mount a plan of attack."

Though her face had softened, she still looked suspicious. "Not years, I hope. I can't keep sneaking out at night forever."

"No, and I wouldn't ask you to. But please… " He swallowed. "Please don't marry Ludwig. Not yet, anyway."

"I'm not going to marry Ludwig, " Marta said, rolling her eyes. "When he proposed I told him quite firmly that I couldn't marry him because I didn't love him."

"You did?" Andras asked hoarsely.

"Yes, and he was very put out. Poor boy, I'm sure he'll find someone who adores him. But did you really think I would have accepted him? I believe I've made it quite clear that I feel nothing for him."

"I know you don't love him," he said. "But I'm also aware that people like you generally don't marry for love."

"Maybe not usually, but I intend to. And that is quite enough arguing for one night, I think." Marta wiped her eyes decisively and smiled at him. "You're quite intimidating when you're angry, you know. I feel like King Henry in that Wagner opera. 'Save us, Lord, from the wrath of the Hungarians!'" she exclaimed, collapsing dramatically back onto the bed.

"They cut that line when we did *Lohengrin*," Andras said. "Thought it might offend any Hungarians in the audience. I can't think why. I find it flattering." He rolled over and kissed Marta on the cheek. "I truly am sorry for losing my temper, though. Of course we'll tell your parents one of these days. Perhaps when I've got more money, and I'm as celebrated as Liszt."

"All right, so next month, then." She laughed. "But I'm sorry too. Wouldn't it be easier if I were someone ordinary, like a seamstress, and my parents understood what a brilliant match you were? With the additional benefit that I would have something to do every day."

"It might make things easier in some ways, but you have a very romantic view of working as a seamstress. My mother was one, and she had strained eyes and sore fingers every day of her life."

"And yet," said Marta, "she seems to have still done a wonderful job of raising you and your sisters."

"I wouldn't jump to conclusions there. You still haven't met my sisters."

"Not yet, but I hope to soon. They don't know about us, do they?"

He shook his head. "I'm nervous about telling them, to be honest. Not that they wouldn't adore you, I just think they would worry. Funny, really, to imagine them worrying over me when it's my job to worry over them." He let out a sigh. "I have this nightmare about them sometimes. Well, sort of a nightmare and sort of a fear. That my father will die, and I won't be able to help them, and they'll lose the flat and the younger girls will end up in an orphanage."

"I understand," she said quietly. "But you must know that I wouldn't allow that to happen."

"You've already done enough."

"Oh, hush," she replied, poking him in the arm. "What's the point of my father giving me a generous monthly allowance if I can't use it to support my second-favorite family? Besides, if I were a nobleman and you were my mistress, I'd be expected to buy you jewels and a fine house and things. You're lucky that I'm restricting myself to medicine and spectacles."

Andras tried to ignore a stab of shame—it still seemed wrong that he needed von Holstadt charity to help his family. "I am, indeed, the most fortunate of men."

He was at that, he thought as he leaned over to the nightstand to adjust the candle, moving a few papers out of the way and tossing them on the bed. What other man in the world could claim that he was loved by Marta von Holstadt?

It wasn't until she picked up a paper he'd put on the bed that he noticed what it was. He flushed with embarrassment. Surely the minute she read a single line of that music she would know it had been written for her, and what if she didn't like it?

"Wait." Her brow furrowed adorably as she scanned the page. "Have you been writing music again? Why didn't you tell me? I've been longing to see something you've composed."

He laughed sheepishly. "I'm not sure it's finished yet. It probably needs a great deal of polishing."

"You're an artist. Nothing's ever really done for you, is it?" She hummed the first few measures. "It's lovely. Makes me think of the color yellow, somehow, and candlelight. What's it called?"

"It's, well, it hasn't got a name yet. But it's yours. Your music."

Marta's eyes widened. "Mine?"

"When I know someone well, I tend to hear a certain tune in my head when I think of them. I don't come up with it consciously, it just occurs to me. I don't always write it down, but this time I couldn't help myself. That," Andras nodded at the sheet music in Marta's hands, "is what I hear when I think about you."

If he'd feared Marta might laugh at him, he was pleasantly mistaken. The look on her face was one of pure joy. "Oh," she breathed. "Do you mean to say I'm your muse? I have always wanted to be a muse. Rather than just amusing, which is what I usually am."

She spoke lightly—jokingly, even—but there was more than a hint of longing in her voice. Not surprising, Andras reflected. Wasn't that what girls like her were brought up to be? Cheerful, amusing decorations on their husbands' arms at formal dinner parties?

That certainly wouldn't be what her life with him would be like, if they ever managed to have a life together. Not least because he had never been a guest at a formal dinner party.

He reached over and brushed a lock of hair out of her face. "I can assure you, my love, that you are both my muse and amusing. And a great many other things, which I spend a lot of time thinking about when I should be working. Now why don't you let me prove how much you…inspire me."

"I think I'm going to die a spinster," Brigita said despairingly as she flopped into the seat across from Ludwig at Witzler's.

This was not how Ludwig typically began conversations with ladies. But, he thought wryly, he didn't usually buy luncheon for ballerinas either. Besides, the more time he spent around Brigita, the harder it was to remember how polite conversations usually went.

Perhaps it didn't make sense, this new friendship. But little enough made sense in Ludwig's life anymore. And he liked Brigita, liked her fiery hair and green eyes and impatient demeanor. She was, at least, a pleasant distraction.

"I'm sure that's not true, Miss Novak," he said, in response to Brigita's unhappy sigh. "Why would you say so?"

"Because," she said, "men in the theatre don't want marrying, they just want a bit of…" She flushed. "Well, you know. Fun."

"Ah." Ludwig could feel his own face heating up. It occurred to him that Brigita most likely knew far more about *all that* than Ludwig did. Not that his own knowledge set such a high bar. He'd learned about *eros* and *agape* and all the other Greek words for love in university, but when it came to actual, physical knowledge of love, he was very lacking.

Brigita, however, did not seem in the mood for talking about *eros* and *agape*. She looked, in fact, very upset. Ludwig cleared his throat and said, "My apologies, Miss Novak. Has something unfortunate happened?"

"It's my…friend, Franz," Brigita said. "He's a nice lad and all, and we've kept company for a few years on and off, but he's got the maturity of a schoolboy."

Ludwig tried to ignore the hot flash of jealousy that flared at the mention of a *friend*. "Do you love him?"

"I thought I did, but these days I just don't know. I can't shake this desire for more, somehow. And I know I'm not a lady or anything," Brigita said quickly. "But surely that doesn't mean I don't deserve a home and family someday, does it?"

"Miss Novak," Ludwig exclaimed, impulsively grabbing her hand. "You most certainly are a lady. You mustn't let anyone treat you badly just because you work for a living."

She looked up at him with tearful, shining eyes. "You mean that?"

"Of course I do." He usually only half-listened when Sophie Stein started going on about the dignity of labor, but it was starting to make more sense. Brigita might not have eaten with much dignity, but she had backbone all the same, and morals. If only she'd been born into a family with more background, it would make things so much simpler. He wouldn't have to spend so much time trying to get Marta to marry him, not when he already had...

No, he absolutely could not start thinking like that. He was supposed to marry Marta, and so he would. Indulging in this kind of idle speculation would only cause trouble.

"It'll be all right, I'm sure," he said lightly. "But I've just remembered. This colleague of yours, Andras Király. We never got around to discussing him last time. Good friend of yours, is he?"

"Right, right. Yes, he's a good sort, you can tell your father that. Always on time, very rarely drunk, and hardly ever tells a dirty joke. And he's very devoted to his family, always sending home money. And that's quite a task, you know, considering his poor father."

Sensing he was about to be privy to important information, Ludwig settled in to listen.

CHAPTER TWENTY-ONE

(*In Which Heini is a Terrible Liar*)

STUMBLING INTO THE kitchen for breakfast, Andras was greeted by the sight of Franz hunched over the table, looking considerably worse for wear. A half-empty bottle of Riesling sat in front of him, accompanied by a very full wineglass.

"Isn't it a bit early to be drinking?"

"I've been drinking since I woke up," Franz replied, refilling his glass. "And with good reason. Brigita's jilted me."

Andras blinked. "Pardon?"

"She's done with me," Franz said heavily. "Told me last night. She wants to be with someone who can give her a home and family, someone who's her *intellectual equal*. Said it nicely, of course, but her meaning was clear."

"Lord, Franz." Andras ran a hand through his hair, unsure what to say. "I'm sorry."

Franz took a long swig of his wine. "Should have seen it coming, really. She's been sneaking off during breaks half the week, always laughing over letters she won't show me. If you ask me, she's found someone else already, some rich protector who'll make her a lady. I suppose it's for the best, but it's still a blow. I was awfully fond of her."

"I know you were, and don't blame yourself," said Andras. "I expect you just wanted different things. It'll be all right in the end, though. There are plenty of girls who fancy you."

"God, don't be so smug."

"I'm not."

"Of course you are, because you're *happy*. Do you really think you're any better off than me? You and your countess are having a fine time now, but how long will it last? I may not know much about high society," Franz said, "but I do know they don't condone their precious daughters spreading their legs for the staff."

Andras winced. "I know it's a strange situation, but Marta and I will sort it out. I love her."

"I always knew you were a romantic," Franz replied dryly. "For your sake, I hope you're right about her." He downed the rest of his wine in one gulp and pushed back his chair roughly. "I need a walk. Don't wait up."

"Listen, Franz, if there's anything I can do...I know I'm not much use lately, but I hate to see you suffer."

"I'll be all right. I never saw myself as much of a husband. There is one thing you can do for me, though." At Andras's quizzical expression, Franz laughed hollowly. "Enjoy it while it lasts, my friend. Enjoy it while it lasts."

July 27

The next Tuesday's lesson was particularly difficult to get through without some extremely bad behavior on Marta's part. She'd awoken that morning thoroughly unsatisfied after a particularly delicious dream, and it was nearly impossible to have Andras sitting so close to her in the music room without touching him at every possible opportunity.

This made it difficult to actually learn anything about the violin, but his sharp intake of breath and the way his eyes darkened as she ran her hand up his arm more than made up for it.

"With respect, milady, are you planning to actually play any music this morning?" Nella inquired from the corner.

"That's a good question, Nella," said Marta. "One without a clear answer, currently. Would you mind getting us a pot of coffee from the kitchen? I suddenly find myself quite parched."

Nella rolled her eyes good-naturedly and departed, thankfully locking the door behind her.

The minute they were alone, Andras pulled Marta into his lap, an impressive feat, considering her crinoline, and covered her mouth with his. As usual, all thought flew from Marta's mind, and all that remained was the glorious sensation of his lips and hands driving her mad with want.

"This is torture," she groaned, when he finally pulled away to take a breath. "If we only had a little more time to ourselves."

If they had, it certainly wouldn't have been wasted. They'd only managed to make love in the music room once so far, on a day when Nella had been struck down with a bad cold and Marta had sent her away to rest. The sheer thrill of being bent over the piano while Andras took her from behind, coupled with the knowledge that someone could catch them at any moment, had brought Marta to climax almost instantly, and she'd been longing to repeat the experience ever since.

"We'll have to wait until tonight, my love," Andras whispered, nipping gently at her ear. "Only we can't go to the garret, I'm afraid. Franz is going to be home, and I'm trying to give him some space. Poor chap. He's been unlucky in love lately."

"Oh," Marta replied, disappointed. "So what are we to do instead?"

"Well," he said thoughtfully. "There's always the theatre."

"The theatre? You mean the one you work at?"

"Why not? We haven't got any performances tonight, and I know how to get in. One of the doors round the back has a lock that doesn't work. No one really takes advantage of it because we haven't got anything worth stealing."

There was something deliciously awful about breaking into a theatre in the middle of the night for a tryst. "It'll have to do. What time?"

"After rehearsal, I should think. Would ten o'clock do? If I have to wait any longer than that," Andras said with a wicked smile, "I'm likely to explode from pure frustration."

"You're terrible," Marta said, rolling her eyes. "Very well, then, ten o'clock at the theatre. Now make yourself decent before Nella comes back. She puts up with a lot from us, but we needn't traumatize the poor girl."

Ludwig had not come to the von Holstadt mansion to see Marta. Really, he had come to borrow a book, a translation of minor Latin poets written by the fourth Count von Holstadt, and to talk with Count Heinrich about the running of Schloss Braumark. If Marta was around, it would naturally be pleasant, though of course Ludwig had no expectations. Even if they did talk, he had to be quick. Brigita was expecting him for lunch, and while she had many wonderful qualities, patience wasn't one of them.

Brigita was, to Ludwig's surprise, much easier to talk with than most of the people he knew. True, she'd never had much formal education, but somehow she was a better conversation partner than anyone else. She had a natural gift for philosophical discussions, and was never shy about expressing her opinions. Spending time with her was a welcome break, what with his father still breathing down his neck about Marta. And she'd cut things off with that friend of hers, which was probably for the best. He didn't sound like a gentleman…

A small figure zoomed down the hall towards him, shocking him out of his thoughts. Little Heini, of course. He ought to know where Marta was.

"Hello, Heini," said Ludwig, holding out an arm to slow the boy down. "Have you seen your sister?"

Heini slid to a stop and shrugged irritably. "I just heard her, down the hall. She's with her music teacher. They aren't playing any music, though, just talking about going to the theatre."

"Going to the theatre?" Ludwig frowned. "Do you mean together?"

In the blink of an eye Heini's expression changed to one of guarded blandness, like a spy hiding state secrets. "I don't know," he replied, his voice slightly higher than usual. "I only heard a bit; I'm not a donkey, you know. They have good hearing because their ears are so big."

Having never had any younger siblings, Ludwig was not particularly good with children. An adult hiding something could have been reasoned with, but a ten-year-old boy— Nonetheless, it was necessary to try. "Heini. I'm sure your nanny and the priests at church have taught you that it's a terrible thing to lie."

"I'm not lying," said Heini unconvincingly. "I don't even know if they were talking about tonight, it wasn't very clear. I'm not a d—"

"I know you're not a donkey," Ludwig snapped. Heini took a step back, looking shaken, and Ludwig took a deep breath to steady his nerves. "My apologies, that was very rude. I'm not upset with you, just worried about your sister. If she's in some kind of trouble and you won't tell me about it, she could be hurt."

Heini shifted from foot to foot guiltily, biting his lip. "I don't think she's in trouble," he said at last. "Not the dangerous kind, anyway. But I think our parents would have been angry if they'd heard what she and Mr. Király were saying."

"Which was?"

"It was…" Heini hesitated again, before words began pouring out of him. "Marta was complaining about something, I think, and then Mr. Király said… he called her *my love* and said something about going to the theatre, and I think he said something about someone named Franz, and that's it, I promise."

Ludwig sucked in a sharp breath. "It's very important that you remember. What exactly did Mr. Király say about the theatre? When did he say they were meeting?"

"Ten o'clock," Heini mumbled. "I think. But I don't even know where…"

"Thank you, Heini." Ludwig patted him firmly on the shoulder. "It's going to be all right. Run along, now." The boy departed, clearly relieved to have escaped. Leaving Ludwig behind, lost in thought.

They can't expect me to marry her now.

The notion hit him like a bolt of lightning. If Marta had been conducting an affair with her violin tutor, there was no way anyone could still insist on the match. No one would judge him for not marrying a girl who behaved so badly.

He should have been brokenhearted. And in a way, he was. It was infuriating that Marta, whom he'd trusted and admired, would be so dishonest. But at the thought that his hopeless quest for her hand in marriage could finally be over, all Ludwig could bring himself to feel was relief.

He was free.

Still, benefits to Ludwig aside, what Marta was doing was wrong. Lying to her parents, carrying on an affair…no one could call that morally correct. As an honest and ethical man, Ludwig knew he had a duty to do the right thing.

He had to tell her father the truth.

The theatre was an odd place late at night, almost frightening. Marta wouldn't have been surprised to see the ghost of Hamlet's father drifting out from the shadows somewhere.

"It's a bit spooky, being here in the middle of the night, isn't it?" Andras said, echoing her thoughts. "Not to worry. I think I know how to make it better." He pulled a small matchbox out of his pocket and set to lighting a few of the candles around the stage until the theatre was bathed in a soft glow.

"This is much better," she murmured. "Goodness, I never had any ambitions to be an actress but I can see the appeal now. It's a powerful feeling, being up here."

"I have to say, I think you'd make a rather good actress," he said. "Go on, give us some Shakespeare."

Marta thought, then cleared her throat and loudly declaimed, "Against my will I am sent to bid you come in to dinner!"

"Marvelous. Go on."

"That's the whole speech, on Beatrice's part," she said. "Benedick says a few more things afterward, but I don't have that part memorized. I imagine I'll need a few more rehearsals before I'm a star of the stage."

"Ah, well, we'll have plenty of time to worry about that later. For now, you have much more important things to worry about. For example," he said with a wicked grin, "dancing with me."

"That might be difficult," Marta pointed out, "seeing as we haven't got any music, and you didn't bring Clara."

Andras laughed and pulled her close, arranging her arms as though they were about to waltz. "Then we'll just have to hum."

And hum he did, leaning close to her ear and sending ripples of excitement through her as they slowly swayed together, their feet barely moving. She leaned into his embrace, enjoying his scent and the firmness of his arms. She might have been perfectly happy staying like this forever had it not been for the itch of lust that had been tormenting her for most of the day. Interrupting their dance, she grabbed his hair and pulled his mouth down to hers.

He responded eagerly, one hand unbuttoning the bodice of her dress with practiced ease while the other reached around to cup her bottom. Marta let out a groan of delight and wriggled against him, reveling in the feel of his warm, strong body and the delightfully obvious effect she had on him. The stage was probably too hard for her to lie on, but she could still drop to her knees and use her mouth as he'd taught her. She wanted to see his refined features flushed with ecstasy, his brilliant gaze hot and desperate.

"I love you," she gasped, as he bent to kiss her neck. "God, Andras, I love you so much, I can't…"

And then, suddenly, there was light.

Bright light, the shock of it almost blinding her. Marta stumbled backwards out of Andras's arms, blinking and shading her eyes with one hand to see what the source was.

Adjusting, her eyes made out two figures, both male; one tall and of solid build, the other shorter and thinner. Night watchmen, perhaps? Or cleaners? Either way, how embarrassing, being caught at it with Andras like this. Not that they'd actually got anywhere yet, but still.

Then one of them lowered his lantern, causing the glare to fade from her eyes and revealing the horrified face of who had caught them.

Her father.

There was someone else with him. Hermann, perhaps? But Marta barely registered their presence. All her attention was focused on her father's face, contorted with rage, as he stood frozen in the aisle and stared at his misbehaving daughter.

"Marta," Andras whispered urgently. "Am I imagining things, or do we have company?"

"We do," Marta replied, her voice dull with despair. "I think you'd better go."

"I can't leave you, not like this…"

"You have to!" she choked out. "I can't risk having you tossed in prison, or God knows what. If you love me then leave, before it's too late."

He glanced over her shoulder to her father's rapidly approaching form, hesitated, then nodded. With a last quick squeeze of her upper arm he turned on his heel and fled.

When she was certain he'd gotten away, Marta squared her shoulders and, affecting a calm she absolutely did not feel, turned to her father.

"Good evening, Papa," she said coolly. "It seems we have a few things to talk about."

CHAPTER TWENTY-TWO

(In Which Our Heroes are in a Great Deal of Trouble)

July 28
The worst day of the year so far

UPON WAKING THE next day, Marta had only vague memories of what had occurred the previous night, and briefly hoped that it would turn out to have been a nightmare.

These hopes were cruelly dashed the first thing in the morning when she was summoned to meet with her parents in the blue parlor.

She prepared as well as she could for the inevitable battle. Poor Nella was undoubtedly aware of the scandal and looked on the verge of tears as she dug out Marta's most innocent-looking dress, a high-necked ivory affair that suggested young-lady-at-a-garden-party rather than musician's-mistress, and arranged Marta's hair in the most sensible, severe style possible. Surely the more respectable she looked, the less likely her parents were to murder her.

Sweeping into the parlor with her head held high, she took one look at her parents and her heart sunk. She barely recognized her loving, indulgent mother and father: the countess's pale face was red and blotchy, and the count was slumped over, clutching a nearly-empty glass of brandy. And for the first time in ages—really, since Andras had kissed her in the park—Marta was consumed by regret.

Blinking back tears, she forced herself into some sort of composure and sat. "Good morning, Mama, Papa."

"Good morning?" exclaimed her mother, almost hysterically. "Good *morning?*"

Her father patted his wife's hand and glared at Marta. "We may as well skip the pleasantries. What do you have to say for yourself, Marta?"

"I…" Marta swallowed hard. "I'm sorry?"

"You're sorry," he said coldly. "I imagine you are. Quite immeasurably sorry, after what you've done. How long has this…" He waved a hand in disgust. "*Business* been going on?"

Breathe, Marta. Looks can't actually kill you. "Four weeks, just about. Since Andras got back from Hungary."

"Four weeks?" said Hannelore. "How have you been carrying on like this under our noses for a month?" Her eyes widened. "Did Nella know?"

"No," Marta lied quickly. "Nella had no idea. Please don't do anything to her." If she was in disgrace, at least she wouldn't drag her maid down with her.

"If she didn't know, which I doubt, she still ought to have noticed you sneaking about like a criminal," Heinrich replied. "Clearly, we'll need to find you a more responsible maid. For God's sake don't look at me like that, Marta, she won't be on the streets. We'll just send her to the country. I'm sure your grandmother will find work for her."

"Why are we discussing the maid's future?" Hannelore cried. "Our daughter has been compromised. Unless… Marta, you must be absolutely honest. Did you… did he…" She waved vaguely, cheeks flushed. "Was this affair… consummated?"

"Honestly?" Marta nodded. "Yes."

Hannelore let out a piteous wail and buried her face in her hands, shoulders shaking. Heinrich, meanwhile, looked as though he might be sick. "Good God, Marta," he grated out. "Do you have any idea what a disaster this is? If you'd had an affair with someone you could marry, it would have been bad enough. But this Király fellow, he's no one. A pauper."

"Now wait just a moment," Marta said. "I know Andras isn't the sort of person I'm supposed to marry, but I've got enough money and breeding for the both of us, I should think. If you would just calm yourselves we could talk to the bishop, get a license, and have this entire thing sorted within a week."

"You must be out of your mind if you think we would let you marry that peasant, even if he wasn't simply using you for your money. Not to mention the family he comes from." Heinrich sat back and crossed his arms, not without a certain satisfaction. "According to Ludwig, your Andras's father was one of those revolutionary thugs who nearly burned down Baron Messerschmidt's mansion in Budapest. You think we would allow that kind of bad blood into our family?"

"The revolution was decades ago, Papa, and… Wait. Ludwig told you this? *Ludwig?*" How had Ludwig known about György Király, about any of this? More importantly, how difficult would it be for her to strangle him?

"Yes, Ludwig. He's been most helpful. Without him, who knows how long this would have gone on?"

"Not that he would marry you now, of course." Hannelore shook her head mournfully. "It'll be impossible to find anyone to marry you if this gets out."

"Then let it get out," said Marta, lifting her chin. "Because I'm not marrying anyone other than Andras."

"You are never going to see him again, Marta." There was no hesitation in Heinrich's voice, no hint of remorse. "He's going back to whatever Hungarian gutter he came from, and I'll be paying a visit to the Landfeld Theatre this afternoon to make sure of it."

"You're, you're going to make him lose his job?" Marta's mouth dropped open in horror. She'd known her father was strict, but this was beyond the pale. "Papa, that's despicable. He has a sick father and three sisters to support."

Heinrich slammed his brandy glass down furiously, his face scarlet. "Then you should have thought of that *before* all this, shouldn't you!" he roared. "Before you decided to let him seduce you. He deserves every punishment I see fit to inflict on him and more. I am being *merciful* compared to what I could be." He slumped back in his chair, suddenly looking very tired. "I have to protect this family, Marta. I have to protect you. And since you seem so determined to ruin your future, I have to protect you from yourself."

The noise Marta let out was somewhere between a sob and a laugh. "How do you plan to do that? Lock me in a tower? Drown me in the Danube and say I died from consumption? Or marry me off to someone so old and confused he won't be able to tell I've been compromised?"

"Stop being so dramatic," said Hannelore, completely without irony. "If you ask me, Heinrich, some time abroad would be a sensible solution. I don't think we can trust her not to do something foolish if she stays in Vienna. My cousin Johannes and his family could be an improving influence on her."

Heinrich stroked his mustache thoughtfully. "Professor Achterburg? He wouldn't let her get away with much, that's true, though Oxford is far away."

"If you ask me," Hannelore said, "the farther away from *him* she is, the better."

"Indeed, though he may object if there are certain extenuating circumstances."

"You mean if she is…" Hannelore gestured to her midsection, making Marta's cheeks burn with humiliation.

"Precisely. But once we find out whether she is, you may write to Professor Achterburg and see if he's willing to play host to our wayward daughter."

"Mama, Papa, no, please don't send me to England," Marta begged. "I'm sorry for what happened with Andras, truly I am, but I can't leave Vienna. If…" She trailed off, knowing her parents would not be swayed by the argument that if Andras came back, this was where he would look for her. "You can't send me away. You don't have all the facts, for one thing."

"The facts," Hannelore said. "And what facts, exactly, have we missed? I think we've learned all we need to know."

There was only one fact that her parents had not been made aware of, and it was this that Marta offered up now. "I love him," she whispered. "Please, Mama, Papa, I love him."

For one glorious, agonizing moment her father's face appeared to soften, and she allowed herself to hope. Until his scowl returned full force. "Whether you think you love him or not, you relinquished all right to make your own decisions when you chose to throw away your virtue with that scoundrel," he said. "And once we find out if you're carrying his child, we will send you wherever we damn well please, be that to England, a nunnery, or the blasted Siberian tundra."

"What are you going to tell Heini? And what about Sophie? I can't just leave her with no warning."

"Heini's got more than enough to think about with starting school this year. He doesn't need any of your nonsense dragging him down," Heinrich growled. "We'll tell him and Sophie what we will be telling everyone else. That you've gone to England for your health, that you're having a wonderful time, and you'll be back when you are feeling better. If I catch you telling them anything else, believe me when I say there will be consequences. Am I clear?"

He was clear. Terrifyingly so. And so as much as she wanted to argue, to shout, to fight back, she did not. She kept her mouth shut, and nodded.

There was one thing she could still do to preserve her dignity, though. Which was to leave the parlor with her chin up and her eyes dry, and wait until she'd returned to her own room before bursting into painful, noisy sobs.

Six Hours Later
The Landfeld Theatre

The minute he was summoned to Glöckner's office halfway through rehearsal, Andras knew what was about to happen. The mournful look on the director's pale face only confirmed his suspicions.

"Andras," Glöckner said, as soon as the door had closed. "Count Heinrich von Holstadt paid me a visit earlier today."

"I thought he might have," Andras replied quietly. "What did he have to say?"

"He certainly wasn't happy, I can tell you that much. Had quite a lot of thoughts on your supposed immoral conduct. And while he wasn't willing to give me many details, he seemed to be concerned for his daughter's reputation." With a heavy sigh, Glöckner removed his spectacles and wiped them with his handkerchief. "Please be honest with me, Andras. Did you have some sort of friendship with the young lady? Beyond what might be proper, I mean? I would believe you if you denied it. You've never given me any reason to distrust you."

"I appreciate that, but I'm afraid I can't deny it. Count von Holstadt is correct." Somehow it was more upsetting to admit this to his director than it had been to be caught by the count. "Mart… Countess Marta and I have had a relationship of sorts for some time now. We hoped to keep it quiet, though unfortunately we didn't succeed."

"God almighty. But why?" Glöckner asked. "The Odysseum was on its way up, Andras. People were finally starting to take notice of us, and your connection with the von Holstadts could have brought us a proper patronage, real money. You could have made a better living, sent your sisters to a good school, hired a nurse for your father. Why would you throw all that away for an affair?"

"Because I loved her," Andras said heavily. He couldn't bear to meet the other man's eye, so he kept his gaze fixed downward. "I still do. There's no justification for how I've behaved. It was selfish and impulsive and utterly mad. But what's done is done, and I can't change my feelings."

A pained look passed across Glöckner's face, and Andras remembered the rumor he'd heard about the Odysseum's founder: that many years before, young Oskar had fallen in love with a shepherd from his village in the Alps. The resulting scandal had driven him away from his home and to Vienna to make his fortune, so if anyone knew about love and tragedy, it was he.

"I understand," Glöckner said at last. "But I am in a difficult situation here. The count has made it clear that if I don't want to lose the lease on this building—indeed, lose the opera company—I can no longer keep you in my employ. If there was another way."

"I doubt there is. But it's all right." Andras managed a weak smile. "This opera company has been my home for four years, and I'd hate to be the one who brings it down. If it'll protect all of you, I'm happy to leave." A part of him longed for Glöckner to insist that he stay, that Andras was like a son to him and couldn't possibly leave, but he knew it wouldn't happen. Business was business, after all.

"Thank you, Andras," said Glöckner. Though he still looked sorrowful, his shoulders slumped with relief as he pushed a thin envelope across the desk. "Take this at least. It's two weeks' pay, the best I could do. I would leave town as soon as possible, if I were you. You won't be finding much work here anymore. Go back to Budapest, that's my advice, look after your family."

"Of course. And thank you, Mr. Glöckner. I will never forget how kind you and the rest of the company have been to me. This isn't how I wanted to repay you. But, well..." Andras trailed off, throat tight. "Once again, thank you."

"It's been an honor. Goodbye, Mr. Király. And," Glöckner added, as Andras rose from his seat, "good luck."

Andras left the theatre immediately, without stopping to say goodbye. There was no point in sticking around, not if he didn't want his friends to see him cry, something he felt dangerously close to doing.

Almost automatically, his feet found their way to the servants' entrance of the von Holstadt house. Perhaps it was futile, but he had to try to see Marta, tell her what had happened, explain why he had to leave. To promise he was neither abandoning nor forgetting her.

His poundings on the door were finally answered by Hermann the butler, whose face seemed even more hatchet-like than usual as he glowered down at him.

"Yes?"

"I'm here for Marta," he said, not even attempting formality. "I know she isn't supposed to see me, but I don't care. I have to talk to her. You're a butler, you're good at being discreet."

"No." Hermann's expression did not change in the slightest. "I cannot help you, Mr. Király. Please leave."

"I'm not leaving, damn it. Well, I am—heading back to Hungary—but not before I tell Marta."

"Even if I did let you into this house, which I am not going to, it would do you no good. Countess Marta is not here. She has gone abroad."

"Abroad?" Andras's heart thudded in worry. "Abroad where?"

"I am not at liberty to divulge that information." The butler crossed his arms. "Is there anything else you would like to discuss?"

Yes, you bastard. Tell me where Marta is or I'll strangle you with a violin string.

"No," Andras said after a beat. "I suppose not."

Back at the garret, Andras set about packing, tossing only the essentials into his faded carpetbag. He wouldn't need much, especially if he wasn't going to be a musician anymore. He briefly contemplated leaving Clara behind before concluding that this would be akin to abandoning his right arm.

Franz arrived home early, apparently having left the opera house in a rush after he'd heard the news. Open-mouthed, he took in Andras's half-packed bag.

"You're leaving?"

"Yes," Andras said curtly. "I've been sacked, Franz, haven't you heard?"

"I can't believe it." Franz shook his head furiously. "I always thought Glöckner had some integrity. I'll give him a piece of my mind all right."

"Don't risk it. Do you think Glöckner would have got rid of me if he had any other choice? I can guarantee Marta's father is breathing down his neck, and if you stand up for me you'll be thrown out by your ear." He shoved a pair of socks into his bag. "Believe me, you'll be better off when I'm back in Budapest."

"But I don't understand why you have to leave Vienna. There are plenty of other places who could use a talented chap like you."

"It's good of you to say so. But my talent doesn't mean anything in this city anymore. I'll be blacklisted from every theater in Vienna by now."

"I don't accept that. My God, you're Andras Király. You can't just give up and go back to Budapest." Franz raked a hand through his hair. "You're my best friend, damn it all. This isn't how I thought we would be parting ways."

Unbidden, tears pricked at the corner of Andras's eyes. In spite of everything, Franz remained one of the best friends he'd ever had.

With any luck, his job would be safe once Andras left.

"Don't worry," he said. "You know me. I always land on my feet."

As he snapped the carpetbag shut and looked around the garret for the last time, he could only pray this was true.

PART THREE

"Zwei Dumme, ein Gedanke."
(Two fools, one thought)
-German proverb

CHAPTER TWENTY-THREE

(In Which No One is Having a Good Time)

July 31
Szerdahelyi Street

THE ONLY PLACE in the neighborhood where it was possible to get any peace, appropriately enough, was the cemetery at the end of the street. Anna Király was buried here, but it wasn't to her grave that Andras went. Silly as it might have been, he felt ashamed to face her after everything that had happened. Instead, he wound up sitting on a bench in front of the grave of someone named Albert Fejes, who had apparently died at the age of forty leaving behind a wife and seven children.

That wouldn't be Andras anytime soon. After recent events, he couldn't see himself marrying or producing children at all. The dying at forty part might be doable, though.

His family still didn't know the details of what had happened in Vienna. They didn't know anything, except what Andras had seen fit to tell them. That he'd been sacked, that Glöckner had no longer been able to pay him (which was not technically a lie, because if Glöckner had continued to pay him, Count von Holstadt would have had the director's guts for garters), and that he was doing absolutely fine.

The latter was a lie. But with any luck, it wouldn't be for long.

Hearing the sound of leaves crunching, Andras glanced over his shoulder to see Jozefa approaching. He scooted to one side of the bench to make room for her, and she plopped down beside him.

"So," she said without preamble. "Are you ever planning to tell us why you really lost your job?"

"I told you," he replied, avoiding eye contact. "Glöckner couldn't pay me anymore. Happens all the time in the wonderful world of opera."

"You're a fool if you think we believe that. No one has called you out on it because you're clearly miserable, but we are your own damn family and we know when you're lying."

"Don't swear," he said automatically. "And I'm not lying."

"You absolutely are, and I think I know why. It was that girl you were teaching, the countess. You got sacked because you fancied her, didn't you? I mean, you practically swooned every time you talked about her last month."

How did a fourteen-year-old girl become so insightful? Maybe he shouldn't have convinced her to stay in school. "In a manner of speaking, yes. Though it was a bit more complicated."

"I could kill her," Jozefa said passionately. "That horrid woman. I could kill her for what she's done to you. I expect she thought of you as some charity case, paying for Pa's medicine so she could brag to all her rich friends about how generous she is, but the minute you get ideas above your station she has you thrown out."

"Jozefa, stop," Andras ordered. "It wasn't like that, not at all. It was—" He swallowed hard. "It was my fault. She wanted to tell her family about us, get them on our side, convince them to let us get married. But I wouldn't let her. I wanted to wait until I was rich and successful and worthy. Then her family found out anyway, and they made damn well sure that we can never see each other again."

"Ah," his sister said, her face softening. "So she loved you too."

Andras let out a heavy sigh. "Apparently she did."

"So what are you going to do about it?"

"What can I do? I don't even know where she is. After Glöckner sacked me I went back to the von Holstadt house to talk to her, but that snob of a butler told me Marta had gone abroad and he couldn't say where. Rather a dead end, don't you think?"

Jozefa rolled her eyes. "Call yourself a Király, with an attitude like that? The other girls and I looked up to you, you know. Here you are, the one member of our family to get a proper education and move to Vienna to make something of himself, and you're sitting here blubbing about dead ends. Shouldn't you have more backbone?"

"Now that's harsh, I must say," Andras retorted. "Let me tell you, young lady, that if I had sufficient time, money, and information, I'd go fetch Marta and be married to her by next week. But as I believe I've mentioned, I have no idea where she is."

"Then figure it out," said Jozefa. "Do I have to do everything around here myself?"

August 16
Oxford, England

"Bless today, oh Lord, the fruits of thy goodness we are about to receive."

Marta stifled a yawn and surreptitiously pinched the inside of her wrist to stay awake as Johannes Achterburg's droning prayer entered what felt like its tenth minute at least. Really, she didn't see much point in blessing this particular food. Everything in the Achterburg household was completely flavorless.

Or maybe it was just that she couldn't be bothered to taste much anymore.

If only she had been pregnant. It was unlikely her parents would have allowed her to marry Andras even then, but it would have thrown a wrench in their plans. Let them try and cover that up by sending her to England. Everyone in England would notice anyway.

But Andras had been careful, and it was confirmed a few days after they were discovered that no baby was forthcoming. This fact established, there was nothing preventing the von Holstadts from sending her, along with her stone-faced new maid and a trunk full of the plainest clothes in her wardrobe, to Oxford. When she had first arrived she'd been full of fire, practically snarling at her hosts, mind full of plans to escape. But with eyes on her every moment of the day, escape proved impossible, and a dark, heavy despair had settled over her that she hadn't been able to shake off.

The only thing keeping her from giving up that last, tiny bit of hope was the memory that she had been loved by someone who was far better than the von Holstadts and the Achterburgs put together. Whether he still loved her after she'd cost him his job was debatable, but he had loved her. And with this in mind, Marta was able—just about—to keep from falling into utter misery. Though the Achterburgs were not making it easy.

Professor Johannes Achterburg was a distant cousin of her mother's, and taught German and Austrian history at Oxford University. These days he was settled in a dark, drafty house on Queen Street with his English wife, Clementine, and their nine-year-old twins, Wilhelmina and Charles. And when Marta's father had said the Achterburgs would keep Marta in line, he'd clearly meant it.

With the possible exception of a Siberian work camp, there were few places Marta would have enjoyed less than the Achterburg household. The family did not light fires in the fireplaces because they didn't want to waste money on wood. They did not put spices on their food, to avoid digestive troubles. They did not go to parties with dancing, because dancing was frivolous. And they did not allow novels in the house, because novels were a bad influence. With this complete and utter lack of entertainment, it was no surprise that young Mina and Charles had to resort to being the most ungovernable children Marta had ever met.

Unfortunately for her, it became apparent upon her arrival that her primary duty was to act as an unpaid tutor. Their last one had quit two months earlier, Clementine had explained, and of course Clementine herself was far too busy with her own work, whatever that was, to continue teaching them. A disgraced cousin who couldn't demand a salary was just the solution to their woes. Marta's parents, meanwhile, could rest assured their daughter was being thoroughly punished for her terrible behavior.

"…amen," Johannes finished at last. He ceremoniously picked up the carving knife and began cutting hair-thin slices of the unappetizing grayish-brown roast. When she'd first arrived, Marta had briefly considered becoming a vegetarian, but the vegetables served in the Achterburg household were even more bland than the meat.

"You're welcome to take your dinner in the nursery if you're not happy down here, you know," Clementine offered dryly, glancing with disapproval as Marta picked at her dinner. Wasting food, like nearly everything else, was a grave sin in the Achterburg household. "Charles and Mina would be glad of the company."

"That's quite all right," Marta said quickly. Earlier that day, when she'd eaten lunch in the nursery, Mina and Charles had managed to spill both their bowls of soup onto an expensive antique rug and not consume a single morsel of anything else, for which Marta had subsequently received the blame. In fact, something similar had happened at nearly every meal she'd had with the twins during the two weeks she had been in Oxford. "I'm sure they'll be fine with Nanny."

"Hmm." Clementine obviously found this difficult to believe. "All for the best, I suppose. Johannes and I had something we wanted to discuss with you, didn't we, Johannes?"

Professor Achterburg made a vague noise of assent, barely glancing up from the notebook he was studying. Undeterred, his wife went on.

"I am worrying," she said, "that you are not settling in here."

"Really, Mrs. Achterburg? Why would you think that?"

Fortunately, Clementine remained oblivious to the sarcasm in Marta's voice. "You've been very glum, Marta. Always drifting about the place with a sour face. I haven't once seen you smile since you arrived here."

"With respect, Mrs. Achterburg, I've been sent away from my home, and not by my choice. You and Professor Achterburg have been very kind to me, but I don't feel I have much to be pleased about."

"Well." Clementine sniffed. "There's gratitude for you. Let me tell you, missy, I may not know all the details, but I know perfectly well that you behaved like a proper hellion back in Vienna, otherwise you wouldn't have been sent to stay with us."

Marta nearly laughed. A proper hellion, indeed. She was almost tempted to tell them everything that had happened, just to see the looks of horror on their faces.

But she couldn't, not even to give Johannes and Clementine a shock. What had happened between her and Andras—that was sacred. The Achterburgs weren't going to sully it with their narrow-minded snobbery.

"My behavior in Vienna is neither here nor there," Marta said, lifting her chin. "I'll stay here, since I don't have much of a choice, and I'll look after Charles and Mina for you. But I won't be happy about it. My emotions are entirely my own business."

"Emotions, indeed." Professor Achterburg looked up from his notebook, adjusting his glasses with a disgusted air. "I suggest you keep those to yourself."

In this, unlike nearly everything else, Marta thought, she and the professor were in perfect agreement.

It seemed like centuries before dinner drew to a close, and Marta was finally permitted to retreat to the tiny upstairs bedroom she had been assigned. The room had clearly been intended as a servant's quarters, with a narrow bed and tiny window, but Marta wasn't complaining. Not only did it afford her the only privacy she experienced in this horrible house, it reminded her of the tiny Leopoldstadt garret where she and Andras had spent so many happy hours.

Now, as she slipped on her soft cotton nightgown, the only truly nice piece of clothing she'd been allowed to bring from Vienna, and sat in the rickety chair by the window, she wondered for the thousandth time what had become of Andras. Small comfort though it was after he'd lost his job, she was glad that he was probably with his family back in Budapest. They'd be able to look after him.

Perhaps it was selfish, but she did hope he missed her, even half as much as she missed him.

"I love you, Andras," Marta whispered to the night sky, in the vain hope that even if he couldn't hear her, he would somehow know. "This isn't going to be forever. I'll figure out something."

Andras had found a new job. Not as a musician, though that wasn't shocking. Even if there had been millions of orchestra jobs available, Andras didn't seem to be able to summon up his usual passion for music at all. He couldn't compose a single note, and every time he took Clara out of her case, he found himself just staring at her, wishing she could reverse time, bring back both Marta and his inspiration.

Ordinary, non-music jobs weren't easy to come by either, considering his fairly limited skill set. It was his father, at last, who came up with a solution, just before Andras's severance pay from the orchestra was about to run out. A friend from the tavern, Erik Orban, ran a tobacconist's shop two streets over and needed an assistant. Andras, who did not smoke, was initially reluctant, but as no other work was forthcoming, he found himself standing behind the counter in a striped apron, trying to tell different types of tobacco apart. It was a task at which he did not excel.

He'd been trying not to think about Marta, considering how futile it was. She was gone, and there was no telling if he'd ever be able to find her again. His frantic letters to everyone he knew in Vienna had yet to yield results. Yet think about her he did, every time he let his mind wander for more than a minute, every single night before he went to sleep on the too-short cot in the kitchen. If nothing else, he had his memories.

As the days went by and the weather grew colder, though, he found his memories of Vienna becoming ever fuzzier, as though he was trying to recall a dream. He could remember what Marta looked like and the sound of her voice, but it was becoming harder to remember the scent of her skin and the feel of her hands, and a dozen other things he'd hoped to hold on to forever.

Maybe, he reflected glumly, a dream was exactly what it had been. Beautiful while it lasted, but impossible to sustain.

Maybe it was best if Marta forgot about him too.

CHAPTER TWENTY-FOUR

(In Which Hope Protects Us)

August 7

DEAR MARTA,
 I'm aware I can't send this letter, as I don't know your current address. But I'll write it anyway.

You may know by now that I've lost my job at the opera company. Glöckner was kind about it; he didn't have much choice but to dismiss me. Your father had something to do with it, and if the count was that hard on me I expect he was just as hard on you. I shouldn't have left the theatre, even if you did ask me to. I should have stayed with you no matter what.

It's good to be back with my family, at least. But I miss you more each day.

Love,
Andras

August 18
Dear Andras,

This may not be a surprise, but Oxford is dreadful. It's far worse than the last time I was here (though that was twelve years ago, when I was more easily entertained). Bland food, annoying young cousins, and the only people I ever socialize with are professors' wives whom Clementine knows. One might think they would be learned and interesting, but one would be wrong.

My letters are being very strictly supervised, so I'll have to burn this one. But I'll inquire after your circumstances anyway. Are your sisters and father glad to have you back? Are they looking after you? How is Clara coping with all these changes?

I love you. And I am so, so sorry about your job.

Your star-crossed lover,

Marta

August 21

Franz,

How are you? I'm as well as can be expected, by which I mean terrible. Is the opera company still functioning? Who have they gotten to replace me? I know Nick in second chair's been after my spot for a while, though I never thought his playing was very precise.

Please give everyone at the theatre my love, particularly Brigita and Leo (I know chatting with Brigita is awkward these days, but do it for me).

Does good old Dietrich miss me? I miss him, and you, and Vienna in general.

—Andras

PS: Could you do a bit of digging and see if the von Holstadts own any houses abroad? Asking for a friend.

PPS: The friend is myself.

September 1

Dearest Sophie,

I wish I could write you an honest letter like this one, not one of the false cheerful ones my family insists on. As it is, I won't be able to send this. I'm not in England for my health, as you've probably already deduced; I've been exiled, to preserve my reputation. Hopefully I'll be able to tell you the whole story in person soon, though I'm not sure if you'll laugh or throw something at me for being so foolish. Perhaps both.

I miss you so much. In one fell swoop I've been cut off from everyone I care about. In a way it's worth it, for what I had with Andras—but it still hurts.

You would like him, Sophie. He's nearly as witty as you are. And talented and gentle and kind and a thousand other things that it almost tortures me to think about. If all three of us are ever in the same room again...

No. When all three of us are in the same room again. We'll have a brilliant time, Sophie, I know it. Just think, you'll finally have an actual working person to be friends with!

Love from your unfortunate friend, Marta

September 15

Marta,

I've been actively trying to avoid becoming the cliché of the tormented musician separated from his true love, rather like Beethoven and that letter to his "immortal beloved." After a few drinks, though, clichés become harder to avoid.

Do you remember that morning alone in the music room, when Nella was sick? The combination of you and that beautiful piano. I can't stop thinking about it. If we ever reunite I'll make love to you on a dozen pianos. I'll make you sing with pleasure, and we won't get out of bed for a month if you don't want to. You won't need to wear anything but your hair.

This letter should be burnt immediately, I think. I certainly don't want the girls reading it.

I love you. Please don't forget that.

September 26

Dear Andras,

I love you. I love the way you think of tunes for everyone and the way you talk about Clara like she's a person. I love how you run your fingers through your hair and how you switch to Hungarian when you talk to animals. I love how even though you don't have strong opinions about things like clothes and sewing, you let me ramble on about them without interrupting. I love your eyes and hands and long legs and red hair. I love how despite the fact that I am spoiled and frivolous, you still love me. Or did.

I love you for all these reasons, and try to repeat them to myself daily, because I refuse to forget a single detail about you. Even if I'm trapped in England for the next ten years.

Yours forever,

Marta

Andras barely noticed the bell on the shop's door ringing as it swung open. In his defense, the smell of tobacco had a tendency to cloud his thoughts, and not in a pleasant way. It took several polite throat-clearings from the customer, a young man in a fine blue suit, before Andras finally realized his presence.

"Can I help you, sir?"

"My goodness," the young man said. "Andras? Andras Király? That can't be you."

Andras let out a long-suffering sigh as he recognized the customer. Of course it was Laszlo Klasky, of *course* it was. The other Hungarian lad from the Academy, whose moderately wealthy family had always helped Andras pay for his train tickets home over Christmas. They'd been good friends, but of all the people he wanted to witness his current situation, Laszlo was not one of them. "Laszlo. How are you?"

"Andras Király, working for a tobacconist," Laszlo said, apparently not having heard the question. He let out a low whistle. "Whatever happened to you? Last I heard you were still in Vienna working for some opera company."

"Yes, well. Times change," said Andras. "How have you been?"

"Oh, you know. Can't complain," Laszlo said with a shrug. "Been traveling a bit, writing a few tunes, same old thing. Not famous yet, but then again, I never had your talent." He leaned forward conspiratorially. "Listen. If you don't want to tell me what's happened that's your business. But it would be nice to catch up. I'm heading to Café Royale around the corner. If you want to meet me when your shift is over, coffee is on me."

Andras hesitated, then nodded. "All right. I'll see you in an hour."

The events of the last few months, thankfully, did not take too long to explain. Laszlo was polite enough to listen without interruptions, though his eyes did nearly bug out of his head when Andras described his affair with Marta. When the tale was all told, Laszlo said nothing at first, only sipped his coffee thoughtfully.

"It's a tricky situation, all right," he said. "But there's no reason for you to be working for a tobacconist. You don't even smoke. I wonder…" He snapped his fingers delightedly. "That's it. I might be able to help you after all, Andras. My father's got this friend, British fellow, something of a philanthropist. He's had this idea for a series of concerts to raise money for an orphanage he's opening up somewhere in England, and he told my father he's looking for a few European musicians to make the whole scheme more sophisticated. I can't go myself, unfortunately, but I could give Mr. Cunningham your name. 'Course, you'd have to go abroad, but a job's a job."

"Indeed it is." Andras's heart had leaped at the thought of once again actually playing music, but he stayed outwardly calm. "Where would we be performing, exactly?"

"A few different places, I think. Cambridge, Exeter, Oxford." He frowned at Andras, who had suddenly gone very still. "I say, are you all right?"

Andras was very much all right, though his mind was racing. At Laszlo's words he'd suddenly remembered a line from a letter Marta had sent him, what felt like ages ago. *I was in Oxford some years ago visiting Mama's cousin…*

And the butler had said Marta had gone abroad. Could it be at all possible?

It had to be worth a try, anyway.

"I'm in," Andras declared. "Tell Mr. Cunningham I'm ready when he is."

Perhaps, he thought ruefully, he should have admitted how lacking his musical inspiration had been of late. But what did it matter? A job was a job, and a chance to find Marta… it was nothing short of a miracle.

It was raining.

It was always raining in Oxford. Marta had seen perhaps two clear days in all the time she'd been there. Which was not having a positive effect on her mood.

Under more auspicious circumstances, she might have found Oxford an interesting place to visit. There were students from all over the world, and university buildings and medieval churches and practically everything she would usually have enjoyed exploring. But there was no exploring to be done when one lived with the Achterburgs. There was only trudging.

On this particular day, the trudging in question was to the post office. Clementine did not trust the servants to deal with the family's correspondence. Marta couldn't be sure of the reason why, since it seemed unlikely that the Achterburgs' letters contained anything interesting. Instead, her cousin insisted on dealing with the post herself. Marta accompanied her, partially for fresh air and partially to serve as a witness when any employees inevitably annoyed Clementine.

As Clementine argued with the post office clerk, Marta's attention drifted to the notice-board just inside the door, plastered with advertisements for used prams and rewards for lost kittens. One flyer, printed with an image of a grand piano, drew her eye in particular.

Charity Concert for the Benefit of Saint Jude's Children's Home, it announced. *A Selection of Hymns Performed by the Continent's Finest Trio. Bruno Pichler on Piano, Albert Menken on Cello, Anders Kiroly on Violin. October 6, Asquith Hall.*

Marta's heart pounded rapidly as she took in the last name on the list. There was no need to get excited, she told herself. Dozens of men had Hungarian names and played the violin, hundreds. And it said Anders Kiroly, not Andras Király.

And yet.

Everyone knew the English were hopeless at spelling foreign names. Professor Grimes's wife still seemed to think Marta's name was Martha von Hulstate. Anders Kiroly was far too much of a coincidence to be worth ignoring.

"I say, Mrs. Achterburg," Marta said as casually as she could manage, when Clementine had finally browbeaten the clerk sufficiently. "That concert looks interesting, does it not? Perhaps we could go? I am so very fond of music."

Clementine eyed the flyer with suspicion. "A public concert? I don't know, Marta. There will be tradesmen and shouting children and sticky floors."

"But all in the name of Christian charity," said Marta. "Mina and Charles will like it, I think. And even if they don't, it will be very educational for them."

"Hmm." Clementine pursed her lips, her expression less skeptical than before. Proving herself charitable in public was a difficult temptation to resist. "I have never much cared for these string groups. Rather florid for my taste. Still, if it is hymns they're going to play…"

Marta crossed her fingers behind her back, not daring to make any more remarks. It had been so long since she'd had any hope, and now it was almost agonizing to have it again. *Please, Clementine, please.*

Finally, after an agonizingly long wait, Clementine nodded. "Very well. But I expect this to be an educational opportunity for the children. Perhaps you can teach them some music history in preparation for it. You play a few instruments, don't you?"

"Yes, I can play the piano, and the violin a bit…" Marta trailed off, as Clementine had clearly stopped listening.

That was all right, Marta thought with satisfaction. There wasn't any need to discuss things further.

Not when she had this much scheming to do.

October 6

Marta was doing her best not to get her hopes up, but after she'd been deprived of the emotion for so long, she was feeling dangerously thrilled at even the slightest prospect of seeing Andras again. She'd barely got a wink of sleep the night before the concert, her mind abuzz with plans. Plans that might not work, but what did that matter? For the first time in weeks, she felt alive again.

Now, though, as she, Clementine, and the children took their seats in the hall and listened to someone named Mr. Cunningham earnestly discuss the school he was opening for orphans, doubt began to seep into Marta's mind. Surely it was far-fetched that Andras would have somehow wound up all the way over here in Oxford after he'd been exiled to Budapest. She was behaving like a silly little girl, wishing for a magical coincidence that would solve everything.

And then the musicians came out and took their places, and Marta had to stifle a gasp of joy. Because the young man with the violin, though he looked thinner and more tired than when she had last seen him, was unmistakably Andras. Her Andras. Marta barely noticed as Clementine guided her towards their seats, so consumed was she by absorbing every detail she had missed—those long, graceful fingers, the sensitive mouth, those glowing turquoise eyes that used to fill with heat when they looked upon her. It was all she could do not to leap up from her seat and throw herself into his arms.

Instead, she waited in the audience, barely listening to the music as the wheels in her mind turned rapidly. If she was going to get a chance to speak with him, she'd need to pull off something very clever. And she couldn't do it alone.

Fortunately, she thought, glancing over at Mina and Charles, she had a pair of built-in accomplices.

There were, to Marta's relief, refreshments of the tasteless-biscuit-and-tea variety following the performance. Marta was equally grateful that Clementine had spotted Professor Grimes's wife and gone to chat with her, leaving Marta in charge of the children. If anyone could cause a distraction, it was Mina and Charles.

Marta bent over and looked first Mina then Charles in the eye. "Listen, children," she said gravely. "I must have your help with something. I see a very dear friend of mine, but your mother will not permit me to speak to him, due to many terrible and boring reasons. And so I wonder if the two of you might cause some small distraction for me."

Mina and Charles looked at each other thoughtfully. "What will you do for us?" they chorused.

"I will…" Marta contemplated the few things in her power to bargain with. "I will give you all my pudding every dinner until January."

"Every dinner until February," Charles corrected her. "And if

Mummy punishes us by making us weed the garden again you have to help."

Marta shook his hand. "Agreed. Thank you, children. I will leave you to think about your plan."

After depositing the children at their mother's side, Marta made her way to the back of the hall, close to the doorway she had seen the musicians disappear behind earlier. She knew she would have to move quickly when the children started their distraction, and remaining undetected by Clementine was a difficult proposition. Fortunately, that lady did not seem to have noticed Marta's absence yet as she stood by the refreshments table chatting with Mrs. Grimes. Finally, Marta saw Mina and Charles glance at one another before scurrying to each end of the refreshments table.

Mina said something Marta couldn't quite make it out, but whatever it was, it made Charles grin and Clementine gasp. Before their mother could do anything, the children grasped each end of the tablecloth and, in one sharp movement, swept everything flying off the table and crashing onto the floor.

Recognizing her cue, Marta fled.

CHAPTER TWENTY-FIVE

(In Which a Doctor's Credentials are Not Questioned)

ASQUITH HALL WAS not a large building, but in Marta's frantic search, the back rooms seemed like a maze. Marta found herself wandering in circles like Theseus lost in the Minotaur's labyrinth, hurriedly opening door after door, finding nothing except tables and broom cupboards. She didn't have time for this. She needed to hurry, before Clementine realized she'd gone missing. If she lost her only chance to see Andras again, she had no idea what she'd do.

Finally, after opening yet another cupboard, she heard a sound from across the hall. A very familiar voice, humming—humming not just anything, but a song she'd recognize anywhere.

The song he had written her.

The tune that made her feel loved and important and *understood*, even when hummed through a wall.

She crossed the hall in two strides and didn't bother to knock. Instead, she simply threw open the door.

And there he was, her Andras, clear as day, standing in front of the mirror and frowning at his reflection. When he heard the door open he turned to face her, eyes wide.

"Marta?"

"Andras," she breathed. Now that she saw him in the flesh, only a few feet away, it was almost too much to bear. She wanted to throw herself at him, run her hands through his hair, kiss him until she ran out of air.

"Marta?" he said again. "Is that really you, or am I having a hallucination?"

She took a deep breath and stepped inside, closing the dressing room door behind him. "No hallucination. Andras, listen," she said hurriedly. "I know how angry you must be with me. I cost you your job, and you loved your job, and I ruined your entire life. So if you never want to see me again, I'll go. But if there's any chance you still love me then please, please tell me, because I am miserable without you."

Andras's brows drew together in a severe frown, and Marta's heart sank. She'd been sure that he would forgive her, be overjoyed to see her, and yet.

"Let me make something very, very clear, Marta," he said, his voice low and fierce. "If I ever hear you say anything like that again, I will have you sent to the nearest lunatic asylum because you have clearly lost your mind if you think it is possible for me not to love you anymore." He stepped forward and took her face in his hands. "Understood?"

"Yes," she whispered. "Absolutely understood."

"Good. Now hush, I'm going to kiss you."

And he did. Gently at first and then, when she made her enthusiasm abundantly clear with months' worth of pent-up passion, his hands roamed over her body as if to assure himself she was real. With a desperate groan of longing he picked her up at the waist and sat her on the edge of the dressing table, pushing apart her knees so she could wrap her legs around him.

Caught up as she was in a fog of almost agonizing desire, it took Marta a moment to realize, reluctantly, that this was not what they should be doing.

"Wait, wait. Andras, *wait!*"

He abruptly let go of her, frowning. "Is something wrong?"

"Absolutely not, but Mrs. Achterburg will be looking for me soon and we need to talk. How much longer will you be in Oxford?"

"Two more days, I think. Why?"

"Because," she said, "the last two months have been the worst of my life, with only one bright spot. I have had a lot of time to think about what I would do if I saw you again. And while those plans involved kissing, they also involved escaping."

"I recognize that look. You've got a scheme, haven't you?"

"I most certainly do," she said. "One of my finest."

Hurriedly and in great detail, she told him.

He was silent for long moments afterward. "It could work," he said at last. "Mind you, I'm not saying it will, but it could. I have some concerns, however. First, my English may not be good enough."

"Nonsense, people from all over the world live in Oxford. You just need to sound confident. Have you got a pen?" He handed her one, and she scribbled a few sentences on the back of a program. "Just memorize these, like you're in a play."

"Fair enough. Second, where am I meant to get a false mustache?"

"I don't know. Don't you work in the theatre? Surely there's a costume shop somewhere in this awful city."

"I'll ask Mr. Cunningham. Finally, concern the third. This all sounds rather expensive."

"Now that," she said, "is something I actually do have a solution for." She reached into her hair and pulled out the pin hidden in one of her braids, silver and topped with a cluster of sparkling stones.

Andras's eyes widened. "Are those diamonds?"

"They are. Grandmama Dorothea gave me this. But I don't need it," Marta said firmly, pressing it into his hand. "Sell it. It'll pay for our train tickets with plenty left over."

"Marta," Andras said softly. "Are you sure?" His hand remained outstretched as if he expected her to snatch the pin back. The thing glittered as if taunting her.

Take a good look, Marta. You sell me to pay for this stupid scheme, and you'll never know wealth and privilege again.

She picked up the pin, hesitated, then laughed, tucking it into the pocket of his waistcoat.

"Of course I'm sure," she said. "It's just a silly piece of jewelry. Go sell it, buy a false mustache and some train tickets, and meet me at St. Aloysius Church on Sunday morning."

"I will. But wait, before you go." He grasped her hand. "If this goes wrong, if we're separated again, I need you to know several things. I do not blame you for what happened with my job, I have thought of you every day since I left Vienna, and I will not give up on being with you. Ever. And if I have anything to say about it, this is the last time we will ever be apart."

"How wonderful that we are in agreement once again." Marta reached up and pulled his face down to hers, kissing him briefly but passionately. "I'll see you soon, my dear. Don't be late."

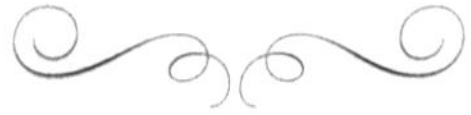

October 9

Sunday dawned bright and early, a day much like any other. An autumn chill was in the air, and the Achterburgs and their guest were bundled up as they made their way to St. Aloysius Church.

If Johannes and Clementine had been more observant, they might have noticed that in spite of the weather their young cousin was considerably more flushed and bright-eyed than usual. But no one had ever accused the Achterburgs of being detectives. During the carriage ride to church, Marta did not detect a hint of suspicion from them.

Which, frankly, she had banked on.

Mina and Charles were fidgeting the minute they sat in the family pew, as usual, and Clementine frowned at Marta as the priest began a reading from Matthew. Marta, however, did not reprimand the children. Instead, she glanced about the aisles, searching for any congregants who appeared out of place. If Andras had understood her instructions, he would be there— though not looking quite like himself.

The organ began to play a dolorous hymn, and the congregation stood, lining up to partake of the Eucharist. Marta stumbled as she and the rest of the family filed forward, earning a sharp look from Clementine.

"Careful, Marta. Walk like a lady."

"I'm sorry, Mrs. Achterburg," Marta whispered. "I'm feeling a bit dizzy, that's all. I don't suppose I could be excused from communion this time?"

"Absolutely not," Clementine replied. "This is church, not a tea party. There will be plenty of time for sitting later."

Marta nodded obediently and took a deep breath, taking a step towards the priest and swaying just slightly on her feet.

And then she collapsed, falling onto her back on the floor.

"Oh!" Clementine shrieked. She fanned Marta's face weakly. "Is there a doctor here?"

There was a shuffling of feet from a nearby pew, and a man's voice with a vaguely European accent spoke up. "I am a doctor, madam. If you'll allow me, I can examine the young lady."

Clementine made a noise of assent, and Marta could feel a hand pushing up her sleeve. The doctor's fingers rested on her wrist for a moment, taking her pulse, and he let out a dissatisfied murmur.

Then he seemed to retreat, and Marta wondered what he was doing—until a splash of cold liquid hit her face, and she had to suppress a gasp.

Holy water. Of course.

The congregation gasped at this sacrilege, and fell silent, undoubtedly waiting to see if a miraculous revival was imminent. Marta remained as still as ever, to all appearances in a deep faint.

"This young woman is very sick," the doctor declared. "This sort of fainting, coupled with the irregular heartbeat, is a sure sign of female hysteria. She will require immediate attention."

"Hysteria," Clementine gasped. "Johannes, that's terribly serious. What are we going to do?"

"We must treat her as soon as possible," the doctor said grimly. "If a course of medicine is administered very soon she ought to recover. My clinic is not far away. I will be able to look after her there, but we must leave immediately."

"Of course, Doctor," said Johannes. "We'll get her into our carriage right away. Where is your clinic located?"

"Ah." The doctor's voice was disapproving. "With respect, sir, it will not be a good idea for the young lady to ride in your carriage with the children. Excitable young people tend to disturb the environment. A wiser course of action would be for her to come in my carriage, with you following behind. I assure you, she will be quite safe."

Clementine and Johannes were silent. Marta could tell what they were thinking: putting their young cousin alone in a carriage with a man really was not the done thing, that was true. But he was a doctor, and the matter *was* urgent.

"Yes, all right," Johannes said grudgingly. "No funny business, mind you. We will follow behind, once we deposit the children at home."

"Excellent. You will find my premises at 145 Henry Street." The doctor bent and lifted Marta in his arms. "My apologies, Father. Please carry on."

And with that, they were out the door.

In the doctor's carriage, which was in fact a hired cab, Marta irritably wiped her face with a handkerchief and scowled at Andras. "Was the water really necessary, *doctor*? I'm soaking."

"I didn't have any smelling salts," said Andras reasonably. "And what kind of a doctor would I be if I didn't try to wake you before declaring you have a life-threatening condition?"

"I'm amazed they weren't suspicious. Was the faint too dramatic? I was up half the night practicing."

"It was a perfect faint. I nearly believed you myself." He thoughtfully ran a finger across the false mustache he had yet to take off. "You know, I think this mustache looks rather dapper. Maybe I should really grow one."

"Andras," said Marta. "If you grow a mustache I will divorce you."

"We're not married."

"All right, so I'll marry you and then divorce you. No mustaches, please. I like your face how it is." She leaned against him and sighed. "How long do you think it will take them to catch on?"

"No idea. But with any luck, we'll be on the train to London by the time they realize anything is amiss." He squeezed her hand. "You could go back, you know. It isn't too late. If you're having any regrets…"

She swallowed hard. "No. My parents will be furious, but I've made my decision. I want freedom, and I want to be with you, and I'm willing to accept any consequences that come with that." She looked at him questioningly. "Are you upset about leaving your latest job? I feel awful. I was so worried about our plan, I didn't even think to ask."

"I do regret not collecting my latest paycheck. But they'll find a replacement for me quickly enough. Besides," Andras said with a grimace, "I hate to say this about fellow musicians, but they really weren't up to Odysseum standards."

"Mmm." Marta wrapped an arm around his waist and, for the first time in what felt like days, allowed herself to breathe. "Where are we going next? Not Vienna, of course, it would be much too dangerous. Were you thinking Budapest, or somewhere else entirely?"

"Budapest," he said decisively. "My family will look after us. Pa will grumble, I'm sure, but he'll recover. And my sisters will be pleased to finally meet you."

"Do they know about us?"

"Jozefa managed to wrangle part of the story out of me. Not sure how much she's told the other girls. But they know what you did for Pa, and they'll be delighted to have you as a sister." Andras bent and kissed the top of her head. "Trust me?"

There was no need for her to reply. They both knew the answer.

The Achterburgs had one final communication with their guest, in the form of a letter left on Marta's bureau.

Dear Professor and Mrs. Achterburg,

I am very grateful that you have been my hosts for the last few months. Your unique form of hospitality is one I will not soon forget.

Unfortunately, the time has come for me to move on, as I feel England is no longer the appropriate place for me to remain. While I cannot at this time reveal my destination, you may rest assured that I am perfectly safe and much, much happier. And while I know my parents will be deeply saddened by this news, for which I'm genuinely sorry, I would like to point out that they sent me away in the first place, and this really is the best solution for all of us.

Yours respectfully,

Marta

PS: I have not been kidnapped. Really, I cannot stress that enough. My leaving is of my own accord and something I have been looking forward to for months.

CHAPTER TWENTY-SIX

(In Which Everyone is Very Surprised)

October 11

FOR THE THIRD time that year—which had to be some kind of record—Andras stood outside the door to the Király family flat and knocked.

The circumstances of his coming home seemed to get stranger and stranger every time. Deathly illness, getting sacked, arriving with no warning and his aristocratic mistress in tow. If they wrote an opera about his life, it would most certainly be derided as too far-fetched.

"Is anyone home?" Marta said. She leaned against his side, close enough that he could feel her trembling from nerves, hunger, exhaustion, or all three. He couldn't blame her. "Because if we're locked out I may have to go to sleep right here."

"Jozefa and Kitti are at school, and Ilka is at work, but I think Pa..." Andras paused, listening carefully. Sure enough, from somewhere behind the door he heard a muttered curse followed by the sound of footsteps, accompanied by a cane. "Yes, Pa's home."

Marta froze stiff, her already pale face going white as a sheet. "Oh, Lord," she whispered. "Your father is going to hate me."

There was no time to reassure her, for at that very moment the door creaked open to reveal György. His face went from irritated to astounded in approximately half a second.

She dropped into a stunningly graceful curtsy, and György stared at her like she was some creature of a species he'd never seen before. *Homo aristocratus*, in the flesh.

After a shocked silence, he shook his head. "Good God, boy. What have you done?"

On the train from Paris Andras had explained in no uncertain terms that their destination would be different from what Marta was accustomed to.

"I wasn't exaggerating when I said we were poor," he'd said, still clasping her right hand in both of his. He'd barely stopped touching her since they left Oxford, as though he was worried, as she was, that if they let go for one minute they would lose each other again. "We only have two rooms. Pa and I sleep in one and the girls sleep in the other. We do all the cooking and cleaning ourselves, the windows leak when it's rainy, and our building is full of noisy, interfering neighbors. I'll do whatever I can to make it easier for you, but it may not be comfortable at first."

Though she had assured Andras she'd be comfortable anywhere as long as they were together, Marta's willful imagination had conjured up a vision of a cold, damp, ugly tenement populated by thieves and tramps. And cockroaches. Enormous cockroaches.

It was for this reason that when she entered the Király family home for the first time, the first emotion Marta felt was relief.

True, Andras hadn't lied about the place being cramped. The room in which they stood had a bed in one corner, a stove and a cupboard in another, a faded red armchair in a third and, in the center, a table surrounded by mismatched chairs. Marta had never seen a room that served this many purposes. But what really drew her attention were the walls.

At Burg Holstadt, the walls were a vast collage of shields and portraits and hunting trophies, things collected and revered over the past two and a half centuries. The walls in the Király home were similarly crowded, but it was obvious that no piece of their decor had been chosen to impress anyone. Above the stove was hung a needlepoint sampler with a phrase in Hungarian that might have been a Bible verse, next to a child's messy but arresting drawing of a snarling tiger. Scattered around the rest of the walls were a wreath of dried flowers, sheets of music, a roughly carved wooden cross. And in what was clearly the place of honor just above the bed, a single photograph in an oval-shaped frame. A photograph of Andras, chin held high and lips quirked in a faint smile. Against this backdrop, he looked like a prince.

Everything on these walls, every seemingly random object, was part of what had turned Andras into the person Marta loved more than anything. Which meant she could love his home too, no matter how small it was.

Mr. Király let out an irritated grunt, yanking her out of her reverie, and sat down with a thump in the sagging armchair. He waited until she and Andras had taken seats by the table before barking out something she could not understand. It sounded disagreeable. Andras responded with something that sounded equally irritated, and battle was joined.

Really, she thought as the argument continued, she did not have to speak Hungarian to know what Andras's father was upset about. Fleeing England with her would have to have cost Andras his job again, and the whole affair was entirely her fault. And here she was, showing up to the Királys' already crowded flat with nothing but the clothes on her back and nothing to recommend her but her status as Andras's lover. It would be perfectly fair for the man to demand she leave, and then what would she and Andras do?

If she'd seen them on the street, Marta thought, desperately trying to distract her worried mind, it might have been difficult to tell that Andras and György were at all related. They certainly didn't look alike. In contrast to Andras's red hair and tall, lean frame, his father was short and stocky, with short-cropped brown hair and a round, ruddy face. The only thing that marked them as father and son was the fact that under his bushy eyebrows, Mr. Király unmistakably had Andras's bright turquoise eyes. How strange it was to see that vivid gaze in another face.

Finally, the two men appeared to reach a conclusion. Andras turned to Marta, taking her hand. "Don't mind my father," he said. "He's worried your relatives will think I've kidnapped you."

"That's ridiculous," Marta objected. "I left a note for the Achterburgs explaining as much as I could."

"Yes, but there's always the possibility they'll think I forced you to. So it's best if we get married as soon as possible."

"Married? Can we do that?"

"If it's what you want." Andras smiled at her hopefully. "It's certainly what I want, and it shouldn't be too hard. We're both of age, and it needn't be expensive. We just need to sort things out with Father Jonas. I'll start looking for a flat right away so we'll have somewhere to set up house. We'll be free, Marta, a proper married couple."

She took a deep breath, trying to keep from panicking. The whole situation had seemed so romantic when she and Andras were on the train fleeing the Achterburgs. But now the reality of the situation, that she was in a foreign country with a hasty wedding coming up, was hitting her full force.

Married?

"I think," she said slowly, "I need to lie down."

"Well," György said, as soon as Andras shut the door to the girls' bedroom where Marta dozed on Ilka's bed. "You've put your foot in it this time."

"Will you stop it?" Andras rolled his eyes. "I'm aware you don't approve, and I know Marta and I have had plenty of trouble. But it's been worth it."

"Worth it." György snorted. "Certain of that, are you? I thought I'd taught you more sense. Then again, I suppose eight years living among those soft-headed Viennese has ruined any sense you had."

"Enough, Pa," Andras said, narrowing his eyes. "Good Lord, I know you're bitter about the revolution. I understand. But I will not have you hating my future wife because of her nationality."

"Her nationality, perhaps not," György said. "But I think you're forgetting that she is a countess. She's used to living in mansions, being waited on hand and foot. How long do you think your fancy new Austrian wife's going to last, living like an ordinary person? Once the thrill wears off, she'll bolt back to her posh relations in Vienna."

"I don't think she will. Marta may come from a rich family, but she is not a snob, Pa. She's good, and kind, and generous."

"Generous!" György exclaimed. "The girl who ruined your career is generous. Well, a man learns something new every—"

"She saved your life," Andras said quietly.

His father's mouth dropped open. "She did what?"

"Saved your life. Did you never wonder where the money for the sanatorium this summer came from?"

"Picked up some extra work, you said."

"I lied, because if you knew the truth you never would have accepted the money. Marta paid for the sanatorium, Pa. She knew nothing about you except that you were my father and fought in the revolution, but she insisted on helping you, because she's a good person."

György let out a long, resigned sigh, his face the very picture of wounded pride. "Aye, if she did that I'm not denying she has a kind heart. And mind you, I was young once. I can see the appeal of a lady like that—bright and pretty and charming. But I was here when you came back from Vienna in July, so miserable you were practically a ghost. I was half worried you'd fade away altogether. It's a powerful hold this woman's got on you, and my mind's not easy about it."

"It's only natural that she has a hold on me, isn't it? Considering that I love her."

"Oh, that's plain enough. Though I always thought, well." His father's voice took on a more wistful tone. "I reckoned you would fall for someone more suited to our family, that's all. Someone like your ma."

A sudden memory flashed into Andras's head of ten years prior, the Christmas after Kitti had been born. The family had been struggling more than usual, and Christmas presents had seemed out of the question until Anna had shown up one evening with an enormous box of animal-shaped marzipan candies, seemingly conjured out of nowhere. She'd never explained where she got the money, but it was the happiest Christmas Andras could remember.

And he knew, without a doubt, that Marta would have done exactly the same.

"Marta is like Ma," he said firmly. "I know you don't believe that yet, Pa, but you will. And until then, you'll have to get used to Marta being here, because she's staying."

It was four in the afternoon before Andras's sisters finally returned home—all three of them, to his pleasant surprise. The girls had clearly been to the shops as their arms were full of groceries, which they nearly dropped at the unexpected sight of their brother.

"Ilka!" Andras exclaimed. "What are you doing home?"

"The Grubers are on holiday this week and didn't take me along," Ilka said. "So the housekeeper let me take a few hours off today. But what are you doing home? Last I heard you were in England."

"I was in England. Though not anymore, obviously."

"But why?" Kitti asked. "Did something bad happen? Was there a war, or…"

"Kitti, darling, please keep your voice down. We have a guest."

"A guest?" said Ilka. "What sort of guest?"

Their father, who had been entirely absorbed in the newspaper, snorted. "Guest, my foot. Your brother's gone and brought his fancy woman here, and what he plans to do with her is anyone's guess."

"Fancy woman?" Jozefa's eyes lit up. "Andras, do you mean to say—"

She was cut off by the sound of the door to the other room creaking open. Marta emerged, rubbing her eyes, her hair adorably tousled.

"Andras?" she asked sleepily. "What's going on?"

"Hello, darling." He went to her and slipped an arm around her waist. "You've woken up just in time. Marta, these are my sisters, whose names you already know. Girls, this is Marta von Holstadt. My fiancée."

To the Király girls' credit, they were not shocked into silence. Instead, they immediately launched into a chorus of indistinguishable questions, all in Hungarian, making poor Marta look even more bewildered. Andras rolled his eyes and held up a hand to silence his sisters.

"Girls," he said, in slow, deliberate German. "I know you must have lots of questions, but if you'll please calm down, I can explain. Also, Marta doesn't speak Hungarian, so I think we should stick to German for now, all right?"

The girls quieted, chastened. And so for the second time that day, Andras explained the situation in which they now found themselves.

When he'd finished, Ilka—who was remaining admirably calm—gave Marta a brisk nod. "Welcome, Marta. We're very pleased to meet you at last. Would you like to come help us make dinner?"

With a hesitant smile, Marta gave Andras's hand one last squeeze before following Ilka and Kitti over to the stove. Jozefa, though, lingered behind for a moment.

"You sly dog," she said approvingly. "I didn't think you had it in you."

"Had what in me?"

"Eloping! With her! Must have taken some brains to pull it off."

"Most of the scheming was Marta, really. I just bought the false mustache and played along."

"The false…never mind, you can tell me later. I'm proud of you, is what I'm trying to say." She shot him a mischievous grin. "And I can see why you went to all the fuss too. She's very attractive. Better get married quick, before someone else snatches her up."

"You're terrible, Jozefa. Go help your sisters."

Ushered into the small kitchen area alongside the three other girls, Marta experienced an

overall sensation of strange familiarity. She'd heard so much about Andras's sisters and listened to all his stories about them, at this point she felt like she knew them a bit. But here they were in person, and it was extraordinary.

She found herself scanning their faces, picking out all resemblances to their brother. Kitti was the only one of the girls with Andras's dark red hair. Jozefa and Ilka both had light brown hair like their father's. Ilka and Kitti both had gray eyes, while Jozefa's were the same bright turquoise as her father's and brother's. But there were definite resemblances among all of them: the wide mouth, the long eyelashes, the air of compressed energy.

Marta was prepared to love them for that alone. She *would* love them, when they actually started talking to her.

All three of them were undoubtedly shocked, from the way they looked at her, barely saying a word. Marta couldn't blame them. It wasn't every day one's brother reappeared with his ex-countess fiancée in tow, though it was a tad embarrassing to have Kitti and Jozefa stare at her like she was an exotic creature from the Schönbrunn Zoo.

Ilka, at least, was reasonably composed. "Do you know how to chop onions?" she asked briskly.

Abashed, Marta shook her head. "Er… no. I'm sorry. I've never had the chance to learn."

Ilka chuckled, not unkindly. She was the musical one, Marta remembered Andras saying, the one who played the piano. And she was quite pretty too, sensitive-looking. "That's all right, it's not hard. Kitti, Jozefa, you can get out the rest of the groceries."

Jozefa followed orders, casting one more interested glance at Marta before setting about unpacking the groceries. Kitti, however, stayed in place, eyes narrowed.

"Are you really a countess?" she demanded. Her German was good, though she rolled her r's far more than her older siblings.

Finally, this was a question Marta could answer. "Yes, I am."

"Why?"

"Why am I a countess? Because my father was a count, I suppose. That's how titles work in Austria."

Kitti crossed her arms and frowned in a manner so reminiscent of Andras that Marta barely held back a laugh. "Why is your father a count?"

"Because, well, because one of my great-grandfathers saved the emperor from choking on a fish bone two hundred and fifty years ago, and got a title as a reward." How ridiculous that sounded, particularly when she was saying it in the kitchen of a two-room flat in Pest.

Kitti maintained her frown for approximately two seconds

before she broke out in peals of laughter. "A fish!" she cried. "Jozefa, did you hear? Marta is a countess because one of her grandfathers saved the emperor from a *fish*."

"Oh, I heard," Jozefa said wryly. "I almost wouldn't believe it, except I think ladies like Marta must be trained from birth not to lie. It sounds like something from a children's story."

"Yes, perhaps you'll put it in a book someday," said Ilka. "With Marta's permission, of course. We wouldn't like to give the von Holstadts a bad name."

"I don't want to be rude," said Jozefa, "but their daughter has just eloped with our brother, who is not only poor but spends all his time worrying and playing the violin. I don't think anything I could write about emperors and fish bones could cause any more of a scandal than that."

"Now, Jozefa, please."

"She's right," Marta cut in. In all the fuss, she hadn't given much thought to what her parents would do when they discovered her escape. Would they pretend she was still in England? Say she'd died? Or, perhaps, tell the truth? Probably not the latter. "My family will be doing their utmost to make sure this doesn't get out, I expect, but it's definitely the sort of thing that would cause a scandal. It's not me I'm worried about, nor Mama and Papa really. Everyone will just sympathize with them for having a mad daughter. But my brother, Heini, he…"

To her embarrassment, Marta felt tears welling up in her eyes. Her family was far away, undoubtedly furious with her, and perhaps she'd never see them again. "I miss him terribly. I don't want him to think I've abandoned him."

There was a long silence, before Ilka reached over and cautiously put an arm around Marta's shoulders.

"Well, you are here now," she said. "But this is not a good time to be thinking about the future. You've had a long journey, and you must be very hungry. Come, you can help us make goulash. I'll show you how."

That evening, sitting on the roof with a blanket spread out beneath him, Andras reflected on the events of the day.

Dinner had gone as well as could be expected, under the circumstances. True, Pa had been unable to understand most of the conversations in German and thus spent the meal in taciturn silence, but the girls had seemed to accept Marta as one of their own. György, well…he would come around in his own time.

Soft footsteps from behind caught his attention, and Andras turned to see Marta, wearing one of his mother's old nightgowns with Ilka's green shawl around her shoulders. Her loose dark hair whipped around her shoulders, and once again Andras marveled that someone so beautiful had given up so much for him.

"Good evening, my love," he said, smiling broadly. "How did you find your way up here?"

"I followed you, naturally. And I must say, it's entirely too easy to get up here. It would be child's play to rob this building."

"It would be indeed, if anyone who lived here had anything worth stealing. But come have a seat." He patted the blanket next to him. Marta obediently sat, arranged her nightgown modestly, and leaned against his shoulder, sending waves of warmth through his body.

"Have the girls been friendly?" Andras asked. "I know they can be overly curious, but they seem to like you a great deal."

"Your sisters," she said with a smile, "are everything I expected them to be. I can see why you're so devoted to them. And Ilka's a brilliant cook. It was very kind of her to teach me how to chop onions." She sighed. "It seems there's a lot I need to learn."

"Are you all right? I know this has been the oddest week of my life, and it must be even harder for you. After all, here you are in a foreign city, you don't know the language, our home is shabby at best…"

"It's not those things, not really. I can adapt, you know that. I can," Marta said fiercely, sounding as though she was trying to convince herself. "I just feel so guilty."

"About running away from your family? I understand, but remember, they sent you away in the first place."

"Not about my family. That's for me to come to terms with when I can," she said. "But you can't imagine how awful I feel. I show up to your family's home and throw myself on their mercy with nothing to give them in return, after costing you your job—twice. It's no wonder your father hates me."

"You've helped us plenty, and my father doesn't hate you."

"Perhaps hate's too strong a word. But he doesn't approve of me, and why should he? I'm not the kind of wife anyone around here expected for you."

"And I'm hardly the husband Viennese society wanted for you," Andras replied. "So that makes things even, doesn't it? In this neighborhood people don't spend their days fussing over who wore peacock feathers to a ball. Yes, it will take them some time to get used to you, especially my father. But once we're married, especially as long as we invite everyone, they'll soon get over the shock."

"Married." Marta sighed and rested her head on his shoulder. "It seems surreal, doesn't it? Not that I don't want to marry you, but somehow it hasn't sunk in yet."

"Hmm," he said. "I can't blame you for feeling that way. I haven't even proposed to you yet, not properly. However, that's easily rectified." He withdrew from his pocket the last thing he'd purchased in England. A thin, cheap, gold-plated ring.

She could still say no. She could realize he didn't deserve her, turn back, return to her family. But Andras knew he had to ask anyway.

"I was waiting for the right moment to do all this," he said, "and now seems as good a time as any. I know it's redundant after all we've been through, but will you marry me, Marta? Even if all I can offer you is a cramped flat and shared custody of Clara?"

"Yes," she said immediately. Her smile broadened and her eyes sparkled with pure delight. "Yes, please. And as quickly as possible, if you don't mind. I'm very tired of not being a Király."

Andras laughed and pulled her closer, feeling a shiver of desire run through him at the feeling of her lush, warm body pressed against him. There would be plenty of time to think about that later, though, once they were husband and wife and their bed was no one else's business.

"You're going to love it here," he murmured against her hair. "I'll make sure of it."

CHAPTER TWENTY-SEVEN

(In Which Szerdahelyi Street Celebrates)

THE KIRÁLYS MIGHT have been short on money, but they certainly weren't short on neighbors. Once it had become public knowledge that Andras Király was not only back in town but getting married, no force on earth could have stopped the entirety of Szerdahelyi Street from contributing in any way possible.

Mrs. Farkas from downstairs, upon hearing of the upcoming nuptials, browbeat her brother who owned the local beer hall into hosting the post-wedding party for free and providing all the guests with his least expensive wine and beer. Not to be outdone, Mr. Smirnov, who had been a deserter from the Russian army in 1849, dug ten dusty bottles of vodka out of his cupboard. The Lakatos family from down the street offered to provide all necessary music while the Turkish Kartals insisted on providing köfte and baklava for all and sundry.

For Marta, who had been silently dreading a hasty and severe ceremony with no celebration, the generosity of the Királys' neighbors seemed like nothing less than a miracle. These people knew nothing about her, didn't even speak the same language, and yet they were offering their time, money, and effort to give her and Andras a proper wedding. Proof, she supposed, of how well-loved he and his family were.

There was, of course, the matter of what Marta would wear. The glorious white wedding gown of the type worn by Queen Victoria did not seem likely to manifest itself, and there was little money to spend on new clothes anyway. In the end it was

Kitti who discovered a solution, digging about in one of the cupboards until she found a carefully wrapped bundle, which she deposited on Marta's lap.

"What is it?" Marta asked, sniffing it carefully. It smelled a bit musty, but not unpleasant.

Kitti shook her head and bounced eagerly up and down on her heels. "Open it," she said. "It's brilliant."

Marta untied the frayed ribbon that held the bundle together and carefully unfolded the contents. She took a sharp breath as she saw what Kitti had given her.

It was a peasant costume, and quite a beautiful one at that. The pleated red skirt, puff-sleeved white blouse, and finely woven apron had been meticulously sewn, and nearly every inch of fabric was covered in the most beautiful embroidery Marta had ever seen. She delightedly ran a hand over the intricate patterns of flowers and vines on the hem of the skirt.

"This is beautiful! Was your mother's family from the Kalocsa district? The clothes from there are wonderful. I've always wanted to make an apron like this. The embroidery is so detailed."

Kitti giggled. "Andras said you knew a lot about clothes. Ilka, Jozefa, look." She waved urgently at her older sisters, who had just come in and were chattering eagerly in Hungarian.

Jozefa stopped short, eyes wide. "Is that Ma's old festival dress?" she asked.

"It is," Ilka said breathlessly. "I haven't seen it in years. Did you get it out of the cupboard, Kitti?"

Kitti nodded and launched into a rapid explanation in Hungarian before Ilka held up a hand. "In German, please. So Marta can understand you."

"I think," Kitti said, in careful German, "that it can be the wedding dress. Ma will like it. Won't she?"

Ilka and Jozefa glanced at one another hesitantly, Jozefa's eyebrows drawing together in what Marta assumed was disapproval.

"I won't wear it," Marta said quickly. "Not if you don't want me to. It's obviously irreplaceable."

"Ma wore that to every wedding and party in the neighborhood," Jozefa said quietly. "You were too young to remember, Kitti, but she would always sit next to Pa so that he wouldn't feel left out during the dancing. And then Pa would tell her to go ahead and dance because he wanted everyone to know that his wife was the handsomest and most talented woman in the room."

Ilka let out a giggle. "And if Andras was around Ma would always dance with him, and he would look so serious and try to get every step right, and he would always trip over his own big feet!"

"He would get so embarrassed." Jozefa snickered. "And Ma would pretend to trip over something too to give him a laugh." She turned to Marta, who had been listening intently. "I think Kitti is right. Ma would like it if that dress was worn to one more wedding. Especially if you plan to make Andras trip while wearing it."

"Thank you," Marta whispered, a lump rising in her throat. "You can't possibly know what this means to me."

I will be worthy of it, she told herself firmly as the Király girls laughed and fell back into conversation. *I will.*

October 15
Marta's Last Day as a Single Woman

The day of the wedding dawned bright, early, and chilly, the sunlight weakly making its way through the patched curtains in the Király girls' bedroom. Marta awoke early, stretching carefully to avoid hitting Ilka, whose bed she was sharing. On the other bed, Jozefa and Kitti were still asleep, Jozefa snoring loudly while Kitti pulled most of the blankets over to her side.

Beside Marta, Ilka yawned and stretched, lifting herself up to a seat on the edge of the bed. "Good morning, Marta. Ready to get married?"

"Of course she is," Jozefa called sleepily. "Can't wait to get out of this flat, I expect. Even if she has to marry our worthless brother to do it." She yawned and stretched, elbowing Kitti awake. "Get up, Kitti, we'll make some breakfast. You'll need to keep your strength up for today, Marta."

Andras wasn't at breakfast. To avoid any potential bad luck, he'd spent the night in the Farkases' flat downstairs. This was sensible, but Marta still wished he was with her. The last time they'd spent the night together had been on the train from Paris. The second-class car was too public for them to do anything but hold each other, but they'd stayed up half the night anyway, talking about everything that had happened since they'd been apart and agreeing that it was never allowed to happen again.

They were so close to not having to be separated again. Once they were married, nothing and no one would be able to keep them apart.

"Are you nervous, Marta?" Ilka asked, misinterpreting Marta's silence. "I would be, if it were my wedding."

"Not too late to run away," Jozefa said, through a mouthful of *kifli* pastry. "I'd still like you."

"I'm not nervous," Marta said quickly. "More impatient. I just want to be married, and not have to sit around waiting."

Ilka grinned and stood, pushing her chair away. "I know just the cure for that. Let's get you dressed up."

Anna Király's peasant costume had fortunately needed few alterations to make it fit. The hem of the red skirt was shorter than what Marta was accustomed to wearing, but not indecently so, and combined with the white blouse and floral apron the effect was very charming. Ilka helped Marta dress her hair, dividing it into two braids which she twisted into a knot at the base of Marta's neck, and pinned a small lace cap on top while Jozefa helped Kitti get dressed.

Finally, Marta stood in front of the old, spotty mirror in the girls' bedroom, staring at herself—or a version of herself, if she'd been born a Hungarian peasant girl—in surprise.

Ilka sighed with happiness. "You look beautiful, Marta. It's a perfect wedding dress."

"At least it will be until Andras rips it to shreds," said Jozefa, with a rude laugh. She, like the other girls, had changed into her best dress, a frock of dark blue wool with only one patch on the elbow. "Don't all men—"

"Jozefa, not in front of Kitti," Ilka ordered. "If you're not going to behave you can go downstairs and sit with the men."

Jozefa wrinkled her nose. "No thank you. Have you seen Andras when he's nervous? He looks like a ghost and gets all… what's the word? Twitchy. Like a rabbit. Why are you marrying him, Marta?"

Marta shrugged. "Because I have nothing better to do with my time. Besides, even twitchy ghosts need someone to look after them." She frowned at her reflection and adjusted the lace cap over her hair. It was so strange, wearing Anna Király's old dress, as if she'd been part of the family for decades.

"Are you sure you want me as a sister?" she asked suddenly. "I can't be the sort of person you imagined your brother marrying."

Jozefa snorted. "True, but only because you're not a violin. Humans aren't allowed to marry instruments, are they?"

"I doubt the church would condone it," said Ilka. "But really, Marta, the answer is quite simple. We want you as our sister because our brother loves you. You weren't here before he went to England, but we were, and he was miserable."

"He cried sometimes," Kitti put in helpfully. "I heard him."

"And I was the only one he complained to." Jozefa rolled her eyes. "Marta, you are doing us all a very large favor by marrying him. Please take him off our hands and keep him happy so we don't have to deal with that again. I promise we will love you for it."

It was sheer force of will—and the desire to not have puffy eyes at her own wedding—that prevented Marta from bursting into tears.

She wasn't allowed to see Andras before the wedding, but as it happened, he was not the Király man she wanted to see when she arrived at the small, simply decorated neighborhood church.

György Király sat in the front pew, wearing a long white tunic and a gray waistcoat with embroidery similar to Marta's apron. Anna Király's work, presumably. He glanced towards Marta as he heard her approach, before looking away again sharply.

"Mr. Király?" Marta said hesitantly. If only she could actually speak Hungarian. As it was, she'd have to hope he could understand her tone. "May I talk to you?"

He gave her a gruff nod, and Marta sat in the pew next to him. "The thing is, Mr. Király, I want to thank you."

His bushy eyebrows drew together in suspicion. "Thank, eh?"

At least he'd understood that part. "Yes, thank. You and your family have been very good to me since I got here, and I am so grateful. I know you don't trust me yet. I understand, I do. But I hope you will soon."

"Hm." He looked at her appraisingly. "Tell me, Countess," he said, in heavily accented German. "You lof him? Andras. You lof my son?"

Marta could not have definitively answered, at that moment, any inquiries about who she was or what would become of her. But the question her future father-in-law asked was one that she could answer without hesitation.

"Yes," she said. "Yes, I love him very much. Always." She boldly reached out and put a hand on his shoulder. "*Tántoríthatatlanság.*" Her pronunciation was probably dreadful, but hopefully he had understood: *Unshakeability.*

He seemed to understand, and his ruddy face creased in a wide smile. "Good," he said, patting her hand. "Very good."

The wedding ceremony was, in a word, efficient.

Not unpleasantly so. There were flowers scattered around the church, and hymns sung, and those of the Királys' neighbors who were present were full of good cheer. And while Andras wasn't dressed in a top hat and silk coat, the peasant suit he had on was just as flattering. Distractingly so, in fact. The pomp and circumstance Marta had experienced at so many aristocratic weddings, though—the hours-long speeches, the family jewels brought out from vaults, the suffocating air of superiority—was conspicuously absent.

None of that mattered. Nor did the many unfamiliar eyes upon her, or the chill in the air, or the fact that her wedding blouse and apron were slightly too tight across the chest. What mattered was, when the priest asked something in Hungarian, and when Andras nodded at her and smiled, Marta squared her shoulders and answered.

"*Igen.*"

Which, if she hadn't been misled, meant: "Yes."

Whatever she'd said, it seemed to work. Father Jonas said a few more phrases in Hungarian and gave them a beatific smile, and the organ started up again as Andras led Marta back down the aisle. People were calling good wishes from the pews, but Marta, deep in thought, barely noticed. Much as she might have felt like the same person on the inside, in the eyes of God and the Austro-Hungarian Empire, Marta von Holstadt no longer existed. That woman had been replaced by Mrs. Marta Király, wife of a Hungarian nobody.

It was the end of her old life. She would be dead to everyone in Vienna now. Even Sophie would probably be forbidden from speaking to her. And yet, somehow, Marta had never been happier.

At the beer hall where the post-wedding party was being held, there was no time for feeling any sadness. The place was packed to the limit, noise and color and laughter filling up every corner. There was food to be eaten, drinks to be imbibed, and neighbors to meet. After, on Ilka's instructions, taking off her shoes and placing them on one of the tables for no reason she could determine, Marta had her cheeks pinched by Mrs. Farkas, received an incoherent lecture from Mr. Smirnov, and received effusive congratulations from what seemed like a thousand different families. The experience would have been much more overwhelming if she hadn't had at least one of the Király siblings with her at all times to translate and guide her about the room.

"I can see I'm going to have to learn Hungarian quickly," she remarked to Jozefa at one point, Andras having been dragged off by a few other young men from the neighborhood, presumably to drink and sing bawdy songs. "After all, I can't ask your family to translate everything I say to your neighbors for the rest of my life."

"No indeed," said Jozefa solemnly. "Especially as I've been mistranslating half of what you say. I told Mrs. Lakatos that your family owns Croatia."

"You did what?"

"Nothing. Oh, something's happening!" Over the last few minutes the center of the hall had been cleared, with all the guests gathered at the sides of the room. Jozefa waved eagerly at Ilka, who slid to a stop in front of them. "Ilka! Is it time?"

"Yes." Ilka grinned, her cheeks flushed prettily. "Marta, you've got to get out there, it's the coin dance!"

"The what?"

"The coin dance," Ilka repeated. "It's a tradition. Didn't you wonder why we made you leave your shoes on the table? The men drop coins into them in exchange for a dance. I had a peek and it looks like every man in the room has put in one."

"Ah." Marta did not entirely like the idea of this. Tradition was one thing, but dancing for money…

Noticing her discomfort, Ilka laughed. "I promise, there's nothing sordid about it. It's simply a nice way for the neighborhood to give you and Andras a wedding present. And just think what a thrill it'll give all the old men, dancing with a beautiful Austrian countess."

"Former countess," Marta corrected her. "I'm a Király now. But if it'll give the old men a thrill *and* help us pay the rent, who am I to refuse?"

"That's the spirit." After allowing Marta to put her shoes back on, Ilka took her arm and marched her to the center of the floor, raising her hands and calling something out in Hungarian. A few laughs and cheers rose up from the guests, and an elderly man in peasant costume stepped out of the crowd, politely holding out one hand.

"Király Marta," he said, in gruffly accented German. "You will dance?"

Marta grinned and took his hand, nerves subsiding. He looked as though he would go easy on her. "*Igen.* I most certainly will."

For the next hour, or possibly longer, Marta's feet barely stopped moving for a second. This wasn't like the stately balls she'd grown up attending; this was proper, boot-slapping Hungarian dancing, without the least bit of restraint. The men were kind, though, and helped her through all the steps, and not once did anyone laugh at her for stumbling, which she did frequently.

It wasn't until her feet were hurting like mad and her head

was spinning enough to fall off that she was deposited back in a familiar pair of arms.

"Hello, darling," said Andras with a grin. "Enjoying yourself?"

"Oh!" said Marta. "It's you. I haven't seen you for a while." Her new husband looked unbearably handsome. He always did, but something about that white shirt and embroidered waistcoat—so much less somber than his usual clothes. She could hardly wait to get back to their new flat and pounce on him like a cat in heat.

"Surely you didn't think you were going to dance with every man in the neighborhood and not your husband?" Andras's eyes twinkled, and he looked Marta up and down admiringly. "I haven't yet had a chance to say this, but you look incredibly ravishing. Apparently you dressing like a peasant girl is fulfilling an unconscious fantasy of mine. Don't say anything in Hungarian until we get home, though. I'm trying to maintain some dignity. It was bad enough thinking all those unholy thoughts about you in church. Have you noticed that blouse is *very* tight?"

She had noticed this, but the way his hot gaze raked over her body made her clothes feel even tighter. The only comfort was that judging from the look on her husband's face, he was nearly as uncomfortably aroused as she was.

Well, no reason not to torture him a bit more. With a wicked grin, Marta leaned in and whispered "*Igen, drágám.*"

Andras groaned deeply. "Now you're just trying to humiliate me. It's a good thing I'm wearing a long shirt." He put a hand on Marta's back to steady her as she nearly stumbled. "Are you all right?"

"Just dizzy. Lots of spinning, combined with a bit of Mr. Smirnov's vodka."

"A dangerous combination. Perhaps we should switch to some slower music."

He nodded at the band, who struck up a lively tune it took Marta a second to recognize.

"Andras!" she exclaimed. "This is the song you wrote for me, isn't it? The one you were working on back in Vienna?"

"It is indeed," he replied. "Not the venue I'd imagined for the premiere of *The von Holstadt Waltz*, but I thought it might add some elegance to the proceedings. And oddly, in all the time we've known each other I don't believe we've ever had a proper dance together."

"We've really gone about this backwards. Most couples start by dancing together, then get married, and finally go to bed together. We've done things in the exact opposite order."

"Yet I wouldn't change a thing. In fact, I think we've had a finer wedding than any of your high society friends could hope for." Andras bowed deeply, holding out his hand. "May I have this dance, Mrs. Király?"

Smiling, Marta took his hand. "You may, Mr. Király. You absolutely may."

CHAPTER TWENTY-EIGHT

(In Which Several Suspicions are Confirmed)

1869 WAS CERTAINLY a year of firsts, Marta thought. Her first time making love, her first Hungarian wedding, and now, not long into her life as a married lady, her first job interview.

It was thanks to György that she had an interview at all. He'd been more kindly disposed to her ever since the wedding, which Marta attributed partially to her own efforts and partially to his desire for grandchildren. Whatever the reason, her father-in-law seemed to consider it his duty to keep her sensibly occupied.

"I've heard about a job that might suit you," he'd explained at one Sunday dinner, via Andras. "Old Aliz Nagy from the linens shop on Prater Street has been looking for girls who can sew. Mrs. Farkas knows her, she'll arrange an interview. After all, you do know about sewing." He'd added something in Hungarian afterward that Andras hadn't translated—probably "even though you can't do anything else."

Naturally, Marta was grateful. Andras had regained his job at the tobacconist, which was wonderful, but it didn't pay much, and Marta had been longing to contribute. Besides, hadn't she always wanted to be gainfully employed? Being paid to sew was practically a dream come true. She repeated this in her mind over and over as she was shown to the small, neat office in the back of Nagy's Fine Linens on Prater Street.

Madame Aliz Nagy was a wiry, gray-haired woman of middle years, who spoke German with a clipped accent and sat at her desk like a queen on a throne. Marta had heard she was an excellent and highly efficient businesswoman, something that was easy to believe. Hopefully she wouldn't be able to tell Marta was terrified of her.

"You have no employment experience whatsoever, Mrs. Király?" Madame Nagy frowned at Marta's uncalloused hands. "Never worked at all?"

"I wouldn't say that exactly," Marta replied. "I've *worked* very hard before. It's only that I've never had a job, so to speak."

"But you can sew, I take it."

"Oh, yes," said Marta eagerly. From her reticule she pulled a linen handkerchief embroidered with a pattern of roses, made with Anna Király's old embroidery materials. "This is my work."

Madame Nagy adjusted her monocle and inspected the small, neat stitches. "Not terrible," she said. "But I expect my girls to work. This won't be like sitting in the parlor and sewing while you gossip."

"I understand, truly." Marta tried hard to keep the desperation out of her voice. "I promise I'll work hard."

"Hmm." Madame Nagy shook her head. "It's unfortunate that you don't speak Hungarian."

"Not much," Marta admitted. "However, I do speak German, French, Italian, and English, which may come in handy. Besides, Andras is teaching me Hungarian."

"Andras?"

"Yes, my husband. Andras Király."

"Good heavens. Not the little red-haired boy with the violin? György's eldest?"

"He's not really a little boy anymore, but yes."

"How extraordinary," Madame Nagy said in astonishment. "Little Andras. When my late husband was ailing Andras would come over every Saturday to play the violin for him. Janos always said that music was better than any medicine. But I heard he'd gone to Vienna, to play for the opera. How did he wind up married to an Austrian aristocrat?"

Marta froze. "Aristocrat?"

Madame Nagy snorted. "My God, girl. You come in here, never having had a job in your life, speaking four languages, and you expect me not to realize your background? If you want me to consider hiring you, you had better tell me your story."

Taking a deep breath, hands twisting nervously in her lap, Marta told her.

Madame Nagy was quiet for a long time afterward, and Marta sat utterly still, willing the *langos* she'd had for luncheon to stay put in her stomach. Andras had been so kind as she was preparing for this interview, assuring her that if Madame Nagy didn't give her the job he wouldn't blame Marta at all, but she couldn't bear to go home and tell him she'd failed.

"Well, Mrs. Király," Madame Nagy said at last. "You can sew well enough, and the Királys are a good family. I won't have folk saying I didn't help them when I could have. I'll take you on for a month's trial at four forint a week, and if you work hard I'll consider keeping you permanently."

"Oh, thank you, Madame Nagy," Marta exclaimed. "You won't regret this, I swear."

"I regret it already," replied Madame Nagy, with the slightest of smiles. "One more thing. If someone were to come in here and ask if I employ a Mrs. Király, I would have to say yes. I don't hold with lying. Unchristian habit."

"Naturally."

"But if someone were to ask me if I knew of a Countess von Holstadt, I would say no. This is a humble establishment, after all. We do not employ countesses."

Marta nearly fainted with relief. "No, no. Of course you don't."

"You got the job?" Andras said delightedly, upon Marta's arrival home. "Good old Madame Nagy. Did you have to drop my name?"

"I am deeply offended that you think she wouldn't hire me based on my skills alone," Marta teased. "As it happens, I did drop your name, and she told me all about how you used to play the violin for her sick husband. She insisted we come by for dinner sometime."

"I remember Mr. Nagy," said Andras wistfully. "He told absolutely awful jokes. I truly am sorry, Marta." His voice suddenly was serious. "This can't be how you imagined life as a newlywed, living in this poky flat and both of us having to work."

"Oh, my darling," she sighed, wrapping her arms around his waist and leaning her head on his chest. "You're right. This is not precisely what I pictured. But we are together, and married, and close to your family, and all things considered it's really not bad at all."

He buried his face in her hair. "It won't be like this forever, I promise," he said. "One of the local opera companies will have an open spot one of these days. It'll be all right."

"Of course it will," said Marta with a confidence she did not quite feel. "This is you and I we're talking about."

The reasons for Marta's exile had not been explained to Sophie Stein with any degree of honesty; the hastily scribbled letter Marta had sent claimed she was going to England "for her health" with no further elaboration. This was so patently ridiculous that Sophie did not believe it for a minute. People left England for their health and, if they had any common sense at all, never returned.

Jacob and Rachel Stein were annoyingly unwilling to entertain Sophie's primary theory that Marta was being punished for something. Even after Sophie laid out her concerns—that Marta was neither a professor nor a poet and thus had no business in Oxford, that the only illnesses people were treated for in England were hysteria and insanity—Mrs. Stein hadn't listened. Instead, she had simply rolled her eyes and explained that the von Holstadts were lovely people who surely knew what they were doing, and if Sophie didn't calm herself people would start thinking *she* had hysteria.

With no familial support, Sophie resigned herself to gleaning what information she could from Marta's occasional letters, which were far from encouraging. While generally Marta's correspondence would be full of witty remarks and interesting anecdotes, the notes she sent from Oxford were colorless and dry, relating the same information over and over. Yes, she was well enough. Yes, the Achterburgs were kind hosts. Yes, the weather and food were considerably different from Austria. And there was nothing more to say about any of it.

This, Sophie considered to be proof. Her friend was being punished for something.

But for what?

A few weeks later, she very much found out.

This revelation took the form of Ludwig von Braumark arriving at the house unannounced in mid-October and demanding to see her. He looked the worse for wear, his usually neatly combed hair sticking up in bunches and his eyes hollow, and were his spectacles *smudged*?

"I need to speak to you alone, Sophie," he said breathlessly. "It's nothing improper, but it is an emergency."

"I can tell," Sophie replied, looking him up and down with raised eyebrows. She nodded at the footman who had let Ludwig in and the man reluctantly departed, hopefully not to tell Mrs. Stein that Sophie was having a rendezvous in the sitting room.

"All right, Ludwig," said Sophie as soon as the servant's footsteps had faded away down the hall. "What's got you kicking up such a fuss?"

Ludwig collapsed onto an overstuffed, floral-patterned chair like he'd just run thirty miles. "Sophie," he said. "You need to tell me. Do you know where Marta is?"

"Where she is?" asked Sophie. She did not like the ominous tone of Ludwig's voice. "She's in Oxford visiting relatives. Mind you, I don't believe it's for her health. There's absolutely something fishy going on there, but…"

"But she's not in Oxford anymore," Ludwig said miserably. "That's the thing. I've just been at the von Holstadts' and according to them, the Achterburgs haven't seen her in days. She's disappeared."

"Disappeared?" Sophie swallowed, trying to ignore a prickle of fear. People didn't simply disappear, especially not ones as rich, pretty, and loud as Marta. "What do you mean?"

"I mean what I say. According to Count von Holstadt, the Achterburgs received a note from Marta last Sunday saying she couldn't stay with them anymore, and no information on where she'd gone." Ludwig sighed and rubbed his forehead. "The count and countess are out of their minds with worry, as I'm sure you can imagine. Only they're not sure what to do, because they're desperate to keep a scandal from breaking."

"Marta is missing and they're worried about a scandal?" Sophie exclaimed, wrath flaring up inside her chest. "You know, I shouldn't be surprised by this point but I truly am. Why are everyone in our parents' generation such absolute fools?"

"Now, Sophie, I completely understand you're upset, but…"

"You're damn right I'm upset." Sophie snarled. She paced back and forth in front of the coffee table. "My best friend has gone missing and her family's worried about a scandal! And why was she sent to England in the first place, Ludwig? Do you have any idea?"

"Of course I know why Marta was sent away," Ludwig said glumly. "It was my fault."

Sophie stopped in her tracks, blood running cold. "*Your* fault?"

"Yes. Marta was… well, it turns out she was in love with that music teacher of hers. The Hungarian one."

"Andras Király?" Sophie frowned, not certain if she could believe him. Surely if Marta was in love, she would have told Sophie about it, unless she thought Sophie wouldn't approve… but how could Marta have so little faith in her? They were supposed to be friends. "I know she was fond of him…"

"She was in love with him. Really, properly in love, and he loved her too. And when I found out about their affair—I expect I was jealous, really."

"You…" Sophie choked out. "Ludwig, please tell me you didn't tell her parents."

"Worse than that," he whispered, hands twisting. "I helped the count catch them together. It was awful, Sophie. I thought he was going to kill one of them. I felt horrible immediately, but what could I do at that point? Ouch!" He rubbed his shoulder, where the teaspoon Sophie threw had hit him. "What was that for?"

"You idiot. You selfish, jealous fool! Poor Marta's been exiled to England because you couldn't keep your mouth shut, and now we might never see her again. I should take you to the zoo and throw you to the lions."

"There's no need to try and make me feel guiltier, I couldn't possibly feel worse than I do now," Ludwig said. "And you don't know the half of it. Mr. Király's been sacked from the Odysseum, the count made sure of that, and now Brigita will barely speak to me."

"Brigita?"

"One of the dancers from the opera ballet," he said, without further explanation. Sophie had a feeling there was plenty he was neglecting to tell her, but truthfully, she didn't care much.

"Well, Ludwig," she said. "You've made quite a hash of things. I think you know what you must do now."

"Become a monk, I think," Ludwig said despondently. "I'll look a right fool with half my head shaved, but if it's my only chance at penance…"

"No, you simpleton, you're not going to become a monk. You are going to help me find Marta. Use those two brain cells of yours and tell me where you think she would have gone."

He wrinkled his brow. "Hmm. If she's disappeared from Oxford, it must be something to do with that Király fellow, yes? And I think… yes, I'm certain he has family in Budapest, I heard Brigita mention it once." He looked up at Sophie hopefully. "Do you think that's where she's gone?"

"I wouldn't be surprised." Sophie paced back and forth, thinking. "But Budapest is a large city. We'll need more information." She reflected, then snapped her fingers. "Your friend Brigita. She knows Andras, doesn't she? Perhaps she'll have an address for his family."

"She may not listen to me. As I mentioned, we're not on the best of terms."

"Obviously not. This is all your fault. But it's possible she'll listen to me. I'm a fellow woman, and it's my best friend who's gone missing. Get your father's carriage, we're going to the theatre."

The young copper-haired woman who met them at the stage door—Brigita, presumably—did not seem pleased to see them.

"No," she said, before Ludwig even had a chance to say

anything, and started to shut the door. He bravely stuck his foot out, wincing as the door pinched his toes.

"Brigita, I know you're upset with me," he said. "I deserve to have you upset with me, but we should discuss that later. I—we—need your help."

She pushed the door open a bit wider and cast a suspicious glance at Sophie. "Who's this?"

Sophie held out a gloved hand. "Sophie Stein. And you are Miss Novak, I assume. I believe we have a friend in common."

"Ah," said Brigita, giving her a limp handshake. "You must mean Marta."

"I do. And I'm not sure if you've heard, but she's disappeared."

"Really!" Brigita exclaimed, glaring at Ludwig. "Because the last I heard, she'd been kicked out of the country and my dear friend had got the sack after Baron von Braumark here decided to go about telling people things that weren't his business." To Sophie's surprise, Brigita's lip trembled, and her eyes sparkled with what might have been tears. "I cared for you so much, Lud… sir. All that time we spent talking together, you were so kind to me, and I thought we could have… but it seems I was wrong about you."

"Brigita, you must believe how sorry I am," Ludwig pleaded. Sophie had never seen him so overcome with emotion. His face had gone red and blotchy, and he was actually gesturing. "I want nothing more than to be the man you thought I was, but we can discuss that at a later point. Marta's not in Oxford anymore, she's vanished."

"Vanished? Good for her. I hope she stays well away from the lot of you for the rest of her life." She tried to close the door again, though Sophie stopped her.

"Miss Novak, I completely understand how you must feel," said Sophie, summoning up her most diplomatic tone. "But I can promise you I don't mean Marta any harm, I just want to know if she's all right. Your friend Andras is the person most likely to know where she is. Haven't you got a way to reach him?"

"Maybe," said Brigita with a shrug. "If I trust you, what's in it for me?"

Sophie had to admit, she liked this girl's spark. Perhaps that was why Ludwig was so obviously infatuated with her. "I'm happy to reward you for your help," she said, taking out her purse. "Name your price, Miss Novak."

"I don't want your money," Brigita spat out. She turned to Ludwig, arms folded authoritatively. "I think you know what I want, Ludwig. And you won't be getting the Király family's address until I get it."

Ludwig and Brigita stared at each other for a long moment, something Sophie didn't understand passing between them. Finally, to her shock, Ludwig dropped to his knees on the dirty cobblestones.

"All right, then. I was planning to do this somewhere nicer, but considering the circumstances." He cleared his throat. "Brigita Novak, will you…"

Sophie returned home not long afterward, feeling as though she had wandered into a dream. Mrs. Stein looked up from her newspaper in surprise as Sophie stumbled into the parlor.

"My goodness, dear, you look odd. Are you feeling quite all right?"

"I just witnessed one of the strangest interactions of the nineteenth century," she said. "But that's not important. I think I need to go visit Aunt Johanna in Budapest."

Several streets away, Ludwig von Braumark returned to his rooms, walking with a sense of purpose he hadn't experienced in a long time. There was no time for abstract contemplations. He knew what he was doing, and he'd have to do it quickly, before he lost his nerve.

As he dug through the piles of academic papers on the floor to find the clothes he would need, Ludwig caught sight of himself in the mirror and laughed. His face was flushed, his hair stuck up, his spectacles were smudged—and he didn't think he'd ever looked better.

No more duty. No more shame. Nothing but a bright future ahead of him.

"I'm marrying Brigita Novak," he told his reflection cheerfully. "As soon as possible. Because I love her."

CHAPTER TWENTY-NINE

(In Which it Transpires that Being Poor is Not Very Nice)

DESPITE HER EXPENSIVE education, as she settled into her new life Marta discovered a great many things she couldn't do.

She couldn't cook.

She couldn't mop the floor without trapping herself in a corner.

She couldn't do laundry, couldn't speak Hungarian, and could never get the frying pan entirely clean. In short, she was the most useless new bride Szerdahelyi Street had ever known.

Her job at Nagy's Fine Linens was the only area of her life where she felt remotely competent. Madame Nagy hadn't lied about the work being hard—it was, and Marta came home nearly every night with tired eyes and aching fingers. But sewing was something she had been doing her entire life. Sitting in the back room of the shop and painstakingly embroidering roses onto pillowcases was the one part of the day where she wasn't going to set dinner on fire or fail to remove a coffee stain from Andras's shirt.

The work was demanding but doable, and the shop itself was a pleasant enough place. Madame Nagy was a brisk but kind employer, and Marta's colleagues had done their best to be welcoming. Of the three of them, only Valeria spoke much German. She'd gone to primary school with Andras and her mother was the local midwife. With Valeria's help and occasional translation, Marta found having a job was beginning to feel ordinary rather than terrifying.

Over the two months since their wedding, she and Andras had

settled into something of a routine. After a long day at work for both of them, Andras would usually cook dinner. Never anything elaborate, but always delicious. In the evenings they would play music or read to each other before falling into bed and, as Andras put it, "getting to work on our family."

Sundays were the best day of the week by far. Each Sunday morning they would join the other Királys at the neighborhood church, where Marta was finally beginning to understand parts of Father Jonas's sermons. Afterward they would head to the elder Mr. Király's flat to cook a hearty Sunday lunch and spend the afternoon playing cards. Andras and his sisters had introduced Marta to a game they'd invented in which the stakes were embarrassing secrets instead of money. Despite their differences, Marta remained astonished at just how welcome the Királys had made her.

It wasn't easy, her new life. She hadn't expected it to be easy. But she had a family, and that counted for a great deal.

Now, as the temperatures dropped and the days grew shorter, Marta bent over a pillowcase, carefully tracing a design of ivy leaves onto the ivory linen. She bit back a curse as her hand slipped. This was the third time today, which was concerning. Her head had been fuzzy all morning, and nothing she did seemed to improve it. And her stomach felt dreadful.

At Marta's hiss of annoyance, Valeria glanced up from her work, eyes narrowing in concern. "You all right, Mrs. Király?"

She did so enjoy being called Mrs. Király. "Quite all right, though I've been dizzy all day. I'm probably just tired."

Valeria pursed her lips, thinking, then nodded. "Go make some peppermint tea and rest for a few minutes before you sew your fingers together. Madame Nagy doesn't like dawdling but she likes injuries even less."

With a sigh of relief Marta stood, one hand clinging to the edge of the table for support as she inched towards the back room where the teapot was kept. Really, it was unacceptable for her to behave like this when she was still so new to the job. Hopefully a hot drink would get her back to normal.

Approximately two steps away from her goal, though, a wave

of dizziness hit her so hard that she stumbled and dropped to her knees in the middle of the floor.

Vaguely, she heard Valeria exclaim in surprise and rush over to help her to her feet. "Mrs. Király, you can't work like this. We've got to get you out of here before you fall to pieces."

"I can't leave, Madame Nagy would be furious."

Valeria called out something in Hungarian over her shoulder, guiding Marta gently towards the door. "It's all right," she told Marta. "Madame Nagy's not upset. Let's go."

"Go where?" Marta murmured. Her head felt like it was stuffed with wool, and it was difficult to put one foot in front of the other. "Home?"

"Soon, but not yet," Valeria replied briskly. "First we've got to visit my ma."

Andras was not surprised when he arrived home to see Marta sitting at the kitchen table. She usually arrived before him. What was concerning was the way she sat, her head down as though she was crying.

His stomach twisted in familiar panic as a thousand horrible possibilities flooded his mind. "Marta. What's wrong?"

She lifted her head, and as she met his gaze Andras realized that the look in her eyes wasn't sorrow or fear.

It was joy.

"I learned something today, darling," Marta said quietly, a dazzling smile lighting up her face. "We're going to have a baby."

Oddly, what first leaped into his head was not a thought, but a sound that resembled all the instruments of the orchestra warming up at the same time. It was only when the noise had faded that he was able to absorb Marta's words.

"I…" He all but collapsed into the other chair. "A baby, really? Are you sure?"

"Fairly sure, yes. Valeria Pataki took me to see her mother, and apparently I'm showing all the signs. I know it's a shock, but are you happy?" Marta smiled up at him hopefully. "Because I am. Quite overwhelmingly happy."

Andras leaned forward and seized her hand. "Of course I'm

happy. It'll be a big change. I won't deny that I'm nervous, but I'm delighted, I truly am. I've been hoping for this ever since we got married." He should have known weeks ago that something was different just by looking at her face. He'd always heard that pregnant women glowed, and Marta certainly did, even this early on. He felt a sudden rush of desire at the sight of her sparkling eyes and the rosy flush that spread over her face, her neck, the skin of her breasts revealed by her partially unbuttoned blouse. She was utterly beautiful, and she was the mother of his child.

As though she'd read his mind, she let out a faint whimper and ran her free hand down his chest. "You're going to be a wonderful father," she whispered, "just as you're already the most perfect husband…"

Much as he appreciated the sentiment, he did not permit her to finish. Instead, he pulled her into his lap and covered her mouth with his, something to which his wife did not object in the slightest.

Sanity unfortunately returned before things could progress, and Andras pulled back quickly. "Wait. We won't hurt the baby, will we?"

"Oh, no. I specifically asked Valeria's mother and she said it's absolutely safe. Healthy, even." Marta leaned up to kiss his jaw. "And I've had quite a long day. Indulge me, won't you?"

In the back of his mind, he was aware that his impending fatherhood would bring with it a whole host of new worries. However, as Marta's lips found his once again and her warm hands began to unbutton his trousers, all fear and anxiety seemed a thousand miles away.

"Do you think we'll ever bring our baby to Vienna?" Andras asked idly, as he and Marta lay exhausted on the narrow bed.

She looked up at him, frowning. "Why would you ask that?" she said, voice strained.

"I don't know," he said. "I just thought it would be nice. Our baby will be half-Austrian, and I'd like it to meet our friends."

She sighed. "Andras, believe me, I'd love to bring our baby to Vienna. I'm sure it would be the darling of the Odysseum

Opera Company. But my family, my old friends, wouldn't even acknowledge our child. I would have to go back to my home city with my husband and baby and know that no one from my old life would dare to congratulate me for fear of scandal. It would hurt." She shook her head. "I couldn't bear to go back. Not unless I can convince my parents to love me again, or stop caring whether they do. And I don't think either of those is likely for a long, long time."

You're better off without them. Andras wanted to say it, but didn't. "I'm sorry. I wish…"

She gently put a finger to his lips. "It's all right. I've made my choice, and I'm glad of it. Now stop fussing, and let's be happy with what we have."

CHAPTER THIRTY

(In Which We Witness a Touching Reunion)

SIX WEEKS AFTER her confrontation with Ludwig, which was as soon as she could escape her duties in Vienna, Sophie set out on her quest.

It was fortunate she had a spinster aunt who lived in Hungary. Had this not been the case, it would have been difficult to put her plan in motion. But Johanna Stein did live in Budapest, and she was a single woman who prided herself on living a life full of amusements. She was distractedly fond of her niece and more than happy to invite Sophie for a visit. So when Sophie left to search for Marta, it was with her parents' misinformed blessings.

Of course, she had to explain the situation to Aunt Johanna. Not all of it, but enough that her activities wouldn't be seen as too suspicious. Precisely as she'd suspected, Johanna was delighted by the entire scandal and offered her full and enthusiastic help. Thus Sophie found herself traveling the streets of Pest accompanied by her aunt's driver, who knew the city well and got them to Szerdahelyi Street with a minimum of fuss.

The address Brigita had given was Number 27, third floor, the flat on the left side of the hallway. This may very well have been accurate, but when Sophie knocked on the door of the flat on the left side of the hallway, there was no reply whatsoever. She knocked again, louder, in vain hopes that someone would hear her this time. If they didn't, she was prepared to wait all afternoon.

No one came running to answer the door from the Király flat, but her knock had apparently been loud enough to disturb the neighbors across the hall. The door of the opposite flat creaked open, revealing an old woman with a face so wrinkled she resembled a walnut.

"*Ezek nem otthon,*" she croaked.

"I'm sorry," said Sophie. "I don't speak Hungarian."

The old woman laughed, showing toothless gums. "They not home," she informed Sophie in heavily accented German. "The little ones at school and Mr. György go to the pub."

"Ah. And what about Mr. Andras Király? Is he about?"

"He don't live here no more," the old woman replied. "He got married, move down the street."

Married! Sophie tried to keep her voice as calm as possible. "Thank you, ma'am. Do you have his address?"

"*Igen,*" croaked the old lady. "Number Ten."

Number Ten, Szerdahelyi Street was a smaller building than Number 27, and it took only a few taps on the wrong doors for Sophie to be directed to the second-floor flat where the Királys supposedly lived. When she knocked, the door was opened by a pale young woman in a blue dress, her dark hair falling out of a messy knot. It wasn't until her mouth dropped open in surprise that Sophie recognized her.

"Sophie!" Marta exclaimed. "Is that really you?"

"Marta!" Sophie stepped back, astonished. This couldn't be her friend, could it? Her face looked much the same, but she'd lost weight and there were dark circles under her eyes that Sophie had never seen before. And that *dress.* The old Marta never would have worn something so plain and itchy-looking. "It is you, my goodness. What on earth are you wearing?"

"Really? We haven't seen each other for four months and you're making jibes about my frock?" Marta shook her head with a laugh. "I can see we have a lot to discuss. Come in. I'll make some coffee."

Sophie tried to keep her face neutral as she entered her friend's new home. It wasn't that the flat was terrible, not at all. In fact it looked rather nice, as Marta had clearly put effort into decorating. It was just so small, and dark. Like a mouse's hole.

"It's a nice place you've got here," she said, with all the cheerfulness she could muster. "Very…cozy."

"There's no need to be coy, I know you're horrified," Marta teased as she bustled about the tiny kitchen. "Though you should be proud of me. I've become part of the proletariat now, haven't I? Even got calluses on my fingers."

"Impressive," said Sophie, taking a seat at the kitchen table. It was, at that. Of all the people she knew, Marta had seemed the least likely to ever have calluses. "Listen, I did just want to check. The old lady from Number 27 said you were married. Is that true?"

"I am indeed. No living in sin for me, I assure you." Marta held up her left hand, upon which glimmered a thin gold ring. "Not a countess anymore, sad to say. Just good old Mrs. Király."

Despite her worries, Marta's face was lit with such unadulterated joy that Sophie couldn't help but return her smile. "Allow me to be the first of our circle to congratulate you."

"Thank you. As a matter of fact, you picked exactly the right time to visit." Marta's eyes sparkled with excitement. "I found out last week I'm going to have a baby."

"A baby!" Sophie cried, all other concerns temporarily forgotten. "My goodness, Marta, a baby. How far along are you?"

"About two months," Marta said with a beatific smile, pouring two generous cups of coffee. "You should have seen Andras when he found out. I thought he was going to faint. But he's delighted, and I think he'll be an excellent father. We like the name Sofia for a girl, and Zoltán for a boy."

"You've got to let me be a godmother," Sophie laughed. "I'm joking, but if you are naming her after me?"

"At the very least, you can be an honorary godmother." Marta took a sip of coffee and looked at her friend with interest. "How did you track me down? I'm not upset, it's lovely to see you. I'm just surprised."

"Actually, you can thank Ludwig for that."

Marta wrinkled her nose. "Ludwig? I'm not inclined to thank him for anything."

"Believe me, I'm just as furious with him as you are. But he was actually quite helpful in this respect. He got in touch with a friend of his, a ballet dancer named Brigita…"

"Wait," Marta interrupted. "Brigita *Novak*? How in the world does Ludwig know Brigita Novak?"

"Your guess is as good as mine. Anyway, Brigita told us Andras's family's address in exchange for Ludwig proposing to her."

"Proposing?"

"Yes. And so I came here under the pretense of visiting my aunt Johanna, and here we are."

"Forgive me for being stuck on one topic," said Marta. "But do you mean Ludwig von Braumark is engaged to a Moravian ballet dancer?"

"Oh, no," said Sophie. "Not engaged. They were married over a month ago, and his family is still furious. It was amazing, though, I've never seen Ludwig so resolute. Or so happy, at that."

Marta buried her face in her hands, her shoulders shaking. Sophie leaned over and gave her a sympathetic pat on the shoulder. "I'm sorry, Marta, I'm sure you're upset."

"Upset?" Marta lifted her head. Far from crying, as Sophie had thought, she was laughing so hard she could barely get the words out. "This is glorious. Shakespeare himself couldn't have written a better ending."

"It is rather poetic," Sophie said, grinning. "But I'm still sorry. Here's Ludwig, doing almost the same thing you did, and no one is exiling him to England. The things men get away with. And of course Brigita gets a title now, whereas your poor husband is stuck as a commoner."

"You're right, it is unfair," Marta agreed. "I should be much more annoyed, but somehow I can't. After all… " She glanced down at her abdomen and smiled. "I got what I wanted."

"I'm glad you're being so philosophical about it," said Sophie, rolling her eyes. "Personally, I still can't think about Ludwig without wanting to pull his hair. But if you're happy, then I'm happy for you. I just wish you had told me about all of this."

"I wanted to, believe me. It was horrible, doing something scandalous and not being able to discuss it with my best friend. Still, I hope it comforts you to know that I really am happy being married to Andras. He's a good husband."

"I'm very glad for you. But I have to be honest. I came here hoping to convince you to come back to Vienna with me."

"Come back?" Marta looked horrified. "Sophie, I can't just go to Vienna. What would Andras say?"

"I don't mean permanently. I was just hoping you would come see your family, give them a chance to apologize."

Marta's face crumpled, and this time she truly did look about to cry. "Don't torture me. I'd love to see my family, but they'll never let me through their door again. Not after I've managed to do practically everything I spent my entire life being trained to avoid."

"True, you haven't exactly been well-behaved lately. But the thing is, Marta, I visited your parents before I came here, just to say hello. They didn't know I was looking for you. And they were quite unhappy." Unhappy was putting it mildly, in fact. Both Heinrich and Hannelore had looked ten years older and couldn't quite manage to smile even when talking about Heini's successes in school. "They truly do miss you, and I wouldn't be surprised if they were feeling more forgiving. It's worth an attempt, isn't it?"

It was some time before Marta replied, and when she did her voice was flat and heavy, her eyes not lifting from her coffee cup. "It's strange, Sophie. I should be ecstatically happy. I'm married to the man I love, we have our own home and freedom and a baby coming. But I'm not happy, not entirely. I miss my family. I want them to meet their grandchild and the rest of the Királys. I want to forgive them, and I want them to forgive me."

"Of course you do," Sophie murmured. "That's nothing to be ashamed of."

"But that's not all." Marta exhaled deeply. "Ever since I found out I'm pregnant, all I can think about is Andras's sisters. Ilka had to leave school at thirteen to work as a maid, Jozefa desperately wants to go to university but it's much too expensive, and the only reason Kitti got the spectacles she needed is because my family's money paid for them."

Sophie opened her mouth to speak, but Marta barreled on. "I ran the numbers last week when I was alone, just trying to see how much it would take to keep our child fed and clothed and comfortable, and it's bad, Sophie. Andras and I can't support a baby on our wages. We can barely support ourselves. I know his family would help us, but things are hard enough for them as it is, and I can't…" She gulped. "I can't be more of a burden. I keep thinking that if I could talk to my parents, get my dowry money, it would change everything. We'd be all right."

"Have you discussed this with Andras?"

"Of course not," Marta said. "He puts himself under so much pressure to keep me happy here, and if he knew about all this he'd probably do something drastic. Sell his violin, maybe. It would kill me to make him suffer any more."

Sophie swallowed hard, staring down at her lap. She'd spent years worrying about people less fortunate, but had never considered that her best friend might someday be one of them. It was, to say the least, eye-opening.

"You are not a terrible person, Marta," she said gently. "What you are is frightened, and why shouldn't you be? Anyone in your situation would."

"What should I do, then?"

"I can't tell you that, unfortunately. But I can tell you this. There's no shame in asking for help when you need it. Not from your family and certainly not from me." Sophie stood and smoothed her skirt. "I'll leave now so you can think things over. Aunt Johanna has said I can stay with her as long as I like, so there's no rush." She reached into her reticule and handed Marta a card. "That's Aunt Johanna's address. Come by anytime."

Marta pulled Sophie into a tight hug. "Thank you, Sophie. I can't believe you traveled all this way to find me."

"You're my best friend, you absolute fool," said Sophie. "What else was I supposed to do?"

When Sophie had gone Marta remained seated, staring into her half-empty cup of coffee while Sophie's words ran around in her head like horses on a racetrack.

They miss you.

They're unhappy.

There's no shame in asking for help.

It felt shameful, though. Shameful how much she longed to

hear her father's voice and be hugged by her mother again, to listen to Heini talking about farm animals and to gossip with Nella. Much as she told herself not to miss them—they'd sent her away to England and they'd cost Andras his job—it was still unbearable to think that her parents might never know their grandchild. Not to mention the resources her family had that her baby desperately needed.

What was the joke Andras had made about the family motto? *Money protects us.* He'd been far more right than he knew.

Which meant the situation required her most daring scheme yet.

And so when Andras finally arrived home, Marta was ready.

"I have some interesting news, darling," she said lightly, as he hung up his coat and hat. "My friend Sophie stopped by today."

"Sophie?" He frowned. "Sophie from Vienna? The one you told me about, who was always going on about redistribution of wealth?"

"That's the one. Sophie Stein. She—"

"Hold on. What is Sophie Stein doing here? And how did she find us?"

"She found out from Ludwig, who found out from Brigita."

"Brigita as in Brigita Novak? How the hell does Ludwig von Braumark know Brigita, let alone go about getting our address from her?"

"It's a long story. But Sophie's not going to betray us, I promise. She did have a request, though."

"I'll bet she did," he replied. "And this request was?"

"Ever since I left, my family has been scared out of their wits not knowing where I am. Sophie was hoping I would come back for a visit, to see if we can make amends."

"No," he said immediately. "I don't think that's a sensible idea at all. Probably quite disastrous, in fact."

There was, of course, a distinct chance that he was right. But disaster or no, Marta's mind was made up. "I understand why you wouldn't want to go back to Vienna after everything that's happened. But Sophie came all this way to find us…"

Andras shook his head. "She came all this way to find you, not me. I know she's your friend, and it was kind of her to come looking for you, but I don't see how that translates to us having to go and face your family."

"It translates because according to Sophie, my family has been going out of their minds with worry ever since I disappeared. For all they know, I could be dead."

"That would be awfully convenient for them, wouldn't it?" he bit off. "Better dead than married to a pauper, isn't that their attitude?"

Marta clenched her fists and took a steadying breath. "That's not fair. You know the background my family comes from, that I come from. My whole life, all my education was specifically to prepare me for a suitable match."

"And when you married me it was a terrible match. I see. How unfortunate."

"Don't talk nonsense. You're a wonderful husband, but you're not wealthy or titled."

"No, I'm certainly not," Andras replied coldly. "And I'm glad of it, the way the aristocrats I've met carry on. Why would you go back to those people? You have a family who loves you here. We're going to have a baby, a baby who'll be free from your parents' ridiculous expectations. There's no reason for you to placate people who hate the life you've chosen."

Marta let out a wordless noise of frustration. "Fine, then. There's no need for you to come along. I will go back to Vienna and assure my parents and brother that I'm alive and well, and you can stay here and revel in what a proud, stubborn Hungarian you are. I can do as I please, and what I please is to see my family and ask for their help."

"Help?" His voice was full of disdain. "What could they possibly help us with?"

"Money," she said quietly. "They have my dowry, and we don't have anything."

"We have each other," Andras choked out. "We have our freedom. I thought that was enough."

His features were twisted with pain, and Marta felt a desperate urge to throw her arms around him and promise that their love was strong enough to solve every problem, and they needed no one but themselves. But she remained still.

Because fighting with her husband was one thing, and lying to him was quite another.

"It's not about what's enough for me," she said, as gently as she could. "I love you, and always will. But I will not bring up my child in dire poverty, not if I have a chance to prevent it. I'm going back to Vienna, and I will do whatever it takes to solve this."

Andras simply stared at her, eyes wide with fear and anger. At last, he let out a deep, defeated sigh. "Go, then," he said. "I wash my hands of it."

This pronouncement made, he threw his coat back on, grabbed his violin case, and exited the flat, the door slamming behind him.

Marta choked back a sob, wiping angrily at her eyes. Much as she wanted to, she wouldn't—couldn't—go after him. Heavy, dull resignation settled over her as she went to pack her bag.

She knew what she had to do and would see it through to the end, no matter what.

And when she saw Andras again, she could only hope he would understand.

CHAPTER THIRTY-ONE

(In Which Sophie is Disappointed, but Not Surprised)

ANDRAS WASN'T SURE how long he spent walking, Clara's case in hand for moral support, his collar turned up against the chill. It must have been quite some time, because when he finally reached the river, the last rays of the sun were fading from the sky.

If he got his hands on a boat, he mused, he could sail upriver and be in Vienna in less than a day. Wouldn't Franz and Brigita and Leo be surprised to see him? They could have a drink at Café Voltaire, gossip about Kristina Eisen, pretend the last three months had never happened.

There were times he missed his old life so much it was physically painful, and he knew Marta felt the same. She'd told him as much when she'd first learned about the baby. He wanted her to be happy, loved her ability to take action, but not like this.

Whatever it takes, Marta had said. The trouble was, he knew what it would take. The von Holstadts were easy enough to understand. They loved their daughter, as they well should, and would happily welcome her back into their family on the condition that she abandon her worthless, penniless husband. If Marta agreed, then with her family's resources it would be easy enough to have his and Marta's marriage annulled. Send the baby away to be adopted by people who wouldn't raise it in poverty. Erase the last few months from von Holstadt history. Of course Marta could refuse such a drastic course of action, but the thought that she might agree was the purest form of torture.

If Andras lost her again, it would kill him. He could see that as clearly as he could see the Danube in front of him. Not physically, perhaps, but in every other way. It would be as though…

As though all the music had left his life.

Perhaps he was hallucinating from cold and anger, but when he looked down at his beloved violin he imagined he could hear Clara's voice in his head, sharp and judgmental.

Is that the kind of life you want, you stubborn fool? You may as well throw me in the river for all the good I'll do you then.

"No," he replied aloud, startling several roaming pigeons. "That's not the life I want. Which means I'll have to fix this. I'm a Király, damn it, and I won't lose my family. Not if I can help it. If Marta will do whatever it takes, then by God I will too." He let out a low groan. "She's going to tear me apart, though. Suppose I deserve it."

If Clara had been a person, he was certain she would have smirked. *Thought you'd see sense.*

"Oh, quiet, you stupid violin," he growled. "You've made your point."

With that, he turned on his heel and strode back into the darkness, making his way home.

There was no sign of Marta when Andras stumbled back into the flat, exhausted and chilled to the bone. Presumably she'd gone to visit that friend of hers, Miss Stein, to talk about Vienna and complain about what a fool Andras had been. She would be back in the morning, and then…

Before he could contemplate what the morning might bring, though, he had collapsed onto the bed and fallen into a deep, dreamless sleep.

He awoke with a start only a few hours later, the sun just peeking over the horizon and his head feeling as though a horse had stepped on it. It took a moment to register the sound that had disturbed his sleep. A rapid, repetitive pounding on the door.

Marta.

He leapt out of bed, nearly tripping over his own feet in his rush. She was back, and he could apologize, try to sort things out…

It felt like a slap in the face from God when the face that greeted him was not his wife's. Instead, the visitor was a young woman he'd never seen before. She was tall, dark-haired, olive-skinned, clad in a purple dress that looked extremely expensive. Everything about her was impeccably put-together, and he was suddenly very aware of the wrinkled clothes he'd slept in and the unkempt state of his hair.

"Are you by any chance Sophie Stein?" he asked, trying to keep the disappointment out of his voice.

"The very same. And you must be the famous Mr. Király." Sophie looked him up and down appraisingly. "I suppose I can see the appeal, though I thought you'd be a bit more dignified. The way Marta talked, one would think you were a Greek god."

Andras blinked in surprise. "She said that?"

"Oh, yes. Why do you think she was so keen to hire you?" Sophie shrugged expressively, pushing past him and dropping uninvited into a chair. "Now that I think about it, eloping with you is just the sort of thing she would do. Marta's never been known for her rational decision-making. I remember when we were nine she decided to build a time-traveling machine out of a wagon with clocks tied to it."

"Really?" Andras asked with interest. "Did it work?"

"Of course not! What's wrong with you?"

He sighed as he sank into the other chair. "Nearly everything, to be honest."

"You don't say," she replied dryly. "But I came here to talk to you about Marta."

His heart dropped so quickly he thought it might fall through the floor. "Where is she?"

Her sharp blue gaze softened, making his stomach lurch in terror. "She's gone back, Andras. I'm sorry. I offered to go with her, but she begged me to stay behind and talk to you."

"Gone back? I thought." His mouth was dry, his hands shaking. "So soon?"

"She caught the six o'clock train to Vienna this morning. And she told me to tell you she knows how painful it would be for you to see the von Holstadts again, so she'll talk to her family alone." She crossed her arms and shook her head. "You and I don't know each other, Mr. Király, so I should tell you this is my disapproving face."

"I assumed as much." Panic-induced pain was building up behind his eyes again, and he took a long breath to steady himself. "Miss Stein, I've made a terrible mistake."

"I've heard that from a lot of men lately," Sophie remarked. "Something must be going around. Go on, tell me what extraordinary revelation you've had, but make it quick."

Andras stood and began to pace the length of the small room, desperately trying to focus his thoughts. "The thing is, Miss Stein, I need Marta," he said. "And for a long time I didn't realize how desperately I did need someone like her. I've spent my whole life tortured by guilt and terrified of the future, but when I'm with Marta it's as though I can remember everything good about life again. She has more energy and enthusiasm and courage than anyone I have ever met, and it's impossible to despair when she's around, no matter how much I want to."

Sophie muttered something that sounded like agreement, though Andras was too caught up in his thoughts to reply to her.

"It's true that Marta is my opposite in nearly every way," he continued. "But we balance one another. She gives me inspiration and hope, and I…I suppose I help keep her feet on the ground. I don't know what will become of either of us if I lose her. You want an extraordinary revelation?" He stopped pacing and folded his arms determinedly. "If she has gone to Vienna I need to follow her and tell her that whatever happens with her family, I will still love her. I will always love her, even if she chooses to leave me. That's all there is to it."

Sophie said nothing for several seconds, and simply looked at him as though she was trying to see into his soul. Eventually, she nodded.

"Interesting," she said. "I think I understand Marta's recent decisions much better now."

He couldn't suppress a relieved smile. "Thank you, Miss Stein. I'm afraid I have to leave you now. Did you happen to notice when the next train to Vienna will be?"

"It's in an hour and a half," she said. And for the first time that morning, she smiled. "If you hurry and pack, you should get to the station in time. And you'll need this." From her coat, she extracted a small rectangle of paper. Andras's eyes widened in surprise as he realized what it was.

"You bought me a train ticket?"

"I had faith you'd make the right decision. If you hadn't…" She shrugged. "Well. I'll leave you to it. Aunt Johanna is expecting me for breakfast shortly."

"I don't suppose you'd like to come along? It seems you've accomplished everything you needed to do here."

Sophie frowned thoughtfully. "Kind of you to offer, Mr. Király, but I'll have to decline. I don't want to spend a six-hour train journey watching you rehearse an apology. Good luck, and if you upset my dearest friend again I will drown you in the Danube."

With these encouraging words she stood and swept out the door, leaving Andras to pack and pray he wasn't too late.

The train journey, long as it was, seemed to pass in the blink of an eye, though this was largely because Andras fell asleep ten minutes into the trip. When he awoke, it was to the sound of an ear-piercing whistle as the train pulled into Vienna's central station.

On the platform, nearly-empty carpetbag in one hand and Clara's case in the other, he paused and considered his next move. His mind urged him to rush to the von Holstadt house where Marta would undoubtedly be in the middle of a heated argument with her parents. His body, however, reminded him that he had barely eaten all day, and he would strongly prefer to not face his in-laws on an empty stomach.

This being Vienna, a café set a stone's throw away, full of exhausted and hungry travelers. Stepping inside was like going backwards in time. How long had it been since he'd stood in a room full of people speaking German, inhaled that smell of coffee and almonds and baking bread?

Vienna. God, he had missed it, more than he would ever admit to his family.

Almost unconsciously, he found himself scanning the room for anyone from his old life. No sign of any of his opera company friends, though there was a woman in the corner with dark curly hair and a green shawl, bent over a spread-out newspaper, who reminded him painfully of Marta.

Wait.

The tilt of her head, that perfect posture. He would recognize them anywhere, and yet he had to be hallucinating. There was no logical reason for Marta to be sitting in a train-station café rather than being welcomed back into her family. Yet it had to be her. No one else in the world could make his legs shake and his heart pound from halfway across a room.

Had it only been a day since he'd seen her? It felt like a lifetime, a millennium. He wanted to do a dozen things at once: fall at her feet and beg forgiveness, pull her into his arms and kiss her, make love to her until she screamed. In a daze, he wove through the other tables, coming to a halt immediately in front of his wife. He wanted to say something eloquent, apologetic, but when he opened his mouth—

"What are you doing here?"

Marta looked up, her brow creasing. If she was surprised to see him, she didn't show it. "I am having a much-needed afternoon coffee. That is something I'm allowed to do, isn't it?"

He winced at her tone. "Yes, of course. You have every right to do what you like. I'm only surprised to see you here, instead of at your parents' house. That was your plan, wasn't it?"

"Fair question." Marta let out a short, bitter laugh. "It's the strangest thing, Andras. I lived in that house for twenty-one years. Yet for some reason, when I arrived three hours ago and stood outside my parents' door, I couldn't go in. I couldn't even knock. I found myself sitting in the Stadtpark staring up at the house for hours, trying to force myself to do something. But I couldn't."

He nodded, cautiously taking a seat and relaxing slightly when she folded her newspaper to make room for him. "I expect it was nerve-wracking to be back there."

"That's one way of putting it." Marta shrugged. "But we'll get into that later. What are you doing here?"

"Sophie came to our flat this morning," Andras said. "She told me you'd gone home, and I, well, I knew what your parents would ask of you. I know the only way for you to be their daughter again is to leave me. And I couldn't let that happen, not before I at least had a chance to tell you how much I love you."

Marta sat back and crossed her arms. "Interesting. Go on, then. How much do you love me?"

"More than anything," he replied fiercely. Even when on the verge of panic, this was a subject he could discuss with confidence. "I love you more than any opera Mozart ever wrote. I love you more than Clara, even if she is the finest violin a man could hope for. I know I can't give you and our baby the life you both deserve, and if you decide to return to your family I'll understand. But if not, I will always love you, Marta. Both of you. I will work my fingers to the bone to provide for you. I'll fight for every opportunity that comes my way, and I will never let you feel unloved or unworthy as long as I live."

To his surprise, Marta's wide dark eyes glistened with tears. "Oh, Andras," she whispered. "Andras, how could you think that I'd leave you forever? I could barely stand to leave you for a day. I waited at this café for hours, hoping you'd come and find me so we could face my family together. I would never abandon our marriage, and if our parents ask that of me, I'll never speak to them again. Don't you trust me at all?"

"It's not that I don't trust you." He rubbed his nose, aware that he too was close to crying. "But our entire time together has been like a dream—the lying, the sneaking about, the eloping. I suppose even being poor in Budapest had some romantic appeal at first. With the baby on the way, though, and Sophie arriving to remind you of everything you've missed. Rather a rude awakening, isn't it?"

Marta stared at him before, astonishingly, bursting into peals of laughter.

"That's it?" she cried. "I grew up spoiled and naive and if I needed an awakening, these last two months have been enough for a lifetime. I never *said* I enjoyed being poor. I never said it was romantic. What I said was that I loved you. And somehow, after everything that's happened, you still don't seem to believe that."

He looked down at the steaming hot coffee the waiter had just delivered, ashamed at how right she was. There was still a part of him that, deep down, couldn't stop seeing himself and Marta as countess and musician rather than simply themselves.

It wasn't a part he was proud of.

"So I need you to do something for me, Andras," Marta went on. "Before we do anything else, I need you to believe that you're worthy of me. That we're worthy of each other, in fact. Because trust me, I feel extraordinarily lucky that someone as talented, kind, and intelligent as you loves me. Ever since I met you, my life has been the kind of adventure I always dreamed about having, and I regret very little." She looked up at him, wide-eyed and desperate. "Please, please tell me you believe me."

"I do," he said firmly. "At least, I'm beginning to, though it may not always be a smooth journey. Will you be patient with me, as long as I promise to absolutely trust you for the rest of our lives?"

Marta pursed her lips, and Andras just barely resisted the urge to lean across the table and kiss her. "I suppose," she said. "But I will hold you to that promise very strictly. And by the way, you owe me an extremely large apology for being so horrible yesterday, and kindly do not give me any temperamental-artist nonsense because we both know you're better than that."

"Ah, yes." He cleared his throat. "For the second time since we've known each other, I say I am deeply, deeply sorry for behaving like an ass. I was a frightened, insecure idiot, and too much of a coward to have any faith in you or myself. Can you possibly forgive me?"

"I forgave you halfway through my second bun," she said, indicating her crumb-laden plate. "And please know that I'm sorry too. I said yesterday that I would do whatever it took to solve things with my parents, but I was wrong. I'll get up at four o'clock, I'll shout at them for hours, I'll bargain with everything I have, but I will not leave you. Ever."

This time no urges were resisted. Without the slightest bit of concern for the café's other patrons Andras leaned across the table and pulled Marta to him, kissing her beautiful mouth with no restraint, overjoyed when she returned his kiss with equal if not greater passion.

It wasn't a long kiss. They pulled apart within a few seconds after being the target of several annoyed throat-clearings from one of the waiters. Short as it was, though, Andras knew it had set everything to rights. The planets had realigned, the sun had come out, and he and Marta were back where they belonged.

Vienna, together.

"Did you truly wait here for me all afternoon?" he asked, when he'd finally recovered his breath. "Just in hopes that I would realize what an idiot I'd been, and rush to your side?"

With a fond smile, Marta shook her head. "Hope had nothing to do with it. I waited here because I know you, Andras Király. I knew Sophie would lecture you, and I knew you'd be desperate to set things right. Most importantly, I knew after spending the entire morning panicking, you couldn't go a step farther without coffee. Of all my schemes, this was probably the easiest."

"You always are two steps ahead of me, aren't you?" He laughed. "And thank God for that. Where to now, my love? I'll follow you to the ends of the earth. Even England, if it comes to that again."

"That's comforting to know, but not exactly what I had in mind." Marta grinned, her eyes lighting up with that conspiratorial sparkle Andras knew so well. "How would you like to blackmail my parents?"

CHAPTER THIRTY-TWO

(Which Concerns Some Entirely Justified Blackmail)

December 15
The von Holstadt Mansion

THE HOUSE HAD changed.

Perhaps not physically. General Johannes still glared down from his portrait in the entryway, the Chinese vase full of hydrangeas still teetered precariously on its table, and the faint smell of lemons still hung in the air, a sign that the maids had been scrubbing the floors. But it felt far more foreboding than the cozy, home-like place Marta had always considered it. Was this how Andras had felt when he came here for their lessons?

As if he'd read her mind, he laughed softly. "Quite intimidating, this place," he muttered. "I always preferred coming in by the servants' entrance. Not to be rude, but your ancestors have very judgmental faces."

"I never noticed that before, but you're right. Perhaps they're just shocked to see me back."

"That footman who let us in certainly was. He looked like he'd seen a ghost. Do you suppose he's gone to get the butler, or to call the priest?"

This question was answered seconds later, as the terrified footman returned with Hermann in tow. At the sight of Marta and Andras he, too, went pale.

"C… Countess," he stammered. "And Mr. Király. What—"

"It's just Mr. and Mrs. Király now," Marta interrupted gently. "Lovely to see you again, Hermann. Could you please tell my parents we've arrived?"

"Mr. and Mrs...." Something seemed to have broken in the butler's brain, as he sputtered for a moment and then gave up. "Countess… Mrs. Király. May I speak frankly?"

"Please do."

"Mrs. Király, I am delighted that you have returned, and you have my warmest congratulations on your marriage. But I feel I must point out that the count and countess will be surprised by your news. Perhaps a warning more in advance of your meeting is advisable."

"I appreciate your concern, Hermann," said Marta. "But we've come a long way, and we don't have time to wait around for my parents to get used to the idea of seeing us. Would you please take us to them? Best to get this over with, I think."

Hermann hesitated, then nodded reluctantly. "Very well. Mr. Király?" He turned to Andras. "I haven't yet had a chance to apologize to you. Some months ago, when you came here and asked to see Countess Marta, I was under strict orders not to let you enter and to reveal no information whatsoever about her whereabouts. Unfortunately, this resulted in my being rude to you."

"Ah," said Andras, plainly surprised. "Well. Think nothing of it, really. You were only doing your job. Didn't have any reason to think I wasn't a vile seducer."

"Perhaps," Hermann admitted, "I should have been a better judge of character. But what's done is done. If you'll follow me, please."

The butler led them to the blue parlor, in which the table was laid with coffee and cakes that no one had touched. To Marta's embarrassment, her stomach grumbled at the sight of the food. Even with the buns she'd eaten earlier, she hadn't had anything that fine to eat in a while

This was no time to be thinking about food, Marta reminded herself. Because for the first time in four months, she was face-to-face with her parents. And while their expressions were hard to read, they didn't seem pleased.

Was it her imagination, or had they aged since she'd last seen them? Hannelore's eyes looked tired and sunken, and there were a few gray hairs in Heinrich's mustache. Maybe Sophie was right and they truly had missed Marta, and worried about her. She'd wanted to believe it, but she hadn't been sure.

Perhaps they really would listen to her. Perhaps they'd even forgive her.

"Mr. and Mrs. Király," Hermann announced, before bowing and retreating.

"Mama. Papa." Marta looked around the room. "Where is Heini?"

"Upstairs," her mother replied stiffly. "We will tell him you came to visit, if…" She glanced at her husband, whose face remained stoic. "Well. Sit, if you like."

"So. Mr. and Mrs. Király now, is it?" Marta's father said flatly as Marta and Andras took their seats. "Got married, then?"

Marta lifted her left hand, displaying her ring. "Certainly did. I've got a ring and everything."

"I spent two shillings on that," Andras declared unhelpfully.

"Did you?" Heinrich said. "You shouldn't have. I'm surprised they didn't pay you to take it."

"If you're going to make snide remarks, Papa, then we'll leave," said Marta. "Is that what you want?"

"No, it isn't," her mother said quickly. "Let's try to have a civilized discussion, shall we, Heinrich?"

Heinrich's face contorted in annoyance, but he nodded.

"Very well. I've come to you with a request, first and foremost." Marta took a deep breath, steeling her nerves. "I want my dowry money."

There it was, on the table. And it was easy to predict what her father would say…

"Absolutely not," Heinrich said immediately. "I'm surprised you would even ask, after all you've done."

"I rather thought you would say that," she replied. "But once again, you do not have all the facts. Specifically the fact that in a few months, you are going to be grandparents."

The announcement had precisely the desired effect. Her parents looked so comically stunned they resembled pantomime masks. Hannelore composed herself quickly, though there was a pleading note in her voice when she spoke. "A baby, Marta? Are you certain?"

"Quite certain, Mama. According to the midwife I am about two months along."

"Oh, how wonderful," Hannelore breathed. Not for the first time, Marta reflected that for all her mother's faults, she really did love children. "That's lovely news, Marta."

"Thank you. Of course, it goes without saying that if we cannot come to an agreement about my dowry, I won't let you meet our child. I shouldn't think you'd have any interest in a Király baby."

"Are you threatening us?" her father demanded, bristling. "Over our own grandchild? Did he put you up to this?"

"Andras has a name, Papa."

"And frankly, I didn't want to spend any time with you lot," Andras put in. "So if you think I'm after your money you can think again. The Királys have gotten by for generations without your help. I am here because Marta wanted to see you, and where she goes I go. But if you can't forgive your own daughter for making a decision you don't approve of, you can take your dowry and…" He said something in Hungarian that, while indecipherable, was clearly very rude.

Heinrich had been doing an admirable job of ignoring Andras's presence, but at this outburst he could do so no longer. "A decision we don't approve of?" he said. "You have a gift for understatement, Mr. Király. I expect you think it's quite eccentric for us to disapprove of our daughter's marriage to someone who can't support her and whose relations go around burning down buildings."

"To be fair, my father hasn't burned down any buildings for over twenty years," Andras said reasonably. "But to answer your question, I'm not surprised you disapprove. You're not saying anything I haven't told myself a thousand times. Marta certainly would have been more comfortable and better off had she married that Ludwig fellow. However, I must point out one thing. It's too late to do anything about it now."

Another silence, this one even longer and more tense than before. Then…

"Give them the money, Heinrich," Hannelore said suddenly, turning to her husband.

Heinrich's forehead crinkled in confusion. "I beg your pardon?"

"Give them the money. This has gone on long enough. I'm not saying I am not upset about all of this," she said, gesturing vaguely in Andras's direction. "But I've spent two months not knowing where my daughter was, if she was dead or alive, and I never want to go through that again. Least of all when our grandchild is involved. I don't know about you, Heinrich, but I have always quite fancied being a grandmother."

"Personally, being a grand*mother* has never numbered among my goals," Heinrich muttered. "I… will you stop giving me that look? For heaven's sake, I'll draw up the paperwork. I suppose fifty thousand gulden is a small price to pay for having some damn peace in this family again."

Andras's mouth dropped open. "Fifty thousand gulden?" he said, almost hysterically. "Marta's dowry is *fifty thousand gulden*? Holy Saint Cecilia, how rich are you people?"

"Not quite as rich as they used to be," said Marta, with a satisfied smile. Outwardly she was managing to stay calm, but it was difficult to keep from leaping in the air and shouting with joy. Somehow, against all odds and logic, she and Andras had been given a chance at a new life.

And they wouldn't be wasting it, that was for certain.

"Thank you, Papa," Marta said. "And you too, Mama. You can't know how grateful I am."

"Yes, well," Heinrich said. "I suppose I'd rather have my daughter married to a scoundrel than have no daughter at all." He shot Andras a severe look. "You're the luckiest man in Vienna, Király, to have our Marta for a wife. And to have a little von Holstadt on the way. The minute I hear about you putting a toe out of line, I'll have you sent to Siberia, understand?"

"Believe me, sir, I am well aware of how lucky I am," Andras said dryly. "Marta will never come to any harm from me, and if I break my word on that I'll head off to Siberia my own damn self."

"I don't believe there will be any need for that," said Marta. "But I appreciate the sentiment. Could I have a few minutes alone with my parents, darling? I'm sure the housekeeper will have a guest bedroom made up for us, I'll meet you up there in a minute."

After a mildly suspicious glance in the direction of the count and countess, he squeezed Marta's shoulder and departed.

"Well," Hannelore said, as soon as the door had closed behind Andras. "I hope you're happy."

There was no sarcasm in her voice, Marta realized, no malice at all, and it was this that made it far easier to forgive her for everything. "I am happy, Mama. But for what it's worth, I'm also sorry. Not for marrying Andras, but for lying about it, and making you worry when I ran away."

"We were so frightened for you, dear. Not only when you left England, but when we found out about you and…" Hannelore shook her head. "Anyway. It was terribly bad form of us to make Mr. Király lose his job, and I personally hope you can forgive us. Don't you, Heinrich?"

"I can't understand your generation, Marta," Heinrich said helplessly. "After all your education and breeding, you and Ludwig go off and marry musicians, or ballet dancers, as though it's perfectly normal. But what can one do? Nothing but disown you or come to terms with it. And against my better judgment it appears I've chosen the latter."

This, Marta understood, was as close to an apology as she was likely to get for the time being. And for now, it was enough. "It's all right, Papa. I forgive you," she said softly. "And I hope you forgive me too. I'd like a fresh start, if we can have one."

"It won't be easy for you now, if you come back here. And I suppose we'll need to make a very large donation to Heini's school, so his position won't be jeopardized. But I believe—" Her father broke off as the door to the parlor flew open to reveal a flushed, disheveled Heini, bouncing on his heels in nervous excitement.

"Marta!" Heini cried, darting across the room and throwing his arms around his sister's waist. "You're back!"

Marta's heart swelled with joy and pride. How much her brother had grown in the past few months, and how mature he looked in his school uniform. She would never abandon him again, she silently vowed. No matter where she went, he would know about it. "Heini, darling. I've missed you so much, you can't possibly know."

"I just saw Mr. Király in the hall," Heini said rapidly. "And he said you're *married*, Marta, and that you lived in a *flat*! And that you both might come back to Vienna. Is it true? Could you please stay, because I need your help with school, and Mama and Papa are too busy to play checkers with me, and…"

Marta laughed and pulled her brother more tightly into her embrace. "Yes, Heini, it's all true. We're back, at least for now. And I have loads of stories for you. You're going to love Andras's sisters. Which reminds me, Mama, Papa," she exclaimed, a sudden burst of inspiration hitting. "May I invite the Királys for Christmas? My sisters-in-law are such lovely girls, and they would adore Burg Holstadt."

"I suppose they're the only guests we can expect at Christmas now," her mother said. "It will probably be years before anyone from our circle speaks to us after a scandal like this. Heaven knows if we'll ever set foot in Schönbrunn Palace again."

Heinrich turned to her, eyes stormy. "For God's sake, Hannelore, my great-great-great grandfather was arrested for embezzlement. My mother once pushed my father into the Danube in full view of a hundred people. We're still the von Holstadts, and if people we've known for years think they can ostracize us over this… they're damn fools."

Now that, Marta thought, was an apology.

She might have to embroider it on a cushion.

"Well," said Andras, when Marta arrived upstairs. "As you can see, I'm a guest now. In a guest bedroom. I hope you're suitably impressed."

Marta wondered if she would ever stop feeling that thrill at hearing her husband's voice. She certainly hoped not. "I wouldn't get too comfortable, darling. I happen to know that you are only considered a guest as long as you're the most devoted husband in the world."

"Is that all?" he teased, brushing a lock of hair off her forehead.

"I thought they were going to ask me to do something difficult. Like contemplate the fact that your dowry is fifty thousand gulden. When were you planning on telling me that?"

Marta shrugged. "I didn't like to say. It felt like bragging. But listen, while we're doing so well with my parents, I think we should insist my father help you get your old job back. Mama was surprisingly apologetic about getting you sacked."

"Actually, about that, Marta. I've been thinking." Though Andras's voice was cheerful, Marta couldn't miss the twist of his lips that signified anxiety.

"Always a dangerous activity for someone as good-looking as you," she said with a hopefully comforting smile, "but I'm all ears."

"Much as I'm fond of the Odysseum, I'm not sure I want my old job back. I could barely support myself on those wages, let alone a wife and child. Even with your upsettingly generous dowry."

"I see," Marta said slowly. "And what would you do instead?"

"It's like this," he said. "With this new money, after we buy a house here, I thought I finally could strike out on my own. Find some sort of theatrical agent, make a go of it writing and performing music as a soloist. It would make a world of difference to Pa and the girls, even if I'm not a wild success."

It had to be unhealthy, Marta thought, to feel this much joy all in one day. "That's brilliant. You'll absolutely be a success, and everyone will be as much in love with your music as I am. And I'll be with you every step of the way. All these social connections I've built up must be good for something. But…" She paused, frowning. "What about Budapest? I couldn't bear it if we moved back to Vienna and you were terribly homesick."

"You once told me," he said quietly, "that I shouldn't have to choose between my family and my work. And you were right. Vienna is home, and it's the best place for me to launch a musical career, but that doesn't mean I'll abandon Budapest. We'll go back as often as we can. Not to that cramped flat, though," he added. "Someone else can take it. We'll stay in a proper hotel."

"Oh, goodness," Marta groaned. "You've been spoiled by wealth already. I dread the day you become famous."

Andras laughed. "The thing is, if I were to become successful, it might involve traveling, and would probably require me to dress better than I do now. So I'd need someone who knows lots of languages and enjoys adventure and has an eye for clothing." He shot her a grin. "Could you tolerate being my wardrobe mistress, translator, and business partner from time to time? If you're not too busy designing opera costumes and making fancy-dress clothes for rich women, that is."

His words sent a shiver of excitement through Marta's veins. She'd spent so long assuming her future would be an endless round of dinner parties and court obligations, and now… Now she could be anyone, do anything. They could do anything.

With a laugh, she reached up and wrapped her arms around his neck. "Anywhere you can play the violin, I can sew. And with our combined talents—we may be artists, but I don't think we'll ever be starving again!"

EPILOGUE

(Which Resolves Matters Nicely)

June 18, 1870

HAVING MISSED THE pleasure of attending their daughter's wedding, the count and countess von Holstadt spared no expense for Sofia Dorothea Erzsébet Reinhild Király's christening at St. Stephen's. While little Sofia herself did not seem impressed by the church's highly decorated splendor, her grandparents considered the event a success.

It wasn't entirely as grand as Marta's own christening twenty-two years earlier. The emperor didn't attend, nor did a good portion of the city's more snobbish aristocrats. Countess von Holstadt had been right: not everyone could forgive a scandal. As it was, the guests—an assortment of Viennese toffs, opera company members, and denizens of Szerdahelyi Street—were surprisingly tolerant of one another. Frankly, Marta and Andras hadn't given them much choice in the matter.

"I think Mrs. Király will be a wonderful mother," Madame Nagy loudly informed Sophie, who'd been interrogating her about life as a businesswoman. "Though I'm still hoping to convince her to come back and work in the shop when little Sofia is older. The things she sends me to sell are lovely, but it really isn't the same."

"The price of success." Sophie sighed and shook her head. "And the Odysseum Opera Company's got her designing costumes for *The Magic Flute*. I don't think she's likely to sleep for the next year."

"A lot of useless extravagance if you ask me," György Király, sitting two pews ahead and resplendent in an embroidered waistcoat and white tunic, grumbled to his daughters. "Shouldn't think a sensible girl like Marta would go in for such things."

"I expect Andras thinks he deserves all this pageantry now that he's popular," Jozefa said, rolling her eyes. "We'll have to bring him down a few notches next time he comes to visit. Kitti, stop leaning forward in your seat like that."

Kitti, who had been discussing horses with Heini in the row ahead, looked back over her shoulder and stuck out her tongue. "You can't tell me what to do now, I'm an aunt. I think that makes me very grown up."

"We're all aunts, which is an honor," said Ilka firmly, switching back to German. "None of the other guests get to be aunts."

"I think I have every right to be called an aunt," declared Baroness Brigita von Braumark from the pew behind the Királys. "Andras always said I was as good as a sister to him. If he doesn't teach little Sofia to call me Auntie Brigita he's not going to be Uncle Andras to my children." She patted her swollen stomach for emphasis and cast a stern glance at her husband, who was clearly trying to hold back laughter. "I'm not sure about you being Uncle Ludwig, though. We'll have to see if they've forgiven you for all that unpleasantness last year."

"The only one who holds any grudges about last year is you, darling," Ludwig said mildly. "Besides, it all worked out for the best, didn't it? You've adapted to your title in record time, and the other day I heard a colleague at the university calling Andras the new Paganini."

Brigita let out a snort of derision at the idea that a philosophy professor would know anything about music. Glancing over her shoulder, she offered a polite nod to Franz, who sat a few rows back with his latest lady friend, the Odysseum's new mezzo-soprano.

"That girl will keep him in line better than I did," she stage-whispered. "Even he won't dare to cross a soprano."

Little Sofia, meanwhile, had become fussy while waiting for the christening to start. Her parents had subsequently taken her to an alcove in the corner of the chapel to calm her, and were engaged in quiet conversation.

"There should be an equivalent of elopement for christenings," Andras said, as he nervously fiddled with his antique cufflinks, a congratulatory gift from his begrudging father-in-law. "We could have had this at the church where we got married, and it wouldn't have taken half as much fuss."

"We need to indulge my parents after we didn't invite them to our wedding," Marta said, bouncing baby Sofia soothingly. "And surely you can't feel that uncomfortable around my family anymore. Granny Dorothea loves you, and her opinion is very valuable. She's half the reason society's forgiven us as much as they have."

"I appreciate that, but it's still rather overwhelming. I'll be grateful when this is over and we can go home."

Home! Even after a few months, the word sent shivers of delight up Marta's spine. Home could have meant many places, of course. It could have been the von Holstadt mansion, where the servants were still laughing over having to call Andras *Mr. Király*, or Burg Holstadt, where the family had passed a delightful Christmas with only a few snide remarks on Grandmama Dorothea's part. It could even have been the Király family's flat in Budapest, where György was enjoying the attention that came from having a successful son.

But really, there was only one place Andras could mean when he said home. Home was the narrow yellow house on the Wipplingerstrasse, with its cozy nursery and new piano. Home was where Wolfgang the dachshund, son of the venerable Liebchen, dozed by the fire and occasionally woke up to demand treats. Home was where Nella Schmidt, now raised to the position of housekeeper, ruled over the household with the efficient grace of an empress.

Home was… well. It was *home*.

The baby let out a worried yowl, and Marta beamed down at her daughter, kissing her on the forehead. Sofia might technically have been a commoner, but to Marta, she was the most regal baby imaginable. "Don't you fret, my love," she whispered, as the sound of organ music from the chapel indicated the service was about to begin. "We'll be done soon."

Though she might not have understood exactly what Marta was saying, the tone was reassuring enough that Sofia's tiny face calmed, and she closed her eyes peacefully. Confusing as the world could be, she had nothing to worry about.

She was a Király, after all. And everyone knew the Királys were the luckiest family in Vienna.

Author's Notes

(Concerning Matters Historical and Matters Musical)

WHILE MARTA AND Andras and their families are fictional, their story is set during a very real and very complex period of European history: the reign of Emperor Franz Joseph. Eighteen-year-old Franz was crowned Emperor of Austria in 1848 after the abdication of his uncle Ferdinand. It wasn't an easy year to become Emperor; nationalist revolutions were taking place all over the continent, including many parts of the Habsburg Empire. Hungary, which had always maintained a strong national identity despite being ruled by Austria, was inspired by revolutionary successes in France and on March 3, 1848, staged a bloodless demonstration demanding greater national independence. While Emperor Ferdinand originally accepted these demands, Franz Joseph refused to acknowledge them once he was crowned, and in 1849 the Austrian government adopted a new constitution that all but destroyed Hungarian autonomy. This led to an all-out armed conflict, resulting in Franz Joseph requesting assistance from the Tsar of Russia. The Russian military quickly put a stop to the Hungarian revolutionaries, and for some time, that was that.

Even though Hungary's fight for independence failed, the end of the revolution was not the end of the story. In 1867, after unsuccessful wars with Italy and Prussia, Austria faced a financial crisis and governmental instability, and Franz Joseph (with the encouragement of his wife, Empress Elisabeth) agreed to a surprising new plan: the Austro-Hungarian Compromise. Hungary gained greater autonomy, their constitution was restored, and Gyula Andrássy, a former revolutionary, was elected the new Hungarian Prime Minister. For people like György Király, who had lost lives, loved ones, and limbs in defense of their country, the compromise was a victory—if a bittersweet one.

(An aside: For much of Hungary's history, Buda and Pest were two distinct cities separated by the Danube River. While they were not formally combined until 1873, I have referred to the city as Budapest throughout the novel, if only for the sake of clarity. I have done this for you, the reader.)

It's hard to think of any city in Europe more famous for classical music than Vienna. While many of its musical celebrities were not in fact born there (Chopin, for example, was Polish, while Beethoven was born in Bonn, Germany), it was still called home by some of the most famous musicians and composers in history, including Mozart, Johann Strauss, and Joseph Haydn.

In writing about Andras I was particularly inspired by the life of Franz Liszt, the Romantic-era pianist and composer. Liszt was born in Hungary and studied music in Vienna before launching a career as a soloist in the 1830s. By all accounts he was a smashing success; women were even known to throw their underwear at him! It should be noted that Franz Liszt also fell in love with an aristocrat, the French-German countess Marie d'Agoult, with whom he had three children. Perhaps it's something about Hungarian musicians?

However, perhaps the most relevant information about Mr. Liszt was that, while he grew up speaking German, he did attempt to learn Hungarian in his youth. According to one story, his linguistic education was going well enough until he stumbled upon one particular Hungarian word that caused him to give up in frustration. That word, you ask?

Tántoríthatatlanság.

Mr. Liszt's loss is Marta von Holstadt's gain.

GLOSSARY

Carinthia: The southernmost state in Austria, famous for its lakes and mountains.

Cosi Fan Tutte: An opera by Mozart, about two army officers who come up with a scheme to prove their girlfriends are shallow.

Don Giovanni: Another Mozart opera, about the misadventures of a dissolute Spanish nobleman who receives a dramatic comeuppance.

Hofburg Palace: The primary residence of the Austrian royal family, located in central Vienna.

Kifli: A crescent-shaped Hungarian roll, similar to a croissant.

Köfte: Turkish meatballs.

La Sylphide: Ballet from 1832, a tragic romance between a Scottish farmer and a mysterious fairy.

Moravia: Historical region of what is now the Czech Republic.

Paganini (Niccolo): Italian violinist famous in the early 19th century. Rumored to have sold his soul to the devil. Missing most of his teeth.

Saint Cecilia: In Catholicism, the patron saint of music and musicians.

Saint Stephen's: Also known as the Stephansdom, a beautiful medieval cathedral in central Vienna.

Schönbrunn Palace: The summer residence of the Austrian royal family, noted for its zoo.

Vanilla kipferl: Traditional Austrian cookies made with ground almonds and occasionally dipped in chocolate. Popular at Christmas, though delicious all year round.

Acknowledgements

As anyone who has written a book, and most of those who haven't, are well aware, this is an exhausting and nerve-wracking process. The following people and animals have kept me sane during times when I've woken up at three o'clock in the morning convinced I'm a talentless hack.

My dear friends from Discord and the online writing community, who have given me scads of advice and encouragement in this whole adventure. I'd like to particularly thank Erin, on whose digital shoulder I digitally cried more than once, and who never judged me for it.

Mom, Dad, and my brother, none of whom particularly *like* romance novels, but do understand why I feel the need to write them.

My lovely editor Barb, who saved me from having 11,000 incidences of the word "solemnly."

Irish singer-songwriter Hozier. He knows why.

Eva Ibbotson, who is no longer with us, but whose Viennese YA romances defined my teenage years and are probably responsible for Unshakeable existing.

Bungo the cat, for being both soft and fuzzy.

And you, of course, for reading this.

About the Author

Molly MacKenzie is an author, educator, costume designer, and occasional world traveler. She was born on a farm in Wisconsin, but currently lives in North Carolina with her cat Bungo. The last time she was in Hungary, she ordered a veggie burger at a diner and received a square of fried cheese on a bun. This is the best thing that has ever happened to her.

Unshakeable is Molly's debut novel.

Instagram: @msmackenzieauthor
Twitter: @mmackenziewrite
Facebook: @msmackenzieauthor
Website: www.mollymackenzieauthor.com